PASSION'S ABDUCTION

"Why don't ye just tell me what you're doing here, prowlin' about my father's stable like this?" she asked, leveling the barrel of the gun at his chest.

A knowing smile came to Sean's lips. "I told ye last evenin' that I'd be back for ye. And I'm a man who keeps his word." He took a step closer. "Give me that thing, before ye shoot someone's foot off," he growled, lunging at her and snatching the weapon.

An instant later, he pinned her wrists back and spoke hotly into her ear. "Now, listen to me. . . . If I'd intended to spirit ye off, I'd have done it by now. I'd have ye by force in my bed, in fact, if that's how I wanted it . . ."

Heather struggled against him a bit, but something kept her from screaming in those seconds, something about his commanding blue eyes.

"But surely you're bright enough to know that that's not how I want it . . ." With that, his face began moving toward hers. "And ye should know it's not polite to draw upon someone who's come 'round to woo ye," he continued. Then, to her surprise, he pressed his lips to hers with a heedless sort of urgency that left her breathless . . . and wanting even more.

"WILD IRISH HEATHER is a delightful tale taut with sexual tension. Readers will purr at Sean's amorous seduction!"

—Ro

HEARTFIRE ROMANCES

SWEET TEXAS NIGHTS (2610, $3.75)
by Vivian Vaughan

Meg Britton grew up on the railroads, working proudly at her father's side. Nothing was going to stop them from setting the rails clear to Silver Creek, Texas — certainly not some crazy prospector. As Meg set out to confront the old coot, she planned her strategy with cool precision. But soon she was speechless with shock. For instead of a harmless geezer, she found a boldly handsome stranger whose determination matched her own.

CAPTIVE DESIRE (2612, $3.75)
by Jane Archer

Victoria Malone fancied herself a great adventuress, but being kidnapped was too much excitement for even Victoria! Especially when her arrogant kidnapper thought she was part of Red Duke's outlaw gang. Trying to convince the overbearing, handsome stranger that she had been an innocent bystander when the stagecoach was robbed, proved futile. But when he thought he could maker her confess by crushing her to his warm, broad chest, by caressing her with his strong, capable hands, Victoria was willing to admit to anything. . . .

LAWLESS ECSTASY (2613, $3.75)
by Susan Sackett

Abra Beaumont could spot a thief a mile away. After all, her father was once one of the best. But he'd been on the right side of the law for years now, and she wasn't about to let a man like Dash Thorne lead him astray with some wild plan for stealing the Tear of Allah, the world's most fabulous ruby. Dash was just the sort of man she most distrusted — sophisticated, handsome, and altogether too sure of his considerable charm. Abra shivered at the devilish gleam in his blue eyes and swore he would need more than smooth kisses and skilled caresses to rob her of her virtue . . . and much more than sweet promises to steal her heart!

Available wherever paperbacks are sold, or order direct from the Publisher. Send cover price plus 50¢ per copy for mailing and handling to Zebra Books, Dept. 3326, 475 Park Avenue South, New York, N.Y. 10016. Residents of New York, New Jersey and Pennsylvania must include sales tax. DO NOT SEND CASH.

WILD IRISH HEATHER

ASHLAND PRICE

ZEBRA BOOKS
KENSINGTON PUBLISHING CORP.

To my sister-in-law, Jane.
To our godkids, Cory and Steve.
And to Tim, Jennifer,
and the rest of the next generation.

Also, to my good friend,
Helen Bayuk—for all the hours
spent listening and sharing.

ZEBRA BOOKS

are published by

Kensington Publishing Corp.
475 Park Avenue South
New York, NY 10016

First printing: February, 1991

Printed in the United States of America

Chapter 1

"Go shoot a landlord, Rory. Make yourself of use!"

Sean Kerry's dim-witted friend recoiled at the snub, and then his eyes narrowed to a chastising glower. "Who'd'ye think you're talkin' to, mate? I'm as hale as you or Patrick, and I mean to help ye kidnap the lass!"

In an effort to determine whether or not anyone had overheard Rory's words, Sean scanned the sea of wedding guests, who were gathered before him now, in the Cassidys' barnyard. It was a curse of nature, the cruelest of ironies that, ever since Rory's unfortunate collision with a constable's musket butt two years earlier, his voice had grown louder, but he'd had less and less of worth to say.

Sean, therefore, spoke in a whisper as he addressed him again, hoping that Rory might follow suit. It wouldn't do, after all, to have the wedding guests know of their plan. "I brought ye along for the ride,

Rory, and nothin' more. I know you've been shut up in the cottage too much lately and that ye crave the company of others. But Pat and I work alone, don't ye see? You know we'll provide for ye, just the same. We have ever since your injury. But ye simply must go home now and stay out of the way. She's a wee slip of a girl, so she won't put up much of a fight," he assured his old friend.

"No, they're the worst," Rory warned, "the thin, wiry ones. They use their bony elbows and knees to gouge a lad in the most frightful places!"

"*Go,*" Sean urged again. "We get precious little work these days, as it is, so I can't have ye bunglin' the capers we do manage to scare up!"

Rory, though ten years Sean's senior, bore enough respect for him to accept the fact that his "no" really meant "no." So, ever humbled and frustrated by his newly debilitated mental state, he planted his cap on his head and stormed off to where their horses were tied behind the barn, leaving Sean to the thoroughly disquieting task of abducting one Jennifer Plithe.

Sean had seen her at close range twice before this evening. She was a plain girl with dull, brown hair and gray eyes. Hardly a prize it seemed. As the daughter of a wealthy milliner, however, her dowry was sure to be quite sizable; and Sean had come to realize that that was all that really mattered in the vast scheme of things. So, though Miss Plithe was scarcely over the age of seventeen, Sean and his brother, Patrick, would kidnap her and see to it she was a married woman by dawn of the following day—or die in the effort. And given the great number of potential witnesses to the act, Sean realized now that the latter was a distinct possibility.

* * *

Just a few hundred yards away, in the Cassidys' farmhouse, Heather Monaghan and her two friends, Shannon Kennedy and Jennifer Plithe, were busy freshening up in one of the bedchambers, before going down to the wedding dance. Heather stood before the room's full-length looking glass, admiring the glints produced by the metallic yarn from which her V-bodiced gown was woven. The green-eyed beauty tossed her shoulders from side to side a couple of times, watching the candlelight dance upon the garment. "Ah, come on, Jennifer," she groaned, "ye can't travel by the wayside for the rest of your days! Come down to the dance with Shannon and me for a while. There's no reason for ye to go home . . . not *now*, for mercy's sake, when the real fun is just startin'."

Jennifer continued to slump back in the Carver chair, which was situated just beyond the mirror, and Heather, studying her friend's reflection in the glass now, silently acknowledged once more what a frump Jennifer really was, how little she cared about her posture, her hair style, and her clothing. It was as if Jennifer honestly believed that all she wanted from life could be attained simply by virtue of the fact that she was hardworking and excelled in her studies.

Heather, on the other hand, knew better. Even though her mother had died of a fever some years earlier and she'd been without a female mentor ever since, she knew that the way in which a young lady presented herself was all-important in the snaring of a desirable husband. She also knew that occasions such as this one—a wedding dance that included scores of young male guests—were ideal for the kindling of new romance.

Shannon Kennedy seemed to know this too, where she stood, leaning back against the frame of the bedchamber door. She clucked loudly at Jennifer's reluctance and breezed her face impatiently with her blade fan.

"We've no chaperone," Jennifer retorted with her usual banality.

"But I've told ye, my father will be here soon," Heather replied, turning away from the mirror and flashing Jennifer an entreating smile. "And we've got each other till then, so what harm could there possibly be in it? Ah, come on, Jen, just for half an hour or so. Who are we, after all, to be denyin' our diverse beauty to the local lads? I mean, me, with my reddish hair," she said, turning back to the mirror and giving her auburn mane an approving glance. "And Shannon, our blonde, and of course, you Jenny, our brunette. Ah, let's permit the lads to have a good look. What say ye to it?"

"Oh, very well," Jennifer grumbled at last, struggling back up to her feet in her hooped and gathered skirt. "But your father's seein' me home when the time comes," she added, shaking a finger at Heather. "I won't be findin' my way back alone after dark over this ridiculous gatherin'. My mother'll have my hide if I do!"

Heather issued a relieved laugh and clapped her hand to her chest. Jennifer was never easy to sway, but it seemed she'd been even more mulish and sullen than usual lately; so Heather knew that this was

8

quite a victory. "Yes. Yes. You have my most solemn vow that you'll be properly seen home," Heather said gaily. And with that matter settled, the three girls made their way out of the room and down to the festivities in the nearby barn.

Still hidden behind a haystack near the Cassidys' house, Sean Kerry continued to scan the crowd of wedding guests periodically. His facial features were already conveniently concealed beneath the blackening of burnt cork, and soon he would join the band of "strawboys" from the neighboring farms in their traditional raid upon the wedding dance. They'd be a noisy bunch when they rode up on horseback and stormed into the barn to dance with the female guests. Knowing this, Sean sank down to the ground now, his back to the pile of hay, confident that the ruckus the strawboys' arrival would create would be enough to call him to his feet as soon as was necessary.

He went on to reassure himself that, having spied upon Jennifer Plithe's comings and goings for the past five days, both he and his brother, Patrick, would recognize her at a glance this evening. They could also be fairly certain that she'd be at the dance, because she'd been present at the wedding service just half an hour earlier, and one rarely attended a wedding in Ireland without also being present at the nuptial feast and any celebration held thereafter.

The plan was for either Sean or Patrick to persuade the girl to dance. Then she'd be waltzed, as surreptitiously as possible, out the barn's back door and into the hands of the other brother, who would be waiting there to help hie her off in the darkness.

9

And since he and Patrick hadn't botched many of their bride snatchings to date, Sean had to believe that they wouldn't mishandle this one.

Experience had taught them that weddings were particularly conducive to bride snatching, because the "strawboy" tradition allowed them to act incognito, their identities obscured by the traditional face blackening and vagabond clothing of these playful wedding shivareers. He and Patrick were, after all, strangers in almost every county they visited, and of course, they prized their anonymity above all else. It was just a given that racketeers, like themselves, were always safest on the run; for though their crimes were in no way as grave as their father's had been, they would still find themselves quite culpable if the law ever caught up with them. Moreover, Sean had begun to suspect that he and Patrick were being followed of late. Twice in the past fortnight, Sean had spotted a cloaked figure tailing them. And though this pursuer had dropped from sight each time Sean had tried to point him out to Patrick, Sean had definitely seen him and he instinctively knew that he wasn't a man who would be easily shaken off.

It was rumored that bride snatching had actually become a capital offense in some counties, punishable by hanging, and this, of course, was making Sean all the more edgy about their cloaked follower. Patrick, on the other hand, insisted that the rumor was nothing more than that—daft, idle gossip. He had, nevertheless, begun shaking his head in disgust a great deal lately, grumbling about how a lad could scarcely make an honest living at crime anymore.

It was clear that Sean's misgivings about their vocation were definitely more deep-seated than his brother's. Not only did he now fear the possible legal consequences more than ever before, but their work had begun stirring up a torrent of emotions within him. He had had the misfortune of falling in love with their last three captives, and he was beginning to doubt his own sensibilities. What a relief it had been, therefore, when he'd discovered that their next victim, the wealthy heiress, Jennifer Plithe, was so plain-looking. Upon seeing her for the first time, when she'd attended a wake the Tuesday before, Sean was immediately struck by her drabness; and he held the highest hopes now that he'd find his former callousness restored while abducting her. Nevertheless, a measure of uncertainty still swelled in his throat as he contemplated the task.

He looked at his pocket watch for what seemed the fiftieth time that evening. Patrick was probably still off drinking with their thuggish band of friends in Kilkenny, he concluded with an exasperated cluck. Patrick had promised that he'd bring his revels to an end by five o'clock and ride into the wedding dance disguised as one of the approaching strawboys, but Sean was starting to have his doubts, and he looked down now to see his hand closing to a knuckle-whitening tightness about a bit of hay that he'd mindlessly picked up. He gave forth a snarl, once again acknowledging that he'd probably be better off depending upon their dull-witted friend, Rory, for assistance in abducting the girl, than to continue relying upon his brother.

One thing was clear to him; if Patrick left this abduction solely up to him, he might just pass the girl up altogether. It seemed a shame to let such carefully stalked prey slip through one's hands under circumstances as convenient as these. But a partnership was a *partnership,* after all, and the dear Lord knew that Patrick certainly had no trouble *spending* sizable sums of the money they earned at this dubious vocation—which had, from the start, been Sean's idea. It didn't take a clever bloke to know that one could profit greatly by marrying a lass with a large dowry. Young Irishmen had been doing so for centuries. But kidnapping wealthy maidens at the behest of other men, now that was a stroke of genius, and Sean again had to give himself a bit of credit for having thought of it.

On most of their jobs, Sean and his brother received nearly half of the groom's take, and the bride's parents were usually willing to pay out the dowry, in the hopes that their daughter would reap the benefits of it. So, the Kerrys bagged much of the reward, without having to suffer the burdens that marriage generally imposed upon men.

It wasn't, however, all rosy for them. There were some sizable risks inherent in their work. Sean had dodged the bullets fired from the gun of an enraged father on more than one occasion. Then, there were those perilous getaways on horseback, with their terrified captives kicking and clawing them every inch of the way. Now and then, there was even the greedy "groom," who managed to collect his bride's dowry on his own and then refused to dispense the agreed-upon percentage to the Kerry brothers. But as Patrick was always quick to point out, such tribulations were really little more than what the average madam had to endure in order to keep her brothel running smoothly; and all things considered, it was rather a tame occupation for two sons of such an infamous highwayman. In fact, their father, the late William Kerry, might actually have been taking pride in the relative uprightness of his boys' vocation, where he now surely resided in the Heavens. Sean was fairly certain his father had been Heaven-bound, in any case, because he'd made a confession to a priest a full ten minutes before his hanging some twelve years earlier in their hometown of Londonderry.

Sean had been eleven years old at the time of his father's death. In the decade that followed—amid the struggle he and Patrick had waged to stay out of orphan homes and make a meager living picking pockets, under the direction of their dear old family friend, Rory MacKenzie—the details of William Kerry's hanging had grown mercifully dim in Sean's mind. Only one vivid image remained against the gray ground of his memory, and that was of the crimson incision left on his father's throat, once his corpse was removed from the scaffold and the hangman's noose was freed from around his neck. Sean had always thought of hanging as a quiet, bloodless means of execution; but he'd discovered, on that fateful day at the gallows, that it was neither.

He swallowed dryly now, in bitter recollection of it, and he silently vowed that he would never, under any circumstances, allow himself to die in so hideous and *public* a fashion. If he ever managed to verify the rumor that bride snatching had become a hanging offense, he'd waste no time in bailing out of his partnership with his brother. There was no sense in all of the Kerry men meeting their Maker stretching hangmen's ropes. One of them had an obligation to live and carry on the family name, and Sean would just as soon this obligation fell upon him.

He'd never known his mother. According to his father, she had run off with an English lord only four weeks after Sean's birth. Sean's father also claimed that she was not heard from again, save for a note she left pinned to a stray pair of her husband's knee breeches, reprimanding him for his ongoing penchant for crime and expressing her hope that the burden of having to raise young Patrick and Sean alone might cause him to adhere to the straight and narrow thenceforward.

It did just that, as it turned out. At least until the boys were old enough to attend school. Then, unfortunately, William Kerry's relatively stable life as a tavern keeper gradually gave way to spurts of his former highwayman activities, and he ultimately landed himself in gaol on charges of theft and murder.

He was a good man, nonetheless. A proud father and an outlaw of the first order. It was, therefore, difficult for Sean to believe that his father's purported shooting of a coachman during a holdup had been anything but an accident. William Kerry had never displayed one iota of violence where his sons were concerned. He had, however, been given to fiercely glaring at Sean in heated moments and growling about the fact that the boy more resembled the fair-haired Englishman his wife had taken up with, than anyone in the Kerry clan. This skepticism about Sean's paternity was, quite naturally, painful for Sean. But most of the time, his father had treated

14

him with the same nurturing gentleness that he'd shown Patrick, and all in all, Sean's memories of him were fond and heartening.

The thundering of approaching horses interrupted Sean's thoughts now, and he sprang to his feet and circled around the haystack to see the band of black-faced strawboys riding across the east pasture to the barnyard. Patrick was among them, and Sean knew that it was definitely time to rally and take his brother to task for spending so much time off pubbing with his shady cohorts. Even from that distance, Sean could see that he was sitting sloppily, drunkenly in his saddle, his red hair shooting up in the evening breeze like flames about a live coal. And though his face was blackened to conceal his identity, there was no mistaking Patrick's infuriatingly casual deportment, that air about him that bespoke his imagined superiority to almost every man he met.

Patrick threw his head back with a hearty laugh, as Sean became visible to him now at this closer range. He was clearly amused with Sean's concern for punctuality and his constant attention to the details of their roguish profession.

"Where is she, pup?" Pat bellowed as his horse led the way into the muddy barnyard and the mingling wedding guests receded to give the riders space. "Let's grab her and be off!"

Sean clenched his teeth and strode over to his brother as he stopped and dismounted his horse an instant later. "You're drunk again, ye bastard! Why did ye bother comin' here at all?"

Patrick drew his head back defensively. "Tisk, tisk. Need ye ask why I came? To help ye, of course, little mud toad. You know I always do my fair share." With that halfhearted effort at making amends, Pat hitched his horse to a post and gestured for Sean to follow him—along with the band of clamorous strawboys—into the barn.

He'd taken to addressing Sean with all manner of demeaning diminutives through the years. "Mud toad" and "pup" were his favorites at present. This seemed the only way for him to compensate for Sean's being the more valiant and successful of the two of them—despite the fact that Sean was nearly four years Pat's junior. Unlike Pat, Sean almost always kept a steady, sober head about him; and Sean instinctively knew that his brother's patronizing nicknames for him simply reflected the fact that Pat was becoming increasingly threatened by his physical and intellectual superiority. And though neither of them ever dared to give voice to it, their possibly differing paternal lineage could very well have been responsible for making Sean a frightfully formidable combination—a man with the upbringing of a ruthless outlaw and the blood of the most enterprising gentry.

"Ah, come along. Let's get on with it," Patrick coaxed again. "We'll be ridin' for hours as it is, just to deliver her to that baker bugger."

"And who's to blame for that?" Sean snarled. "You'll be late for your own bloody wake, I hope ye realize!"

"Don't start with me, little brother. I'll have none of that tonight! I'm in no humor for it, and we'll be havin' our hands full soon enough, with that she-cat to steal off to a weddin' bed. . . . I'm here, aren't I?"

16

he challenged finally, his eyes widening with defiance, and Sean could tell that, beneath his mask of black, his brother's face was red with indignation.

"All right, so you're here in body," Sean conceded. "But let's just hope ye didn't leave your brain behind in town, 'cause, if ye do aught to botch this thing, I swear to ye that you'll be answerin' to *me* before the local sheriff can even get his hands on ye!"

Chapter 2

They found that the barn was only dimly lit by intermittent lanterns as they entered it seconds later.

"Mother of Jesus, it's dark in here!" Patrick complained in a whisper, his breath reeking of whiskey as he turned back to hear Sean's response.

"Let my eyes adjust, and I'll spot her right off. . . . Ah, there she is, the frumpy one standin' by the far wall."

Patrick nodded and smiled. "Yes. The one in the shimmerin' green gown."

"No. The one just beside her. The one in brown," Sean countered firmly.

"No. No. The one in the green, pup. The one with the flashin' green eyes to match."

Sean shook his head in disgust. "Too much whiskey and wishful thinkin'. It's the dull one in brown, I tell ye."

"Let's go closer," Patrick ordered in a whisper, "and have a better look." He led the way through the crowd of wedding guests as several young men were lining up to take turns dancing with the bride.

Heather Monaghan clutched at Jennifer Plithe's

hand and gave forth a capricious giggle. "We're being watched," she noted under her breath, "by two of those ridiculous strawboys. Do ye see them?" She gasped in horror as Jennifer turned about to look at the two young men in question. "No! Don't *look,* ye fool! 'Tis unbecoming to actually turn full-face and gape at 'em, don't ye know. You should never act too familiar or approachable," Heather concluded with a resolute toss of her auburn curls.

Jenny turned back to her and scowled. "They already know we're approachable, ye nit! Why else would we be standin' in this drafty smelly barn, gettin' straw caught in our flounces?"

Heather nervously withdrew her kerchief from her off-the-shoulder neckline. She dabbed her brow with it and returned it to the ruffled cuff of one of her three-quarter-length sleeves. It was a fetching bit of business, and it seemed to play down the fact that, in spite of any claims she might have made, she was as unversed at flirting with men as her two companions.

"This is most tiresome," Jennifer huffed. "My feet hurt, and there's absolutely nothing to sit upon."

"Beauty knows no pain," Heather said hearteningly. "Just try, if ye will, to remember that."

"Well, I won't dance with any of those filthy strawboys, so don't be thinkin' I will," Jennifer retorted with an uppity expression. "Only savages and groundlin's paint their faces and rove about like hobgoblins, is what—ah, what a backward lot, this!"

"I'll have ye know, Jen, that the Cassidys are some of my father's most loyal crofters, and I have it on the best authority that they are neither savages nor groundlin's!" Though she was trying not to let it show, Heather was angered by her old friend's sudden haughtiness. "Besides," she continued, "if ye didn't wish to come along this evenin', ye should have declined my invitation to the weddin'. Now, you agreed to come down here fair and square, and, as I told ye, it's only for a little while."

Jennifer opened her fan with an abrupt snap and stood breezing her face with a fluttery rhythm. Then she turned her eyes irritably upward. Once again, she'd obviously found herself without a suitable retort for her brighter, glibber friend, Heather. "Well, we're here now, aren't we, Shannon," she grumbled conspiratorially after a moment, "so we may as well be makin' the best of it."

Heather, too, opened her fan and was beginning to catch furtive glimpses of the two interested strawboys from behind its lacy pleats. One of them was quite tall with sandy blond hair. He was wonderfully broad-shouldered, and his statuesque facial features were evident, in spite of his black mask. His large blue eyes were childlike, beckoning, and even from that distance, she could see them reciprocating the twinkle that surely must have shone in her own. A warm rush of arousal ran through her as she noted the silky elegance of the ivory-colored shirt he wore. She studied its full, bishop sleeves and caught herself imagining what it might be like to be swept up in those arms and held tightly to the warmth of that powerful chest.

But these weren't "boys," she suddenly acknowledged. The quaint "strawboys" title was truly a misnomer where these two were concerned. They were men, well into their twenties, she imagined. The second of the two was a carrot top, the freckled, red-haired sort of male who bullies girls and boys alike in his youth and then spends his adulthood trying to prove to the world that he's a wholly civilized gentleman. She'd kept company with her father's cohort, Malcolm Byrne, long enough to recognize a strong-armer when she saw one. And indeed, the redhead did appear to be the bossier of the two, where he stood, snarling out of the side of his mouth now at his courtly-looking companion.

"Oh, dear Mother Mary, here comes the red-head!" Heather exclaimed to her friends as Patrick Kerry suddenly left his brother's side and began weaving a drunken path toward them.

At this, Heather and Shannon started fanning their faces even faster, in nervous unison.

"Sweet Jesus, what shall we do, Heth?" Shannon queried, the panic she was probably feeling pretty well hidden behind her toothy grin.

"Act like ladies," Heather whispered.

The girls reflexively lowered their eyes as the eldest Kerry stood before them a moment later, smelling of a far more potent brew than any God-fearing strawboy would be apt to have at his disposal. But to Heather's amazement in those heart-stopping seconds, it wasn't Shannon or herself whom the stranger invited to dance. It was Jennifer Plithe—by far the plainest of their threesome.

As Heather looked up once more, she couldn't help gaping a bit at this unlikely selection. Poor Jenny, born to great wealth, yet as given to it as a sharecropper's sow. Heather continued to watch in awe as the fierce-looking stranger bent down from his waist an instant later and raised the unwitting Jennifer's hand to his lips.

"Dance with me, my lady," he urged in an amazingly seductive voice. It was a tone so knowing, so suggestive that even the worldliest of women would have had trouble refusing—if only out of curiosity as to whether or not the gentleman's embrace could possibly have been as persuasive as his voice.

A brief, but tense silence ensued. Then, to everyone's surprise, Jennifer slipped her hand from the young man's grasp and answered simply, "No. Thank ye just the same, sir."

When the redhead remained standing dumbfoundedly before her for several seconds more, Jennifer stepped back from him and began eyeing the crowd of eligible males on the opposite side of the barn, as though intent upon saving herself for what she considered to be a better prospect. Heather and Shannon, in turn, simply offered the stranger embarrassed smiles and again began frantically fanning themselves.

Perhaps it was simply her imagination in the heat of the moment, but Heather could have sworn she heard the strawboy curse under his breath as he retreated into the swelling crowd of wedding guests once more. She hadn't actually seen him utter the words, but there was no escaping the fact that they had been ones of disgruntlement, the underlying ferocity of which made a chill run through her. She pulled her heavy shawl up about her shoulders and immediately turned to question Jennifer.

"Why did ye say no?"

"Because I didn't like the looks of him, of course. It's as simple as that," she concluded, slapping her fan shut and crossing her arms over her chest in that scathingly pragmatic way of hers.

"But that might have been the only opportunity any of us will have to dance this evenin'."

"I'd rather be dancin' with a cow pat, thank ye just the same, Heather Monaghan."

Heather indulged in a sideward study of her old friend in those seconds, still amazed at how blunt she'd been with the gentleman. Jennifer might have been callow and unfashionable, but no one could ever accuse her of not knowing her own mind. She stood as firm and undaunted on most issues as a pile of rocks cleared from a planter's field, and no matter what else there was to be said of her, one had to give her credit for that.

"You botched it, didn't ye," Sean acknowledged with an irrepressible laugh as his brother rejoined him on the other side of the barn a moment later. "I told ye not to go off drinkin' before a job. No self-respectin' lass wants to find herself courted by a man who's too sotted to finish what he starts!"

"Finish what he starts?" Patrick echoed in his usual caustic tone. "By that I suppose ye mean that ye don't think my rammer can see it through!"

Sean's laughter faded to a knowing grin. "Crudely put, yes."

"And are you any more the prize?" Pat challenged. "You with quite the opposite problem? Why, you're so wrought up every time we snatch a lass, that we daren't let her ride in the same saddle with ye!"

Sean continued sniggering at his brother. "At least I keep my breeches on. I'm not out whorin' every Saturday night, like you."

"Some of that would do ye good, it would. Maybe if ye did it more often, ye wouldn't be as big as a pistol when ye finally got 'round to it. Don't be thinkin' I haven't heard Madam Bennington's girls cry out so whenever *you* bed 'em. Ye haven't got many secrets in a brothel," he added with a taunting wink.

Sean was too taken aback by this inadvertent invasion of his privacy to reply.

"Anyway," Patrick continued, obviously enjoying the stunned state he'd evoked in his brother, "a little more wenchin' would do ye good, is what. Keep your mind off these sweet things we have to deliver to our clients."

"I can separate business from pleasure as well as the next man," Sean retorted in a cool, deadly growl.

"Ah, well then, lad," Patrick began again in a cajoling voice, "why don't you strut over there and persuade that well-to-do field mouse to dance with ye. I'm sick to death of always bein' stuck with that part of it!"

"Fine. That I will," Sean said with a determined gleam in his eye. And without an instant of hesitation, he strode off to prove that he could succeed where his brother had failed.

A moment or two later, he neared the cluster of wealthy maidens with a gait that was only semiconfident. It was never a woman's response to him which concerned him, but his to her. He found it more and more unbearable each year to have to dance with and woo their quarries, only to be forced to stop before it all went too far. He had, therefore, been recently leaving the seductive portion of their business to his brother. But now, clearly, it was his turn once more, and he knew he would have to do his best to remain emotionally detached.

Yet, mindful of all of this, he couldn't believe what he found himself doing as he stood before the demure threesome seconds later. It wasn't Jennifer Plithe's hand he reached for, but that of her more solicitous, green-eyed *friend!*

The young lady was so startled by his touch that she emitted the most alluring gasp Sean had ever heard, and he stood frozen for several seconds, marveling at her—at how astonishingly verdant her eyes were.

He felt suddenly oblivious to his surroundings, swept away with wondering what had compelled him to take her hand, rather than that of his true target. Was it the paradisiacal fragrance she wore, the winsome perfume that she had been wafting at him with each stroke of her fan? Was it the radiant quality of her ivory complexion, framed, as it was, by her rich, coppery hair? She was, clearly, an unworldly creature, a treasure chest of gemlike hues and seductive scent; and only by the grace of God was Sean able to choke out his invitation for her to join him now in a dance.

His words were immediately followed by a tense swallow and another entreating gaze into her emerald eyes. He searched for some benignity in them, some indication that she would either accept his offer or allow him to simply drown, then and there, in the sea green depths that surrounded her pupils. No other alternatives seemed possible, since he knew he would find himself quite unable to move, should she refuse him.

She regarded him for what felt like an eternity, those hypnotic eyes of hers seeming as all-powerful to Sean as Caesar's thumb in a Roman arena. She appeared, in that instant, to be capable of both cruel indifference and the most heavenly affection, and he silently prayed that it would be the latter.

How old was she? Sixteen. Maybe seventeen, he guessed. Then he sternly acknowledged that he had left himself open to the compassion of a virtual child, and now, fool that he was, he had no choice but to await her verdict.

Then, suddenly, his breath was restored to him and the heart-stopping seconds were ended as a gentle smile began to play upon her lips. She lowered her eyes in a bashful manner, one that hardly seemed befitting such a goddess, and then, at last, she spoke.

"I will," she agreed.

"Ye will?" Sean echoed, no longer feeling the legs that still seemed to be supporting his weight.

As she lifted her face once more, those jewel-like orbs were again revealed. But this time, fortunately, they were mercifully veiled by the black fringe of her long lashes. "Dance with ye," she added with a light laugh that, had it been any longer or louder, would have seemed incredibly heartless in the face of the enervated state she had managed to induce in him.

"Ah . . . yes," he stammered, trying to reciprocate her casual smile, "dance."

While the intensity of her presence was more than enough to drown out all around him, Sean did seem to hear the fiddlers playing a sweet-flowing folk tune in the background, and it began to dawn on him that, somehow or another, he would have to find the strength, the presence of mind, needed to guide this exquisite creature out among the other dancers and lead her through the demanding paces. He knew, however, that he would probably find himself unable to sustain the steadiness such a dance required and that he might not be able to summon the concentration necessary to make congenial small talk with her all the while. Rather, he had, almost magically, transcended the stage of introductory conversation and was more than ready to proceed to the most intimate of exchanges. Indeed, he had an overwhelming urge in that instant to wrap himself up with this angel of a girl, to pull her closely to him and find refuge in her warmth and softness, as one would with an eiderdown quilt on a howling January night.

"I don't know ye under all that black, do I, sir?" Heather asked as he led her out to the rows of dancers seconds later.

Sean wondered at her casual manner, the easy way in which the words flowed from her, while he, on the other hand, was finding himself stumbling over the simplest replies. He tried to smile, but his lips became a quivering, nervous mass, and he was forced to clench his jaw and assume a solemn expression. "I think not, my lady. I would remember havin' met someone as splendid as you."

Heather fought a smile. Not only did he appear to be unusually handsome under his black mask, but he was a true charmer to boot! What a pity he was from lowly sharecropper stock. Her father would never approve of her encouraging the amorous attentions of one from such a humble station in life. He far preferred the wealthy, albeit chilly, variety of male for Heather, his only child. And as far as he was concerned, having won the courtship of Malcolm Byrne, Heather needed to look no further.

Heather didn't agree. Not only did she differ with her father on this point, but lately she had begun to take advantage of every opportunity to meet eligible males on her own. This wedding dance was, of course, just such an occasion, and she found herself curtsying now to one of the most attractive young men she had ever met. He bowed in return, and the sprightly dance began, her hand joined with his. She didn't really care whether or not he was wealthy. He was charming, complimentary, and obviously quite taken with her; and that was a hell of a lot more than could be said for Malcolm Byrne.

"What farm are ye from, then?" she inquired, unable to resist engaging in the fashionable asides that couples usually exchanged during the promenade portions of such dances.

"Farm?"

"Yes. You're a strawboy, aren't ye?"

"Oh . . . aye. I am . . . from the Murphy farm," he added, as convincingly as possible. In all of Ireland, there didn't seem to be a name more common than Murphy, and given that, there was sure to be at least one farmer who answered to it thereabouts. Sean was, therefore, willing to wager that the young lady would believe this claim.

She flashed him a complaisant smile, offering no rebuttal, and he breathed a sigh of relief.

As they began their second promenade a moment or two later, Sean felt her fingers wriggle slightly in his overly tight grasp, and to his chagrin, he saw an undeniably pained look in her eyes.

He instantly loosened his grip. It was an occupational hazard of sorts, he silently consoled himself, this fear of letting a wealthy maiden slip from his clutches. "Forgive me, my lady. I'm sorry if I hurt ye. All I can say in my own defense is that, when a man happens upon one as lovely as you, he may not wish to let her go."

Heather found herself too surprised by his candor to offer an immediate reply. Finally, she emitted a light, unnerved laugh. "I do understand," she assured in a hushed voice. "And thank ye for your kind praise. But as ye must know, my hand is not mine to give."

They now stood at the far end of the line of dancers, and Sean seized this handclapping pause in the reel to raise the young lady's hand to his lips and hold it there much longer than was considered proper.

Heather looked on in silence, appalled at his forwardness, but too enraptured by his engaging blue eyes to protest. To her further amazement, it wasn't just the warmth of his lips that she felt pressed to the back of her hand, but the sudden, sensuous wetness of his *tongue!* Indeed, it seemed as pointed and purposeful an appendage as any she'd ever encountered, and the implications of such an overture left her breathless.

A chill ran through her, and she felt hot arousal

rising from the most unutterable of places beneath her skirts. What an enticer he was, what a shameless tease, as his eyes remained unflinchingly locked upon hers! What was more, he was clearly taking pleasure in seeing the shocked blush that she felt spreading over her face now.

Only the two of them knew. Though they were surrounded by others, no one else could possibly have detected the steamy message that was passing between them. And for what seemed the second time that evening, Heather attempted to pull her hand free of his grasp without calling attention to herself amid the other dancers. Sean held it tightly between his stout fingers, however, refusing to let it go.

"And whom shall I ask for your hand, fair maiden, should I want it?"

"My . . . my father," she answered, her voice cracking. Her eyes would have filled with frightened tears had she not continued to experience the ineffable response in the most intimate parts of her, had his fervent solicitation not filled her mind with a sinful flash of fantasies about the lengths to which he might dare go, were they ever to find themselves alone together. His grip, his eyes, the golden shimmer of his thick blond hair, everything about him held her fast in those seconds.

"And what would your father's name be?" he continued with a blatantly sensual smile playing upon his lips.

She answered reflexively, as though under his spell. "Master Monaghan."

"Brian Monaghan?" Sean pursued. "The Monaghan who owns the hard coal mines to the north?"

She shuddered slightly at the ambitious gleam that suddenly appeared in his eyes. "Aye. The very same . . . I'm Heather Monaghan."

"Ah." He nodded, seeming quite pleased to hear this, and he continued to guide her through the steps of the dance.

"Do . . ." She swallowed back her uneasiness and tried to speak again.

He listened intently, as though her every utterance held some genuine fascination for him.

"Do ye kiss every woman's hand in the way ye did mine just now?" she stammered after several seconds.

He gave her a coy, sideward glance as they again promenaded between the two rows of dancers. "And what way is that?"

The grin he was fighting, coupled with his knowing tone, made her begin to seethe. "Ah, ye know perfectly well what I mean!"

"Did ye find it unpleasant?" he asked in an innocent whisper, his lips hovering close to her ear.

"No . . . no," she choked.

"Then why protest?" His tone was easy and matter-of-fact. "It was meant to bring you pleasure. I tasted of you, and you, in turn, had a taste of things to come."

Were he any other man, under any other circumstances, Heather would have slapped him then and there. But he was so straightforward, so intent upon touching some innermost part of her, that she found herself quite overwhelmed by it all.

"I'm enamored of ye, ye see, dear Lady Heather,"

he added. "So I can take no responsibility for my actions."

"Oh, aye," she clucked, with as much disgust as she could feign. She needed to challenge him, to convince herself of his sincerity. "I know you hooligan farm boys. The sort of 'enamoredness' that springs from your *loins!*"

He suddenly halted them both in the dance and led her away from the others. "No," he replied, and the teasing look in his eyes gave way to something else, something penetrating and real. "From here," he murmured, pressing her trembling fingers to the level of his heart.

Was it her imagination or was this the most poignant gesture she had ever witnessed? She was too moved to do anything but let her hand continue to rest in his, rising and falling with his quickened respiration and subject to his relentless heartbeat.

"Ye really must let me go, sir. I have to return to my friends now."

There was a strange quiver in her voice, and Sean believed she was close to tears. He couldn't imagine, however, why she should feel like crying. Perhaps, he thought, she was simply confused by the jumble of emotions that seemed to be welling up in her. In any case, he released her and watched in wonder as she backed away from him, her lovely green eyes glistening with misgivings.

She had to return to her "friends," she'd said. The words echoed in his mind now as he glanced over her shoulder to see a sinister-looking man standing next to one of her female companions. He was stout and dark-haired, and he was dressed entirely in black, in apparel that somehow reminded Sean of an undertaker's. The man's eyes bore a murderous glint, and there was no escaping the fact that he was looking directly at Sean. But that was not all that disturbed Sean in that moment. Jennifer Plithe was missing from the scene, and a quick scan of the east side of the barn revealed that Patrick was gone as well.

Bloody hell, a voice within him scolded. He had let himself get so caught up with Miss Monaghan that he had temporarily forgotten their objective. "I must go as well," he called out to Heather as she continued to back away from him. "But I'll be back for ye. Rest assured of that." With that, Sean made his way quickly to the back door of the barn and disappeared into the cloaking darkness outside.

Heather stood staring after him for several seconds. She suddenly felt very chilly, and she pulled her shawl up around her shoulders. *"I'll be back for ye."* Was it a threat or a promise? There had definitely been a measure of forewarning in his voice, yet his eyes had shone with such gentleness as he'd said it. She shook her head slightly, as if trying to wake herself from a dream. They were, after all, some most disquieting words for a young man to offer in parting.

Chapter 3

Malcolm Byrne had entered the barn a few minutes earlier and now stood at Shannon Kennedy's side. His nostrils were flaring like those of an enraged bull. To his relief, he realized at this point that his employer, Brian Monaghan, was still too busy socializing with the bride's parents in the barnyard to overhear the angry words he had in store for his daughter, Heather. He, therefore, seized the opportunity to sneak up behind her, where she still stood, staring wistfully after her mysterious dance partner.

"Who was that man with you?" he demanded, noting, with a sadistic sneer, how the sudden thunder of his voice made Heather turn on her heel with a startled gasp.

As she looked up into Malcolm's dour brown eyes, however, her surprise instantly turned to anger. "I don't know who he was. He simply asked me to dance."

"Ye little liar," Malcolm growled. "I saw him holdin' your hand, and I demand to know what he could have said to make ye go so pale."

"What he said to me is no business of yours, Malcolm Byrne! And what are *you* doin' here? I would hardly have thought it possible that you'd lower yourself to anythin' as boorish as a barn dance."

"I'm here with your father. He's outside talking to the Cassidys."

"Well, go back out there and join him, for mercy's sake because *I* surely didn't invite ye!"

He glowered at her, and the blackness of his hair and eyes in that dim light made him look more ominous than usual to Heather. "You're a real little shrew, aren't ye now. Things will change once we're married. You can be certain of that!"

"I don't have any intentions of marryin' ye, Mr. Byrne. So don't be wastin' your breath with talk of it."

"And what do ye think you're doin' out here without a proper chaperone? Even your mollycoddlin' father won't approve when he comes in here and finds ye alone."

"I'm not alone." She turned about and saw Shannon Kennedy engaged in a flirtatious chat with one of the Cassidys' shirttail relatives, a chandler from the town of Kilkenny. "Shannon's here, and so is Jennifer Plithe."

Malcolm skimmed the crowd with a skeptical scowl. "I don't see Jenny anywhere."

"So, I suppose you'll be callin' me a liar again, ye great blusterin' bully!" Heather snarled with her hands planted defiantly on her hips. "Well, Jenny *was* here earlier. I simply—"

"You simply lost track of her while ye went dancin' with that lout," Malcolm interrupted with a vengeful look in his eye.

35

"Shannon," Heather beckoned to her friend in exasperation. "Where's Jenny?"

Shannon looked up from her conversation, and even from several paces away, Heather detected an embarrassed flush in her cheeks. Shannon excused herself from her male companion and crossed to where Heather and Malcolm were standing.

"She's . . . she's *indisposed,*" she answered in a chaste whisper, refusing to look at Malcolm as she spoke.

Heather cocked her head questioningly. "Relieving herself up at the house, ye mean?"

"No." Shannon laughed uneasily. "Well, you know Jenny. She's not proud," she explained, directing her eyes toward the back door of the barn. "I think she just went down the hill to the earth closet."

Heather turned to face Malcolm with an accusing glare. "There now. Are ye satisfied? Now that you've embarrassed this poor, dear girl beyond remedy. Or will ye be goin' down the hill yourself to catch our Jenny with her skirts up?"

"You're a spiteful little cat," Malcolm noted under his breath as Shannon took her hurried leave and went back to resume her tête-à-tête with the Chandler. "I'm going outside to tell your father how I feel about ye consortin' with peasants. And at a *barn dance,* no less!"

Heather waved him off with the fervor of a fishwife. He had an amazing knack for bringing out the worst in her. "Go then! We'll be glad to be rid of ye, is what. Everyone was havin' a grand time, I hope ye realize, till you arrived!"

Malcolm, choosing to ignore her retort, stormed through the crowd and out the front door of the barn, feeling even more enraged than he had when he'd entered. Heather was one of many necessary evils in his life these days. If the truth be known, he couldn't honestly imagine being married to her. She was a frivolous, undisciplined child to whom he was sure to have to take a riding crop on their wedding night. On the other hand, however, Malcolm couldn't imagine life without Brian Monaghan's mines. He had worked in those coal beds ever since he was eight, and for the past decade, he'd acted as their sole foreman, overseeing every detail of their operations. There was, therefore, no doubt in his mind that it had been *his* hard work that had made the mines the incredibly profitable enterprise they were today. It followed, of course, that he, more than any other man, deserved to inherit the business when old man Monaghan died. Naturally, the best way to ensure such an inheritance was to marry Monaghan's only child. So, like it or not, Malcolm was stuck with Heather, and she with him. And he'd be damned if he'd allow some piss-ant plowboy to come along at this late date and interfere with his plan!

Sean was depending more upon instinct than sight to lead him to Patrick minutes later. Though it was a moonlit evening, it was still pretty dark outside, and as he ventured farther and farther from the noisy gathering in the barn now, he found himself relying more upon his heightened, outlaw hearing to guide him to his brother, than upon any real ability to see.

In the seconds that followed, he crept over what appeared to be the exposed gnarled roots of an ancient oak and down the steep slope of a hill. Then he paused once more to let his senses again determine his bearings and gauge his course. Naturally, were he any other man, he'd have brought a lantern with him from the barn. His line of work just did not allow for such luxuries, however. So, over their past six years of bride snatching, he and Patrick had simply learned to embrace darkness as a necessary consociate in their occupation.

He stood in open view now on a grassy knoll below the hill, anxiously awaiting some signal from Pat, yet wary of inadvertently scaring off their quarry. After several seconds, the expected signal came. It was a subtle rhythmic clicking sound, like that of an incensed squirrel, and Sean knew instantly that it had been produced by his brother. He breathed a sigh of relief at this realization and again held himself perfectly still, waiting for Pat to make the sound once more. This time, as Pat did so, Sean was able to place it, and he peered into the darkness to his right and instantly spotted his brother standing with his back pressed to the right side of a nearby outhouse. Pat, in turn, having long since spotted Sean, cautiously waved him on.

Sean rushed to him as soundlessly as possible in the seconds that followed. He could only conclude that Miss Plithe was in the earth closet, because, once he was close enough to see his brother clearly, Pat began gesturing for him to circle around to the other side of it. Sean, of course, did so, realizing that the plan was for them to each take a side and concurrently await the young lady's eventual exit. They'd developed that skill through their years of partnership, the ability to communicate as wordlessly as two wolves collaborating in a kill. And though it was, indeed, a handy skill, it had its drawbacks—like now, as Pat leaned forward and stood glaring across at Sean with obvious aggravation at the fact that he'd, once again, allowed his amorous feelings to interfere with their work. Their telepathic abilities were more a curse than a blessing in such instances.

Sean didn't really know what to do in response. He simply offered his brother an allaying smile and a shrug, and then, assuming a dutiful air, he crouched to a lunging position and readied himself to help tackle their prey the instant she emerged.

In the minutes that followed, there was scarcely a sound from within. Only the occasional rustling of the young lady's skirts offered any testimony to the fact that the facility was, indeed, in use. So, after what seemed an eternity of silence, Sean leaned forward once more, to again lock eyes with his brother. He flashed Patrick a scowl that was meant to convey both his impatience and his male perplexity as to what on earth could possibly be taking her so long in there. Pat shook his head with equal exasperation, and again, the two men positioned themselves to lunge when the fateful moment finally came.

Sean withdrew his watch from his doublet pocket and caught a glimpse or two of its hands in the intermittent moonlight of that cloud-flecked night. To his surprise, he noted that Miss Plithe had been thusly occupied for a full four minutes since his arrival—a veritable lifetime to two such anxious men. Finally, two minutes later, at precisely quarter to eight, their quarry emerged, and to Sean's dismay, she was only now endeavoring to get her billowing frock and kirtles shoved back down about the lower half of her.

He couldn't help wondering why a lady of such fine upbringing would wait until she was outside to undertake so intimate a task. But then, seeing the huge circumference of her raised skirts, the reason became clear: the earth closet simply didn't have the room to allow for the manipulation of such garments. So, Miss Plithe had obviously given up trying to redress inside and had simply elected to depend upon the cloak of darkness outside to preserve her modesty as she did so now.

Sean felt a sudden tightness in his stomach as Patrick lunged out and grasped Jennifer's left ankle an instant later. He couldn't help pitying her in her embarrassingly encumbered state, and he wished, however futilely, that they could have waited to ambush her until she'd gotten her skirts smoothed down more fully. True to his roguish code, however, Patrick was taking full advantage of the situation, and as soon as he grabbed the poor dear, she toppled face first into the muddy expanse that lay just beyond the outhouse's threshold. Luckily, she seemed too startled to scream in that instant. She merely emitted the squishing sound of one who had just had all of the air forced out of her lungs.

Sean was on her in that same second, throwing his body over hers and clamping his huge right palm over her mouth. They couldn't allow her to scream; the barn was too close by and the tune the fiddlers were playing was probably too soft to drown out the noise.

It was a most discomfiting moment for all concerned, as Sean lay prone over her and she struggled with him, her arching form causing her bared legs to jostle against his loins. Sean, in response, ordered Patrick to take over gagging the girl. Then he scrambled back to his feet and pulled her skirts downward to cover her. For an instant, Miss Plithe clearly did not know in *which* direction her gown was being maneuvered, and she issued a dread-filled scream. Fortunately, Patrick's hand was there to muffle it. But then, for some reason, it was Patrick who cried out, and it wasn't until Sean saw blood trickling down his brother's wrist that he realized why. The girl had bitten him! Miss Plithe had sunk her teeth so far into the palm of Pat's hand that she'd actually drawn blood, and the poor chap seemed to be having all he could do now to stifle his response to the pain of it.

Sean grabbled in the darkness to withdraw a handkerchief from the sleeve of his doublet, and he handed it to his brother. Still snarling in agony, Pat accepted the gag from him and tied it rather roughly about Jenny's mouth. Then he pulled away from her and surveyed the damage down to the meaty mound beneath his thumb.

"It's bleeding like the devil," he hissed. "Damned little bitch!"

Sean continued to straddle their captive, leaning forward now to keep her slender arms pinned to the ground.

"She thought we were trying to rape her. You'd have done the same in her place," Sean whispered, trying to quell his brother's anger. He knew that neither of them could risk becoming blinded by rage at a moment as critical as this. And considering the pre-

41

carious nature of their business, it was always preferable for him or Pat to suffer any injuries that might occur, rather than to risk letting their captives be hurt in any way—spoiled goods, as it were. It was, after all, a profession that was akin to the transport of tropical flowers or birds; no damage to their delicate "cargo" was tolerable to their clients.

"I'll get her for it, though," Patrick replied in a growl. With that he leaned over the sprawled body of their captive and ripped a strip of cloth from the flounce of one of her petticoats. Then he hurriedly wrapped the cloth about his wound to stop the bleeding. "Before we hand her over to that ruddy baker, I'll have a go at her. Mark my words!"

Hearing Pat's threat, Jenny once again issued a squeal of distress and strained with all of her might against Sean's weight.

"Stop scarin' her, ye daft bugger," Sean scolded. "And help me get her to her feet!"

Pat, in response, grudgingly bent down and took hold of Miss Plithe's left arm. Sean, meanwhile, eased himself off of her and stooped down to take hold of her right side. Then they lifted her from the cold, muddy ground. In all other matters the Kerry brothers were consistently at odds. They disagreed on everything from which ales to drink with supper, to the relative worth of political uprisings against the Orange. When it came to carrying out abductions, however, they were of one, dangerously unified mind, and few words were needed between them.

"She's covered with mud," Sean complained, having felt from the outset that tackling her on her way out of the privy was rather slipshod procedure.

"And who's to blame for that now? *You* with your taste for green-eyed beauties! If you had danced with this one, the way ye were supposed to, I wouldn't have had to resort to trackin' her down here, I hope ye know!"

"Well, we've no time to bicker about it," Sean countered, knowing full well that Patrick's anger was justified. "We'll just have to get her a bath somewhere along the way, is what."

Miss Plithe gave forth an apprehensive groan at hearing this.

"Ah, she doesn't fancy that idea, does she now," Pat observed with a vengeful grin.

"No. I don't suppose she does."

They walked as far as the old oak that Sean had passed en route. Then Pat relinquished his hold on their captive, and Sean pinioned her scrawny figure up against the tree's trunk.

"Hold her fast," Patrick directed, "and I'll fetch the horses."

Sean, of course, did so; but he couldn't help feeling rather uneasy as he watched his brother trudge uphill to the hitching post. He wasn't sure why he felt apprehensive, but he knew that it had something to do with their captive. It was just him and her now in the darkness, and her eyes, wide with trepidation, were mercilessly fixed upon his face. Her modestly endowed chest rose and fell in the moonlight with the racing respiration of a scared rabbit. He could hardly bear to look at her; yet she appeared to be searching his eyes for any trace of reassurance. She had stopped struggling against him for the moment and seemed to be directing all of her energy into the

43

silent task of evoking some words of comfort from him.

He, therefore, offered her some in a whisper as he continued to straddle her against the tree. "We won't kill you, miss. I give ye my word that we won't hurt ye in any way."

But in spite of this offering, her gray eyes continued to probe his, focusing alternately upon his right eye and then upon his left. She was obviously asking the next question, a question that he knew he could not allow himself to answer.

"I can't tell ye why we're takin' ye or where, Miss Plithe. I'm terribly sorry. But I just can't."

Her eyes remained locked upon his for a moment longer. Then, apparently seeing that he really did not intend to say more, she directed her gaze defeatedly downward.

Sean felt great compunction in those seconds, as a single tear trickled down her right cheek and was absorbed by the gag wrapped about her mouth. Sean, in turn, freed his shackling grasp on her right wrist just long enough to blot her wet cheek with the cuff of his silken sleeve.

At this, her eyes flashed up at him once more, as though she were both surprised and touched. He resisted meeting her gaze again, however, resisted acknowledging this tender exchange between them. He couldn't allow himself to become emotionally involved with yet another captive, and he knew it. So, heaving an exasperated sigh, he stared off in the direction of the hitching post.

What, in the name of God, was keeping Pat? If he didn't return with their horses soon, Jennifer was sure to begin kicking and thrashing again, placing Sean in the hapless position of having to knock her unconscious, something to which he really didn't want to have to resort.

Thankfully, Pat reappeared a moment or two later, sauntering down the hill with their horses in tow and their riding capes draped over his shoulder. His stride, however, was annoyingly languorous and unbothered, as though he were on his way to a picnic or a county fair.

"Make haste, ye laggard," Sean hissed. "I can't hold her still forever, ye know!"

"Comin', comin'," Pat returned calmly, bringing the horses to a halt at the base of the hill. He dropped their reins and pinned them to the ground with his foot, displaying the agility of a true horseman. Then he reached back to Sean's saddle and freed a long loop of rope from around its pommel, and having done this, he tossed it to Sean. "Tie her up, then, and let's be off."

Sean, in turn, caught the rope in his left hand. Then he turned the girl around and began to tie her hands behind her back. It all went amiss somehow in those seconds, however, as Sean looked up once more to see Patrick messing about with his riding cape. He was ceremoniously arranging it around his shoulders and bending down to inspect his mud-caked boots with the absent-minded manner of the drunkard he was, and it was clear to Sean that all the liquor he'd been off drinking before his arrival was finally catching up with him. The next thing Sean knew, Pat's pistol was falling from the waist of his breeches and it landed on the ground near Sean's feet with a conspicuous thud.

Sean's eyes lighted upon the weapon in roughly the same instant as Jennifer's seemed to, and seconds later, Sean found himself diving down upon her in a frantic scramble to get hold of it. But she was a bright one, this lass; and even though it was apparent that Sean would succeed in wrenching the gun from her tiny hands, she had the presence of mind to pull the trigger amid their struggling and fire a shot to signal her distress.

Time became agonizingly protracted for Sean in the seconds that followed. He jerked the gun from her trembling fingers and dealt her a heavy blow upon the back of her head—an act he might not have had the will to carry out, were he given an instant longer to contemplate it. Her head slumped forward, as a result, and she sank to the ground.

Meanwhile, Pat had had the good sense to mount his horse, and he was now just a couple feet from Sean and reaching out to collect their unconscious captive. Sean, in turn, gathered up Miss Plithe's now-dead weight and helped to ease her, sidesaddled, onto Pat's steed. He then took the rope that was meant for her hands and tied it about her ankles in the hopes of minimizing the damage done once she regained consciousness and began kicking and gouging in protest again.

Pat looped his arms under hers and clasped her limp body to his. Then his hands closed about the horse's reins. With that done, he gave his brother a nod, and Sean delivered a stinging slap to his steed's haunch. Pat's stallion responded by galloping around the right side of the barn and off to the southwest, directly on course for their destination of Lismore. Then Sean scrambled to be off as well. He flung his riding cape over his shoulders in the chilly night wind and mounted his horse in one, smooth motion. He knew, however, that his was not to be an easy get-away, because the shot Jenny had fired had, naturally, brought several curious guests out of the barn.

Among the first to reach the barn's back door, as the shot was heard, was Heather Monaghan, and she now stood gaping in wonder at what she'd thought she'd seen happening in the darkness. It had been *Jenny.* Some strawboy had, apparently, made off with Jennifer Plithe, and he was being followed now by a young man who looked frighteningly like the blond strawboy with whom Heather had danced earlier!

Realizing this, Heather reflexively turned and posed a question to the befuddled circle of guests who had gathered behind her to investigate the shot. "That was Jenny Plithe he took, wasn't it?" she croaked.

To her dismay, no one answered, and she turned back to see the fair-haired gentleman taking off like a shot, his regal cape billowing out at his sides and his thatch of golden hair luminous in the moonlight as he disappeared around the right side of the barn.

"It was Jenny," Heather concluded, seeing, out of the corner of her eye, that Shannon was now standing beside her. "It *was* Jenny," she said again, and Shannon offered her a horrified expression and a nod.

Heather knew she couldn't waste another moment. She turned away from the back threshold once

47

more and began making her way through the crowd to the front entrance of the barn.

"Father! Father!" she screamed as she reached the front door, and she found herself breathless as she dashed across the barnyard to where he and Malcolm were still conversing with the Cassidys seconds later. "They've kidnapped Jenny Plithe," she exclaimed. "Two strawboys have taken her off somewhere!" She gasped with relief as she pointed southward and saw that the riders were still visible in the distance. "Go after them, someone, *please!*"

Malcolm, having seen the blond-haired object of his wrath race past on horseback seconds before, was the first to run to the Cassidys' stable and emerge from it again on one of their horses. This was, of course, a careless choice on his part, a reflexive move that seemed more expedient than taking the time to unhitch one of the horses from Monaghan's carriage. A plow horse would never be able to catch up with the steeds that the strawboys were riding, but sadly, chaos prevailed, and Brian Monaghan, not thinking any more clearly than his employee, followed suit— as did the Cassidys' three eldest sons.

Heather, feeling unbearably helpless in those tense moments, simply turned and clutched at Mistress Cassidy's skirts. "It's my fault," she wailed. "I was the one who brought Jenny here. I invited her."

Her kindly hostess hugged her close and patted her back, shushing and rocking her, as the crowd of wedding guests began pouring out the front of the barn and teeming all about them.

"Don't be worryin' yourself about it now, child," Mistress Cassidy cooed. "Our boys will soon overtake them. They know the lay of this land a great deal better in the dark than those strangers ever could, and they'll fetch your friend back here in no time at all. You can rest assured of that."

Heather emitted a pained sigh, and a terrible storm began brewing in her stomach. She wanted Jennifer rescued, but she refused to believe that the breathtaking stranger she'd danced with could possibly have been involved in her abduction. She pulled away from the graying matriarch of the Cassidy farm, just long enough to search her face for a possible answer. "What could they want with her, do ye suppose?"

"Bride snatchers," some gentleman in the crowd declared, and the note of certainty in his voice made Heather's blood run cold. "The Kerry brothers, I'll wager," he continued with a confident nod. "Wanted in every county from here to Derry for it, and their favorite guise is dressin' up like strawboys, or so rumor has it."

Heather furrowed her brow, finding this neighbor's conjecture too unimaginable to be mere fabrication. "And what will they do with her?" she pursued with a shiver.

"Marry her off to some stranger and claim a share of her dowry for themselves."

Heather's mouth fell open incredulously. "So it's not Jenny they want, but her dowry?"

"You're a clever lass, you are," he answered, laughingly elbowing the gentleman who stood next to him.

"But that's outrageous!"

49

"Aye, it is," he agreed, "but mighty lucrative, and not altogether unlawful either."

"So she can never be returned to her family?"

The man looked skeptical about the prospects of it. "Not if they have the chance to lay claim to her, she can't. She's used goods then, ye see, and one night will be all 'twill take for her family to assume so."

Heather scowled at him perplexedly. " 'Lay claim?' What does that mean?"

"*Whisht!* You shush up now, Gordon O'Malley," Mistress Cassidy interjected scoldingly, again hugging Heather to her rotund form. "I'll not have ye discussin' such things with a motherless child in my barnyard!"

Virtually everyone in the region knew of the untimely death of Heather's mother five years before, and Heather had, consequently, found herself being coddled by her older female neighbors ever since. Most of the time she appreciated the attention, but now she wished that her hostess would simply be quiet and let the gentleman speak. She wanted desperately to know what his cryptic allusion had meant. But with Mrs. Cassidy acting so protective, it was clear that she wasn't apt to find out.

In any case, Heather knew that she could safely conclude that he'd been referring to something unseemly. Why else would Mistress Cassidy have responded so vehemently to it? *But what on earth could it have been?* Heather wondered, falling silent now and staring off, like the rest of the crowd, at the five pursuing riders, who had already become mere dots of darkness on the evening horizon.

Chapter 4

Malcolm Byrne was close enough now to get several good shots off at the blond strawboy. He couldn't have known as he fired, however, that Sean's backward glances at him were filled more with contempt than fear.

"You keep goin'," Sean called out to Pat, who was riding at least seventy meters ahead of him. "I'll take care of 'em."

"Don't kill 'em," Pat shouted back at him, not slowing his pace. "The law'll have our hides if ye kill any of 'em."

"I won't," Sean assured. "Just keep goin'."

At that, Patrick spurred his horse on to a run, and Sean fell back just long enough to fire one good shot in his assailant's direction. He recognized the sinister figure as he looked back and took aim. It was the black-haired bloke who'd stood glowering at him as he'd concluded his dance with Heather Monaghan. He was a spiteful-looking fellow, to be sure—obviously someone who had some stake in Heather's future. Because he was too young to be her father and too resentful of Sean's attentions to her to be her brother, Sean deduced that he was nothing less than a fellow suitor, a rival for her hand. That was all he could conclude, and based on this, he sensed now that this man's relentless pursuit and shooting were much more on Miss Monaghan's behalf than Miss Plithe's.

The other men, who were chasing Sean, had fallen far behind the brunet. Their plow horses were clearly unable to maintain the speed necessary to catch up with Sean's bay, but this didn't keep the dark-haired rider from continuing to try. He just kept driving his horse on, pushing it, until its mouth was foaming and its white breath carried on the night wind with the steady swishing of a water wheel.

"Crazy bastard!" Sean growled. Anyone who tortured a harmless beast like that deserved to be shot. He had no qualms, therefore, as he fired at the brunet now. Sean watched as he jerked back an instant later, dropping his reins and slapping a hand to his wounded left shoulder. Then, seeing him hit, Sean spurred his steed and raced on to catch up with Patrick, who was, by this time, well out of sight in the growing darkness and, thankfully, out of danger as well.

All in all, Sean concluded, it had been short work to shake off the men chasing them. In addition to the difference in horses, Pat and Sean also possessed the considerable advantage of having already executed many such getaways.

"Ye lunatic," Patrick bellowed as Sean finally rode up next to him. "Did ye have to resort to shootin' at 'em?"

Sean's voice was rock-steady though he was terribly winded by this point. "I had no choice. They were gettin' threatenin'ly close and I had to clip their feathers a bit."

"Fine solution that was! We were only wanted for bride snatchin' before tonight. And now it's murder, thanks to you!"

"Murder, huh! I'd be surprised if I so much as grazed the bastard. He was such a sop in his fine, ruffled shirt and frock coat! I just knew he'd turn tail at the first bit of bloodshed."

"Well, let's just hope they're gone for good and all," Pat hollered back over the steady thunder of their horses' hoofbeats. "We hardly need 'em on our heels all the way to Lismore, do we now."

"Of course not."

After a few minutes more, they looked back again to make certain they'd shaken their pursuers. With this confirmed, they finally let their horses drop into a slower gait, and they began traveling in easy unison over the moonlit countryside.

"Still, Sean," Pat continued, shaking his head in his usual older-brother-knows-what's-best manner, "ye had no call to shoot at 'em. They would have lost us sooner or later, anyway, on those drag-ass garrons."

"But didn't ye hear him shootin' at me? I can understand a bullet or two, but he shot several times, and I have to tell ye, I found it damned gallin'!"

Pat did not reply, apparently having said all he'd wanted to on the subject. Sean, in turn, found that he, too, was content now to ride without conversing. It was already pitch black out, and he was too cold and tired to care about anything but reaching their destination and bedding down for the night.

Pat was right, of course, Sean silently acknowledged minutes later. There probably had been no call for him to return his assailant's fire. In fact, it was rather an irrational thing to have done. But remembering the brunet's possessive regard as he'd said good night to Heather Monaghan, Sean realized that the shooting had been sheer impulse—the angry clashing of antlers over a coveted doe. Their fray was that basic, that instinctive; and perhaps, on some far-flung level, the shot had been meant to serve as Sean's message to Heather that he intended to claim her as his own, that he would, indeed, be back for her, in spite of any obstacles.

"Well, I hope you're satisfied," Malcolm grumbled to Heather as the physician cleaned and bandaged the gunshot wound in his shoulder forty-five minutes later. "You should be ashamed of yourself, encouragin' the attentions of such a scoundrel! I'm wounded and your best friend is kidnapped, and all because you didn't have the good sense to have a proper chaperone along with ye from the first!"

Heather had been crying off and on over the incident for nearly two hours, and she could do little more by this point than emit a repentant whimper in response. She blamed herself completely for what had happened, and Malcolm's admonishments were only making her feel worse.

"Let her alone," Mistress Cassidy chimed in on

Heather's behalf. "She says she only danced with the lad. So how was she to know he'd steal Miss Plithe?"

It was getting late, and most of the wedding guests, out of concern for Jennifer, had drawn the festivities to a close and gone back to their homes. Only half a dozen of them remained, and they were now congregated in the Cassidys' master bedchamber, looking on as Malcolm's wound was being tended and listening as Byrne indulged in giving an awe-inspiring, if somewhat embellished, account of their brief pursuit of the two outlaws. Malcolm sat on Mr. and Mrs. Cassidy's four-poster bed, stripped to the waist as the physician continued to tend to him. He was clutching a bedpost with his left hand and an open bottle of whiskey with his right, and he took regular swigs of the pain-killing liquid—that was, when he wasn't casting scathing looks at Heather.

"It was good of ye, Malcolm, to go after Jenny . . . to fight for her like that," Heather acknowledged for the third or fourth time that evening, and she punctuated this declaration with an amenable sniffle.

"That it was," her father added, and everyone nodded in agreement.

Malcolm smiled at his employer, glad for the praise. In truth, however, it wasn't Jennifer who had been the cause of his pursuit and consequent shooting; it was his covetous feelings for Heather—or more specifically, for the Monaghan mines. There was, of course, no sense in admitting that. If old man Monaghan and the rest of this naive lot wished to believe that his actions were purely chivalrous, why, Malcolm would do all he could to encourage it.

"Is there no chance of recoverin' the girl?" Mistress Cassidy inquired. "Surely there must be."

"Aye," Malcolm replied, wincing as the physician helped him back on with his shirt. "We'll rouse the sheriff and Jenny's brothers straightaway and ride southwest on some *decent* horses."

"Ah, but don't go after 'em again yourself, though, Malcolm," Mr. Monaghan gingerly advised. "They're murderers, the pair of 'em, and I'd hate to see ye shot a second time."

Malcolm turned to his boss with the bootlicking smile that he reserved for him alone. "But, Brian, one of us must help to put right what our little Heather has put wrong, and ye must agree that I'm far more dispensable at the mines than you are."

Malcolm didn't, for an instant, believe this last part, but he knew that it would strike his boss dumb with gratitude, and a sense of indebtedness was what he always strove to evoke in him.

He was successful as usual. Monaghan looked almost moved to tears now.

"Oh, all right then, lad," he said at last. "But do be careful, won't ye?"

"I shall, indeed," Malcolm declared, rising with a resolute gleam in his eye and making his way out of the room.

Heather was close behind him as he strode down the corridor seconds later and began descending the stairs. "So it was the blond who shot ye?" she asked sheepishly, keeping her voice low so that she wouldn't be overheard by the others as they rose to see him out as well.

Malcolm turned back on his hurried course and

glared up at her, where she stood now, halfway down the stairs. "You know perfectly well it was. And ye also know that it's more your honor than Jenny's that concerns me. I just hope ye weren't foolish enough to let that strawboy's angelic looks win ye over. I've felt his wrath, and I tell ye, lass, that he's a *killer* under the flesh. As deadly as the day is long! And you, ye silly wench, brought him down upon me like a hive of angry bees!" he hissed, reaching the first floor and snatching his frock coat and cape from the wall peg beside the front door.

Heather recoiled at his rage; yet with the thought of the outlaw, she found herself feeling the oddest mixture of remorse and erotic arousal in that moment. She was inexplicably stimulated by the idea of her mysterious dance partner shooting Malcolm— and the cool ease with which such a seasoned felon would surely execute that sort of act. Strangely, she felt almost as seduced by it now as she had been by the way he'd kissed her hand, and the image of his placid blue eyes came flooding back to her. He'd readily shot Malcolm, and she knew that, if given half a chance, he would just as easily have "laid claim" to her—as Mr. O'Malley had phrased it earlier. And though she realized it was rather irrational, part of her genuinely envied Jenny tonight. What an adventure, what a thrill it would be to have such a handsome outlaw steal *her* away into the darkness!

The Kerrys stopped en route at a moonlit creek. They needed to wash the strawboy blackening from their faces. They'd learned, from long, hard experience, that there was no profit in inadvertently scaring their clients with their ominous masks. Sean suggested cleaning up their mud-splattered captive at this point as well, but Patrick seemed unwilling to bother with it. She was still knocked out cold where she sat, slumped over in his saddle, and reviving her with a freezing bath would only lead to a struggle that neither brother cared to wage in the last stretch of their journey. So, they just left her as she was, hoping against hope that their client wouldn't mind their taking the time to bathe her upon their arrival at his abode.

By the time they reached the baker's cottage, Jennifer had finally regained consciousness. She was, however, still very groggy as Sean and Patrick carried her inside. Their client was nowhere to be found, but he'd left his front door unlatched, and there was a hastily penned note affixed to his loop doorknocker. So, after taking their captive inside, Patrick went back, with lantern in hand, to read it aloud.

"It says, 'Due to an unusually large bread order, which was placed with me today by the Fipple Flute Roadhouse, I shall be working late at my ovens. Look for my return after midnight.' Signed, 'Tiernan O'Ryan.' Ah . . . a true romantic," Pat grumbled, tearing the message from the door, crumpling it in his fist, and flinging it to the ground. "Late for his own weddin' bed."

"Humph," Sean replied in befuddlement, continuing to linger beside the settle upon which they'd laid Miss Plithe.

Pat, in turn, proceeded to the fire room, obviously

58

in search of food and drink. Because he still appeared to be seething at Miss Plithe for biting him earlier, Sean knew that the ticklish task of stripping and bathing the girl would be his alone.

Sean continued to stand over Jennifer for several seconds more, dreading the task and simply choosing to observe her now in the amber glow of the baker's fire. She was lying fairly still, but she moaned a bit now and then, like one in the midst of a high fever. Sean, again feeling pity for her, knelt down and untied the rope that bound her ankles. Then he took the gag from her mouth. As he did so, he was sorry to note that there was dried mud splattered over almost every inch of her. Everything from the tiny tendrils of brown hair that framed her face to the lengths of her slender calves bore testimony to the mud bath she'd been through.

Sean went on to remove her shoes. Then he slipped a bolster under her head and stood waiting for any further signs of consciousness from her. But perhaps it was best just to disrobe her before she really came to, a voice within him suggested. *No. No. That wouldn't do at all,* some other part of him admonished. She'd only panic. She'd only conclude that she was being raped, and then he'd have a real fight on his hands. He'd simply have to wait until she came around a bit more, he decided, until she was awake enough to understand that he was simply trying to get her cleaned up. With that, Sean slid her, ever so carefully, farther down on the long settle and sat down next to her reclining form.

After several minutes, Sean looked over again to see that her eyes had finally fallen open. "Jennifer, can ye hear me?" he asked in as soft and unthreatening a voice as he could muster. She didn't respond. She simply stared up at him, glassy-eyed.

Sean rose very slowly and made his way gingerly over to her, bending down once more to look into her face so that he could really assess her cognizance. "Please, Jennifer. I pray thee," he whispered, "answer, if ye can hear what I'm sayin'."

After several seconds, she swallowed dryly and offered him a weak nod.

"We're very sorry about the rap on the head, but I'm afraid your actions made it necessary. Are ye thirsty?"

Again she nodded, but this time, with a pained expression, as though her head ached from the blow.

"Your head, is it hurtin' then?" he asked gingerly.

"Aye," she answered feebly, clearly unwilling to nod again.

At this, Sean called out to his brother to bring the young lady a cold compress and a skin of wine. Pat, however, was far too engrossed in assembling a meal from the baker's well-stocked pantry to give a damn about tending to the needs of someone who had so severely bitten his hand only a couple of hours before. So, Sean was forced to rise and fetch the necessary provisions himself.

He glared at Pat seconds later as he passed by the dining table and saw him finally sitting down before a mouth-watering platter of sliced cheeses, meats, fruit, and bread. "You could have thought to serve me up a plate as well, ye know, ye selfish lout!"

"Oh, mercy no," Pat countered, raising a brimming mug of ale as though to toast his younger brother. "I reasoned you'd be far too busy bathin' our little she-wolf to find time for supper. And don't be thinkin' I'm likely to take over the job in your stead. I'll take a crop to that vixen if ye leave her to me! As God is my witness!" His eyes still shone with rage, and Sean again acknowledged that he really could not rely on his brother for any further assistance that evening.

Pat was terribly predictable that way. He would simply do what he'd done most every evening since he'd reached adulthood: he would sit at the table for half an hour or so, stuffing his face, belching, and getting quite intoxicated on ale. Then he'd pass out and find his repose with his face pressed to his dinner plate.

Sean, with a disgusted cluck, returned to Jenny's side a few seconds later and again offered her some words of comfort. It was very late, and he knew now that he didn't have the energy for a kicking and screaming match with her tonight, so clearly, every move he made had to be executed with the utmost forethought and tenderness.

"Here ye go. Somethin' to ease the pain," he explained, setting down the things he'd brought from the pantry and reaching out to help her up to a sitting position. To his relief, this effort went smoothly, and he proceeded to hand her the cup of wine he had poured for her. She, in turn, raised it to her lips with trembling hands and drank deeply from it. To Sean's dismay, however, he noted that she kept her eyes fixed fearfully upon his all the while.

When, at last, she lowered the cup, he reached out

61

slowly and gently pressed the cold, damp cloth, which he'd fetched, to the back of her head.

She winced a bit, but fortunately, she still wasn't panicking. She seemed a little too disoriented for that, and her expression was rather more like that of a bewildered baby bird.

"Where am I?" she asked softly.

"Lismore."

"Lismore?" she echoed with an incredulous scowl.

"Aye."

"But that's miles from my home," she noted, her brow still furrowed in confusion.

"I know, Jennifer. I know," Sean murmured. "But you're safe, my dear. Rest assured."

Her voice was low and solemn as she spoke again. "And who are you, might I ask? Ye seem to know *my* name, after all."

Sean was hesitant to tell her. But on second thought, he didn't suppose it really mattered. She'd be the baker's problem soon enough. It wasn't as though she'd be returning home, where she could sic a sheriff on him. "Sean. And I don't dare give ye my last name, for obvious reasons, miss," he answered after a moment with a clumsy smile. His voice reflected his genuine regret as he spoke again. "I really can't tell ye more at present, my lady. I'm sorry."

"There was someone else with you," she noted apprehensively. "That redhead who asked me to dance. Where is he?" She strained in her weak state to sit up and look for Patrick.

Sean coaxed her to lie still. "Ah, ye needn't worry about him. He's retired for the night. Passed out from too much ale."

Her eyes moved across his face as though she were skimming words on a page, and he now recognized something in her that a week of shadowing her from a distance could not have told him: she was shrewd and capable of great restraint if she felt it suited her ends. Their brighter captives were always the most troublesome, because they were the most prone to using deception. They would lull Sean and Patrick into laxity with their seeming willingness to cooperate, and then they'd attempt to flee when it was least expected. Jenny Plithe was of such character, and Sean realized now that he would have to be all the more wary with her. He'd have to get her bathed quickly, before she fully recovered her wits and her strength.

"And what, dare I ask, do ye want with me, Sean?" she inquired, keeping her voice amazingly even.

"Well, surely ye remember now, don't ye? My brother and I . . . well, we kidnapped ye earlier at that weddin' dance. But as I've said, you needn't worry. We have no intentions of harmin' ye."

"Kidnapped me?" she echoed. "What? Ye mean for a ransom?"

"Well . . . aye. I suppose ye could call it that," Sean stammered, hesitant to tell her more. At least this way she'd believe that she still had some chance of being returned to her family unscathed, and that was sure to help keep her from panicking. "You need a bath," he continued in a sheepishly low voice. "You're covered with mud, I'm afraid, and I'm goin' to have to see that your clothes are cleaned as well.

Do ye think that you could see your way clear to agree to that?"

He took the compress from her head and braced himself for her reaction, for the thrashing and clawing that were sure to come once she fully realized that a strange man was proposing to disrobe her and sponge her clean. To his amazement, however, she simply remained silent.

"It's all right," he added in a whisper. "I've done this before. It's part of my profession, ye might say, like bein' a physician, if ye will."

She didn't question this claim. She just looked down and scanned the muddy expanse of her body. Then she sat up slowly and turned her back to him, as if waiting for him to undo the seemingly endless row of buttons that extended from her shoulderline to her waist.

Though confounded by her passive response, Sean did not question her about it. He simply began at once to unbutton her frock. He could only assume that her cooperation was due to the fact that she was so cold and miserable in her wet, soiled apparel that she craved a bath as badly as he felt she needed one. In fact, being disrobed seemed to be almost second nature to her, as though she'd had someone else undress her thousands of times. But then, of course she *had,* Sean realized. Wealthy women like her were accustomed to being helped in and out of their garments by others every day. The only difference here was that her "handmaiden" was now a man; a fact that, to Sean's great relief, didn't appear to be causing her any undue concern. And again, Sean simply had to conclude that she was too uncomfortable in her damp, bespattered state to object.

When, at last, he finished unbuttoning her gown, it gaped, revealing the ivory lace of the kirtle the she wore beneath. "I'm done here, then, miss," he noted gingerly.

To his surprise, she rose dutifully in response, letting her frock fall to the floor. Then, with her back still turned to him, she reached down and pulled the entire length of her petticoat up over her head, leaving only her corset and chemise to be removed. She stood quite erect and steady as Sean got up a few seconds later and began the arduous task of unlacing her girdlestead.

His hands began to tremble inexplicably as he did so. Why was she being so damnably cooperative? And if she was this agreeable to having a bath, would it perhaps be for the best if he simply let her tend to it on her own?

With the job of removing her corset finally accomplished a moment later, Sean charily moved to help her out of her smock. His captive, however, was at last ready to bring things to a halt. She turned back to him and snatched the flowing skirt of the garment from his hands with a tremulous smile, and it was then that Sean realized that she was not nearly as at ease with all of this as she was pretending to be.

"Do you mind if I go and sit by the fire?" she asked. "I'm sure it's much warmer there."

"Not at all, Miss Plithe," he replied, relieved to hear that this was all she sought.

He watched as she made her way, on unsteady legs, to the hearthstone seconds later. Then, just before she sat down on it, her eyes focused upon the dining table and she issued a horrified gasp. "Oh, Mother Mary! What's wrong with him? Is he dead?" she exclaimed, clapping a hand to her chest.

Sean laughed. "Ah, Pat, ye mean? God, no. He's just out from too much drink, as I told ye."

"He's the one I bit earlier, isn't he," she acknowledged, sinking down on the hearthstone with flushed cheeks.

Again Sean laughed. "Aye. The very same. But not to worry. He's in no shape to retaliate. And I wouldn't let him do so, miss, even if he were," he promised.

Sean couldn't be certain in that dim light, but it did look to him as though she took some comfort in this pledge, and that brought him comfort as well. The main thing, after all, was to keep her calm. He'd learned, from long hard experience, that their captives were much more manageable if they weren't given cause to get their wind up.

"You've snatched me for my dowry then, haven't ye?" she said after a moment, and her gaze was so incisive that it was Sean who had to fight to stay calm now.

"Well . . . what . . . what would make ye ask such a thing?" he stammered, striving to sound as artless as possible.

"My father's great wealth, of course," she answered matter-of-factly. "It's not unheard of, ye know. It happens quite often, in fact. Or so I've been told. So, I suppose I'd no assurance that it wouldn't happen to me sooner or later."

Sean was so taken aback by her directness that all he could seem to do was nod.

Jennifer swallowed loudly in response, and her apprehension was evident in her suddenly paling face. "Very well," she said after a moment, and the resignation in her voice made Sean's heart begin to ache a bit. "I'm to be yours then?" she pursued, letting her gaze drop demurely to the floor.

"No. Not mine."

She looked disappointed as she stared up at him again. Then her eyes traveled back to where Patrick sat at the dining table. "Not *his* surely. He'll kill me for what I did to him!"

"No. Not his either," Sean answered guardedly.

She was clearly relieved to hear this. But then, an instant later, an apprehensive expression returned to her face. "Whose, then?" she demanded. "I feel I have the right to know!"

"Well, I can tell ye only that he's a baker. And I promise that you will know more soon enough, my lady. But the matter at hand is to get ye cleaned up."

"I can bathe myself, thank ye very much, sir," she said indignantly. "I've been doin' so for many years. Just find me a tub and some buckets of cold water to mix with this boiling over the fire . . . and," she added timorously, "a blanket to cover myself."

Sean stared at her for several seconds, admiring the pragmatic way in which she was dealing with her predicament. Thank God she'd recovered her wits enough to take over bathing herself. He was greatly relieved to be spared the embarrassment of having to do it for her. He withdrew his pistol from the waist of his breeches and pointed it at her, feeling remorse at seeing how she recoiled at the sight of it. "You may bathe yourself," he declared. "But I'm afraid I'll be forced to keep an eye on ye throughout."

She nodded resignedly.

Sean removed his riding cape, keeping his eyes and his gun trained on her all the while. Then he crossed to where she sat and handed the garment to her. "Wrap this about ye, and let your smock fall," he ordered. "I fear we will have to go in search of your tub and water together."

She rose quickly, fearfully. Then her eyes darted up to meet his as she wrapped the cape about her and her chemise descended in a rustling nest about her feet.

"Come along," he directed. "We haven't got all night. Let's have done with, so I can get some sleep."

She led the way hesitantly as he steered her out the front door to the well beside the cottage. Barefooted in the darkness, she cried out once or twice as she apparently trod upon sharp stones along the way.

"You take up one pail, and I'll carry the other," Sean instructed, motioning for her to lower the first of the buckets down to the well's water.

She worked as quickly as she could, with one hand clasping Sean's cape about her neck all the while. She filled both of the empty vessels and bent down to carry one of them back to the house.

Sean followed with the second bucket, clucking in the chilling wind at the tedium of having to draw a bath at such an hour. As usual, Pat was saddling him with the most troublesome tasks, using his wounded hand and his penchant for liquor as his excuses for

68

not doing his half of their work. It was insufferable, and it may well have been the last straw for Sean as he again contemplated retiring from bride snatching once and for all.

And what of Jennifer Plithe? In a short time, she would be warm and dry, bundled off to the baker's bed with all of the mud and strain of their journey washed from her. She'd see her wedding night with a stranger, a self-appointed groom who was motivated far more by greed than any love for her. It was criminal, in a way, this business of plucking young ladies from their families and friends and leaving them to the lusty appetites of mere opportunists. It had never struck Sean, until tonight, just how reprehensible it really was, and as he watched Jennifer trudging defeatedly before him with a swaying bucket in one hand and the impeding hem of his cape in the other, he finally acknowledged that their ruthless profession was all wrong for him and that he could never make it right.

This occupation, which was begun to keep him and Patrick out of debtors' prison, this pursuit that had first sprung from genuine need, was motivated almost solely by greed now, and Sean knew that it was high time he and Pat face it. And even if Pat wasn't willing to do so, Sean had amassed enough money along the way to retire on his own. They'd brought off over a dozen bride snatchings to date, after all—thousands of guineas' worth—and if Sean wanted to get out of it now and try his hand at an honest life—so he could court young ladies like Miss Heather Monaghan on more equal ground—what could Pat do to stop him?

Once they were back inside the cottage, Sean allowed Miss Plithe to bathe herself with only minimal supervision. He simply chose to remain a room away, leaning up against the dining table with his pistol pointed in her direction. There was no sense in humiliating her any more than was necessary, after all. She'd soon find herself mortified beyond words as the baker put her through the ordeal of their wedding consummation, and there seemed no reason to make the evening any more painful for her than it was already certain to be.

Minutes later, she concluded her bath and emerged from the baker's wash barrel. With her back to Sean all the while, she wrapped his cape around her in one chaste, concealing motion. She then bent from the waist, suspending her sudsy hair above the tub, and requested that Sean pour a bucket of clean water over her head to rinse it. He crossed to help her, setting his gun down on the hearthstone as he did so. Then, once she'd wrung out her mane, he picked up the pistol once more and tossed her a towel which he'd found in the baker's fire room. "Feeling better?" he inquired in as cheering a tone as he could muster.

She nodded.

"Let's take ye up to the loft, then. It's very late, and I'm sure you're tired."

She gathered up her clothing and walked before him, crossing the room and making her way up the runglike stairs with obvious difficulty in the trailing cape. Once they reached the second floor, she stood silently beholding the baker's bedchamber. His four-poster bed was neatly made, and the room was surprisingly free of clutter, given the fact that it belonged to a long-time bachelor.

She set her clothes down on a ladder-back chair and turned to Sean with the look of someone who was about to be put to death. He recognized it instantly. It was the heartrending expression of one who had nothing left to lose and would say or do almost anything to save herself.

"Is he old and fat, this man for whom you've stolen me?"

Sean felt his throat constrict slightly at seeing the beginnings of tears in her eyes.

"I wouldn't know. I've never met him. 'Twas my brother who arranged it, I'm afraid."

"So you and the redhead are brothers?"

"Aye."

Her voice wavered as she continued to speak. "I wouldn't have guessed it. You're far more handsome than he, ye know."

Sean felt his face redden a bit at the compliment. Then he gave forth a light cough and forced himself to get a grip on his emotions. With the acquisition of her dowry so close at hand, he knew he couldn't allow her to manipulate him. So he simply dropped his gaze and crossed dutifully to the bed to pull its covers down for her. "Get in. It's late, and I'm sure ye crave some rest."

She hesitantly walked over to him and sank down upon the edge of the bed. Then she arranged the cape out in front of her so she could slip in beneath the covers without exposing herself to him.

"There," he murmured. "That's better than standin' about in drafts, don't ya think?"

71

She clutched the bed linens to a point just below her neck and nodded, tears now beginning to stream down her face.

Sean's heart sank at the sight of them, and he knew he must get out of the room at once or risk falling prey to her surprisingly effective wiles. "I'm goin' back downstairs," he stated firmly, feeling confident about leaving her alone in the windowless loft now. There was obviously no escape from it, and he'd be sure to sleep very near its ladder, so he'd hear her if she tried to sneak down it. "Shout down to me, miss, if ye've need of anythin'," he directed, and with that, he turned to go.

"Does it hurt?" she called after him, and he definitely heard desperation in her voice.

He turned back to face her with an apprehensive chill running through him, and again, he could feel his face flushing slightly. "Does what hurt?" he asked.

Her gaze was exacting. "Ah, ye know very well *what,*" she said scoldingly. "What he'll do to me, this man for whom you've snatched me. Will it hurt? I have no mother to counsel me now, after all. You've seen to that. So, I think it only fair that you tell me," she declared in a voice that reflected that most volatile of combinations—rage and fear. She was right, of course, and what was more, she was proving amazingly persuasive for one in such a powerless position. She was, in fact, succeeding in making Sean feel more pangs of conscience than the entire convent of nuns who had schooled him in his youth ever had.

"Well," he swallowed dryly. "That depends entirely upon whether or not you've done it before."

Her face tightened as she choked out a sob. "Would I be askin' ye about it, dear sir, if I'd done it before?"

"No. I suppose not," Sean conceded.

"So, you come back over here and tell me what I'm in for! I'd sooner have ye shoot me, don't ye know, than to have to lie here all night, dyin' of fright!"

It was, in any case, not a subject to be discussed from across the room. So, realizing this and acknowledging that the young lady was not about to be placated by insouciant replies, Sean walked back over to her and sat down on the edge of the bed.

He shushed her in an allaying tone. "I shouldn't worry myself about it tonight, miss. Really. The baker will likely be too tired for it when he returns, in any case."

"But he'll find strength for it sooner or later," she countered. "If he wants my dowry, he'll have to lay claim to me straightaway, and you know it as well as I. So, you answer me, ye shameless coward! What will be expected of me here?"

Sean looked her in the eye. She deserved some candor in exchange for her own, and he would do his level best to give it to her. "There's nothin' expected of ye, Jennifer. All you'll have to do is lie here, and your husband will know what to do. I swear it."

"And what about my first question?" she pursued, her anger seeming somewhat quelled by his frankness.

"I'm not sure," he answered gingerly, returning his pistol to the waist of his pants. "I've never been on the receiving end, ye see. I imagine it hurts a wee bit.

But it's over quickly enough. And it will all go much easier for ye, I assure ye, if ye don't put up a fight. Some women find it quite pleasurable, in fact," he added hearteningly.

At this she stared pensively down at the bed linens, obviously giving his answers some thought. "Well, if it really is pleasurable, why does no one speak of it?"

Sean furrowed his brow. "Don't they? I hear talk of it often enough."

She scowled at him. "Well, of course you do. You're a man, and I suppose there's no end to what men will discuss. But I meant ladies. Why do I never hear ladies speak of it?"

Sean fought a laugh. "Well, because they're *ladies,* of course." His amusement waned, however, as she reached out an instant later and placed a warm, entreating palm upon his knee. Her eyes were filled with a poignant supplication in that second, a compelling expression that was as seductive as any worn by a damsel in distress.

"Teach me," she implored in a barely audible voice, her slender fingers reaching up to the hollow of his throat and sending tickling shivers running through him with their touch. "I'd much prefer to have you show me, ye know, than some fat old baker-man."

"But if I did that, I'd be layin' claim to ye for myself," Sean countered.

"Ah . . . is that so bad now?" she asked coyly.

"It is when you're promised to someone else."

"I've made no promises."

"No, but my brother and I have."

"So break them."

"Oh, I can't, Jenny. So please don't ask it of me again. A man's word is everythin' in this business. You should realize that."

She lowered her gaze knowingly. "The word of an outlaw is so important?" she asked.

"Aye," Sean replied, inwardly offended at being called such a thing. He'd simply spent too much time among thieves, he guessed, to have his profession derided very often, and he just wasn't accustomed to it.

"Very well. If you say so," she said resignedly, and he did feel rather allayed by this concession. "What can ye do for me then, Sean?" she asked, great trepidation evident in her voice once more.

In so many ways, Sean thought, she was like a lamb readied for the slaughter, a condemned prisoner who should have, at least, been entitled to a last request.

"It's wrong, what you're doin'," she blurted, as if reading his thoughts, and her words were suddenly broken and confused. "It's monstrous . . . to steal a girl and cast her into a . . . a stranger's bed!"

He couldn't bring himself to look at her now. He stared down at the woven floorcloth at his feet. "Aye. I agree."

"Then *why* are you doin' it?"

He somehow found the nerve to meet her gaze once more, his eyes conveying his sincerity. "You're my last, Jenny Plithe. I'm givin' it up, startin' tomorrow."

"Oh, that's all well and good. But what about me?" she retorted tearfully. "Can nothin' be done to save me?"

75

He knew that he sounded almost as tortured as she as he spoke again. "I'm afraid your fate was decided a fortnight ago, when the baker asked to have ye abducted. So please, woman, please stop askin' the impossible of me." With that he rose to leave.

She clutched at his hand in a last, desperate attempt to persuade him to stay. "When is he comin', this intended husband of mine?"

"Shortly. In an hour or so."

Her gray eyes seemed to look right through him, searching his soul for some ultimate compassion. "Will ye stay with me a while, then? Till I fall asleep at least," she implored.

"Well . . . I suppose there's no harm in it." He reached out and brushed the wet strands of hair from her eyes as she settled back upon the pillow. "Let me find ye a comb, Jennifer," he suggested amicably. "You don't want your hair to dry in tangles tonight, do ye? I'm sure ye want to look your best for your groom."

She declined to respond and simply reached up and dabbed her brimming eyes with the edge of the bed cover.

He stood up and surveyed the room for a comb or brush. Then, finally spying a toilette tray on top of the dresser, he crossed to it. As he reached it, a tiny jar of ointment caught his eye and he picked it up to give to Jennifer as well. Then he hesitated for several seconds, wondering whether he should take it to her or not. It was highly doubtful that she would have the slightest notion what to do with the lubricant, and he certainly did not care to have to explain. Nevertheless, such an aid was sure to make her first experience easier, and since the pain of such an encounter obviously concerned her, he figured it was worth a try.

He gathered up a comb as well and carried it and the ointment back to her. Then he set them down upon the bed covers over her lap. She, in turn, reached out, took hold of the comb, and began slowly running it through her damp mane—continuing to sniffle quite pitifully all the while.

"You can return the hand balm to the dresser," she directed. "I've never used it. I find it too greasy."

Sean averted his eyes, feeling, for what seemed the first time in years, rather bashful. "I didn't intend it for your hands, miss," he said under his breath.

She furrowed her brow. "For what then?"

"To ease the pain ye asked of earlier."

Her face appeared to pale a bit in the dim light. "I don't understand."

"I feared ye wouldn't. But I'll show ye, if ye wish."

She stopped her combing and sat staring questioningly at him.

"Well, it is for you to say, my lady," he continued with an uneasy shrug. "Do ye trust me to instruct ye in such a matter or not?"

She dropped her gaze as well, and it was clear that his meaning was finally starting to dawn on her. Then, after several seconds, she gave him a nod.

"I won't look at ye. I swear," he pledged in a whisper, keeping his eyes fixed upon hers, endeavoring silently to assure her that he meant to help rather than to harm her.

Though seeming frozen with misgivings, she again offered her consent by nodding.

"Lie back, then," he whispered as he opened the jar and dipped deeply into its creamy contents.

She swallowed back her abashment and reclined, keeping her eyes locked nervously upon his two, lubricated fingers. She shut her eyes as his hand disappeared beneath the linens a moment later and quickly found its way to her lower lips. He did his best not to touch any more of her anatomy than was absolutely necessary. He was certainly practiced enough with naked females to find what he sought without much delay. Her thighs parted reflexively, and she issued a demure gasp as he applied the chilly balm and his fingers moved up into secret realms that she had, apparently, never had the courage to explore on her own.

Neither of them seemed able to breath in those seconds, both politely restraining their responses to the sensuous contact. It was her first lesson, a tender liaison that left her dumbstruck, but hopefully less afraid of what was to come. His fingers said what his lips couldn't seem to now, that she was capable of finding great pleasure and not just pain in her relations with her groom. Indeed, Sean could see the dread draining from her face seconds later as he finished applying the ointment.

"Sleep now, Jennifer," he murmured as he rose to leave the room. "I promise ye there is really nothin' to fear." With that, he made his way slowly to the nearby dresser and returned the comb and hand balm to it. Then he gathered up the lantern they'd brought up with them, knowing that, if she was like most virgins, she'd want nothing more than solitude now—solitude and the solace accorded by darkness.

He descended from the loft seconds later, happy in the knowledge that he'd probably succeeded in relieving one kind of pain for her. Sorrily, though, he knew that there was little he could do now to stop her suffering at having no say in her fate.

Chapter 5

It was nearly eleven o'clock by the time Heather and her father left the Cassidys' farm. Malcolm Byrne had long since gone off to fetch the sheriff and Jennifer's male relatives, so they could help track down Jennifer's kidnappers. It was, therefore, just the three of them—Heather, her father, and Shannon Kennedy—who boarded the coach to return home now. Mr. Monaghan, probably out of disgust at his daughter's actions that evening, chose to ride up front, on the driver's box, with their coachman. That meant, to Heather's relief, that she and Shannon could finally be alone inside the vehicle to discuss all that had happened.

Shannon, a long, lean blonde, was seated opposite Heather in the cab as the coach pulled away from the Cassidys' farmhouse minutes later and began heading down the dirt road that led toward town. Shannon had one of those faces that could just as easily have belonged to either a lad or a lass. It was one of those lightly freckled faces that was so typically Irish. From the downturned outer corners of her blue eyes, with their crow's-feet laugh lines, to

the straight white row of upper teeth that consti-
tuted her smile, it was Irish through and through.

It was a shrewd, yet friendly face that had been
duplicated twelve times to date, with the births of
each of Shannon's brothers and sisters, and only now,
at the late age of seventeen, was Shannon mature
enough to have added some distinction, some femi-
ninity to it. At Heather's urging, she'd recently
begun to apply a touch of rouge to her freckly nose
and cheekbones, and to set a pair of pin curls at each
of her temples. As a result, Shannon had actually
begun to bloom in the course of the last few months,
to change from tomboy to maiden almost overnight.
" 'Tis a shame about Malcolm," she noted softly as
they rode.

Heather, now cloaked in a heavy, woolen capu-
chin, which Mistress Cassidy had lent her for the ride
home in the late evening chill, turned and stared
coldly out of the coach window to her left. "No it's
not. If I know him, and believe me I *do,* he surely
did somethin' to deserve it."

She heard Shannon gasp a bit in obvious surprise.
"To deserve bein' shot? Ah, come now. Ye can't
mean it! He was tryin' to save our Jenny, after all."

Heather waved her off. "He was just jealous of the
attention that blond strawboy paid to me, is what.
You heard for yourself how cross he was about us
bein' at the festivities unchaperoned, and he saw me
dancin' with the lad when he came in."

"Ah, but ye can't mean it, Heth," Shannon maintained. " 'Tis daft . . . wantin' your own betrothed
shot!"

Heather turned and glared at her, her eyes narrowing with indignation. "He's *not* my betrothed! How many times must I tell ye that?"

"Well, it matters little that ye tell *me,* does it. It's Malcolm and your father who should be told, because they seem to think I'm right."

Heather clucked at her and again turned and directed her gaze out the window, at the night's darkness as it sped past. "Well, you're all wrong, the lot of ye, because I haven't the least intentions of marryin' him."

"And if he'd been killed by that shot tonight, that would have been an end to it, then, wouldn't it," Shannon said knowingly.

Being a God-fearing girl and certainly as superstitious as anyone in County Kilkenny, Heather knew better than to answer this affirmatively. "Well I . . . I don't wish him dead," she stammered, turning back to her friend. "But I do wish him out of my life for good and all, and I don't care who knows it. Heaven help me, though, Father thinks he walks on the water, so God knows there's no point in tryin' to tell him again how I feel."

"Well, you'll have to, sooner or later," Shannon admonished. "Now that Jen's been kidnapped, our parents will want to keep us both hidden away for quite some time to come, and you'll not get a chance to win the eye of another if Malcolm's the only man you're permitted to see."

"Yes. Yes," Heather said pensively, again turning to face the window. Part of her wanted to converse with Shannon now, and yet another part wanted simply to continue staring into the darkness, going over again and again all that the mysterious strawboy had said to her.

Shannon, however, began to speak once more, interrupting her thoughts. "It's dreadful about Jen, though, isn't it," she said with a shiver. "I don't think I really even believe yet that it happened. Just thank the dear Lord that it was Malcolm and not us who was burdened with havin' to tell her family of it. And to think that you actually danced with one of them who took her! Oh, Heth, how terrifyin'. Doesn't it make a chill run through ye just to think of it? I'm surprised ye haven't fainted dead away, in fact." She had Heather's shawl drawn up over her head and neck, as well as her own wrapped about her shoulders in the night's cold, yet her voice trembled as though she was still chilly. Or perhaps, Heather thought, she had been genuinely frightened by the kidnapping.

Heather turned back to face her now with a mischievous smirk, and she knew that Shannon must have been able to see it in the glow from the coach's sidelight. "To tell ye the truth, I found it rather excitin'."

Shannon furrowed her brow in amazement. "Ye did?"

"Oh, aye," Heather said rather proudly. "In fact, I think it might be the most excitin' thing that will ever happen to me."

Shannon continued to scowl. "But *why?*"

"Well, because it was so fraught with danger, of course. I mean, I'll wager I came this close to havin' 'em snatch me instead," she declared, thrusting her

83

thumb and forefinger out to show the minuscule amount she meant.

Shannon looked even more dumbfounded at this. "Ye mean, ye wish they had taken ye?"

A smile tugged at the corner of Heather's mouth. "I half wish it, aye," she confessed.

"Ah, you're daft, Heather Monaghan . . . as crazed as dear Jen was always accusin' ye of bein'!"

"No I'm not. I mean, who better to say, after all, than one who's danced with one of 'em? I saw up close how handsome, how charmin' he was, and I can honestly tell ye that there are worse fates than Jen's."

Shannon raised a knowing brow at her. "Ah, sure. That's what ye say now, now that you're wrapped up, safe and warm and headin' home in your father's coach, that's what ye say. But if it had happened to ye, you'd be beside yourself now, sobbin' and cryin' out."

Heather clucked. "I'd be doin' nothin' of the sort."

"Aye, ye would . . . because I know what they'd do to ye. I know what that 'layin' claim' business means, that everyone was whisperin' about at the Cassidys', and I can tell ye for sure that ye wouldn't like it."

Heather leaned forward, skeptical of her friend's claim, but anxious to have her elaborate. "How do ye know about that?"

Shannon lifted her chin with a suddenly superior air. "Because I have brothers, and I've caught 'em a time or two with girls in the hayloft."

"Hmm," Heather replied, beginning to place more

stock in Shannon's opinion now. "What's it mean, then?"

"Well, it's embarrassin', Heth. I can't just come right out and say it."

"Why not? I won't tell anyone, if that's what you're thinkin'."

"Oh, I'm not worried about that. It's just that it's difficult to put into words, ye see."

"Has it anythin' to do with the way cows are bred?"

Shannon shook her head. "No. I don't think so, 'cause they're standin' up all the while, ye see, and they're not facin' the bull."

"And people do? Face each other, I mean?"

Shannon gave her a decided nod. "Oh, aye. They surely do. And they're huggin' and kissin' and tossin' about all the while, until . . ."

To Heather's dismay, her words suddenly broke off. "Until?" she echoed anxiously.

"Until the man . . . makes water inside the woman," Shannon blurted, blushing from ear to ear by this point.

"Makes water?" Heather repeated with a gasp. "What? Ye mean, as in a chamber pot, first thing in the mornin'?"

"Exactly so."

Heather drew in a deep breath and sat back on her coach seat to give this allegation some thought. "Oh, that can't be, Shannon. Ye can't have got it right," she said after a moment.

"But I did. Why would I fabricate somethin' like that?"

Heather shook her head, clearly lost for an answer

to this. "Ah, but that's horrid. Repulsive! People can't possibly go about doin' such things."

"Well, they do," Shannon maintained. "And if ya don't believe me, you may come and spy on one of my brother's for yourself."

"May I?" Heather asked with a smile in her voice. "Oh, aye, I think I'd like that. You must send for me at once, the very next time you think it's about to happen. . . . Does it hurt, do ye suppose?" she continued.

Shannon again knit her brows, as though having to think this over. "It's difficult to say, because they're both makin' a great deal of noise all the while, ye see. Moanin' and groanin' and such."

"Well, are they pleasureful moans or painful ones?"

"With my brothers, they're definitely pleasureful," she declared. "Not at all like the sounds they make when Father canes 'em. But with the lasses, I'm not so sure. It's a bit more like gaspin'. Ye know . . . like ye do when somethin' startles ye."

Heather settled farther back into her coach seat and began to mull it all over. "I don't know, Shannon. It all sounds most peculiar to me. Perhaps, I wouldn't have wanted 'em to make off with me, after all."

"Certainly not."

"Will ye keep a secret if I tell ye somethin'?" Heather asked after a moment in a wavering voice. She knew that there was probably no need to ask this; she and Shannon had been exchanging confidences for as long as she could remember, and as far as she knew, none of them had ever been divulged.

86

But she simply wanted Shannon to know now that what she was about to say must not be repeated, under any circumstances.

"Of course. Need ye ask?"

"Probably not. But I mean that *no one* must know. Not a livin' soul. Understood?"

"Yes. Yes. Out with it, girl!"

"That . . . that strawboy I danced with," Heather stammered uneasily. "He . . . he said he was comin' back for me."

Shannon's mouth fell open. "He *didn't*."

"Oh, aye. As God is my Witness, he most certainly did."

"Oh, Heather. How frightenin'! Did he mean yet tonight, do ya suppose?"

"Well, I don't know just what he meant. But I do remember him kissin' my hand in the most shockin' of ways and sayin' he was comin' back for me, and I've been atingle ever since, Heaven help me!"

"Ah, Lord, girl. Ye best tell your father, then."

"No. I can't. He'll lock me up somewhere and throw away the key if I do, and then, I'll be stuck with Malcolm forever."

"Well, maybe the strawboy won't know how to find ye. I mean, ye didn't give him your name, did ye?"

Heather felt her cheeks warming with a sheepish blush. "Aye. I fear I did. But that was before we learned that he was a kidnapper, so I'm hardly to blame for it," she added defensively.

Shannon raised a suspicious brow at her. "You gave him your name, but he didn't give ye his?"

"Well, no. Not really. All he told me was that he

87

was from the Murphy farm. And that's a secret as well, Shannon," she added sternly, "so ye mustn't repeat it."

"But ye told Malcolm and the rest that he said nothin' about himself, that ye just danced, and then he was off."

"Well, I . . . I didn't want Malcolm tearin' off to the Murphys' and playin' the devil. And ye have to admit that the kidnappers weren't headed toward the Murphys' as they rode off with Jen. They were ridin' in precisely the opposite direction, in fact."

"So, ye don't think he's from the Murphy farm?"

Heather shrugged. "I don't know, really. I thought I might go over there tomorrow and have a look 'round for Jenny's sake. But I don't want Malcolm or Father to know about this, ye understand," she concluded sternly.

Shannon leaned back with an incisive expression. "What I understand is that you're tryin' to protect the lad. But I can't fancy why."

"Well, he was really quite charmin'," Heather said again. "And if the truth be told, I found myself rather taken with him, and I just don't want him judged too harshly. I mean, what if we've got the wrong lad altogether here?" she suggested hopefully. "What if the strawboy who danced with me wasn't the one we saw ridin' off later?"

Shannon waved her off. "Ah, ye know perfectly well that he was. We all saw him up close for several seconds when he came up and asked ye to dance, and then he couldn't have been but a few yards from us, as he mounted his steed minutes later. What was more, I think he was the only blond strawboy at the dance."

Again Heather narrowed her eyes at her friend. "But ye promised not to tell any of this to a soul, remember. And I expect ye to keep your word, Shannon Kennedy. 'Cause ye know full well that I've enough of your secrets to finish ye, if ye cross me," Heather added in an ominously low voice. She hated having to bare her fangs with her old friend, but she knew, from long experience, that it was the only way to make Shannon know how serious she was.

"Oh, all right," Shannon agreed after a moment. "But just you make sure that ye pay a call upon the Murphys tomorrow and scout for Jen there yourself, or I swear to ye, I'll take it into my own hands."

"I shall. I shall," Heather promised, reaching out and giving her a heartening pat on the knee. "And, too, you've got to consider that, if they really were bride snatchers, as it's rumored, at least Jennifer is sure to find herself married when all is said and done. And ye must admit that, even with all our efforts to make her presentable, that's more assurance than you and I could have given her."

"Aye, well . . . I guess you're right," Shannon conceded with a tentative nod.

There were bread crumbs embedded in Patrick Kerry's forehead now as he lifted his face from his pewter dinner plate. Sean had come down from seeing Jennifer to bed in the baker's loft half an hour before, and he'd sat by the fire for a while, reading one of the baker's books and mulling over what he

89

would say to his brother. But now he knew that their talk couldn't be put off any longer, and he sought to rouse Patrick with a brisk shake.

"What is it?" Pat asked groggily, his eyes still shut as he spoke.

"Wake up, ye lazy sot," Sean ordered. "I crave a word with ye."

Pat forced one eye open and peered up at his assailant. "What? Is the baker finally here?"

"No."

"Well, is the girl givin' ye trouble, then?"

"No. That's not it either."

"Then, what in the bleedin' hell is it, pup? I'm visitin' the land of Nod here, in case ye couldn't see that for yourself."

"What I see is you out cold from drink again," Sean retorted. "And as I said, I want a word with ye now, please, before the baker returns."

"Oh . . . all right," Patrick snarled, heaving his torso up against the back of his chair. "What is it?" he hissed, reaching up and brushing the bread crumbs from his face with a couple angry sweeps of his hand.

"I'm through," Sean heard himself say.

Patrick's brows drew together questioningly, and he leaned forward a bit. "Through with what? With tendin' to the girl, ye mean? Now ye can't have roused me just to say that!"

"No," Sean replied with an uneasy laugh. "I mean I'm through with bride snatchin', Pat. You'll have to find yourself another partner if ye want to go on with it."

Patrick squinted at this as though having difficulty making out what he'd just heard. "What was that?"

Sean swallowed dryly. "I said I'm retirin' from bride snatchin', startin' tonight. I'll take my share of what we get for Miss Plithe, of course. But then I'm through."

Patrick continued to squint at him, as though unable to believe what was happening. "Retirin' on what, pray tell?"

"On all that I've saved thus far."

"Saved? We haven't made enough to save much out."

Sean pulled out the dining chair opposite his brother's and sat down at the table as well, calmly, coolly, determined not to let their conversation escalate into a confrontation. "Ah, yes we have, Pat. We've made a good sum, really, if ye count from when we first started with it. . . . It's just that *I* haven't drunk my share away, is all," he added gingerly.

Patrick's eyes narrowed again, but this time it was into what was unmistakably a scowl. "I'll have ye know that I drink a lot less than most, little brother—"

"Ah, that's not the point," Sean interrupted, waving a palm at him. "What ye do with your share is entirely your business. The crux of it is that I want out of this line of work for good and all, and that's an end to it," he concluded firmly.

"But why? We've been doin' so well with it lately."

"Too well, perhaps," Sean said in a pointed tone.

Patrick rolled his eyes wearily, obviously tired of

his brother's great wariness where their business was concerned. "Now what's that supposed to mean?"

"It means that I'm worried about that elderly gentleman who's been followin' us about. I saw him again this evenin', before I went to the Cassidys' weddin'. He dogged me there, part of the way anyhow, and then, when he realized I'd seen him, he dropped out of sight, as he did the other evenin'.""

"Ah, sweet Jesus, pup," Pat began again irritably. "If he really is a constable from one of the other counties we've worked, why hasn't he put the shackles on us yet, eh? He's surely takin' his sweet time about it, isn't he."

"Maybe he's waitin' to catch us at it, is all. What, with our faces blackened on most of our jobs, it might be the only way he can prove we're the ones."

Pat gave this a couple seconds' thought then shrugged. "Aye. Could be," he conceded. "But that's hardly reason to give up the kind of money we've been seein' at this."

"It's reason enough for me," Sean declared. "That and . . ." His words broke off, as he realized that he really didn't want to finish his sentence.

"And what?" Pat prompted with a determined edge to his voice.

"Well, just that I feel it's time I started livin' an honest life, Patrick."

"Honest, is it?" Pat echoed with a surprised chuckle. "Well, I never thought I'd hear *you* callin' what we do dishonest. I mean, it was you, after all, who first made the claim that bride snatchin' was not stealin' really, just a 'redistribution' of Ireland's wealth. Ye said it was one of the few ways we had of makin' certain that the rich were forced to marry the less fortunate from time to time, instead of always marryin' other rich folks."

Sean felt his cheeks warm a bit with embarrassment at this, and he realized now that he'd taken the wrong tack entirely with his brother. Questioning the legality of the profession might only lead to Patrick choosing to drop out of it as well. And given the number of debts he'd accrued and his endless ability to squander what he earned, bride snatching was about the only thing that paid well enough to keep him afloat. "Yes, yes. I know what I said, Pat, and believe me, I don't mean to disavow it now. . . . I guess 'honest' wasn't the word I was lookin' for. I think what I meant to say was that I just feel 'tis time for me to move on to doin' somethin' different for a livin'. Ye know, the kind of work a lady could respect."

"Ah, who bloody cares about what ladies respect? The brothels take plenty good care of ye, don't they?"

"Oh, aye. If all a fella wants is tail trade."

"Well, what else is there, man?" Patrick asked, his voice rising in amazement.

Sean looked him squarely in the eye. "A great deal more," he said softly, almost reverently. "I'm almost sure of it."

"Such as?"

"Well, such as . . . as love," Sean stammered, growing quite uncomfortable with the subject now. He'd known, even before he'd brought it up, that such feelings would be wasted on his brother. That was the funny thing about drinkers, Sean had noticed through the years; they were strangely unswayed by sentimentality, given their penchants for living in drunken dreams. But then, perhaps, their cynicism was what they were seeking to flee by drinking so much. Well, whatever it was that made one man drink to excess and another choose not to, Sean was different from his brother in this way. Spirits held very little interest for him, except as a beverage with a meal, and try as he had, in his late teens and early twenties, to make himself into a drinker, to fit in with his older brother and his tippling friends, he'd simply had to come to terms with the fact that he wasn't a swiller and he never would be. He just didn't have the stomach for the stuff, and what was more, he didn't even care to try to develop one.

"Love? What? Ye mean as our mother loved us?" Pat asked, interrupting Sean's thoughts.

"Well, you knew her, remember. I didn't," Sean retorted bitingly. This had always been a sore subject between them, one they usually tried to avoid. But since Patrick had been thoughtless enough to bring it up, Sean couldn't seem to help responding accordingly. Though he knew it was rather irrational, he resented the fact that their mother had stuck around to see Patrick from birth through the age of four or so; whereas Sean had been left, from infancy, to the fumbling care of their father and whatever wet nurse he could scare up. So Sean's childhood memories were not of a flowing-haired mother, holding and coddling him—as Patrick's were. Rather, they were of their huge, surly-looking father, forever handling him like a sack of potatoes, cordoning him off, with their dog and pet piglet, in a makeshift pen in their fire room, and endlessly puzzled about what was causing Sean to cry.

Sean knew that, as long as he lived, he would never get the image of his father's questioning face out of his mind entirely. It would always be there, like a huge cumulus cloud, looming down at him from the sky, doing its best to understand, but always falling a bit short of the mark. Sean shook his head in wonder. Such a big, stupid, inquiring face.

It wasn't that he didn't believe that his father had tried to do his best for him and Patrick. It was just that, looking back on it now, Sean could only resolve not to make the same mistakes William Kerry had made, when rearing any children he might have one day. They wouldn't be raised without a mother, he'd decided, and they most certainly wouldn't be raised by a father who had one foot in the world of crime all the while. But his thoughts were again interrupted as he heard his brother speaking once more.

"Well, ye didn't miss much," Patrick was saying with a bitter laugh, and Sean again noted that this was always his response when mention was made of their mother. "She was there in body, maybe," he continued, "but rarely in spirit. In fact, the day she ran off, I remember thinkin' that she'd already done so, for all intents and purposes, years before that . . . Besides," he added awkwardly. "*I* love ye, Sean, and so does Rory . . . though I hate your damnable ass for forcin' me to say so," he concluded in a growl.

Sean laughed under his breath. "Oh, aye. I know the pair of ye would miss me, were I to die. But I'm not talkin' about that kind of love," he continued, sobering. "I'm talkin' about the romantic sort."

Pat waved him off. "Ah, don't delude yourself. It just doesn't exist, that. All a woman wants ye for is to put food in her mouth and children in her belly. You're simply needed to service one end or t'other, is all. You'd do well to learn from our mother just up and leavin' our dad as she did," he added admonishingly.

"Oh really? And are we men any bloody better? Spiritin' off rich girls for their dowries?"

"I didn't say we were better, did I. I'm just sayin' you're daft to think you'll ever find a woman who truly loves ye."

Sean drew back from the table and straightened his posture resolutely. "Well, that's your opinion, not mine. And I, for one, do intend to try."

His brother shrugged. "Ah, fine then. Suit yourself. But I still don't see what any of this has to do with our work. No reason why ye can't go on pullin' off a job or two with me each month."

Sean shook his head and donned an amazed smile. "Christ, Pat. Ye haven't heard a word I've been sayin' to ye, have ye? I want out of this partnership, don't ye see? I want to live aboveboard now, and nothin' you can say or do is goin' to change my tune." With that, Sean crossed his arms over his chest and sank back in his chair.

"Well, then . . . who . . . who would I work with?" Pat stammered after a moment. "Who could I trust with such work?"

"Rory," Sean answered without hesitation. "He was askin' to help us again, just this evenin', and ye know it would mean the world to him if you'd bring him in on it now."

Pat donned an incredulous scowl. "Have ye takin' leave of your senses? He belongs locked in a closet somewhere, is what! Sewn between two mattresses, where he can't do a lick of harm to man or beast! Why, we wouldn't last ten minutes in this business with that temper of his! He's totally unpredictable. Ye never know when he's goin' to fly off into another of his rages."

"He's fine, I tell ye . . . as calm as a lake on a windless day if ye just talk to him quietly, Patrick. It's you who sends him into those fits by raisin' your voice to him."

Pat gave all of this a few seconds' thought, then he shook his head. "Naah. It can't be done. It's far too risky."

"Oh, I admit that there would have to be some changes made," Sean agreed. "You'd have to get to your jobs on time and without so many pints in ye. And you'd have to keep a steady head about ye, and keep an eye on Rory all the while as well. But still, I think it's possible, and I wish you'd give the poor chap a chance at it. . . . In any case," Sean began again, rising from the table, "I'm hereby retirin' from it all, and except for helpin' you and Rory out of the occasional scrape, I'm done with."

As Sean began to stroll off to the fire room seconds later to bed down for the night, he heard Patrick bring his fist down loudly upon the dining table, and he turned back to face him with a startled expression.

"I won't let ye," he declared. "I ruddy well won't let ye walk away from it, pup! Not when it was you, yourself, who first thought of it!"

"And how are ye going' to stop me?" Sean asked

frostily, growing angry now with his brother's unwillingness to accept his decision.

"I . . . I don't know yet," he confessed. "But by God, I shall surely find a way!"

Sean flashed him a sportive smile, sensing—but perhaps, only hoping in those seconds—that his brother was simply seeking to save face by offering such protest. "All right. You do that. In the meantime, though, I thought I'd have some sleep by the fire and keep an ear out for the baker. Do ye find that agreeable?"

Patrick issued an irritable grunt. Then he shoved his dinner plate aside, grumbling all the while, and plopped his face down upon the table once more. They would both get a bit of rest now, and Sean knew that he'd sleep a little better for having finally unburdened his mind with his brother.

Even so, Sean was not naive enough to believe that Patrick would really let him retire without putting up more of a fight. What form that fight would take remained to be seen, of course, but Sean had little doubt that some reprisal was in store.

In the meantime, Sean intended to go on as he'd planned. He would head back to Kilkenny first thing in the morning, both to deliver their "ransom" note to the Plithe family and to round up the lovely green-eyed Heather Monaghan.

Chapter 6

Sean woke with a start half an hour later and found a well-clad stranger standing before him.

"Tiernan O'Ryan," the man declared, extending his right hand to Sean.

Sean struggled up from his supine position on the settle, his brows knit into a groggy furrow. "The baker?" he asked, shaking hands with the gentleman.

"Aye. That I am," he said with a warm smile. "And you'd be Sean Kerry, then?"

Sean nodded and tried to reciprocate his smile. To his great relief, he saw now that O'Ryan was not at all the fat, old bakerman whom Miss Plithe had feared he'd be. He was, in fact, rather young-looking and handsome. Almost princely, really, in his long, curly periwig and burgundy cocked hat. He had dark, almond-shaped eyes, an aristocrat's straight nose, and elegantly high cheekbones. And he stood nearly six feet tall, by Sean's estimation.

"Oh, aye. I guess you would be," the baker replied, "since I already met your brother, Patrick, and I distinctly remember him bein' a redhead."

"Yes. That's him over there," Sean replied, point-

99

ing at where Patrick was still hunched over, asleep at the dining table.

"Oh, yes." O'Ryan laughed softly. "He looks absolutely dead asleep, doesn't he, dear fella."

"Well, ye must admit it's late, sir. Well past midnight by now, I imagine."

The baker reached into the pocket of his frock coat and withdrew a watch. "Aye. Nearly one. I'm terribly sorry to have gotten back this late, but I was so excited about meetin' my bride tonight, ye see, that I fear I burnt a few loaves and had to stay on to bake more," he confessed with a sheepish smirk.

"No matter, I guess," Sean replied, reaching up to run his fingers through his sleep-mussed hair.

"Ye didn't have too much trouble with her, I hope," he said uneasily.

Sean shook his head. "No. A wee bit of a tussle when we first got our hands on her. But that's to be expected. No harm done really. Besides," Sean added with a slightly embarrassed laugh, "they're not much of a catch, are they, if they don't offer at least a little bit of a fight."

The baker looked rather surprised by his candor. "No. I suppose not," he answered with a wavering smile. "Well . . . where . . . where is she, then?" he pursued, and it was clear to Sean that he was more nervous about meeting his bride than most of their previous clients had been.

"Upstairs in your bed, of course. Isn't that where ye wanted her put?"

O'Ryan laughed uneasily. "Aye. I suppose so. If that's what ye generally do with 'em. I mean, if that's your usual procedure."

100

Sean shrugged. "Aye. That it is. Though I suppose ye could move her out of there, if ye wished."

The baker raised a palm to him. "No. No. 'Twill be just fine, I'm sure." With that he reached up, with unsteady hands, removed his feathered hat, crossed to a nearby butterfly table, and set it down. Then he turned back to face Sean once more. "I'm new at this, havin' never been married, ye see. Not quite sure how it's done . . . oh, not the swivin' part of it, mind," he added with obvious embarrassment. "I've experience with that, of course. But I'm simply unsure of the decorum, ye see."

"Well, most of our clients just take it as it comes, I guess, Mr. O'Ryan. I mean, there's no definite way to proceed, really. Just let nature take its course, if ye will."

The baker was silent for several seconds, as though giving Sean's words some thought. "Ye don't suppose that it could be put off till mornin', do ye?" he asked gingerly at last.

"What? Layin' claim to her, ye mean?"

"Yes."

Sean considered this. "Well, it's your decision, sir, of course. But we do recommend that our clients proceed with it as soon as possible, given the nature of the situation. I mean, my brother and I went to some risk to snatch the lass for ye, so it would be a shame if ye waited till mornin' and then we woke to find that she'd crept out of here and run off in the night. We'd all be out a goodly sum, if she got away unclaimed, wouldn't we now."

O'Ryan gave forth a long anxious sigh. "Ah, yes. I suppose you're right about that."

An awkward silence ensued between them, and then Sean finally ventured a suggestion. "You could pour yourself some ale first. Ye know, relax a bit, before goin' up to her, if you'd like. I can't see why it has to be done immediately, really."

The baker donned a relieved smile. "Splendid idea, Mr. Kerry. Just splendid," he said brightly, taking up a lit lantern, which he'd apparently brought in with him, and moving toward the pantry now. "Will you be havin' some as well?"

Sean shrugged and followed him. "Maybe a wee bit. It might help me get back to sleep, come to think of it."

Not wanting to suffer the humiliation of having his brother slumped upon the table while they drank, Sean went over to wake Patrick as the baker disappeared into his larder.

Patrick again greeted Sean's efforts to rouse him with total surliness. "What is it?" he growled.

"It's the baker," Sean whispered. "He's here now. Wake up for a bit, and be civil, will ye."

Pat clucked and slowly brought himself up to a sitting position. Sean could tell, however, that he'd been sleeping too long now to be fully awakened. He would obviously have little to contribute to the ensuing conversation, let alone being of any help in quelling O'Ryan's trepidation at meeting and bedding Miss Plithe.

This was, Sean acknowledged, the first time that any of their clients had seemed in the least bit hesitant to lay claim to his bride, and he realized that Pat's help would come in very handy now. But Patrick just couldn't be counted upon when he was needed, and Sean knew that Pat would, once again, let him down.

"Here we are," O'Ryan announced, returning to the dining table a couple minutes later with two mugs of ale and the lantern still hanging from his wrist. He set one mug down before Sean, then circled around to the other side of the table and sat down with his own mug and his lantern set out before him. "I'd have brought one for your brother, too, if I'd known he was awake," he explained, gazing over at Patrick.

"Ah, don't worry about Pat. He's had enough as it is, haven't ye?" Sean asked, turning to gaze at him as well.

Pat, obviously fighting to keep his eyes open, only nodded and offered a groggy, "Uh-huh."

"Well, it's late, as ye said, Sean," the baker declared with an awkward laugh, surely aware now that Patrick was as drunk as he was sleepy. "He'll probably have more to say, come mornin'."

Sean laughed. "Oh, you can rest assured of that, Mr. O'Ryan."

"So, tell me of the girl," he said suddenly in a wavering voice. "What is she called? Jenny, is it?"

"Jennifer, aye. Jennifer Plithe. But I thought that you and Patrick had already discussed her."

"Oh, we have. I mean, I know what she looks like and that sort of thing, from your brother's sketches. But I was just wonderin' . . . I mean, now that you've actually captured her and all, about her nature, her temperament, ye know."

Sean took a swallow of his ale and fought a smile.

"Well, it's not unlike your own, Mr. O'Ryan, to tell ye the truth."

He leaned forward, great interest suddenly showing in his eyes. "Really? In what way is that?"

"Well, it's just that she was askin' much the same questions about you earlier. Clearly afraid of what lay ahead for her."

He cocked his head, as though a bit surprised by this, and some of his nervousness seemed to drain from his face. "Was she now?"

Sean nodded.

"Well, of course, I guess she would be. This bein' her first time with a man and all."

"Precisely."

"So, do ya think she's still awake up there? I mean, I won't be wakin' her, I hope, will I?"

Sean hesitated before answering. " 'Tis hard to say, really. I put her to bed over an hour ago, so she very well could be. On the other hand, she was so frightened, given the circumstances and such, that she might still be starin', wide-eyed, up at the ceilin'."

The baker gave forth an uneasy sigh. "Oh, aye. I suppose it could go either way, then. . . . So, um . . . do ye . . . do ye think she'll be cooperative about it?" he asked, nearly choking on his words, and Sean knew instantly that this was what concerned his client most about the arrangement.

"Well, there's really nothin' to be afraid of, my good man," Sean assured. "I mean, it's not as though she *bites.*"

In that same second, Patrick issued a groan and

whisked his bitten hand, with its bloodstained bandage, under the table and out of the baker's sight.

O'Ryan stared questioningly over at the elder Kerry, as though wondering what had prompted him to make such a pitiful sound. Sean, however, managed to draw the baker's attention back to their end of the table as he spoke again.

"I mean, she's from very good stock, after all. Truly a gentlewoman, of course, bein' from so wealthy a family. And, too, Patrick and I always stay with our clients till . . ." He broke off, trying to find the most tasteful way to phrase it. "Till things have been . . . made final."

The baker appeared to take comfort in this as he raised his mug and took a sip of ale. "Oh, aye. That's the best way, I'm sure. Though I must tell ye, Sean and Patrick, that I really don't want it to come to a show of force, if it's all the same to you. I mean, after the pair of ye are gone, I'll still be here, havin' to live day to day with the lass, and I'd hate to be findin' ground glass in my food, ye understand," he concluded gingerly.

Sean reached out and placed a consoling hand on his forearm. "Naah, Mr. O'Ryan. You can rest assured that it's not at all apt to end in rape. In fact, I don't think we've ever had a bona fide rape occur in all the years we've been at this. Have we, now, Patrick?"

His brother, looking as though he was having all he could do to keep his head up, let alone to recall any of the details of their past jobs, simply responded with a "nay," an utterance that sounded almost equally like a grunt.

Again the baker seemed to take some comfort in Sean's words.

"Besides," Sean continued, hoping to get his client in even more of a mind to go up and tackle the task at hand, "you're really a fine-lookin' gentleman, sir. Quite elegant in your own way, in fact."

The baker's face lit up almost magically at this. "Do ye really think so?"

"Oh, aye. I mean, it's not that I make a habit of goin' about tellin' other gents how fetchin' they are, mind," Sean explained with a slight flush warming his face. There was, of course, a lot of money riding on this, his final bride-snatching job, and if he had any hope of retiring now, as planned, he knew he couldn't allow their client to wriggle out of their agreement. On the other hand, he told himself that what he was saying was absolutely the truth, and he saw no harm in being candid with O'Ryan about his looks. None at all. "It's just that . . . well, to be truthful with ye, I can't believe that ye haven't heard this said of ye many, many times before; but, well, the lasses must swarm about ye like bees when you're in town."

The baker's grateful glow became even brighter, and his tremulous lips gave way to a broad smile. "Well, no, they don't," he confessed, lowering his voice. "But aye, I suppose I could have won the hand of one of them, on my own, if I'd wanted to. I mean, if an adequate dowry hadn't also been a concern."

Sean leaned forward and gave him a hearty pat on the shoulder. "Ah, of course ye could have. It hadn't occurred to me for an instant that a handsome, hard-workin' man such as yourself couldn't have fared well without us. But needed or not, sir, here we are, Patrick and me, and we'd be most grateful to ye if you'd simply go on upstairs now and show Miss Plithe what a prize she's gettin' in you, as well."

The baker's smile faded, giving way once more to a look of uneasiness, and he stared down into his mug. "Would ye . . . would ye go up with me, then, and see that we're properly introduced?" he asked finally, looking up again into Sean's eyes.

Though he tried not to let it show, Sean was taken aback by this request. In all his years in this business, he'd never once been asked to do such a thing. "Well, I . . . I suppose I could," he stammered. "If ye think it would help."

"Oh, yes. I'm sure of it."

"Well, fine then. Shall we go up now?"

The baker gave forth a clumsy laugh and held up an index finger. "Just one more swallow," he declared, again lifting his mug to his lips. To Sean's surprise, he proceeded to finish off all the ale within it in those seconds, ending with the vessel's bottom tipped all the way up toward the ceiling. "Ah, there," he concluded with a great, breathless gasp. Then he set the mug back down upon the table. "Let's go up, then. I guess I'm as ready as I'll ever be." With that, he pushed his lantern over to Sean. "Prithee, lead the way. I think it for the best if she sees you first."

"Very well," Sean replied, rising, taking up the lantern and heading for the loft's ladder. "But I will have to leave her to ye after a moment or two, Mr. O'Ryan. I mean, I hope ye realize that."

"Oh, aye. That I do. That I do," the baker answered, following Sean up the steps.

Sean extended the lantern well out before him as he reached the second floor. He peered in the direction of the bed, but the loft was still too dark for him to tell whether or not Miss Plithe was awake. So he left off trying to see her and turned back to give the baker a hand up the last of the stairs.

"Is she awake?" O'Ryan asked in a whisper.

"I can't tell yet," Sean replied, keeping his voice equally low.

"You go over first, then, if ye would, sir," the baker directed, giving Sean a nudge in the shoulder.

At this Sean turned and started walking toward the bed, their captive's recumbent figure becoming more and more visible as he progressed. "There's no tellin'," he answered under his breath. "She's turned away, ye see. Facin' the other side of the room."

"Well, you wake her, then. I don't want to be the one to do it," O'Ryan declared.

"Well, of course, I'll wake her. I can't very well introduce ye to her without wakin' her, now can I," Sean hissed, finding himself growing impatient with his client's apprehensive requests now. It was very late, after all, and his body was starting to tell him that it had been too long deprived of both sleep and food. Once he got this absurd task behind him, he'd go back downstairs and fetch himself a fine, overfull plate of supper, just as Patrick had. Then, he told himself hearteningly, he could finally retire—not only for the day, but from this whole sticky business.

"Miss Plithe? Jennifer?" he whispered as he reached the girl at last.

She didn't answer, so he gave her arm a jiggle. At this, the lass rolled onto her back with a groan, and

Sean could see, in the lantern light, that her eyes were falling groggily open. He was surprised to note, however, that her expression was utterly blank. She looked neither frightened nor confused, and he didn't have the slightest idea how she would respond.

"It's me, remember? Sean," he said.

"Oh, aye," she answered, her voice cracking with sleep.

"I've someone I want ye to meet." Sean knew, even as these words were leaving his lips, that this was a ridiculous way to begin his introduction, given the circumstances. But, then again, he reminded himself, the baker's request for such a thing was ludicrous to begin with, so there was probably no dignified way in which to handle it.

Their captive sat up slowly, her eyes widening, as though she was trying to wake herself more fully. "The man you stole me for?"

"Well . . . yes," Sean answered, again caught off-guard by her bluntness. "Your husband," he added firmly. With that, Sean turned back to his client and yanked him up by his side so Jennifer could see him more clearly. "Mr. Tiernan O'Ryan, Miss Jennifer Plithe," he introduced.

Sean watched as Jennifer's eyes traversed the length of her husband-to-be. They traveled from his wig-topped head down to where the edge of the bed hit him, just below his crotch—and Sean could see instantly that she wasn't altogether displeased with him. He was, after all, neither fat nor old, as she had feared, and this realization was clearly bringing her some comfort.

"How do'ye do, miss," O'Ryan greeted, reaching out to shake her hand.

Jennifer, looking taken aback by this gesture, took several seconds to disengage her right hand from the bed's linens. Once she had, however, she quickly extended it to him, and they shook hands in what was, Sean thought, quite a genteel manner—all things considered.

To Sean's surprise, though, they didn't disjoin their hands in the seconds that followed. They simply kept them linked, as each went on staring into the other's face.

"Well, then," Sean said at last, "I trust you can manage from here, Mr. O'Ryan. Can ye not?"

The baker, even from Sean's profile view of him, looked as though he'd slipped into some sort of lovesick trance, and it was clear that he was not about to take his eyes from Jennifer now, simply to address Sean. "I can. Yes. Yes, I believe I can," he answered, with a soft smile coming to his lips, and in spite of being ignored, Sean couldn't help feeling rather touched by the scene. The attraction between them was more than apparent, almost stunning, and he was beginning to half congratulate himself for having played such an important part in bringing the two of them together.

"Well, I'll stay a bit longer, if ye wish," he offered as an afterthought, wanting to make sure that O'Ryan was as certain of success as he now seemed.

"No. No. You go," the baker said, his tone unashamedly dreamy. "We can manage on our own from here, can't we, Jennifer."

Though it was more a statement than a question,

Miss Plithe did offer a nod to it, along with a sweet and suddenly confident smile.

"Well, fine then. Just call down to me if you've need of anything'," Sean replied, feeling as though he were totally alone, as the couple continued their enthrallment.

In the seconds that followed, he took a punk from the adjacent night table and lit the bedside lamp with the flame from the lantern, which he still held. Then he headed back downstairs. Things were obviously going so well between the pair that he didn't care to risk spoiling the mood by saying anything more.

He'd gotten no "thank you" to his offer to wait upon them. But then, he hadn't really expected one. The soon-to-be newlyweds were clearly too smitten with one another to be bothered with courtesies for the time being, and Sean knew better than to be offended by it. On the contrary, he was, in fact, filled with a renewed sense of hope as he reached the first floor. It was a hope that things would go as smoothly between him and Miss Heather Monaghan when next they met. Yes, he thought, with a soft smile playing upon his lips, he would like it very much if she proved even half as cooperative as her friend had.

Chapter 7

Sean had no sooner sat down to eat the late supper which he'd prepared for himself when all hell seemed to break loose up in the baker's loft. It began with O'Ryan bellowing in obvious disbelief. He was ranting and raving, and while Sean couldn't hear it all with complete clarity where he sat, one floor below, he caught enough of the baker's words to get the gist of it. O'Ryan was, apparently, outraged at having been shortchanged by the Kerry brothers. He'd found Miss Plithe unsatisfactory for some reason, and he wanted his "merchandise" exchanged for better at once.

Sean, knowing that Patrick was sure to come up swinging at him if he attempted to wake him a third time, simply sprang from his dining chair and hurried up to the loft to deal with the problem on his own. He found the baker, now dressed in nothing but a nightshirt, right at the top of the stairs, and he looked angry enough to shove Sean back down the steps to the first floor.

"Yes, Mr. Kerry," he growled. "I was just comin' down for ye, in fact. Get up here! Just get up here and see what we've acquired," he added, bending down and tugging at Sean's right wrist, where it preceded his left on the ladder's highest rung.

Sean, though annoyed at having his hand jerked at in such a manner, hurried up the remaining steps and into the loft, with the baker taking a step or two back to accommodate him. "Sweet Jesus, what is it, Mr. O'Ryan? I think you've roused the dead with your hollerin'!"

His client didn't answer. He simply thrust a finger out toward the bed like an enraged schoolmaster directing an unruly child to one of the classroom's corners.

Sean's eyes followed that finger and lit upon Miss Plithe, where she lay, curled up like an infant. Her body was heaving with sobs, which she was stifling against one of the bed's pillows.

"Well, what on earth have ye done to her, man?" Sean asked, turning back to the baker. "She looks as though ye slaughtered her dearest friend!"

O'Ryan's palms opened widely with aggravation where they hung at his sides. "It's not what I did to her, ye ruddy dolt! It's what she's done to us! She's four months pregnant, for Christ's sake, Mr. Kerry! Don't you lads even bother to look into such things before stealin' a girl?" he exclaimed. "Why, it's like me sellin' burnt bread to people! It's an outrage, is what!"

Sean furrowed his brow. "Four months pregnant? But that can't . . . can't be," he stammered, moving numbly toward the bed. "I mean, she was terrified when I left her up here, utterly lost as to what the . . ." He paused and searched for the most tasteful term. "What the marriage act entailed."

"Well, she was deceivin' ye then, because she knew what she was doin' well enough when I climbed in with her! Descended upon me like a wolf on a burrow of bunnies, she did . . . until I saw for myself that swollen belly on her and she finally confessed to being over twelve weeks along!"

Sean continued to scowl, scouring his memory for anything he might have missed while helping the girl disrobe, any hint that she'd managed to girdle in such a condition. But there'd been none, he concluded. She'd had her back to him all the while. She'd kept her naked form hidden from him before and after her bath. And he'd been so careful not to touch any other part of her while applying the balm earlier, that not even a telltale brush of his palm had occurred as he'd traversed her, to offer him warning. "Is that true, Jennifer?" he asked, still astounded. "Did ye tell him what he claims?"

"Yes," she sobbed.

"Well, why would ye confess to such a thing?"

"Because it's true," she bawled again. "Because he was thinkin' I was just fat, and I wanted him to know I'm not usually. That 'tis not my fault." She turned and lifted her face to look at Sean, and the tears streaming down her cheeks were quite visible in the light from the bedside lamp.

"Ah, Christ," Sean exclaimed under his breath. He should have known from the moment they began plotting to snatch her that she was trouble, that she was dangerously different from the rest—a fox who dressed like a mouse. "Well, why are ye cryin' then?"

he inquired softly after a moment. "Is it that ye want to stay with him?"

Her tone was almost pleading. "Yes. *Yes.* But now he doesn't want me, because he says I'm 'spoiled goods,' " she explained like a child reporting some schoolyard mistreatment to her father.

"Ah, Christ," Sean said again, returning his gaze to the baker. "Did ye really say that to her?"

O'Ryan's expression became almost comically defensive. "Aye. Somethin' of the sort, I guess. I really don't recall. . . . But what does it matter what I said?" he added, looking angry once more. "Our agreement, Mr. Kerry, was that you would be bringin' me the *unclaimed* daughter of a wealthy milliner from Kilkenny, and clearly, that is not what happened! Damned harlot," he snarled.

"Harlot, is it?" Jennifer screeched. "How dare ye call me such a thing, ye boar! The three of ye conspire to spirit me off in the night so that you can get your greedy hands on my dowry, and you dare to judge *me?* Well, a pox upon ye! A pox upon the lot of ye," Miss Plithe spat back, and her face was so pale in that moment, so corpselike with its swollen red eyes, that she looked like a banshee come to whisk them off to their graves.

Most unbecoming for a bride on her wedding night, Sean thought, raising his palms and letting his face drop into them. Then he gave forth a weary groan. The muscles in the back of his neck were tightening like the rope on a ship's lowered anchor, and he wished to God he was simply lost in a drunken sleep now, like his brother. "Ah, stop it! The pair of ye," he ordered as he lifted his head once more.

115

"We'll come to naught here if we start hurlin' curses at one another. Now, Jennifer, please tell me, if ye would, why ye went to all the trouble of pretendin' to be chaste with me earlier?" he began again in a diplomatic tone.

Her angry expression melted back into a wounded one. " 'Cause I . . . 'cause I liked the looks of ye," she explained through hiccupping gasps. "And I thought . . . thought maybe there was a chance that you'd change your mind and claim me as your own."

"So, then, you don't want Mr. O'Ryan?"

"Well, it's not that. I like him well enough. It's just that now . . . now that I've told him about the baby, he doesn't want *me,* " she concluded, letting her head fall to the pillow again with a pitiful wail.

"And what about the father? Who sired your baby?"

"I asked her that," the baker interjected, throwing up his hands as though fit to be tied. "Don't ye think I asked her that, ye fool? And she wouldn't tell me!"

"Well, who is it?" Sean asked her gingerly. "Someone who's goin' to want ye returned?"

Again all she could seem to do was sob. "No."

"Are ya certain of it?"

Jennifer lifted her head once more and nodded.

"Does he know about the baby, whoever he is?"

"*No.* And I don't want him to! I'll not tell a soul who he is! Ever!"

"So, ye hate him then?"

"I can't bear the sight of him!"

"And that's why ye didn't resist when I told ye

116

we had kidnapped ye for your dowry," Sean said knowingly.

Again she nodded and, turning back onto her side, clutched the bed's right pillow to her once more.

"So, ye want to stay with Mr. O'Ryan?" Sean asked charily after several seconds.

"If he'll have me . . . aye . . ." she answered, her voice again breaking off into weeping.

Sean shook his head in wonder and fell silent. He'd seen some strange things in his many years of bride snatching, but this topped them all! Ordinarily he would have assumed that such a captive bride was simply claiming to be pregnant in order to get them to return her to her parents. Yet he'd clearly offered this one a chance or two to free herself from the arrangement, and she wasn't taking him up on it. Yeah, she was with child all right, he concluded. Only a woman in such a temperamental state could have produced cries as gut-wrenching as those she was giving forth now.

"Mr. O'Ryan," Sean said finally in a hushed voice, "can I have a word with ye downstairs, sir?"

O'Ryan, still looking quite dissatisfied with the situation, crossed his arms over his chest and gave Sean a grudging nod. "Oh, all right. But, I warn ye, Mr. Kerry, I'm not a man to be trifled with, and I think I've had to endure just about enough for one night!"

Sean offered him a spiritless "uh-huh" and, turning, led the way down the loft ladder. "We shall return forthwith," he called back consolingly to Miss Plithe.

"Now, let's keep our voices low, please," Sean began as he and the baker sat down at the dining table several seconds later. "No need to risk gettin' the lass any more upset than she is already, and I'm sure this can all be wrought out."

"Is that so, Mr. Kerry? Well, I'm not," O'Ryan retorted with a humph, plunking his elbows down upon the table.

"Ten thousand guineas," Sean replied through clenched teeth. "That's what you'll be castin' to the winds if ye let that girl go now . . . now that we've gone to such trouble to snatch her for ye! Have ye any idea, I wonder, how many bloody loaves of bread you'd have to bake to earn that kind of money?" Sean concluded, staring over at him with imploring eyes.

"A fair number, I guess," the baker conceded, obviously moved by Sean's expression.

"Aye. A fair number, indeed. . . . Now ordinarily, sir, I would die before I'd speak ill of my brother to any man. And if ye dare to repeat what I'm about to say, I'll see that ye live to regret it! But given the circumstances and the *hour,* Mr. O'Ryan, let me speak very plainly. Startin' tomorrow, I'm finished with this business, for good and all. And should ye choose to return Miss Plithe to her parents and begin again tryin' to have another wealthy lass stolen for ye, you'll be stuck arrangin' it all with my brother there, since we Kerrys are just about the only ones in this line of work. And as you can probably see, my brother is all too fond of drink and often out of his senses with it." Sean shook his head sorrily. "Take it from someone who's had more than enough dealin's with him to know."

"So what are ye sayin', Mr. Kerry? That you're the headpiece here?"

"The headpiece *and* the sobriety, sir. Now I can hardly say it any plainer than that, can I?"

"I suppose not," the baker replied, looking as though some reason was beginning to return to him. "Well then, couldn't ye stay on with it? For just one more job?" he asked hopefully.

Sean shook his head. "Not for even one more hour, if I had my way. But I don't. I've agreed, with my brother here, to see that this last snatchin' is made final for ye, and I'll honor that agreement, but not a bit more. So, you tell me," he declared, his eyes narrowing as he continued to stare at his client, "which will it be? Either I ride back to Kilkenny in the mornin' to return Miss Plithe to her home—and pray to God they'll take her back after she's been in our hands overnight. *Or* I ride back to 'em with our 'ransom' letter and we all collect as we agreed. Which will it be?" he asked again with a note of finality that struck him as being amply compelling.

The baker fell silent, obviously giving this choice some thought. "Well . . . she's a comely enough lass, I guess," he acknowledged after several seconds. "Though a bit high-spirited. I mean, I really hadn't figured upon havin' to rear some other man's child in the bargain, ye know, Mr. Kerry," he concluded pointedly.

Sean rolled his eyes. "Ah, come now, O'Ryan, just think how many men do so without even knowin' that they are! At least the girl was honest with ye about it. I mean, ye must give her credit for that."

119

The baker bit his lower lip contemplatively. "Yeah, well, that she was, I guess," he agreed.

"And with ten thousand guineas, well, dear Lord, man, you could afford to rear dozens of kids with that much money!"

Again his client nodded. "Aye, well. Maybe you're right."

Sean stood up and gave him a bolstering slap on the shoulder. "Of course I'm right. Though no one's askin' ye to do such a thing. We're just askin' that ye find it in your heart to tolerate the presence of one little baby, an infant who, from its first breath, will come to think of you as its one and only father." Sean could speak with confidence on this from first-hand experience, though he had no intentions of further besmirching the Kerry name by saying so. "And just think how obliged the lass shall be to ye for it. Other men who've stolen brides might have to endure endless reproach from their women, but not you, my good man. No, indeed. In fact, it wouldn't surprise me at all if she simply worshiped ye in the long run."

To Sean's relief, the baker was beginning to look appeased by his words. "Do ye really think so?" he asked after a moment.

"I'm almost certain of it, sir. I'm nearly as sure as I can be that Miss Plithe and her child will be eternally grateful to you to the end of your days. I mean, no man has surety in marriage, Mr. O'Ryan. You knew that when ye hired us. But, I'm tellin' ye, sir, from the depths of my soul, that, given the circumstances, you're apt to know a great deal more matrimonial happiness than most."

"But what if the fella who bagged that child with her should suddenly come 'round claimin' her dowry is his? What then?"

Sean waved him off. "Ah, he won't. Ye heard her; he doesn't even know about the baby."

"But what if she's lyin' and he does know?"

"Lord, man, how's he goin' to prove such a claim? And what good would it do him, anyway, with the three of us havin' pocketed all the spoils by that time? Besides, ye can't end any worse off for money than ye were before ye hired Pat and me."

The baker sat pondering all of this for several seconds. "No. I suppose not."

"Well, of course not," Sean declared. "Now, why don't ye go back up there and start again," he added with a suggestive smirk, his eyebrows angling up in the direction of the loft.

The baker still looked a trifle hesitant. "But do ye think she'll have me now, after all that was said?"

"Have ye?" Sean repeated, feigning amazement. "Did ye hear how she was cryin' at the thought of losin' ye? I think she'll welcome ye as the eighteen trumpeters!"

"Well . . . all right," O'Ryan said, rising slowly. "But I'm comin' back down, mind, if she doesn't."

"She will. She will," Sean assured, rising, circling around to him, and hastening his course to the ladder.

Sean watched as his client disappeared into the darkness above seconds later. Then, he returned to the table to resume his meal.

He consulted his pocket watch as he finished eating, and a full ten minutes had elapsed since the baker's return to the loft, with nothing but heavenly silence descending from above.

He rose, walked over to the hearth, and stooped to stir its embers. Then he went to the settle and stretched out upon it, again using the bolster as a pillow. He was almost certain now that the arrangement with the baker would stand. And as he drifted to sleep minutes later, to the harmonious squeaking of O'Ryan's bed frame overhead, he said a silent farewell at last to the dubious profession of bride snatching.

Chapter 8

Heather Monaghan stood before the wardrobe that adjoined her bedchamber the following morning, trying to decide which gown to wear for her espionage work at the Murphy's farm. Monaghan Manor was as quiet as usual today, with her father off working overtime at the mines. Heather knew, however, that his absence wouldn't make it any easier for her to slip away from the manse. The servant staff had, doubtless, already been told of Jennifer's abduction and warned not to let Heather leave the grounds, lest the same fate befall her. So Heather would have to choose clothing that was as inconspicuous as possible, in order to facilitate her getaway.

As she stood, surveying the tightly packed array of frocks that hung in front of her, she again had trouble believing what had happened the night before. She'd actually awakened with the thought that it had all been some sort of dream, a nightmare that would fade from memory by the radiant light of day. But she knew now that it had been real. Her longtime friend, Jennifer Plithe, her nearest neighbor and frequent confidante, was gone, swept away in the night by two masked men, like an autumn leaf being carried off on the wind. To make matters worse, Heather again acknowledged that she, herself, had been, at least in part, to blame for the kidnapping, and not even the familiar, cheerful surroundings of her lace- and linen-adorned bedchamber could seem to quell the guilt she was still feeling over it.

As if all of that weren't enough, one of Jenny's abductors had threatened to come back for Heather as well, and Heather grew so weak in the knee at recalling this now that she had to drag the joint stool from her embroidery tablestand over to her wardrobe so she could sit down while continuing to try to decide upon just the right garb for the day.

Whatever she chose, she knew it would have to be unimpeding enough to allow her to shinny down the tree outside her bedchamber window, in case either a stealthy exit or return was made necessary by the vigilance of the servant staff. But she was certain that her wardrobe contained at least a few such garments, because she'd found herself climbing up that old oak more than once in the past couple years—being, as Jennifer often put it, "a spoiled and far-too-spirity daddy's girl."

Heather had always chosen to ignore this assessment, deciding, instead, to think of herself as a free and adventurous spirit. A true *bon vivant,* with the wisdom to sow her wild oats before marriage and motherhood made it impossible for her to do so. She'd come to no harm at it, after all. That was the important thing. Visiting the shops in town and poking her head in on what social events Kilkenny had to offer was innocent enough—even without a chaperone. Her virtue was still intact. That was what really mattered. And she knew how to go on protecting it well enough with the pistol she often carried in her drawstring bag.

It wasn't as though she was really "sneaking" out on her own, she rationalized. It was just that she enjoyed getting out and about more often than her governess did, and Heather saw no point in imposing such outings on the dear woman.

How was a lass to acquire knowledge, after all, Heather reasoned, if not by seeing things firsthand, if not by doing? Surely her father couldn't expect her to learn about the outside world entirely from books. Yet, to her dismay, she'd only been out of Ireland once, packed off to a Parisian finishing school, which, her father had been careful to confirm, employed a solely Catholic staff. But between her schoolma'am's complaints about her unruliness and her widower father's, albeit unvoiced, hankering for her company in their lonely Irish manor, she was returned home within six months to complete her schooling with a tutor from Belfast.

Heather had hoped for a male tutor, someone with whom she could play her kittenish games to best effect. Instead, her father's coach had returned carrying the sour-faced Elvina Pritch, a middle-aged spinster so stern that her lips had actually gone permanently pale from having been pursed so much. From Miss Pritch—to whom the rest of the servant staff never tired of referring by the obvious rhyme of her name—Heather had learned that the world was, on the whole, a cold and perilous place. Miss Pritch maintained that the pox, rapists, and thieves were lurking around every corner, just waiting to pounce upon the evil and virtuous alike and that all one could expect from life was to finally be freed from its hardships and miseries by death.

In keeping with this, Miss Pritch was hit and killed by a lightning strike shortly after taking the Lord's Name in vain at a Monaghan family picnic in the summer of 1706. To Heather's great relief, her father decided that, at seventeen, her tutelage was about as complete as it would ever be and there was no need to hire another instructor for her. Unfortunately, however, Miss Pritch's tyrannical sternness had quickly been replaced by the uninvited courtship of Malcolm Byrne. Heather just couldn't seem to escape having a devout disciplinarian in her life. Yet, she knew for certain that the efforts of such people were totally wasted on her, for she, like her mother, was just too vibrant and life-loving to believe a word of what they tried to teach her.

Life to Heather was like a banquet, filled with new adventures and delights for those brave enough to reach out and sample them. And if, once in a while, such daring ended in a scoundrel or two making off with one's girl friend, so be it, Heather thought. The feelings of fear and remorse this evoked made one know one was alive, and such feelings were certainly preferable to the excruciating boredom of spending all of one's days in a manor that was set much too far from town.

Having finally reached this conclusion and, thereby, absolving herself of some of her guilt, Heather rose once more and stepped into the wardrobe. She'd decided upon her tan and green worsted gown. Its neckline was tastefully high, and its unobtrusive shape and color would help her blend in against the dead-grass green of Kilkenny's early-spring landscape. What was more, the frock's cut called for so little of the usual underskirts and corseting that Heather would be able to slip into the garment on her own, without needing to enlist the help of her overcurious dresser.

Her auburn hair would, of course, also have to be worn in as unostentatious a fashion as possible. She would sweep it back, she decided, into a bun and fix it with the tortoiseshell combs that her father had brought back for her after a business-related sojourn in Madrid. Spanish hair accessories, the rage of the previous decade, were still considered quite stylish in Kilkenny, and though Heather had never liked how the combs blended with her natural hair and had always preferred to wear them when her mane was powdered—today was an exception. The less visible they were, the less visible she was, and the less visible she was, the better.

She'd have to dress quickly though, she realized, as she heard the striking clock in the manor's entrance hall gonging the hour. According to the stablehands' weekly schedule, her gelding, Nigel, would be in his stall for grooming at present. If she hurried, she could sneak in and make off with him before he was returned to the croft, where getting hold of him was sure to draw too much attention to her.

* * *

Sean had stopped in the town of Lismore that morning and had a tailor fit him for a set of dress clothes. This was, after all, the first day of his new life as an honest man, and he wanted to make certain he looked the part. He was, he'd been told by a tailor or two, of fairly average height and proportions, so fitting him hadn't been difficult, and while the necessary alterations were being made, he went off to purchase a periwig for himself. He wanted something flowing and elegant, of course, but not too far from his own hair's color. The town's wigmaker managed to oblige him as well, as did its shoemaker, and within three hours, he was newly clad from head to toe and on his way back to Kilkenny.

As planned, he paid a Kilkenny street urchin a tidy sum to take the "ransom" note to the Plithe residence, leave it at their doorstep, and dash away without being seen. Then, having gotten this last bit of bride-snatching business out of the way, he wasted no time in heading for Brian Monaghan's manor, outside of town.

He rode as far as Monaghan's front drive. Then, not wanting to be seen or heard by any of the household or staff, he dismounted, tied his horse to a nearby tree, and began traveling the rest of the way on foot.

Monaghan Manor lay a third of a mile before him now, atop a grassy plateaulike hill. Its vine-strewn, Neoclassical facade shone with a comforting brightness in the late-morning sun, and its numerous front windows seemed to be staring out at Sean, across the front grounds, like so many quizzical eyes. It was really quite a grand domicile, Sean acknowledged as he neared it—more befitting royalty, actually, than someone as lackluster as a coal-mine owner. But no matter, a reverent voice within him said; this was *her* house, the home of the lovely lady Heather, whose emerald eyes were far finer gems than any royal personage could ever hope to possess.

This was *her* house, he told himself again with veneration as he continued moving cautiously toward it and its features became more visible. This estate, with its white lace curtains, circular carriageway, and three widely spaced chimneys, was, as far as Sean knew, where she spent her days and nights, where she ate her meals and dreamed her dreams and said her prayers at eventide. This was where she dressed and undressed and sat brushing through her lovely coppery mane. And somewhere, quite probably on the second floor, was her room, that sacred chamber where she lay at night in sweet, heavy darkness, with the unclaimed depths of her waiting, secretly seething to be ravished by just the right man.

But what if, like her friend, Jennifer, Heather had already been claimed? Sean stopped in his tracks at the sheer horribleness of this thought. What if that black-haired brute he'd shot was betrothed to her? What then?

No. *It couldn't be.* He started walking again with a brave, determined swallow. She had accepted his invitation to dance without reservation, something no respectable lass would have done were she promised to another. What was more, he'd seen the look on her face, the shock in her eyes, when he'd kissed her hand, when his tongue had swept over her soft, ivory skin, and no young lady of real experience was likely to have looked that taken aback by such an innocent act.

It suddenly dawned on Sean, as he continued walking, that in all of his musing about Miss Monaghan, he hadn't yet taken the time to work out the details of his approach. He couldn't simply knock on the estate's front door and ask for her. That was just too risky, too direct.

So, what were the alternatives? He could simply keep watch over the place for a while, he imagined. Hide himself in some nearby bushes and observe Heather's comings and goings off and on for a day or two. Then, perhaps, he'd be well enough acquainted with her routine to engineer a clandestine intersection of her path. Or better yet, maybe he could simply do what he'd done with the Plithes: leave a note at the front door, one that was so cryptically worded that only Heather would have any idea who had sent it. Yes, he decided. That seemed the best course of action now.

In the note, he would suggest a rendezvous, a time and place where they might meet, away from any witnesses. Nevertheless, he'd still have to observe her comings and goings for a couple of days, he realized. He would have to be able to determine what time was best for the young lady to slip away and where they might be allowed to speak privately, without arousing the suspicion of her family and servants. But that would be easy enough, Sean told himself. Spying upon maidens was second nature to him now, after all his years of bride snatching. What was more, he thought, with a soft smile coming to his lips, tailing this particular young lady was sure to prove especially enjoyable, because, in the end, she would not be delivered to another man, as all the others had been. Rather, she would be Sean's and Sean's alone.

He began heading toward the east now, in the direction of the stable, which stood off to the right of the manor. Since there was no sign of Miss Monaghan out front, he would sneak around to the rear of the estate on the off chance that she was back there. Perhaps she was out strolling through the gardens or eating a late breakfast on some terrace or other. He knew, from long experience, that these were among the ways in which wealthy maidens spent their mornings.

Just as he was moving to do this, however, something far off to the left caught his eye. It was sudden movement, a streak of tan against the duller ground of the manor. As he turned to get a better look, he fully expected to discover that it was an enormous dog of some sort, sallying forth from the manse with the intent of stalking Sean, just as he was stalking the daughter of its master.

He and Patrick had encountered enraged watchdogs more than once on their jobs, and Sean certainly didn't relish the idea of tangling with another. Such dustups had sometimes ended in their having to shoot the beasts in their own defense, and Sean knew that a gunshot would call far too much attention to him now. What was more, he acknowledged, he wasn't apt to better his chances of winning Miss Monaghan's heart by killing her pet.

To both his relief and amazement, however, Sean saw, upon a closer look, that it was not a dog at all. It was the master's daughter herself, Heather Monaghan! She was dressed in a frock of beige and green, and she was moving along below the first-floor windows of the estate in an odd skulking manner.

Sean instantly dropped to his belly, praying she wouldn't spot him, and he lay watching her for several seconds more. "What luck, what great fortune!" a voice within him sang: to have the very object of his heart's desire appear to him so readily. It was the will of Heaven for sure! And realizing this, a smile lit his face again.

She was positively creeping along now, her hunched form a great contrast to her proud carriage of the night before, and Sean realized that she was sneaking out of the manor. She was seeking to avoid the notice of all within the dwelling by staying tightly to its facade and by hovering, for several seconds, in front of each of the intermittent bushes she passed along the way.

He studied her very carefully, doing his best to determine whether or not she was really Heather or simply some sibling who closely resembled her.

She looked different, granted. She was dressed much more staidly than she had been on the preceding evening, and her flowing auburn hair was now swept up into a matronly bun. But even across the many yards of land that separated them, Sean could see that it was Heather and not a look-alike. He wasn't sure how he knew this. He certainly wasn't close enough to see if her eyes were as verdant as he remembered them being or whether or not her lips were as invitingly full and pouty as he recalled. He simply sensed it somehow. He just *knew* it was her, and his heart began to pound with excitement at seeing her again.

She was headed for the stable, Sean realized in those wonderful, palpitating seconds. The drawstring purse she was carrying and the urgency in her movements told him that she was going to make her way to the stable and flee on horseback. He'd certainly executed enough of such getaways in his time to recognize one when he saw it.

Keeping his body hunched, he slowly got back up to his feet and began moving farther toward the east. He would go around to the stable's back entrance and lie in wait for her within. If she, in her obvious efforts to avoid notice, thought it safe enough to go into the stable, then surely it would be for him as well.

Sean heard only the faint sounds of someone sweeping as he snuck around the side of the stable to its back door a minute or two later. He was terribly winded from the run, so he had all he could do to keep his panting from being heard as he crept over to the rear entrance. Once he reached it, he looked about to make sure no one had seen him. Then he darted across the opened doorway and stood just on its other side, listening for anything more from within. There was nothing, however. He heard only the continuing sound of someone sweeping, and he could tell now that whoever was making it was far enough inside the stable that he could probably slip in unnoticed.

He did so, again pressing his body tightly up against the stable's back wall and biting his lip to keep his labored breathing as soundless as possible.

His nostrils were immediately assailed by the smell of leather, and as his eyes began to adjust to the dimness of the stable's interior, he saw that he was in the tackle room. To his great relief, it didn't appear to be occupied.

Having made certain of this, he dashed across to the doorway that led to the horses' stalls. Again he hid himself just off to one side of the threshold and peered around to see who was within. All he saw was a stableboy mucking out a stall which was several yards down on Sean's left, very near the front entrance.

To Sean's surprise, he found the stablehand's presence anything but threatening in those seconds. On the contrary, the servant's sweeping was so rhythmic, so methodical that Sean couldn't help feeling strangely comforted by it, and he seized these seconds of calm and used them to gather his wits about him and slow his racing heart.

A moment or two later, a figure darkened the stable's front doorway, and Sean looked up to see Heather standing there, her hands and, consequently, her drawstring purse hidden behind her.

"George?" Sean heard Heather call out to the stablehand in a cautiously low voice.

The servant, obviously not having heard her enter, looked up from his work with a start. "Aye, miss?"

"Has Nigel been brushed, do ye know?"

"Aye, miss. And I was just about to take him back out to the croft."

"No. Don't bother," she blurted with a nervous laugh. "I'll see to it."

Sean saw the stablehand shrug. "As ye wish, miss."

134

"George," Heather said again as the servant resumed his sweeping.

"Aye, miss?"

"The steward was just askin' for ye, over at the great house."

The stablehand stopped his work once more and simply reached up and scratched his head at this claim. "At the great house, ye say? Why would he be lookin' for me there I wonder . . . I don't work over there, now, do I," he added with a befuddled laugh.

Sean's eyes traveled back to Heather and saw her offer the servant a shrug.

"Ah, all right, then," the hand said after several seconds, stepping over to an adjacent stall wall and propping his broom up against it. "Thank ye, miss." With that, he turned on his heel and, to Sean's horror, began heading for the stable's back door.

Sean moved like lightning, pivoting on his heels and flattening himself back against the tackle room's inner wall. To his great relief, the hand strode right past him in the seconds that followed, past him and out of the stable without so much as a backward glance.

When he was fairly certain the servant was gone, Sean turned back to the doorway and continued watching Miss Monaghan. He would wait to see what she'd sought in coming out to the stable, and if the circumstances felt right, he would reveal himself to her.

She had wasted no time in moving down the center passage, and her eyes were fixed upon the one and only horse in the place: a fine-looking black gelding who was tethered in the last stall down on Sean's right.

Time seemed to freeze for Sean, as he was again allowed to behold her jewel-like features at close range. Every glorious inch of them was getting more and more distinct as she approached. He stole those secret seconds to let his eyes travel over her now-covered bosom and drink in the porcelaneous beauty of her face, framed today by the spit curls at her temples and ears. Even dressed and coifed this sedately, there was no hiding the fact that a true beauty smoldered beneath. Sean had seen for himself the night before the ample cleavage that presently lay under her high-cut worsted gown and the temptress's mane that peeked out at him now from behind the prison-bar teeth of a brown-colored comb, as she turned and headed into the horse's stall.

She was cooing something as she went up to the gelding and reached out to stroke his right thigh. And the endearing sounds she was making, coupled with the sight of her caressing ivory fingers, were enough to make Sean's knees give out from beneath him with imagining those same gentle attentions directed to him.

He clenched his teeth and tried to get a grip on himself. What was she saying? a voice within him demanded to know. He knew that he must force himself to keep track of all that she was saying and doing now, so he could best determine how to proceed.

"Nige," he heard her say again in an adoring undertone.

It was probably the horse's name, Sean deduced as she repeated it a few times more. Yes. He'd heard her say it to the stablehand just a minute or two earlier. It was definitely the gelding's name, Sean concluded, as she finally added the suffix "ems" to it.

"We're goin' for a ride, Nigems lamb. Just a short one," she whispered, obviously afraid of being overheard. "But we must be *very* quiet," she continued as though addressing a small child. "Heather shall lead her Nigel out of the stable a ways, and then we'll be off to Murphys' farm to have a look 'round."

Sean could see little more than her gown's skirt as she rounded the horse's right side seconds later and moved to the back of the stall to untie him. Then she guided the animal out of the compartment by the lead rope that was about his neck and started moving toward the tackle room door.

A *saddle,* a voice within Sean exclaimed. She was going to need a saddle from the tackle room for her ride to the Murphys', and *he* was going to need somewhere else to hide! But there wasn't time to seek another place of concealment, he realized in those frantic seconds. So he simply flattened himself back against the left side of the doorway once more and prayed he'd again go unnoticed.

She strode right past him a moment later, she and her cooing and the rhythmic clops of her horse's hooves. Then the two of them came to a halt, and she hurried over to the shelves to grab a saddle for herself—for that lovely, curving bottom of hers, Sean thought with relish as she bent down to withdraw it. And as her posterior spread the folds of her skirt out to a revealing flatness, he found himself imagining a lifetime of fondling what lay beneath that woolen gown.

"Murphys', is it?" he heard himself blurt an instant later, and he realized that some part of him couldn't bear the thought of letting her leave now, and thereby disappear from his sight for God knew how much longer. In that same second, he somehow found the presence of mind to reach up and ceremoniously remove his hat in deference to her.

She spun about and faced him with a gasp, letting the saddle fall from her grasp. "Oh, dear God! Ye scared me half to death," she exclaimed, clapping a hand to her chest.

His smile conveyed a roguish knowingness. "I fancy I did, miss, the way you were sneakin' about."

Heather studied him for several frenzied seconds. He was quite expensively dressed in a long white waistcoat which was garnished with gold embroidery, and his navy blue frock coat was so official-looking, with its accenting rows of white piping, that she would almost have thought him a military man, if not for the garment's generously flared cut. But it was the color of his periwig that made his face really come into focus for her. It wasn't gray or reddish or brown, as they usually were, but a golden blond. And that particular shade, coupled with those unforgettably large blue eyes of his, brought recognition to her in a shuddering flash.

"Oh, sweet Jesus! You're that strawboy who abducted Jennifer, aren't ye," she acknowledged in a terrified whisper, backing away from him.

Sean raised an allaying palm. "Ah, now, don't go gettin' all wrought up on me, lass. No need to cry out and give *both* our plans away. I won't . . ." He was about to assure her that he meant her no harm,

138

that there really was no reason for her to panic, but his words broke off as her right hand dove into her purse and emerged with a pistol.

Mother Mary, a voice within him exclaimed, these Kilkenny girls were just brimming with surprises!

"Now, you stay where ye are, ye hooligan," she snarled, leveling the weapon at him. "Make one move and I'll fire. I swear it!"

Sean froze, as requested, but it was not so much out of fear that she'd shoot as it was out of utter amazement that this angel of a girl, this sweet, gentle goddess, who had haunted his every thought since he'd met her, could possibly look as ferocious as she did now.

"Yes. Yes. All right," he replied, wanting to put his hands up to help convince her of his benevolent intent, but worried that she would, indeed, shoot if he indulged in even that much movement. Judging from the looks of things, she was sure to make a bloody botch of it. She was holding the pistol in just one trembling hand, its muzzle wobbling in such a way that God only knew what part of him or *herself* she'd hit, if she did manage to fire it.

She wasn't calling for help, though. That was one thing in his favor. If she really wanted him hauled away, she'd have done at least that much by now. Rather, she looked as though she wanted to handle him on her own for some reason, and Sean couldn't have been more pleased at this revelation.

"Where's our Jenny, then?" she demanded, still keeping her voice low. "What have ye done with her?"

"Well, it's a long story, Miss Monaghan. Are ye

139

sure ye want to hear it standin' out here in horse droppin's, holding' me at the point of a gun all the while?"

The green eyes he'd found so entrancing suddenly narrowed to angry slits. "A simple answer will suffice, sir. Now, you tell me where she is or I'll blow ye to high heaven!"

"Well, not at the Murphys', miss. I can save ye havin' to make that trip, in any case."

"Where then?" she demanded again.

"Lismore," he answered after several seconds, fairly certain that matters were well enough under way now with the Plithes that telling her this much wouldn't endanger the deal.

She furrowed her brow. "Lismore? But that's hours of ridin' from here. Ye can't have gotten there and back in so little time."

Sean donned a slightly sheepish smirk. "Ah, you'd be surprised how fast a gent can travel with armed men chasin' him."

"Oh, I don't know," Heather retorted. "Judgin' from the wound ye left Malcolm with, ye couldn't have had that much of a lead."

Sean pursed his lips. "So that's the bugger's name, is it? Malcolm?"

She nodded.

"And who the devil is he, pray tell? Your brother?" he added hopefully, having sensed from the start that the man was some sort of suitor.

She shook her head, keeping her eyes locked upon him as though he were a carnival lion, poised to pounce upon her at any moment.

"Well, what then?" Sean pursued. "I'd have killed

140

him, ye know, if not for you . . . if not for bein' worried that he was someone whose death would have wounded you as well." This wasn't true, of course, but Sean thought it might help to keep her and her gun in their places.

She looked quite unprepared for this question. "He's my . . . my father's assistant at the mines," she stammered, with, Sean observed, an odd note of annoyance in her voice.

"Sure seemed too possessive of ye to be nothin' more than your father's hirelin'."

"Well, he thinks I'm goin' to marry him," Heather confessed, rolling her eyes and clucking as though she found the subject not only irksome but embarrassing for some reason.

Sean bit the inside of his lip, trying not to laugh at her adolescent display. "So, if I may be so bold, miss, I take it the feelin' is not mutual."

"Not in the least. Now, where's Jen?" she snapped. "Where in Lismore are ye holdin' her?"

"I can't tell ye that," Sean replied, lifting his chin resolutely. "I'm sorry, but ye must wait a day or two before I can answer that question. And if that is not satisfactory to ye, you'll simply have to shoot me," he concluded, fixing his jaw.

To his relief, no shot came. Her grip on the gun seemed to ease, in fact, as she continued to hold it on him. "But why can't ye answer it now?" she asked, sounding childishly disappointed.

"Because, were I to tell ye, you'd go and tell her parents. Then they'd tear off in search of her, and my brother and I couldn't collect on her as intended."

141

"Collect what? A ransom, ye mean?"

"Yes, miss. Her dowry, to be precise."

"So then, it was true, what some of the guests at the Cassidys' were sayin'; you're a bride snatcher," Heather acknowledged with a dry swallow. She really hadn't been able to bring herself to believe it until now . . . now, with one of the very culprits standing before her, confessing to it.

Sean nodded, casting his gaze downward rather ashamedly in those seconds.

"So, who's to . . . to have her?" Heather asked, knowing that this was yet another question to which she wasn't sure she truly wanted an answer. "You?"

To her great relief, he shook his head as he lifted it again. "Oh, no, miss. Not me."

"That redhead who was with ya then?"

He laughed at this question, but Heather couldn't imagine why. "God, no. My brother take a bride?" he asked incredulously. "What a ridiculous notion."

"Well, who did ye snatch her for?" Heather asked impatiently.

He looked somewhat sheepish again. "I can't tell ye that yet either, miss. I'm sorry."

"Well, what can ye tell me?" she asked, again with a juvenile cluck.

His eyes suddenly seemed larger somehow, filled with compassion, as was his voice. "Just that she's in no danger, and that she'll be a married woman by day's end."

A chill ran through Heather at recalling what Shannon Kennedy had told her the night before about the laying of such claim to a woman. "So,

142

you've already done it to her?" she acknowledged, her face hot now with a spreading blush.

To her chagrin he looked as though he didn't know what she was referring to. "Done what, miss?"

"Well . . . ya know," Heather replied, waving her hands about in the hope that some gesturing might relieve her of having to put it into words. "Made . . . made water inside of her," she concluded, letting her gaze drop and feeling as though she might die of embarrassment.

To her horror, he didn't answer, and he still looked puzzled as she lifted her face once more. His brow was furrowed, and his eyes moved from one side to the other, as though he were searching his mind for some tag that might help him figure out what she was talking about. "I am sorry, my lady. But I've lost ye, I'm afraid."

"I knew it," she suddenly growled, shaking her head with annoyance. "Damn that Shannon! I knew she had it wrong!"

He continued to look perplexed. "Had what wrong?"

"About how you'd be layin' claim to Jennifer."

"Oh, she's been claimed well enough," he confirmed, his matter-of-factness in that instant again sending a rush of chills through Heather. "But it hasn't anythin' to do with makin' water. I can't imagine where this Shannon ye speak of could have gotten that."

Heather swallowed loudly again, her legs beginning to tremble. There was something about discussing such things with a man as attractive as he that was leaving her quite unnerved, and she knew she had to get a grip on herself or wind up falling into his clutches as well.

"Well, enough said about it," she declared, again leveling the barrel of her gun so it was pointed at his chest once more. "Why don't ye just tell me what you're doin' here, prowlin' about my father's stable like this."

A knowing smile came to his lips. "I told ye last evenin' that I'd be back for ye. And I'm a man who keeps his word."

"Back . . . back for me? *Why?*" Heather stammered, feeling as though she were about to swoon.

His smile broadened, and his eyes became more penetrating, more intolerant of her schoolgirlish line of questioning. "Oh, come now, Miss Monaghan. A fine, educated young lady like yourself, can't ye fancy why?" he asked, taking a confident step toward her.

In daylight now, at such close range, the manly shadow about his chin and cheeks was apparent to Heather, and she realized that, in spite of his huge urchin's eyes, he was no strawboy, no fair-haired lad come simply to steal a kiss behind a haystack. He was a fully grown man with all of a man's appetites, and toying with him would be as dangerous as toying with fire. She locked both her hands upon the gun and jabbed it in his direction. "Don't come any closer, ye scoundrel," she hissed.

Sean could see fear in her eyes, but he didn't care if he scared her now. He'd had about as much of her tomfoolery as he could handle for one morning, and he knew it was time to take matters into his own hands. "Give me that thing, before ye shoot someone's bloody foot off with it," he growled, lunging at her and snatching the weapon from her grasp. Then he set it down on the shelves that stood just behind her.

An instant later, he pinned her wrists back against the wooden saddle case and spoke to her from behind clenched teeth. "Now, listen to me, ye little tease, standin' out here like this triflin' with me when we both know ye could have called out for help at any time. If I'd intended to spirit ye off, like I did your friend, I'd have done it by now. I'd have ye tied to my bed, naked as the day ye were born this very minute, in fact, if that's how I wanted it. And ye know it as well as I!"

Heather struggled against him a bit as his grip tightened about her wrists. But something kept her from screaming in those seconds, something about his commanding blue eyes. They seemed to lash her there, insisting that she listen to reason—such as he perceived it to be.

"But surely you're bright enough to know that that's not how I want it . . . that a man doesn't dress to the teeth and come callin' upon a lass if all he wants is to rape her in some stable. And as for Miss Plithe, why, my brother and I did her a good turn by snatchin' her. She was in need of a husband. More than you shall probably ever know. . . . And I'll thank ye not to pull any more guns on me either, miss—you and that Malcolm friend of yours! 'Cause I must confess to havin' lost all patience with bein' drawn upon in the last twenty-four hours, and while slow to anger, I have been told that I make rather a formidable foe."

145

With that, his face began moving toward hers, and Heather, not knowing what he might do to her in those seconds, turned away.

"So, just you conduct yourself like a gentlewoman when you're with me," he continued, whispering heatedly into the ear she'd inadvertently turned to him.

All she could seem to do was moan at the feel of his hot breath as it poured into her in those seconds.

"It's not polite to draw upon someone who's come 'round to woo ye," he continued. "And I warn ye, lass, I'll have no more of it!"

"Who says I want ye wooin' me, then?" she retorted, somehow finding the courage to face him once more. She was sorry to note, however, that her voice was far too tremulous now, too dreamy—with the feel of him pressed up so tightly against her—to sound particularly defiant.

"Your eyes told me so, last night," he whispered. "And just minutes ago, too, as they traveled over me, stoppin' along the way at some rather unmentionable points, I might add," he concluded with a sportive smirk.

Heather's blush deepened. Had he really noticed? How embarrassing! She had prided herself on being much more subtle than that. "My eyes don't speak for me, sir," she replied, somehow managing to keep her voice steady. "If it's my hand ye seek, you'll have to discuss it with my father, as I told ye at the Cassidys'. And it's most unlikely that he'll say yes to ye," she added derisively.

Sean was stung by this, but he tried not to let it show. "Either way," he began again, with a deathly determined look darkening his handsome features, "I want ye, and I intend to make ye mine, my dear. Ye certainly haven't denied wantin' me, and by God, I shall make it so!"

Then, to her surprise, he pressed his lips to hers. Still keeping her pinned to the case, he kissed her with such force that her head bent back and she could feel her bound-up hair coming to rest upon the shelf that was situated just behind the nape of her neck. There was room enough between the shelves for his head to fit in over hers, and it felt almost as though they were reclining as he continued to kiss her with a heedless sort of urgency. But there was something tender about the kiss as well, something that told her that it was the most natural thing in the world for him to be doing to her.

After several seconds, she realized that he wasn't pinning her there anymore, that his hands had relinquished their hold on her wrists and traveled down to spread themselves open over her shoulder blades. There they hugged her to him with a breathless firmness. Oh, Heaven help her, how she adored the feel of him holding her!

"No. I won't have to bind and gag ye like all the others, will I, Heather," she heard him whisper as he finally lifted his lips from hers.

Her eyes were pressed shut, and she was still too entranced by his embrace to utter a word.

"No. When the time comes, you'll unfold to me like a blossom on a sunny day. I could feel it just now," he concluded, his tone confident and seductive.

Then, an instant later, Heather opened her eyes

to see that he was backing away from her with a challenging smirk.

"So, should I call out for a stablehand now, my dear? Do ye want me to shout for someone to come and rescue ye from me now that I've taken your gun away? You were so frightened just now, as I held ye, that I could feel your heart racin' in my ears."

When, after several seconds, she didn't respond, but stood staring rapt up at him, he cupped his hands about his mouth, as though planning to call out, as he'd threatened to do. She, in turn, lunged at him and clapped a palm over his lips. "No. *Don't*," she implored. "Ye mustn't. Please!"

His eyes offered her a look of acquiescence, and she slowly withdrew her hand from his mouth.

"Why not?" he asked in a low voice. "It's me who'll suffer for it. I'm the intruder here, not you."

"Yes, but there will be all manner of questions asked, don't ye see? They'll want to know who ye are."

"So tell them," he said evenly.

"What? And let them have ye arrested? For that is surely what they'll do if they learn you're one of the men who took Jen."

"And ye don't want me arrested?"

"N—No," she choked.

"Why not? Don't ye think I deserve to be after what I've done?"

Heather scowled at him, at his cool, calculating expression. "It is *you* who's doin' the triflin' now, sir."

He gave forth a soft laugh. "Ah, so I am. But then again, ye can't blame a fella for tryin' to learn whether or not his feelin's will be requited."

Heather dropped her gaze and clasped her hands behind her back. Then she extended her right foot and stood coyly drawing doodles in the dirt floor before her with the toe of her riding boot. "Well, if it's my devotion ye seek, why don't ye show me your trust and tell me your name. Because in all fairness, ye know mine and where I can be found," she concluded, looking up at him through her thick dark lashes.

It was a look he couldn't refuse. "It's Kerry," he said in a voice so low that only she could have heard. "Sean Kerry. And I'm sorry, my dear, but I can't tell ye anythin' more. I will simply have to continue to come to you, I'm afraid."

She smirked and blushed. "So, ye saw me comin' down the tree from my bedchamber earlier?"

He knit his brow. "The tree?"

"The big old oak just outside my window. Ye said, when I first entered the tackle room, that you'd seen me sneakin' about, so I thought that meant you had seen me leavin' the great house."

Sean smirked as well. "No. But now, at least, I know where your bedchamber is, don't I . . . as, surely, ye intended me to."

At this, she dropped her gaze once more, her face feeling as though it were aflame with embarrassment. "I didn't," she quickly retorted.

"Ye did," he maintained, crossing to her once more and lifting her chin, so she was forced to face him. "And 'tis quite all right, my dear. I would have found it in any case. I would have wanted to know before very long."

To Sean's surprise, her expression changed in those

149

seconds from one of enamourment to one of great concern. "Ah, but ye mustn't risk it, Sean. 'Twould be the end of ye if my father or any of his staff found ye up there. Let me come down to you."

He laughed under his breath, a dry laugh that once again told her that it was a seasoned outlaw with whom she found herself alone now. "I'm not afraid of your father, love."

No. On second thought, she didn't imagine he would be, not given his obvious proficiency with a gun. "Yes, but it will only lead to trouble, don't ye see? And then, next thing ye know, you'll find yourself in the hands of the sheriff."

He wrapped his arms around her waist. "So, I'll court ye openly. I'll go to your father and ask for permission to do so."

She bit her lip and again dropped her gaze, as though hesitant to say what had come to mind. "He . . . he'd never agree to it. Even if he doesn't find out that you were one of the men who abducted Jen, he—"

"He what?" Sean prompted, when her words broke off.

"He wants me to marry someone . . . someone who's well shod," she explained, looking up at him apologetically.

Sean smiled. "Good enough, then. I'm well shod. Quite well shod, in fact. You'd be amazed."

"You are?"

"Aye. Bride snatchin' is a very profitable business," he added with a wry laugh. "So much so that I can now retire from it. Your friend Jenny was my last."

150

"You're givin' it up then?" Heather asked, her voice reflecting both her surprise and approval.

"Aye."

"And what will ye do henceforward?"

Sean shrugged. "I haven't givin' it much thought yet, I'm afraid. There's no rush, ye see. I've plenty to live on."

"But you'd have to tell my father somethin', wouldn't ye."

Again he shrugged. "I'd lie, I suppose. Tell him I inherited it."

Heather gave this some thought, then shook her head sadly. "No. That wouldn't do. He'd learn about ye on his own. He's got many friends in authority."

"So, what are ye sayin'?" Sean asked, easing away from her. "That ye don't want me to come back for ye?"

Her lips quivered a bit, and she looked as though she deeply regretted her circumstances. "No. That's not it at all. It's just that I'm worried about ye . . . worried that your comin' here will lead to your undoin'. Perhaps what ye said earlier, about stealin' me away as ye did Jen . . . perhaps that wasn't simply somethin' to be said in passin'."

He scowled at her. "Ye mean, then, that ye think I *should* abduct ye?"

She couldn't help flinching slightly at having the proposition echoed back to her. Maybe he would think she meant that he should up and spirit her off right then and there, and she knew that, deep down, the very thought of it terrified her. "Well, not right here and now, mind," she added with a nervous

151

laugh. "But yes, maybe in the end it would prove the best solution."

He lifted a fist to his lips and began pacing pensively about. "But I had my heart set on givin' it up, ye see."

"Oh, I'm sure ye did," she said, raising a sympathetic brow. "I mean, that's no way to live, really, is it? Bein' chased from county to county."

He stopped pacing and glared at her. "County to county? How would ye know about that?"

She recoiled a bit at his threatened tone. "Well, I—there was someone at the Cassidys' who said the name 'Kerry' when ya made off with Jenny. Somethin' about how infamous ye were . . . are," she amended, "throughout Ireland."

Sean continued to scowl. There was a time when news of such notoriety brought him pleasure, but he knew now that that time had clearly passed. "What? Ye mean he recognized us?" he asked uneasily.

"Oh, no," Heather assured. "He was standin' out in front of the stable. He couldn't have even seen ye. He was just takin' a guess. That was all."

Sean breathed a sigh of relief. "Ah, well, that's different, isn't it."

"Even so," Heather began again gingerly. "I suppose you'd do well to take warnin' from it and leave Kilkenny if ye can, before the authorities overtake ye."

His defensive expression suddenly gave way to one of longing as he continued to stare over at her. "Is that what ye really want? For me to leave Kilkenny?"

His eyes were so big and heartrending in those seconds that a lump formed in Heather's throat, and her nostrils stung a bit as though she were on the verge of tears. "Well, I . . . I don't know what I want. Except that I know I don't want to see ye arrested."

They both stood staring wordlessly at one another for several seconds. Then suddenly, a male voice was calling Heather's name from the direction of the great house.

"Ah, dear God, it's the steward," Heather exclaimed. "The stableboy must have told him I was out here. You'll have to go. *Now,*" she declared, rushing over to him and trying, in vain, to push him toward the back door. "Please," she entreated, again feeling as though her eyes might fill with tears.

"Very well," he conceded. Then he squared his shoulders. "I'll go, if ye think it too dangerous for me to stay. But I'll be back for ye, Heather Monaghan," he declared again, pressing another masterful kiss to her lips.

An instant later, he was gone, slipping out the back way and disappearing from view around the side of the stable.

Heather, still very shaken by his visit, pressed her eyes shut for several seconds and tried to steady herself. Then she went out front to answer—and distract—the steward.

Chapter 9

Sean's horse lost a shoe en route from Monaghan Manor to town, and Sean had no choice but to dismount and walk the rest of the way. He soon found, however, that *his* new shoes weren't serving him much better. They were torturously tight, and he had no doubt that they were starting to draw blood; but the truth was that he was so disheartened by his encounter with Heather that the pain he was suffering barely fazed him.

The dear girl had been kind enough to wrap her arm about the steward and head him back to the great house so Sean could slip away toward the road unnoticed, and for that he was most grateful to her. However, it didn't seem to erase the fact that her words of warning about her father and all his friends in high places had completely dashed Sean's hopes of courting her in a conventional manner.

The lass probably hadn't meant for it to demoralize him, Sean told himself. Clearly, she had seemed to like him and to be concerned for his well-being. Nevertheless, he did feel quite discouraged about it all, convinced that he would be forced to assume the

154

role of bride snatcher one last time and make her his final quarry. She herself had actually suggested this course to him, after all. So perhaps she'd find it in her heart to forgive him if his pursuit of her ended in her being hied off in her nightshift one evening soon.

He could, indeed, provide for her now. Perhaps it wouldn't be in quite as grand a style her father always had, but certainly she'd want for nothing—especially once Sean procured her dowry. Then, if she was willing to move with Sean to some distant county, where he and Patrick were not branded, she would receive the respect that a well-born young bride deserved. It simply all hinged upon how cooperative she intended to be.

But what a pity it would have to come down to abducting her, Sean thought, giving his head a sorry shake. He certainly wasn't looking forward to all that sneaking about in the darkness, dodging gunfire, trees, and rough terrain in the mad dash to get beyond the Monaghans' grounds before he and his bride-to-be were overtaken.

He'd just have to run the gauntlet one more time, he decided, clenching his jaw. He would simply have to pretend she was merely another of the lasses whom he'd been hired to spirit off. And more importantly, he'd have to turn a deaf ear to any protests she might offer as he did so. Then he would convey her to the cottage which he shared with Pat and Rory outside of town and lay claim to her with the same merciless avarice that most of his clients had displayed. He would have to bed her and have done with, before anyone could rescue her. The rest of the details could be sorted out later, he told himself with a wince as he finally stopped to inspect his blistered feet.

He was just on the edge of town at this point. He would stop by the smithy's and leave his horse to be reshod. For now, however, he simply wanted to get off his feet for a few minutes. He, therefore, led his steed over to a nearby stone fence, atop which he could be seated. Still hanging on to the horse's reins, he hoisted himself up onto the craggy wall and perched there, letting his feet dangle blissfully below him. Just having gotten his weight off them seemed remedy enough.

But it wasn't, of course. One look down at his bloodstained hose was enough to bear out that he was definitely in the cobbler's stocks today. He, therefore, kicked off his right shoe, lifted his foot up onto the fence top, and began rolling down his stocking to have a closer look.

It wasn't good. There was a ring of oozing blisters about the back of his ankle, and the tops of his toes looked as though they'd been scraped with a file. He didn't even have to look to know that his other foot was in roughly the same shape. But all in all, it wasn't so bad, he supposed. The abrasions wouldn't be nearly as lasting as those left on him by the leg irons at the debtor's prison in Derry, where he and Pat had served time briefly after their father's death.

Fortunately, Rory had come to their rescue within a fortnight, helping them to escape and then teaching them all they needed to know in order to survive on the streets of Londonderry. And to their credit and Rory's, they had managed to remain free citizens ever since.

In the midst of this retrospection, however, Sean suddenly heard something that once again warned that they might not be for long. It was the unmistakable sound of footsteps several yards behind him. He turned and, in an instantaneous glance, spied a figure standing in back of the partially masking width of a huge tree trunk. It was his cloaked pursuer again, Sean acknowledged, in the second it took him to return his gaze downward to his upraised foot. In spite of Sean's periwig and new mode of dress, his shadower had recognized him and was hot on his heels once more.

The only blessing in all of it was that the stranger hadn't seen that Sean had spotted him. Sean was certain of that now as he sat massaging his feet, each in its turn. And provided the chap wasn't fool enough to try to sneak up on him and grab him from behind, all would be fine. No need to do anything about it just yet, not when there were so many ways for Sean to turn the situation to his advantage.

The town of Kilkenny was quiet at present. The sky had become overcast in the last hour, and a light rain had begun to fall, coaxing the usual traffic of playing children and chatting neighbors off the streets and back into their homes. Sean was, therefore, relatively certain that there would be no witnesses as he moved to turn the tables on his pursuer.

With a pained breath, he slid himself slowly down from the fence, picked up the two instruments of torture that rested on the ground beneath him, and again began walking, with his horse in tow, toward the heart of town.

The cloaked figure followed. Sean could hear the

telltale crunch of pebbles upon the dirt road behind him. He wasn't much good at tailing, really, Sean thought with a wry smile. It seemed he and Patrick had been more proficient at it in toddlerhood than this fellow was as an adult. Given this, it was almost certain that the old "doorsill slip" wasn't part of the stranger's repertoire. Sean decided, therefore, that, if the man was still on his heels once he emerged from the blacksmith's shop, he'd give the maneuver a try.

He began swinging his shoes nonchalantly from his left hand and whistling as he walked. He knew he shouldn't rush or appear in any way ruffled. It wasn't as though the gentleman was apt to attack him, after all. Surely he'd have done so by now if he intended to, Sean reasoned. And even if he did attempt such a thing, Sean was certainly prepared. Though he hadn't pulled it on Miss Monaghan, his trusty pistol was hidden beneath his frock coat, tucked into the waist of his breeches where he could grab it in a flash. But there was really no need for matters to escalate to such a point. He would simply take his sweet time. He'd merely go on putting one throbbing foot out before the other, gingerly, deliberately, until he reached the smithy's.

Once he did so, he found the blacksmith inundated with work. So he prepaid him and, giving him an assumed name, promised to return for his horse the following day.

Then he went back out onto the street and, with a mix of anger and almost sadistic amusement, again heard his shadower walking closely behind him. He traveled as far as the second set of crossroads. And when he reached them, he took a casual turn to the right. Then, making certain he was out of his pursuer's sight, he picked up his pace to a run and darted into a deeply receded doorway, which was just far enough down the street to allow him the time he needed to get ready for the passerby.

Sean flattened himself up against the left wall of the entrance. Then he bent his knees until he was low enough to soundlessly deposit his shoes upon the stone stoop beside him. Having done this, he eased back up to his full height, and his fingers worked with lightning speed to undo the lacy white cravat about his throat. Once it was free of his neck, he stretched it out between his fists to a threatening tautness. Then he waited until he heard just the right footfall: one that was heavy and hurried enough to be that of a man who was in pursuit of someone of whom he'd lost sight.

The minutes that followed seemed an eternity. Sean's heart was racing, and he was growing angrier by the second about the fact that so little had gone right for him on this, his first day as an honest, upright Irishman. The object of his heart's desire had all but thrown cold water in his face with her rather teary-eyed explanation of her father's matrimonial expectations for her. The expensive new shoes he had bought had thanked him for his purchase by gnawing his feet raw during his trek back to town. And now, the cloaked stranger, who'd had him on edge for the past several days, was on his heels again, completely undiverted by his new costume and disguising wig.

One-step. Two-step. Three-step, and reach! Rory's faultless instruction in street crime had served Sean long and well, and it was still coming in handy now as Sean's shadower strode into view and Sean threw the scarf over his head. The shrouded form, in turn, came flying back against Sean's in the doorway, and their muffled struggle ensued.

He was quite old, Sean noted, as two vein-corded hands reached up and fought to free the strangling cravat from his throat. Old, indeed, Sean acknowledged again, as the cloak's hood slid downward to reveal a head covered with real white hair. Old enough to be no match for Sean's youthful strength; that much was clear.

"Who are ye?" Sean growled, easing up enough on the scarf to allow the stranger to choke out a reply.

"An ally," he answered, his voice hoarse and desperate.

"I have no allies in Kilkenny, sir," Sean said sternly, fighting the man's continued efforts to slip free of his stranglehold.

"You . . . you do now."

At this Sean, having had his fill of people toying with him for one day, threw the old man back against the door of the shop and pinned him there so he could get a good, long look at his face.

He had to admit to himself that it was surprising, not at all what he'd expected of a constable's henchman. It was an aristocrat's face, amazingly well preserved and powdered. No scars. No razor stubble. Markedly different from what Sean had anticipated.

"Who do ye serve?" Sean demanded through gritted teeth. "And I warn ye, man, I can strangle just as easily from the front as from the back." He punctuated this threat by moving one of his hands onto the gentleman's throat.

"I work for no one, Mr. Kerry," the stranger gasped, fighting to catch his breath under Sean's grasp.

This answer only served to further infuriate Sean. "How do you know my name?"

"Eve—everyone knows your name, sir. You're famous. A hero," the man explained in an allaying tone.

"Well, you're mistaken. You've the wrong man. Now leave off followin' me at once, or next time, I shan't spare ye. Do ye hear?" Sean hissed, his knuckles whitening as his hand again tightened about the man's throat.

The stranger managed a throaty "aye" before Sean banged his head back against the shop's door, knocking him unconscious. Sean didn't like having to get that rough, but he knew he couldn't risk having the man follow him home. From the sounds of things, the location of their cottage was probably the only secret he and Pat had left in Kilkenny.

Having reached that dismaying conclusion, Sean tied his cravat about his neck once more. Then he bent down, gathered up his shoes where they rested beside the stranger's slumped form, and continued on his way.

He wasn't even five minutes from where he'd left his pursuer when trouble again seemed to cross his path. He was just a few yards from Finney's Public House now as he heard its occupants singing a ballad to which he'd prayed he would never again be subjected. He froze in his tracks and simply stood listening. Its melody was ridiculously simple, thoroughly forgettable. Its words, however, would stay with him until the end of his days. They stung him like a brand, in fact.

"Beware, you fathers and mothers,
of two dangerous, thieving brothers
whose fortunes are sought
through girls sold and bought
for dowries more grand than most others.

Take care in your riches and leisures,
as the sun descends on night's pleasures,
that masked riders don't snatch
maiden daughters and fetch
them off to grooms seeking treasures."

Sean grimaced and slunk over to the far end of the pub's facade, bracing himself for the refrain, one he'd always found particularly wrenching.

"They dread not the grope
of the hangman's rope,
fearing poverty more than the Pope."

Sean shut his eyes and gave his head a weary shake. He did his best not to listen, but the song just kept flowing, and he realized he should hang about and try to find out who had prompted it. He was already fairly sure, however, that he knew.

"If in their keeping for even an hour,
these rogues will surely deflower
the homeliest of lasses.

In this war of the classes,
they seek gold and fame and power.

So keep watch for these brothers named Kerry,
who come from the County of Derry,
wielding knives and guns
on their nightly runs,
stalking maidens their clients can marry."

Sean's eyes fell open once more, and he let out a groan as the patrons apparently caught their breaths between stanzas. There were certainly more words to the song, but Sean knew now that he couldn't bear to hear them. He would simply go inside, grab Rory by his collar, and haul him out of there with all possible haste. Why the daft bugger insisted on passing the dreadful ballad on from county to county as they traveled wasn't entirely clear to Sean, but whatever his reasons, he had to be stopped.

It had all seemed rather laughable to Sean and Patrick several years before: how Rory had paid some bard, who'd frequented their local den of thieves, to compose the song for them and how quickly it had caught on with the clientele. But it wasn't funny anymore. In spite of any prestige Rory may have vicariously derived from it, it certainly did nothing to enhance Sean's view of himself. On the contrary—it was lunacy, a warning to sheriffs and parents alike that the Kerry brothers were nearby and about to strike again.

Sean decided not to remove his hat as he entered Finney's. He wanted to do everything he could to keep his features hidden, in case trouble erupted.

163

He'd never been in this particular pub, and it took his eyes a few seconds to adjust to the darkness of its interior. Once they did, however, he was able to survey the place in just a second or two. It was the typical tavern: a stone fireplace in the back wall with its flame burning low, a bar nearby with shelves of ales and distilleds up behind it, and a clientele of slags and crofters seated rather intermittently at the tables provided.

Sean could tell at a glance that it was a more respectable establishment than Rory usually chose to haunt. This was a relief because it meant that trouble was less likely to break out here. But in spite of the relative respectability of the place, the patrons seemed no less enthusiastic than others had in the past about canonizing the Kerry brothers in song. And as Sean spotted Rory seated at a table back beside the fire, he could see that their enthusiasm was bringing his father's old friend no end of satisfaction.

Rory's pockmarked face was lit with an ear-to-ear grin. His dark, beady eyes flashed with mischievousness, and his spiky black bangs were plastered to his forehead by the sweat he had obviously worked up with all of his rhapsodizing.

"Rory," Sean called out with a scowl as the bloody ballad started up again.

Rory didn't seem to hear or see him. Though several patrons had looked up when Sean entered, Rory had not been one of them, and he continued to seem oblivious to Sean now as he sat surrounded by eight or nine men—their mugs and voices all upraised with the tune.

Sean gave forth an exasperated cluck and began

making his way back to the table. He had hoped it wouldn't be necessary to go too far into the place, but it was clear to him now that it was unavoidable. He tried, nevertheless, not to draw too much attention to himself as he sidled past the clusters of customers in the minutes that followed. He kept his face down as much as possible, and he hugged the left wall of the place until he reached its hearth. Then he stopped and stood waving and "psst"ing in Rory's direction.

Again Rory seemed not to notice. Fortunately, however, a fellow just off to his left caught sight of Sean and was good enough to tell Rory so.

At this, Rory stood up slowly and, after squinting at Sean for several seconds, donned a grin. "Come over here," he said, seeming completely undaunted by Sean's glare and waving him on enthusiastically. "I hardly knew ye in those high-flown clothes."

Sean shook his head and continued to scowl. "No, ye bastard! *You* come over here. I want a word with ye!"

Rory leaned toward him a bit and cupped his hand behind his right ear. "I can scarcely hear ye over all this singin', lad. Come closer, will ye."

Finally realizing that Rory had already drunk too much to be reasoned with, Sean swallowed back his anger and made his way over to him. "For Christ's sake, what are ye doin'?" he snarled as he reached him.

Fortunately, the singing had died down; but Rory still seemed not to hear him.

"Just look at ye . . . so bedecked," he said, continuing to grin. "You'd be your father's pride and joy, ye would, if he were alive to see ye today. But mighty glad I am to see ye as well," Rory added, sitting down once more, "because I was just tellin' these fellas that I know the Kerry brothers personally, and they don't seem to believe it. Now, isn't that the damnedest thing?" he asked, giving Sean a wink.

"Isn't it just," Sean retorted, still doing little to hide his displeasure.

"So tell them then, will ye. Tell 'em I've known the Kerrys since before they were old enough to crawl!"

"Ah, it's malarkey," one of Rory's fellow singers interjected. "No one's ever gotten that close to 'em. They'd likely have been hanged by now if they let others know who they were."

"It's not malarkey," Rory countered, with, Sean noted, a tremor about his lower lip that indicated he was dangerously close to having one of his outbursts.

Sean bent down to whisper to him. "All right. If I tell 'em 'tis true, will ye get up at once and leave with me?" he growled.

"I will."

"Very well," Sean answered, and his next words came forth in a bold, self-assured stream. " 'Tis the absolute truth, gentlemen," he declared with a diplomatic smile. "I've got it on the best authority that Rory here was brought up in Derry, not three doors down from the Kerrys."

There was a hush at the table, and Sean offered up a silent prayer that Rory's companions would simply take his word for this and allow him to whisk Rory out of there before he found reason to fly into one of his rages.

"Ye see, Rory," he coaxed, easing his way back behind his old friend and taking hold of one of his arms. "They all heard me, and they know now 'tis true." With that, Sean peeled Rory's fingers off the handle of the ale mug that rested on the table before him. Then he brought him up to his feet and began leading him away from his companions. Though lumbering as usual, Rory didn't seem to be fighting him. Only a few more yards to the door, Sean assured himself, and they'd both be safely outside.

"Well, *I* don't believe it," someone shouted from behind them. "Not for a moment!"

Sean's eyes fell shut at this, and he cursed under his breath. He did his best to keep his grip on Rory's hand in that instant, but his effort was in vain. What Rory had lost mentally since his injury, he'd seemed to gain in brawn, and he broke away from Sean with one violent jerk. Then he turned back to the crowd of patrons, spotted the man who had risen to issue the challenge, and went storming over to him with his hands raised out before him like the paws of a charging grizzly.

"Rory, *don't*," Sean shouted, rushing after him. "Don't do it!"

Before Sean could reach him, however, Rory had his hands around the offending party's neck and was thrashing him about like a chicken who was to be plucked and served for Sunday dinner.

Without another thought, Sean leapt across the yard or two that still separated him from his old friend. He came to rest upon Rory's back an instant later, his arms wrapped about his neck and shoulders and his legs curled around Rory's hips.

167

Rory let out an enraged roar and tried to free himself from his rider with several explosive shrugs. It was no use, however. Sean was holding on to his shirt with such tenacity that he was certain he had several of the hairs on Rory's chest in his grip as well.

Rory, still failing to shake Sean loose, threw himself backward, onto the floor, apparently in the hope of crushing Sean in the process. Sean wasn't sure, at this frantic point, whether or not Rory realized who was clinging to him. Nor was Sean certain if it would have made the slightest bit of difference, if he had known. The only thing Sean knew for sure was that he was now lying beneath Rory's awesome weight, fighting for his breath and any opportunity to gain the upper hand. What was more, he knew that it would end as the frays of outlaws like themselves always did, in a heedless, senseless tumult comprised of kicking, gouging, and punching. He'd been drawn into enough of them to know all too well how they ended; the loser was left dead or out cold, and the victor, with any luck, narrowly escaped being thrown in gaol. So there seemed no point in delaying the inevitable.

Before Rory could get back up to his feet, Sean again took the cravat from his throat and tossed it around Rory's neck. He was, as a result, managing to keep Rory down now with a fairly standard strangle hold. The only problem was that Rory was certainly strong enough to break free of the hold in time. Just another minute or so was all it would take, Sean estimated. So Sean knew he'd be forced to fight foul. And with that decided, he slipped one knee between Rory's and snapped it up into his crotch with smashing rapidity.

Rory responded with a piteous outcry and fell back even heavier upon Sean. Then Sean made his next move, seizing those seconds in order to slide himself upward, out from beneath this giant of a man, while the getting was good.

Rory managed to outmaneuver him, however. Despite Sean's continued hold on the scarf about his throat, Rory took one of his hands from the effort to free the cravat and thrust it upward, catching Sean squarely in the mouth with his fist.

Sean saw blood on Rory's knuckles as he pulled his hand away an instant later, and he knew it was his own. But in spite of the numbing blow, he still had the presence of mind to lean back and get out of the way before Rory's next punch was thrown.

Rory snarled at this and began swinging wildly with both arms. Sean, meanwhile, reached down and snatched his pistol from the waist of his breeches. With one crowning blow of the weapon, Rory's body fell still.

Sean managed to wriggle the rest of the way out from underneath him in the seconds that followed. His new hat was gone. His periwig, too, had gotten cast off to the side in the scuffle, and a cursory feel about his lower gumline confirmed that one of his front teeth was in danger of being lost as well in the days to come.

He reached out, snatched his wig up from the floor, and threw it back onto his head. Then he got to his feet with as much dignity as was possible after such a savage display.

No, indeed. This wasn't the lowlife variety of patrons with whom Rory usually chose to carouse. Sean could tell, from their gapes and their humiliating silence now, that the scrapping of thugs was, by no means, an everyday occurrence here in Kilkenny.

"Your hat, sir," someone behind Sean said finally, ending the horrible hush.

Sean turned about and dabbed his bloodied lip with one of his ruffled cuffs. Then he offered the gentleman a wincing smile as he reached over to accept the huge feathered chapeau.

"And thank ye kindly, sir, for peelin' him off of me," another voice called out from the opposite side of the room.

Sean turned around and saw that it was Rory's first victim. "I . . . I hardly thought my comment was enough to make him go to such lengths," he continued, his voice still hoarse from the attack.

Sean took a few steps toward him, his face growing hotter with even greater embarrassment. "Ah, he's a bit tetchy, that one. Can't be helped, I'm afraid. Just flies into these rages from time to time," he explained apologetically.

"A friend of yours, is he?" the gentleman inquired.

"Aye. A very old friend. I—"

"Couldn't have told it from your bandyin' just now," he interrupted.

Sean gave forth an uneasy laugh. "Well, as I was about to say, sir. I do try to keep an eye on him, but I fear he slips away from me now and then."

"Well, see that he doesn't slip back in here, will ye," the publican called out rather bitingly from behind the bar.

Sean turned and offered him an amenable smile. "That I will, sir."

Damn that Rory! Sean had been trying so hard to keep a low profile; yet here he was, winding up having to look them all in the eye and apologize.

"Need any help gettin' him out of here?" Rory's strangulation victim asked, eyeing the body of his assailant as though afraid he might regain consciousness before Sean could remove him.

"No. I can manage it," Sean quickly replied. "Thank ye just the same."

He probably could have used some help, he realized, as he went back over to where Rory lay and began hoisting his now-dead weight up over his shoulder. He knew, however, that he couldn't risk having any of them escort him and Rory home. If he hoped to continue to keep their place of residence a secret, he'd simply have to handle Rory on his own, he resolved, coming back up to his full height seconds later with his old friend slung over him.

As he staggered to the door and made his exit, he became aware once more of his smarting feet. He didn't even want to contemplate what condition they'd be in once he walked the rest of the way home under the weight of *two*. There really seemed no alternative, however. If he chose to haul Rory off into some alleyway and leave him there until he could get back to town with a horse-drawn cart for him, he would be running the risk of Rory coming to in the meantime and going on another of his rampages, and that was something that neither he nor Patrick could afford to have happen.

The ruddy bugger, Sean thought, clenching his jaw

as he began heading westward, out of town. He had told Rory not to leave their cottage. Yet here he was, out rabble-rousing once again at the local pub, out letting one-too-many mugs of ale loosen his tongue and get him swaggering about his friends, the Kerry brothers, like a bloody carnival barker!

Maybe getting him more involved with the bride-snatching business would be just the thing to make him see how precarious an occupation it was and how very foolhardy it was to go around bragging about taking part in it. Then again, Sean thought with a weary sigh, maybe it wouldn't be.

All Sean knew for sure was that, though it was still relatively early on this, his first day as an "honest" gentleman, he had already had to choke and knock out not one, but two men! Despite his proud resolution, there had been no difference in him, when push had come to shove. He'd reverted to the violent ways of the scamp he was at heart. His instincts had gained control, and he'd settled his problems in the same kicking, gashing manner in which he always had.

It appeared he was no better suited to the straight life than his feet were to his new shoes. It was just inevitable, he realized, like rainwater collecting in a gutter. He'd been sucked ever downward since the moment he'd risen from the baker's settle at dawn, and now he would have to commit the coup de grace and get out of town before it all caught up with him.

There probably was no other course for him but to leave Kilkenny. Too many people had seen his face, and his cloaked follower had gotten too close for him to risk staying. But he wouldn't leave without Heather Monaghan, he silently vowed. By God, now that he knew that abducting her was really the most viable route, he'd snatch her without a second thought and make his swiftest getaway ever!

Chapter 10

Even though it had been over eight hours since Sean Kerry's visit, Heather was still feeling shaken by it. She'd managed to quell the steward's concerns, telling him that she'd simply dressed and gone out to the stable because she wished to pay a call upon Shannon Kennedy. He, in response, had been good enough to consent to this outing and to insist that Heather's governess escort her. Consequently, Heather and Shannon hadn't had much of a chance to talk together alone.

In what time they did manage to steal, however, Heather had poured forth an account of how the bride snatcher had suddenly appeared to her in the tackle room. She'd told Shannon of Sean's curious claim that Jennifer was very much in need of a husband and of his promise that he would once again be back for Heather.

Shannon had been dazzled by it all. Her face had paled with what appeared to be an expression of awe, and she had wanted to hear every detail of the encounter. She'd asked how Mr. Kerry had been dressed, what he'd said to Heather, and how he'd kissed her. Heather, eager to share the specifics with the one person she knew she could trust with such information, had answered each of the questions with relish—at least until her governess had come bursting into Mr. Kennedy's study, where the girls had sequestered themselves, and announced that it was high time she and Heather returned home.

Now Heather had only her memories of it all as she sat before the mirror on her lowboy, brushing out her freshly washed hair. It was chilly in the breeze of that early-April evening, but she wanted to keep her bedchamber window, the one nearest the oak tree, open. She both feared and thrilled at what might come of it, and in the end, the thrilled part of her was winning out. She would keep her candles burning tonight, she decided. Even at the risk of having her father come up and scold her for it, upon his late-night return from the mines, she would let her room remain lit in anticipation of her lover's return.

Lover, she thought with a curious gaze into her looking glass. Did she really think of him that way? She wasn't sure. His kiss had been wonderful. Positively leg-melting, in fact. Yet there had been such a brashness about him, an outlaw edge that not even his dearly bought costume could seem to soften. Then again, she told herself, no matter how much she feared him, she would always fear Malcolm more, because Malcolm didn't love her. He didn't even seem to like her, and given that, the prospect of being wed to him was much more frightening than being swept away by the likes of Sean.

Sean, by contrast, seemed almost to worship her. She had seen it in his face, both that morning and

175

at the Cassidys'. She liked the dreamy gaze that glazed his blue eyes as he beheld her, the catch in his throat when he'd first tried to address her, and the locking of his jaw that said he was struggling to hold something back, something almost bestial. It was as though her very presence tortured him somehow, made him ache inside. She'd never seen such a stirring look from a man, and for some reason she didn't fully understand, it had made her ache as well. She had wanted to reach out to him as one would to a wounded soldier, offering sympathy and care.

His words echoed in her mind now: "When the time comes, you'll unfold to me like a blossom on a sunny day." Heaven help her, she thought, biting her lip, she probably would. Without giving a second thought to the consequences, to her future, she would very likely go completely limp in his arms and beg him to have his way with her.

But he was trying to give up bride snatching, he'd said. Jennifer had been his last victim, and he was obviously trying to mend his ways. Yet if that was really the case, why had he been so receptive to the idea of climbing the tree to her bedchamber? Was it simply to despoil her and run? To take what he wanted and then not even have the decency to claim her as his own?

Heather stopped brushing her hair and swallowed dryly. Perhaps he felt that, as the daughter of so wealthy a man, she could afford to take the risks of such dalliance. Maybe her not calling for help in the stable had led him to believe that she really was the tease he'd accused her of being. At this, she rose abruptly, crossed to her casement window, and pushed its two halves shut with a snap. Then she turned her back to it and stood with her arms crossed over her chest.

She was so flimsily dressed that she couldn't help sliding her hands up to warm her shoulders in the nippy air. She was wearing her most costly nightshift this evening, a teal-colored gown of the sheerest silk. It was a garment which made her blush a bit. In fact, she was embarrassed to let even her dresser see her in it, and she knew better than to risk the same with a self-confessed bride snatcher. Yet here she stood with it on. Knowing full well that she might be swept away by an infamous kidnapper before the night was through, she had donned it. What was more, she hadn't felt even an instant of remorse over having done so—until now.

But she had to stop this, a voice within her scolded. After so many hours of mulling over Sean's visit, her stomach was churning with emotion. The salmon steak she'd eaten for supper seemed to be hovering dangerously near the base of her throat, and she knew she couldn't afford to find herself sick this evening. It would only lead to her governess being called up to spend the night with her in her room, and then her poor caller, if he did dare to come, would find himself stepping right into a snare.

She simply had to get a grip upon herself and go on as usual. The crucifix that hung about her neck really did stand for something, she reminded herself as she reached down nervously to finger it. She was, at heart, a good, God-fearing young lady, one who knew better than to give herself to a man before she was properly wed to him, and she had to continue to conduct herself as such. If Sean came and took her at gunpoint . . . well, then, it just couldn't be helped, she supposed. But until and unless he did, she knew she must go on with her life in the upstanding way that was expected of one of her station.

Her thoughts were suddenly interrupted as her bedchamber door swung open and her father stood calling her name.

"Heather?" he blared, scanning the room for her with his usual hurried squint.

To Heather's continuous dismay, he had never been one to knock. This wasn't because he didn't believe in being courteous to others. It was simply that he was always in such a rush, so mired in the responsibilities of running the mines, that he seemed to carry that role home with him, bursting into every room in the house, occupied or not, with the brusqueness of a boss about to issue orders to a scrivener.

"Oh, Saints help us," he exclaimed as his eyes finally lit upon his daughter's sheerly draped figure where she still stood before the window. "I didn't know ye weren't dressed!"

Heather, who had long since covered herself with her hands, turned to the side now to further shield her body from his view.

"Well, I am, Father," she said with an embarrassed laugh. "But not for talkin', just for bed."

Master Monaghan clapped a hand over his eyes. "Well, go and fetch somethin' from your wardrobe, lass. I crave a word with ye."

Heather, grateful for the chance to put something more on, dashed over to her adjoining wardrobe, stepped inside, and withdrew a robe linge from the

178

clothes rod. Then she threw it on and stepped back out to face him with the hope that her hot blush would soon fade.

"It's all right. I'm decent now," she announced.

Mr. Monaghan took his hand from his eyes with a sigh of relief and launched into the topic that had brought him to her door. "It's bad news, I'm afraid, Heth," he said, shaking his head.

Heather couldn't imagine what he was referring to. "Is it?"

"Aye. Malcolm and the sheriff and the rest had no luck with trackin' down those two strawboys last night, as the steward probably told ye."

Heather shook her head ruefully. "Aye. I wept at hearin' it. 'Tis a pity."

"That it 'tis. And I fear it's only gotten worse."

"Has it?"

"Oh, aye. Malcolm was in town, askin' 'round all day today about any more clues as to where they've taken Jennifer, and sadly, he learned naught."

"God help us," she choked, trying to look amply worried about her friend.

"Indeed. Especially since the Plithes received a note this mornin' askin' for Jennifer's dowry."

Heather did her best to appear surprised. "So, it's true then, what that man at the Cassidys' was sayin'? They *were* bride snatchers?"

Her father nodded. "Yes. The Kerry brothers. They're the ones who've been plaguin' the counties to the north for so long. We'd all hoped they wouldn't find their way down here and torment us as well, but it seems our prayers have gone unanswered. Even had the gall to *sign* the note to the Plithes! The scoundrels! Should be boiled in oil for stealin' dowries as they do! Instead, our local slags loll about, singin' their praises in the pub. Ah, well, they can afford to praise them, the crofters," he continued bitterly. "Haven't got much to lose if one of their daughters gets swept away by those hoodlums. But then, of course, they wouldn't, because the wily dogs only prey upon the wealthy. . . . Anyway, my warnin' still stands, daughter," he said, shaking a finger at her sternly. "You're not to leave the grounds without Nurse or one of the other servants along. Do ye hear?"

After over a decade and a half of their having had no nurse on the premises, Heather was always tempted to laugh at the way he continued to refer to her governess as such. But this was clearly no time for tittering, so she offered him an obedient nod. "Yes, Father. Ye have my word."

"Good. Good enough," he concluded, taking a couple steps back, out of the threshold, and drawing the door shut as he went. "And, Heth," he began again a second later, always one for afterthoughts.

"Yes?"

"Malcolm has somethin' he wishes to discuss with ye," he declared with a smirk. "I don't want to spoil the surprise, mind. But I think it has to do with a ring," he added with a telling wink.

Heather's voice wavered with dread at this announcement. "When?"

Her father shrugged. "Tuesday night, I believe. I invited him for supper, as usual."

Heather drew in a deep, steadying breath. "And if I should . . . should refuse him?"

Her father threw his head back and laughed as though this was the most preposterous question he'd ever heard. "Don't be ridiculous. Of course ye won't refuse him." Then, after an instant, there was a knowing twinkle in his eyes, as though he suddenly understood why she'd make such an inquiry. "Ah, ye dear, blessed lass. Ye've got your darlin' mother's wit, ye do!" And with another roar of laughter, he was gone and the door was solidly shut behind him.

Heather didn't go after him. She'd known him long enough to realize that, when his mind was made up about something, it was next to impossible to change it—especially with an approach that was too direct. It would simply have to wait until she could think of some way to soften him, some way to make him understand that, while Malcolm might be good for his business, he wouldn't be good for his daughter. And that would take some doing. But then again, Tuesday night was just forty-eight hours away, so she knew she had to come up with something fairly quickly.

In the back of her mind, of course, was the hope that Sean Kerry would come and spirit her off, thereby rescuing her from the predicament. Yet she couldn't help wondering what sort of "rescue" that would really be. Where could a man like that, a fleer of justice, possibly live, after all? Where would he take her if he did come for her? And most importantly, how would she feel after he had ravished her?

It only stood to reason that, well-shod or not, his couldn't have been much of a life to lead: running from one town to the next, always having to keep an eye over one's shoulder for the local sheriff. It had seemed to Heather such an exciting existence when she'd first heard about it the night before. It had seemed so daring and colorful when it had simply applied to Sean and his brother. But now that there was a chance that she might be swept into it, she wasn't finding it quite so appealing.

Still wearing her robe linge, she padded over to her huge four-poster and sat down on the edge of its mattress. As she did so, she silently began scolding herself once more. Here she'd dwelt, year after year, in her lacy bedchamber, musing about being a world traveler, yearning for the chance to learn about life from something more than books. Yet now, when the opportunity seemed to be presenting itself, when a renowned wayfarer had appeared and made overtures to her, she found that all she really wanted to do was crawl under her bed and hide!

What did she truly want in all of this? she wondered. A man with Sean Kerry's build and comeliness yet Malcolm's promise of lasting wealth and stability, some part of her retorted with amazing decisiveness. But that just didn't seem possible, given the circumstances. Ah, hell, she didn't know what she wanted, she concluded with an exasperated cluck, standing up to pull off her clingy robe.

With another cluck, she tossed it onto the end of her bed. Then she took the candle snuffer from her night table, bustled over to each of her room's candlestands, and extinguished their tapers, leaving the one beside her bed for last.

Once she'd returned to her bed and all was in darkness, she threw herself onto her mattress and lay staring up at the ceiling. It was the second night of the full moon, and its bluish light was now streaming in through her windows. Her eyes, therefore, took only an instant or two to adjust, and everything about her became visible in a roomscape of moonlight and silhouette.

She hoped she'd sleep, but she doubted she would. Between Sean's claim that he would return for her and the pressing threat of betrothal to Malcolm, it seemed unlikely that her mind would even stop racing, let alone allow her to drift off into slumber.

Sean had watched with relish seconds earlier as his beloved Heather had moved about the room, extinguishing each of her candles. Even through the blurriness of her window's glazing, he had been able to see that she was wearing the most exquisite nightshift he'd ever laid eyes upon. It was aqua-colored, like a shallow pool of sea water splashing all about her. To his delight, it had seemed every bit as transparent as she'd scurried from one source of illumination to the next, snuffing out each in its turn. Then, finally, she'd been lit by nothing but moonlight. Her curving breasts and bottom had been visible only as the darker form within the airy envelope of her flowing shift, and she'd gone and flopped down upon her bed like a disgruntled child.

Ah, what a gem she was! What great pleasure he'd take in bedding her, he thought with an amorous sigh where he continued to balance, atop an arching limb of the oak she'd been good enough to point out to him.

Was she asleep yet? he wondered, continuing to

watch her with rapt attention. She was lying very still, so it was hard for him to tell. He'd simply have to wait until he was inside to know for sure, he concluded. Then, too, he'd have to pray that, if she was awake, she wouldn't be so startled by his sudden entrance that she'd call out for help.

He'd just have to be exceptionally quiet, he told himself, like a cat springing from limb to windowsill in one, fluid motion. He'd have to do what he'd done so many times before: go in soundlessly, gag and bind his quarry, and be off with her. It was as simple as that.

He'd done his groundwork, of course. Not even his great infatuation with this particular target would have blinded him to the need for that. Consequently, he knew all there was to be gleaned from the exterior of a house at nightfall.

Brian Monaghan had gotten home a full hour before. Sean had watched him pull up to the manor and get out of his coach. He'd proceeded into one of the front chambers, obviously a dining room, and he'd sat down for his evening meal. After thirty minutes or so, he'd gone upstairs, and the staff had begun extinguishing the first floor's candles. So surely, by now, the master of the estate was settled in for the night. Probably off sleeping in his suite, Sean deduced, because as far as he knew, Heather's lights had been the very last to be snuffed.

Ah, dear Heather, he thought again with a sigh. How he longed to get his hands on her! Perhaps if she proved cooperative enough, he might even slip in and claim her then and there, right under her father's roof. But only time would tell, he reminded himself once more. First he'd have to see if he could get a steady enough grip higher up on the tree, one that would enable him to push the window open.

But what if she'd had second thoughts about letting him in and she'd left it latched? In that case, he'd just have to break through it, he resolved, silently chiding himself for not continuing to think of this as simply another of his snatchings. He hated having to damage any part of his dear Heather's domain, but a job was a job, after all, and he knew he must do anything that was necessary in order to claim her.

Keeping his left hand locked upon the tree's trunk, he jumped up and caught the branch just above him with his right. As he dangled there, a full foot from the cradling safety of the limb his feet had just left, he took his hand from the trunk. Then, offering up a prayer that the branch he held was, indeed, sturdy enough to support his full weight, he brought it to rest near his other hand. There he hung for several seconds more, adjusting his grip and summoning the strength he needed to make his next move. Once ready, he began to swing the lower half of himself to and fro, building up momentum, until his feet were finally able to reach both halves of Heather's casement window.

It fell open with one firm stamp, dispelling his fears that it might have been locked. With another shove from his toes, the window opened much wider, and he seized that instant to let go of the branch and let his body slip down into the room.

He landed with an unavoidable thud; but at least he hadn't banged the blazes out of his back or head in the fall, as he'd expected to. What was more, the noise apparently hadn't been loud enough to wake Heather. Sean's eyes were fixed upon her shadowed form now, and he was positive that she hadn't stirred at all since she'd lain down.

Sean rested there for a moment or two longer, readying himself for whatever might befall him. He slid one palm down onto the handle of the pistol stashed in his waistband, and he put the other up on the windowsill, where it could facilitate a speedy exit, should one prove necessary. After several seconds more, however, he began to believe it would not. There wasn't a sound from anywhere in the house. Not so much as a creaking floorboard or door hinge to indicate that anyone was astir. All Sean heard— and continued to hear in the minutes that followed— was the anxious beating of his own heart, and even that became quieter as he began to believe that this last bride snatching would prove a rub-free success.

Heather had frozen with fear as she'd heard the first thump at her closed window minutes earlier. To her amazement, the sashes had burst open and a dark figure had come sliding into her room and landed upon the floor beneath her window with the soft thud of an overfull sack of flour. Now, roughly three minutes after this curious entrance, she still lay with her eyes locked upon the individual, half wondering if his stillness could have meant that he'd knocked himself unconscious with his fall.

The intruder was definitely a male; that much was clear to her. Even now, with him sprawled so, she could see the considerable length of him. His long torso and legs were splayed out before him, and the billowy, gathered sleeves of his thin-spun chemise were tucked into the darker, tighter surface of what appeared to be an underdoublet. Unfortunately, that was about all she could make out in the darkness, and she knew she shouldn't risk getting up and going over for a closer look. If it was Sean, the noise of her rising and crossing to him might cause her governess or one of the other servants to come and look in on her. And if it wasn't Sean, she knew she'd be an even greater fool to chance stepping into the fellow's reach.

Under any other circumstances, she would have wanted to laugh. There was something inherently humorous, after all, about seeing a man come swinging into one's bedroom window like an ape. But for some reason, she didn't feel the slightest bit amused by it tonight. Quite the contrary, all she felt at present was fear, fear that her father or someone on the staff might have heard the stranger enter and might be on the way now to investigate. And that was why she continued to be so silent and still. She didn't want to risk calling any more attention to the situation by attempting to converse with the gentleman.

She would simply hold her tongue, she decided. The intruder was certainly long and lean enough to be Sean's red-haired brother or some other fellow, and on the off chance it wasn't Sean, she knew she shouldn't risk betraying their liaison by uttering his name. The Kerry brothers were the experts at this sort of thing, she reminded herself—not she. So it only stood to reason that she should allow the gentleman to take the first step.

But what if it wasn't Sean *or* his brother? a panicked little voice inside her queried. What if it was some village lad, who, all fired up by the news about the Kerry brothers being in Kilkenny, had decided to try a little bride snatching of his own. How dreadful, she thought with a shudder. Swept off in the night by a faceless amateur!

This chilling supposition was interrupted, however, by the stranger's sudden movement. He had one hand resting on the windowsill behind him, and he turned a bit and brought himself up to his feet now with a whisper of a groan. Then he began moving toward her bed with the soundless stride of a seasoned burglar. And even though the moon's glow was to his back and his face was in shadow, she could see that it was Sean. This was the height and the broadshouldered build she remembered. The decisive feature, however, was his hair, the way the moonlight reflected off his obviously light-colored crop. This was, without a doubt, her beloved Sean, and she let out a long, relieved breath at finally realizing it.

For some reason, he'd gotten rid of the fancy wig and dress clothes he'd had on that morning and he'd gone back to wearing the peasantly sort of garb she'd first seen him in at the Cassidys'. But if the truth be known, she liked him better this way. Heaven help her, she liked how such simple, groundling dress seemed to enhance, rather than hide, what was most attractive in each gender. She'd tingled with excitement at seeing his muscular chest peek out at her from beneath the drawstring closure of his flaxen

188

shirt as they'd danced the night before. And though she would rather have died than admitted it, she'd tingled even more at how the tightness of his brown breeches had inadvertently revealed so much of what was beneath.

But he'd see that she was awake, she silently warned herself. With only a step or two more, he'd surely be close enough to realize that her eyes were open and she was fully aware of his presence. So acknowledging this, she squeezed her eyes shut, and turned her face back up toward the ceiling with the sleepy languor of one who was deep in slumber.

What would he do to her? Part of her was most eager to just stay quiet and find out. Yet another part was terrified and kept warning her to get up and dash out of there while she still could, while she still had some control over the situation. But there was something titillating about it, she acknowledged, as she finally heard him reach the side of the bed. She could actually *feel* him there, staring down at her, and she suddenly realized how wildly wonderful it would be simply to go on lying there, leaving herself to his mercy. Devil take her, she'd never felt so aroused in her life as she felt now, and she knew she wouldn't do a thing to spoil it.

To her surprise, however, he just continued to stand there for several seconds more. She heard his rather heavy respiration, and she could tell that shinnying up the tree and breaking into her bedchamber had left him a little winded. It was nice, though: the sound, the warmth of him breathing over her. She didn't know exactly why she liked it, but she did, and she sensed that it must simply have been instinctive, one of those unexplained parts of the secret realm of lovemaking.

The next thing she knew, she was feeling something, a soft, almost imperceptible mix of sensation and motion against her right shoulder, like a summer breeze slipping through the finest strands of her hair.

His fingers, she realized an instant later, his fingers were brushing up and down, gently, lovingly over a stray lock of her auburn mane where it streamed down her pillow.

How sweet, how dear, she thought, having to bite her lower lip now in an effort to keep herself from smiling.

He then went on to press his lips to her forehead. They felt wet and warm, and again, she had all she could do to stay silent and still beneath his penetrating presence.

Maybe she should cover herself, the more prudent half of her suggested. Here she was, after all, with little more than a veil draped over her, and what was he to think? Perhaps he'd think her worse than the tease he'd accused her of being earlier in the stable. Maybe he'd think her a woman of easy virtue and force himself upon her without a second thought.

But there had been no way she could have known for sure that he was coming tonight, and a lass could hardly be blamed for what she chose to wear in the privacy of her own room. What was more, his actions thus far had been anything but chastising in nature. In fact, his touch, his kiss, his gentleness clearly conveyed a reverence for her, the same sort of worshipfulness she'd thought she'd seen in his eyes that morning.

So it was probably best to stay still, she concluded—stay still and pray that the darkness, coupled with the shadow he was probably casting over her now, was enough to keep most of her body from his view.

Her thoughts were again interrupted as she felt him sink down beside her on the bed. This would have seemed an innocent enough move on his part, were it not for the fact that his weight had caused the mattress to slope to the right a bit, and this, in turn, had made her body roll up against his.

She lay there for several seconds, trying to come up with a sleeper's response to such a thing. She'd just roll over onto her left side, she finally concluded. She'd give her torso a groggy toss in the other direction and thereby land herself on higher and *safer* ground.

Once she did so, however, she discovered it was to no avail. He simply followed her, pulling himself farther onto the mattress, and again she found her scantily clad body lying face-up, next to his.

She now realized that, unless she intended to reveal that she was awake, there was no escaping him. But she also realized that she didn't want to escape. She liked the feeling of him lying next to her. She relished his warmth and the soft rise and fall of his chest as he breathed. And she knew that continuing to feign slumber was her only salvation, for one could hardly be blamed for sins committed in one's sleep.

This resolve was put to the test an instant later, however, as she suddenly felt one of his palms close down upon her right breast. It was big, encompassing, and its heat and moisture seemed to seep in through her shift in the seconds that followed.

She wanted to hold her breath, to keep this unspeakable part of her from rising and falling so suggestively in his cupping grasp. Nevertheless, she knew she had to go on breathing normally or risk betraying the fact that she was awake—something she feared her pounding heartbeat might already be telling him.

There his hand rested for several seconds more, caressing her with a possessive sort of firmness. And there she lay, doing her damnedest not to show how shocked she was, how aroused at having him get to the point so quickly.

Dear God, she thought with maidenly pride, Malcolm would have tried to tear Sean limb from limb had he seen what was transpiring. Even with all his imagined claim to her, Malcolm himself had never dared to touch her in so forbidden a place, so she shuddered to think what action he'd take at seeing another man do so. All hell would have broken loose! That much was certain.

Hell *and* its nether regions, a voice within her added, as this venturesome stranger laid yet another hand on her, this time his right palm upon her other breast. In truth, she realized, they would both have the devil to pay, should Malcolm or anyone else walk in on them: Sean for the doing and Heather for the letting.

But why was she thinking of Malcolm and the others at a time like this? Perhaps it was simply in her own defense. To keep from thinking of the exquisitely handsome gentleman who was actually doing

MORE PASSION AND ADVENTURE AWAIT... YOUR TRIP TO A BIG ADVENTUROUS WORLD BEGINS WHEN YOU ACCEPT YOUR FIRST 4 NOVELS ABSOLUTELY *FREE* (AN $18.00 VALUE)

Accept your Free gift and start to experience more of the passion and adventure you like in a historical romance novel. Each Zebra novel is filled with proud men, spirited women and temptuous love that you'll remember long after you turn the last page.

Zebra Historical Romances are the finest novels of their kind. They are written by authors who really know how to weave tales of romance and adventure in the historical settings you love. You'll feel like you've actually gone back in time with the thrilling stories that each Zebra novel offers.

GET YOUR FREE GIFT WITH THE START OF YOUR HOME SUBSCRIPTION

Our readers tell us that these books sell out very fast in book stores and often they miss the newest titles. So Zebra has made arrangements for you to receive the four newest novels published each month.

You'll be guaranteed that you'll never miss a title, and home delivery is so convenient. And to show you just how easy it is to get Zebra Historical Romances we'll send you your first 4 books absolutely FREE! Our gift to you just for trying our home subscription service.

BIG SAVINGS AND FREE HOME DELIVERY

Each month, you'll receive the four newest titles as soon as they are published. You'll probably receive them even before the bookstores do. What's more, you may preview these exciting novels free for 10 days. If you like them as much as we think you will, just pay the low preferred subscriber's price of just $3.75 each. *You'll save $3.00 each month off the publisher's price.* AND, your savings are even greater because there are never any shipping, handling or other hidden charges—FREE Home Delivery. Of course you can return any shipment within 10 days for full credit, no questions asked. There is no minimum number of books you must buy.

this to her and there by preventing her from responding the way she wished to . . . yes. That had to be the reason, she decided, still trying to keep her feelings in check.

Sean was leaning over her now. He was letting his palms rub up and down with a roughness that, to her chagrin, had the friction-heated peaks at her beginning to stand at shameless attention.

But she had to keep breathing, she told herself. If she didn't get the lump out of her throat and draw in another breath soon, she was sure she'd pass out for lack of air. And she knew, at the core of her, that she didn't want to lose consciousness for even an instant and risk missing that much of his amorous attentions to her.

"Ah, ye like it, *asthore*," she heard him whisper in response to her inhalation.

Asthore. It was the Gaelic word for one's "beloved" or "treasure." She didn't know him well enough yet to be certain which meaning he was assigning to it. But at this point, she didn't honestly care. What mattered was the satisfaction in his tone, the joy he seemed to derive from the realization that he was bringing her pleasure. What was even better was that his voice had indicated that he still believed he was addressing a woman who was sound asleep, oblivious enough to think of him as nothing more than some portion of an erotic dream.

Heather had those from time to time, she thought with a flush running over her, and she'd surely be having one again, at this very moment, were it not for that fact that she was awake and knew that what she was perceiving was real.

But something was happening to her, she suddenly realized. His stroking was starting to make her nipples uncomfortably warm, and the lower half of her was beginning to burn with the need for the same sort of stimulation. She, therefore, drew away from him again, turning sleepily onto her side and curling up into fetal position.

This was a better choice, she decided. It was wiser to roll away from such fondling and appear to drift off into another sort of dream than to risk doing what his touch had made her really want to do: arch the lower half of herself up toward him, like a kitten seeking affection by rubbing against his legs. Acting on such an impulse would have just been too indecent, too humiliating for her ever to live down, should he somehow discover that she wasn't sleeping.

To her relief, however, he responded by gently rolling her onto her back again. "Ah, too hot, too sore, are they?" she heard him murmur in a sympathetic tone.

He'd known! He'd somehow realized what she'd been feeling, and to her utter amazement, he punctuated his words of comfort now in a way she would never have imagined. It started with a strange sensation at the peak of her right breast, the one he'd first begun fondling. It felt pleasant, but odd all the same, and she suddenly realized that what she was experiencing was great wetness and warmth, more than his hand could have generated. His mouth had closed around her nipple and he was soothing it with the moist caressing flicks of his tongue—much as he had her hand the night before.

This was different, though, because he was doing

it right *through* her silken shift, like a man so hungry for a meal that he'd eat it right out of a steaming kettle. What was more, he was drawing her now-tender flesh upward with every stroke. He wasn't just kissing, but sucking, as an infant would from its mother. And this, try as she might to fight it, made Heather give forth a slight gasp.

It was just too much for her, more loveplay than she'd dared even to contemplate—especially during what was only her third encounter with this man. So she rolled away from him again, this time with a pained groan.

"Oh, I won't hurt ye, angel. Surely ye must know that," he whispered, pulling back lightly on her right shoulder.

She noted that his tone was still artless, as though he honestly believed he was addressing some sleeping childlike part of her, a part that certainly couldn't be held responsible for what she was allowing to happen. And hearing this, hearing that he still seemed to think her an innocent and that he meant her no harm, she gave in to his second tug and again fell back upon the mattress.

It was rubbish, she realized in those seconds: what the church had always taught her about the spirit being stronger than the flesh. It was a barefaced lie when one came right down to it. The only truth at present was that Sean wanted to touch her where she wanted to be touched, and she'd be damned if she'd do a thing more to stop him now . . . now, as she felt him lean over her once more and place his fingers down by her ankles, on the hem of her shift . . . as she felt his hands slip in beneath the garment and slide up her calves and thighs to the ineffable region above.

Her breath caught in her throat again, and she had to bite her lip to keep herself quiet, but by God, she knew now that she wouldn't discourage him from doing whatever it was he had in mind.

His fingertips paused, just beneath the area that Shannon said her brothers called the "pleasure garden." Heather had always giggled with embarrassment whenever this crude bit of male jargon had crossed her mind. It had struck her as both humiliating and shamefully provocative to realize that men actually sat about coining names for such intimate portions of the opposite sex—and names that were so telling at that!

But as embarrassing as this term had always seemed to her, she hoped to God that that was how Sean was thinking of it now: as something sweet and deep, something inviting enough to make him want to touch and explore. And then, too, she prayed that she'd have the courage to simply let him do so, that she wouldn't end by panicking and trying to stop him.

But this might be the only opportunity she'd have with him, she reminded herself, and certainly it would be her only chance to enjoy it and then disavow having done so.

Should she ease her legs apart? she wondered. Should she, *could* she do anything more to make it easier for him, without letting on that she was awake?

But before she could give these questions another second's thought, she felt him slip his hands under each of her thighs and, in one smooth motion, spread them so widely that she knew that she'd opened to him like a gaping door.

He definitely needed no counsel, she thought with a stunned swallow. He was obviously quite proficient in this area. And realizing this, Heather surreptitiously reached down and dug her fingers into the bedding beneath her, bracing herself for his next move. To her surprise, however, it wasn't what she thought it would be. She'd expected some sort of thrust from him, some indication that he was finally getting on with it. Instead, she felt the whisper-light sensation of him simply tracing the orifice with a fingertip or two.

She had everything she could do to refrain from laughing at how it tickled in those seconds, and she bit the inside of her cheek in order to keep silent. Was he just testing her? Was it possible that he knew she was awake and was doing what he could to make her confirm it?

It didn't matter. Whether it was intended to elicit a response or not, she wouldn't give in, she resolved, digging her nails even more deeply into the bedding. It was he who had come to her, after all. It was he who had dared to take things this far, and she would surely see to it that he, and he alone, bore the responsibility for where this might lead.

But he certainly seemed more than willing to do so, she realized an instant later, as he finally stopped his torturous foreplay and began easing the two fingers into her. And how experienced they were! So stout, so warm, so stimulating amid her ready wetness.

As they began stroking her inner surfaces, she was forced to conclude that they were as at home within her as anywhere else. They were as nonchalantly adept as if they were curled about the handle of an ale mug or the trigger of a gun. They seemed to know, based on touch alone, what could only have been learned from having probed several women before her. And as the seconds sped by, with them directing such unrelenting attention to the most sensitive parts of her, she found herself arching up toward them, surrendering to their commands like those of an invading army. And, the saints help her, she couldn't keep from letting a soft moan escape, a moan of ecstasy at being brought to such unimaginable heights.

Then suddenly it was over, that instant or two of rapture, and as he continued his stroking, she felt great apprehension welling up in her, a fear that he might take things too far and do some sort of irreparable damage to her virtue if she didn't free herself from him soon.

"No," she protested in a slumberous tone, doing her best to roll away from him once more. To her surprise, however, he held her fast, pinning her to the mattress.

"I'm takin' ye with me, love," he whispered. "I've come for ye, and I don't intend to leave without ye, so get up now and find a cloak or somethin' with which to cover yourself."

Her eyes fell open, and they were instantly met by his, where he hovered over her.

"No," she said again, shaking her head. "I can't."

"Ye can," he insisted. "Ye can and ye will, lass,

unless ye relish the idea of bein' knocked out cold and hauled off like the rest. Now get up," he ordered, easing off of her and taking hold of her left arm with a viselike grip. "I've a gun, and I'm prepared to shoot anyone who gets in our way, mind, so be wise enough to keep quiet and not call anyone in here."

"I . . . I didn't realize . . . I didn't mean it when I told ye out in the stable earlier to come back for me," she explained, continuing to keep her voice cautiously low.

He jerked her up to a sitting position and spoke to her through clenched teeth. "It doesn't matter whether or not ye meant it. I've come for ye. I've put my life on the line to take ye, and this is my last warnin' before I start to use force!"

His hand tightened even more painfully upon her upper arm, and she finally realized that he was deathly serious. How could she have forgotten that she was dealing with a bona fide outlaw? Now she was finding her memory amply refreshed.

"And this is how ye want me?" she whispered. "By force, by rape?"

"I came to ye as a gentleman this mornin', remember, and ye flatly told me your father would have none of it. So this is the alternative, my dear. As simple as that. And as for me rapin' ye," he added with a roguish sort of smile in his voice, "well, that's entirely up to you, now isn't it? I mean, if you've a willing heart, ye might even find it more enjoyable than what ye just let me do to ye!"

She reflexively reached up to slap him with her free hand. Even in that dim light, however, he saw the blow coming, and he caught her wrist before she could deliver it.

"I was asleep," she hissed defensively.

He gave forth a soft laugh. "No ye weren't, ye little jilt! Ye lay there all the while, knowin' perfectly well what I was doin' to ye and not even pretendin' to try to stop me. So just ye see to it you're as obligin' later on!"

She made another attempt to break free of his grasp and strike him, but he remained in control.

"Ah, ye don't want to resort to strugglin', now do ye, love? Not with me hoverin' so near a foul mood this evenin', surely," he said in a growl. "I did have my heart set on us bein' kind to one another, it bein' our weddin' night and all."

"No," Heather said again, this time in a pained undertone as he pulled her from the bed and dragged her up to her feet.

"*Yes!* Now walk with me to your wardrobe, and fetch what ye need to cover yourself as we ride. 'Tis a mite cool this evenin', and I wouldn't want my beloved takin' ill."

"I'm not your beloved," she whimpered. "And it's not right, your stealin' me off this way!"

"Wasn't right of ye to lead me on if ye really don't fancy me either, but ye did it none the less, now didn't ye," he acknowledged, propelling her toward her wardrobe door.

"I wasn't simply leadin' ye on," she explained tearfully. "I do find ye comely. It's just that I don't want ye . . . not this way," she quickly amended.

To her surprise, his grip on her loosened and he stopped to stare down at her in the flood of bluish light from the window. "It's the only way, Heather. I'm sorry," he said softly, and she could tell that he honestly was. "Now go and fetch a cloak, will ye, before someone hears us and we're *both* caught."

She hesitated, weighing the alternatives. She was frozen by the frightening possibilities that lay ahead for her, no matter which course she chose. If she left with him, she knew she would find herself deflowered and utterly unreturnable that very night. What was more, she might be stuck living the life of a fugitive's wife, having to stay apace for the rest of her days. If, on the other hand, she decided to stay, she probably wouldn't see Sean again, and it was very likely that she'd end up married to Malcolm—a fate she could hardly bring herself to contemplate.

There was a sound from somewhere outside her room, like a door opening far down the corridor, and again, Sean's grip on her tightened.

"Come with me now, I say. This instant, lass, or you'll not lay eyes upon me again. I swear it," he said in an urgent whisper.

Heather hesitated for a second more. Then, hearing footsteps coming toward her room, she knew she had to decide. "Very well," she blurted with a crazed rush of emotion. It was the oddest sensation, like suddenly diving off a seacliff with absolutely no idea if she'd be alive and able to swim when she touched down below.

He released her in that same second, and she dashed to her wardrobe and grabbed the first garment that came to hand. It was too dark to tell with any certainty what it was, but it felt very much like one of her loosely knit shawls. She threw it over her shoulders and rushed back to the window.

Sean had already made his way out to the tree and was beginning to head downward. "Come on out with ye, then, love," he called up in a low voice. "Ye said ye climbed down it just this mornin', so ye must know your way."

"Yes. But not in the dark," she exclaimed.

"Can ye see my right hand? Here on this branch?" he asked, lifting his middle fingers, each in its turn, so that she could better spot it.

Heather winced as she heard the footsteps drawing closer. "Aye."

"Well then, put you right foot out here next to it, and I'll brace it for ye, while ye get a good hold on the trunk."

Heather's heart was racing, and she felt as though she might faint as she climbed out of the window and the chilly evening air hit her. She did as she was told, however, putting all her faith in Sean's ability to come to her aid during their precarious descent.

True to his profession, he seemed to have eyes like a hawk. Even in that faint light, he spotted footholds for them both that even her many trips up and down this tree hadn't revealed to her, and he made it to the ground in no time.

With his whispered guidance, Heather reached the lowest of the tree's limbs seconds later, and she jumped down to his open arms, where he waited below.

"Ah, there's a darlin' girl," he said in a winning tone as he set her down. "Come along now to where I've hidden my horse, and we'll be off."

She couldn't help yelping a bit as the tender soles of her bared feet tread upon several sticks and stones en route to the nearby thicket where he was leading her. But once they reached his steed and he pulled her up to sit behind him in the saddle, she consoled herself with the knowledge that at least her part of the navigating was over for now.

She looked back at her still-darkened window as the horse trotted out from behind the cloaking bushes seconds later. To her surprise, she saw no one there. Apparently, the footsteps they'd heard were only those of a restless servant, up to raid the larder or visit the earth closet. And she realized that that also meant that she and Sean weren't apt to be pursued as they fled over the many acres of Monaghan grounds ahead of them.

She probably wouldn't be missed until breakfast, she thought with a wistful sigh as Sean brought the steed to a gallop and the night wind began to whip about her.

She tightened her hold about his waist and ducked down to let his shielding form break the cold for her. She probably wouldn't be missed until breakfast, she thought again with mixed feelings, and by then, it would definitely be too late for her father to recover her.

Chapter 11

It seemed to Heather that they had ridden for hours in the freezing wind before Sean's horse finally began to slow. Sean only laughed at this observation as Heather voiced it, and he assured her that his cottage was little more than half an hour's ride from her home.

Heather had thought about trying to get some sleep along the way. She had tied the long ends of her shawl around Sean's waist to anchor herself, in case she dozed off and lost her grip. Unfortunately, however, she'd scarcely been able to rest her eyes en route. She was just too cold and too apprehensive to relax.

"Ye live here with your brother?" she asked as she spotted the lone cottage that lay several yards dead ahead of them now.

"Aye," Sean answered evenly. "When he's here. But he isn't tonight. Luckily for us," he added with a soft laugh.

She swallowed uneasily and rearranged her grip upon him, doing her best to ignore the implications of what he'd said by peering up over his shoulder at the dwelling they approached. It was a tiny place, barely the size of the stablehands' lodge at Monaghan Manor. But however humble, she was glad at least to see the smoke that trailed from its chimney and the soft glow within that said that a fire was still burning in its hearth.

She was in desperate need of warmth. Her fingers and bare feet felt positively numb. She'd even developed a nasty case of the sniffles in the past few minutes and had, sorrily, been forced to begin dabbing her nose with the upper edge of her shawl.

It wasn't easy, she concluded, this being an outlaw's consort. But for all its inconvenience, she had to admit that it was proving less distasteful than being holed up in her bedchamber. At least her suffering made her know she was alive, and she'd come to prize that awareness above all else through the years.

"That's it, then? Just your brother and you livin' here?"

She'd expected another quick "aye" from him, but instead, she heard him give forth a chary laugh. "No. Unfortunately. There is our friend Rory as well. But I suspect he's out cold from drink by now. He usually is by this hour."

"A friend, ye say? From here in Kilkenny?"

"No. From Derry, as we are. A dear old friend of our father's, he was."

"Was?" Heather echoed. "Not anymore, though?"

"No. Not anymore, I'm afraid."

"Why not? I mean . . . if ye aren't offended by my askin'," Heather added, sensing that she'd hit upon a rather touchy topic. But she knew so little about him, a voice within her rationalized, and given the leap of faith she'd just made for him, she felt she had the right to learn much more.

"Ah, no. I'm not offended," Sean replied. "It's because my father's dead, ye see. Died years ago, when Pat and I were just boys."

"Of what?"

Sean could feel his posture stiffening at this question. It wasn't one he'd had much call to answer in the past several years, and he realized now that, given who was asking, he'd be rather ashamed to tell the truth. "Of chokin'," he answered flatly.

Heather was silent for several seconds, and Sean knew that she was stymied by this response.

"What? On a piece of meat, ye mean?" she asked finally.

"Somethin' of the sort," Sean lied. There'd be time enough to tell her the ugly truth, he reasoned. Time enough *after* he'd bedded her and officially made her his.

"Ah, that's a pity," she replied with a sympathetic tsk. "And your mother?" she inquired as they finally reached the cottage and Sean guided the horse back to a lean-to stable that stood behind it.

Sean bit the inside of his cheek, wondering which of his parents' fates was the most disgraceful. "Never knew her," he said, bringing his horse to a halt and reaching down to untie Heather's shawl from around his waist. "What was this about, then?" he asked with a laugh. "Tyin' yourself to me, Miss Heather Monaghan. Were ye afraid I'd try to get away from ye?"

"No," she answered bashfully. "That I might fall as we rode."

"I'd have come back for ye, ye know, if ye had," he continued, dismounting and smiling up at her. His teeth were a handsome yet eerie flash of silver in the moonlight. "You'd not get away from me that easily."

She dropped her gaze as he continued to stare up at her. "No. I know, Sean," she said under her breath.

"And ye still find that agreeable?" he asked in a tentative tone.

She simply nodded, again feeling torn. The only thing she sought for certain now was a fire. She wanted a big heavy quilt and her half-frozen fingers and toes pushed up as close to the cottage's hearth as she dared push them.

Seeming satisfied with this answer, Sean led the steed into the lean-to and hitched it to a post within, beside two other horses. Then he came around to help Heather dismount as well.

"Sweet Jesus, like a block of ice ye are, lass," he said with a grimace as he held her there, suspended over him for several seconds. "Ye should have grabbed more than a shawl, ye know."

"I know," she answered, again staring downward. And how well she knew! She'd have given almost anything now to have had more clothing with which to shield herself from his view once they stepped into the fire's light in his cottage.

"Take my cloak, then," he offered as he set her down. "I'd have stopped and given it to ye sooner if I'd known how cold you were gettin'."

Heather eagerly accepted it from him and stood sighing with satisfaction as she draped it about her and its warmth—the warmth his body had left upon it—enfolded her.

"We'll get ye some mulled ale and warm ye by the fire," he declared, wrapping an arm about her and leading her to the cottage. "I know some wonderful ways to do that," he added with a sportiveness to his voice that made her want to run off somewhere and hide. She didn't though. She'd come this far in the bone-chilling night, and there certainly was no turning back now—not until she'd had a chance to warm herself anyway.

" 'Tis best to let me go in before ye," Sean said gingerly, stopping as they reached the front door. "I'll just make certain old Rory is down for the night."

Heather stepped back from the threshold and let him slip inside, and he scarcely allowed her a glimpse of the place before he shut the door behind himself.

She stood shivering for several seconds as she awaited his return. The front stoop was so cold that she had to shift her weight from foot to foot. But then, blessedly, he reappeared, and he swept the door open to her with a smile and a bow.

"Welcome, miss, to our temporary abode."

"And your friend?" she inquired cautiously as she entered.

"Out cold up in the loft, as I suspected. He's had a difficult day, ye see, so I'm sure we won't be hearin' from him till mornin'."

Heather took in the place in an instantaneous scan. It was an odd little dwelling with a length far greater than its width. Back to the left was a ladder that led up to what appeared to be a loft. Just to the right of that, on the first floor, was an enclosure that must have been a larder or some such thing, and farther forward to the right was an open pantry.

Everything looked neat and clean, but the fire room was strangely devoid of furniture. Except for a dining table and its four chairs, the first floor was empty, and it began to occur to Heather that this was what it meant to live life on the wing—having to set up camp in leased or abandoned cottages and make do with what furnishings were provided.

She swallowed back her reservations, however, and once again becoming aware of her freezing fingers and toes, she made a beeline for the hearth. "What's he do, this Rory, that he finds so difficult?" she asked, throwing her hands out over the flames.

"Lolls about in taverns and such."

"And that's difficult?" she asked incredulously.

Again Sean laughed. Then he shut the front door behind him and, to Heather's dismay, barred it as well. "It can be, when ye find yourself with the wrong lot."

"He does that, then? Lolls about with the wrong gents?"

A smile tugged at the corner of his lips. "Well, think it through, lass. He lives with two bride snatchers. Can't go much further wrong than that, now can ye."

He crossed to the pantry. From it he withdrew a large earthenware jug, a tiny kettle, and a small cloth pouch. He carried these over to the dining table and poured a generous amount of ale from the jug into the kettle. Then he withdrew a pinch of what appeared to be ground spice from the pouch, and he dropped it into the kettle and gave the mixture a quick slosh.

He walked over to where she stood before the fire and hung the vessel from the pothook. "To mull it," he said in response to her questioning expression as she sidled out of his way. "There's nothin' like it to warm ye."

"I wouldn't know," she said, pulling her shawl more tightly closed over her chest. "I've never had it."

He gave forth a dry laugh. "No. I don't suppose ye have, come to think of it. You're a little too young and refined for such brews. Still, I think you'll like it if I sweeten it a bit with honey. Just the thing to take the chill off ye, love," he added, moving up beside her and cupping his large palms over her shoulders.

He felt her stiffen with obvious misgivings, but he didn't care. He had her in his possession at last, and he wasn't about to let her wangle out of being claimed.

Heather bit her lip and shut her eyes as his mouth closed down upon her an instant later. He was planting a trail of hot, ardent kisses from her right shoulder up to her neck, and she had all she could do to keep her legs from giving out from beneath her.

"Your . . . your mother," she blurted, pulling free of him and pivoting around to where she'd stood before, directly in front of the fire.

He seemed amazed that she'd had the presence of mind to move away from his mesmeric kisses. "My mother?" he repeated blankly, looking as though he'd just been catapulted out of a very deep sleep.

Heather thrust her hands out over the warming fire again, and she drew in a deep, bolstering breath. "Aye. Ya didn't really answer me about her. Is she still alive?"

Sean shook his head slightly, but more to rouse himself than in response to her question. Why all these queries from her? he wondered. They put him on edge. If he didn't know better, he'd have thought her a spy for the local sheriff. "No. She's dead, as far as I know," he said, not sure if this was true and, quite frankly, not caring.

To his surprise, Heather responded with a sad smile. "Aye. So's mine. Died of a fever when I was little. So, my father's all I have."

"Not all," he replied, again moving over to embrace her. "You've got me now, love," he said in a whisper that sent chills running clear up to the crown of her head.

"Ah, well, that's not really final yet, is it," she retorted, using one end of her shawl to shield her hand as she reached up to remove the little kettle from the heat. "Looks to me as though this is plenty hot already," she announced, whisking away from him once more and crossing to the table with the steaming brew. "Where might I find some cups?"

"I'll fetch 'em for us," he replied, clucking under his breath. This was the third time that day that he'd found himself aching with arousal for her, and his body was beginning to lose all patience with the situation.

But he had to remember a young lady's penchant

for chat and romance, a voice within him counseled as he walked back to the pantry and withdrew two mugs from its cupboard. The poor girl was being robbed of a wedding night in the fancy suite of some expensive inn; and though he planned to use some of the wealth he'd amassed to provide many such luxuries for her in the future, he knew that he should at least take the time now to answer her questions and get her properly tipsy before having his way with her.

With this in mind, he set the mugs on the table as he returned to it, and he pulled out one of the dining chairs for her with a chivalrous bow.

"Ah, thank ye kindly," she said with a smile, sitting down like a duchess in the seat he offered. "You've lovely manners, ye know . . . for an outlaw, I mean," she added awkwardly. "Well, I didn't mean to say outlaw, exactly," she quickly amended, and Sean could tell from her reddening complexion that what had obviously begun as a compliment was rapidly sucking her down into a quicksand of explanations. "I mean, from what I've heard, most of Ireland thinks of you and your brother as heroes—"

"I know what ye meant, love," he interrupted, reaching down and pressing a finger to her lips. "No need to go on with it. Just take a sip of this, while I find ye some honey for it."

She was young yet, he reminded himself, and thankfully, still rough enough around the edges to commit such blunders and to have avoided becoming the priss that only a year or two more in such a well-to-do station might have made her.

Heather lifted the hot mug to her lips with trembling fingers an instant later. She hadn't realized, until she'd caught herself babbling so, just how ill at ease she truly was with the situation.

Perhaps he was right, she thought. Maybe her only hope now was simply to drown her apprehension in the drink he had poured for her. But one sip of the strong ale made her nostrils flare and her throat burn, and she returned the mug to the table with a telling thud.

He was just coming out of the pantry with the honey as she did so, and he responded with a laugh. "Ah, take heart, my dear. You'll like it much better with a bit of this in it." Once he reached her, he used a honey dipper to ladle a generous amount of the sweet goo into her mug. Then he pushed the ale back toward her. "There now. Give it another try, and you'll see."

She rather doubted that this addition would help, but she raised the mug to her lips again and, crinkling up her nose with repulsion, took a second sip. To her surprise, he was right. It wasn't bad at all. There was just a bit of a nip to it, like the liquor-flavored candies her father had brought back from France a few years before. And she had to admit to herself that, though she'd been equally skeptical about those at first, she'd grown quite fond of them.

"Ah, there, ye see," he encouraged. "Ye took a few good swallows there, now, didn't ye."

She nodded and smiled shyly over at him as he sat down in the chair beside hers.

"And just feel how it takes the chill off ye. Like buildin' a fire inside yourself, isn't it."

Again she nodded, and she drank a little more.

"Tell . . . tell me . . . if ye will," she began, nervously fingering her mug, "what it was ye meant this mornin' when ye said that Jennifer was in need of a husband?"

He looked caught off-guard by the question. "Oh, well . . . I shouldn't say anythin' more about that. I'm sorry."

She glared at him. "Why not?"

He shrugged and smiled. "I just shouldn't betray our client's trust. Even we kidnappers have our principles. I'm sure ye understand."

Heather put her hands on her hips and clucked at him. "No. I'm afraid I don't. I mean, I've come all the way here with ye, in the dark of night . . . in nothin' but my shift," she sputtered. "And given that, I should think you could see your way clear to put a bit of trust in me as well."

"Are ye sayin' you'll keep it to yourself then? No matter what happens?" he asked tentatively.

Heather returned her hands to the table and nodded. "I am."

"Well then, I'll let ye guess at it, and I'll tell ye if you're right. But that's all, love. . . . So, then," he began again with a sportive smile playing upon his lips, "what is it ye think I meant by it?"

Heather furrowed her brow in annoyance and took a long angry swallow of her ale. "I haven't the slightest idea. That's why I'm askin' ye, for Heaven's sake."

"Ah, think about it," he coaxed, looking exasperated. "Why would a girl be in need of a husband?"

Heather continued to scowl. "I don't know. . . . Because she'd gettin' old, I suppose. Or her parents have died and left her penniless. But none of that was true of Jennifer."

That annoying smirk continued to tug at the corner of his lips. "Right ye are. So what's that leave then?"

Heather felt her cheeks warming, and the silence between them suddenly seemed like a mocking roar in her ears as the answer finally occurred to her. "Ah, *no*," she gasped. "Sweet Mother Mary! Ye can't mean it. Not our Jen!"

To her astonishment, however, he simply nodded and continued to smile. "I wouldn't lie to ye about such a thing, now would I?" he asked, his eyes twinkling with sincerity. "She actually confessed it to me herself," he added, raising an imperious brow. Then he laughed and shook his head as though hardly able to believe it himself. "First bride we've ever had in that condition! Felt almost as though we were doin' the Lord's own work with that job!"

"Well, I'll never believe it! Jennifer would scarcely agree to dance with a lad, much less . . ." Her words broke off, and her cheeks grew warmer.

"Much less *what?*" he asked teasingly.

"Whisht, ye scoundrel! Ye know perfectly well what," she snapped. "You'll not trick me into sayin' it!"

To her surprise, he didn't look the slightest bit abashed at her reproof, and he reached out in that instant and began caressing her fingers where they rested on the handle of her mug.

"Ah, Heather, ye must realize that I'm not nearly as interested in the sayin' as in the *doin'*."

She felt an aroused tingle run through her, and she

215

drew her hands away and hid them under the table. "Who was the father, then? Did she say?"

Sean shook his head. "No. She wouldn't tell us. . . . Wouldn't or couldn't," he added pointedly.

"Oh, that's ridiculous. How could a girl not know that sort of thing?"

"Well, though I'm sure ye won't believe me, my dear, I do pride myself on bein' a gentleman. So I shan't even attempt to answer that."

Again the silence between them was unnerving to Heather, and she had all she could do to keep from slipping under the table and hiding as the answer to this dawned upon her as well. "Ah, Lord, Sean! That was a dreadful thing to imply. I mean, Jennifer and I have been friends since we were babes, and ye would think I'd have known if she had even one suitor, much less two!"

"Well, it doesn't matter now, does it. We did the poor girl a favor, as it happened. And God knows that can't be said of us very often. So naturally, we're pleased when it can."

Heather wanted, with all her heart, to believe him—if just for Jennifer's sake. "Really? Do ye really think ye helped her?"

"Oh, aye. She honestly seemed to like the man for whom we stole her. Actually said she *wanted* to stay on with him," Sean added with a note of pride in his voice. "Of course, they'll never make the pair you and I will," he continued, leaning forward in his chair and kissing her forehead. "But at least now, knowin' that it came to a happy end, ye might be more willin' to forgive me for it and for my draggin' you off as well."

"I chose it too, remember," she said stoically. "Ye gave me every opportunity to stay behind."

He smiled. "That I did."

She looked up at him through her dark lashes, and her schoolgirlish air of uncertainty seemed enough to make his heart melt. "So, do ye really think it, Sean? Do ye really believe us to be a good match?"

There was not a hint of his previous jocularity on his face now. "With all my heart, love." But as he rose and circled around to embrace her, she lifted her face, and he could see that she wore a deeply pained expression.

"What is it?"

She drew some air in through her teeth, making a pitying sound. "The corner of your mouth. What with it so dark in here, I thought it was just the shadow of a beard. But I see now that you've bruised yourself, haven't ya? Someone's left ye black and blue."

Sean drew back from her slightly, from her odd tone. It was sympathetic, yet a bit scolding, like a . . . a mother's. Yes, he realized after a second. He'd never had enough experience with one to know for certain. But it seemed to him that she sounded like a mother who had caught her son sparring with a neighbor boy. Yet the obvious concern in her voice kept him from feeling defensive. In fact, he found that his only response now was to fight a smile.

"Aye. Rory and I had a difference of opinion earlier. 'Tis nothin'."

"Ah, but it is," she insisted, and to his utter amazement, she raised her fingers to his mouth, parted his lips, and began feeling around his bottom row of teeth. "He's knocked one or two of 'em loose on ye, the ruffian! And I think ye ought to fetch this Rory, so I can do the same to him!"

Sean laughed. "Not bloody likely! He's three times your size, love. Besides, I can fight my own battles, thank ye just the same. I've been doin' so since well before you were even born."

"Ah, still," she continued, shaking her head sadly. "That lovely smile of yours, Sean. All white and cool as snow against your sun-browned skin. I'd hate to see it ruined . . . . Let me get some ice for it," she declared, rising.

He caught her wrist and held her there. "No. Stay here with me. We have no ice, and besides, it's too late for that, isn't it. Our row took place hours ago, so the damage is done."

She tugged a bit, trying to free her hand. "But there must be somethin' I can get for ya. It looks so terribly painful."

"It's nothin' that the ale and your compliments can't soothe," he returned with an imploring glimmer in his eye, and she was so moved by it that she found herself compliantly sinking back into her chair.

"There now, that's better, isn't it," he murmured. "I mean, a fella can hardly ravish a girl when she's up tryin' to play nursemaid, can he. . . . So, tell me more about how you'd hate seein' my smile ruined," he prompted with a smirk, knowing that she found him attractive, but anxious for more specifics.

She smirked as well. "Well, yes. I would, because next to your eyes and your bonny, gleamin' hair and wide shoulders, I think it your best feature."

"Well, then," he began with a provocative note in his voice, taking his pistol from the waist of his breeches and setting it on the table, "ye won't object if I show ye a bit more of myself now, will ye. Ye just might find some parts ye like even better." With that, he took hold of her silken shift and pulled her over to him.

Though still reluctant, Heather let herself be drawn into his embrace, and an instant later, she was thankful she had, because the words he spoke brought her surprising comfort.

"I know you're frightened," he whispered in her ear, "of what I'm goin' to do to ye. But ye needn't be. It's not somethin' to be feared. Just give me a few minutes, and I'll show ye . . . and I'll provide for ye as well as your father ever has. You'll see. You'll not want for a thing, in my bed or out of it."

His tone was so intimate in those seconds, so earnest, that she found herself believing him, and she didn't fight him as he swept her up into his arms and rose to carry her over to the fire. The ale she'd drunk was beginning to take its dizzying effect upon her. It was already starting to fog her thinking, and now, more than anything else, she wanted to know what Jennifer apparently did: how it felt to make love—especially with a man as attractive as Sean.

He kissed her as he walked—as passionately as could be expected after such a blow to the mouth. She, in turn, found herself clinging to him, her arms locked about his neck and her lips and tongue playing about the periphery of his with empathetic delicacy.

"That's it, my dearest Heather; you be gentle with

me, and I'll return the favor," he said under his breath as he set her down upon the hearth rug, very near the warming fire.

He was silently elated that she was finally cooperating, that the ale seemed to be breaking down her resistance. And he had every hope of deflowering her without too much of a fight. He'd done all the fighting he cared to for one day.

She didn't move as he stood over her in those seconds, slowly untying the drawstring neckline of his shirt. She only stirred enough to remove the cloak he'd given her, and slip it behind her head for use as a pillow. Then she flung her long hair up and over it, and lay back down with her arms cast above her head.

In that position, with her auburn mane streaming upward, she looked to Sean like a mermaid floating down into the ocean's aqua depths. And all he knew for certain was that he wanted her—right then and there. He'd kept his body waiting too long, and he knew it wouldn't be refused again.

Heather continued to watch him rather dazedly in those seconds, noting his every move with the objectivity of a mere observer. She saw him pull off his shirt, thereby unveiling the gloriously brawny chest beneath. Then she saw him step out of his shoes and shove them aside with one of his feet. Finally, there were his breeches and hose, and to her surprise, he chose to leave those on as he dropped to his knees and straddled her supine form. She didn't know why he chose this, and she felt sure she'd be too embarrassed to ask. Yet the next thing she knew, the question was leaving her lips.

He laughed softly at it amid the kisses he was showering upon her neck. "So as not to frighten ye," he answered simply, and she didn't have the slightest idea whether he meant it or had said it in jest.

"Why would I be afraid?" she asked. But again, it seemed to be another part of her speaking—the daring, drunken part. And the real Heather, the more cautious Heather, simply continued to lie there and observe.

"Ah, ye just might, is all. Some lasses are, I've found, and I don't want ye judgin' until you've had a chance to . . . to feel it."

"Then can I stop ye, if I change my mind?" she queried in a tone so coquettish it surprised even her.

His words were a hot, fervent stream in her ear once more, a compelling, almost irresistible force. "Ah, ye won't, ye won't, ye won't. Trust me."

Trust him? a voice within her echoed. He was a kidnapper, for mercy's sake! A fugitive! Why on earth should she trust him? But then again, why on earth had she dared to come *this* far with him?

Because she loved him? Yes. Perhaps, this was the way love felt: all tingly and melting and insanely impulsive.

She felt him push the shawl away from her shoulders as he continued to kiss her, and she closed her eyes, offering up a prayer that she wouldn't live to regret in leisure what they were both about to do in haste. There was something about his manner, however, about the careful way in which he peeled the garment from her, like one easing back the delicate petals of a rose—something about the way he kissed the flesh on her chest and shoulders as he bared it, that told her that she was doing the right thing. It was clear that he adored her and would cherish her in a way that Malcolm never could.

In the seconds that followed, he drew her nightshift upward, well past the point to which he'd lifted it in her bedchamber, and to her amazement, she was actually helping him do so. She was arching her back, lifting herself from the hearth rug, and enabling him to pull the silk well up above her breasts. Then he and his wounded mouth closed down upon one of the rosy peaks with a gratified groan, and she couldn't help groaning as well as his lips began pleasuring the upper half of her and his fingers the lower.

What delicious sin this was! What ecstasy! To be alone before a crackling fire with a man like this and far too inebriated to have the good judgment expected of her.

Sean was so wonderful to behold from head to toe and so blatantly disregardful of every law she'd ever been forced to live by. He just didn't seem to care. He wasn't afraid of her father or the local authorities, and clearly he didn't fear doing those things to her that would surely see him hanged, were he caught. And because he didn't care, neither did Heather anymore. She was becoming shamelessly attached to him, and she knew she'd follow him to the ends of the earth if that was what it would take to keep him.

She opened her eyes once more as she felt him withdraw his fingers from her. Then his body shifted over hers, and as he bent down to finally open his breeches, she saw how the firelight played upon his golden hair. It was so beautifully distracting, so like the sunlit crop of a child or an angel, that she didn't really see what his hands were releasing beneath. He was neither a child nor an angel, some tiny, distant voice wanted to scream out in warning. But she wouldn't listen, because she wanted this now. She wanted, more than anything, for him to finally lay claim to her and put the terrible possibility of marriage to Malcolm behind her forever.

It would hurt. She'd deduced that much from her discussions about it with Shannon and her other girl friends. But whatever the pain, she told herself, it could never compare to a lifetime of torment in the bed of a man she didn't love.

She thought she might shut her eyes again and begin saying the rosary or some other invocation to dispel her fear and any discomfort. Yet she found now that she couldn't do so. She found she couldn't take her eyes off what was happening below. She simply stared downward, through the space between their bodies, as his fingers opened her and his firm, muscular posterior began easing this alarmingly large part of him into her with a series of penetrating nudges.

Then, at feeling how her body hungered for it, how it seemed to give way beneath him, granting him admission with disgraceful passiveness, her eyes closed once more, and she heard herself whisper a shameless "aye" up into his ear.

Just as he seemed to have slipped nearly all of himself into her, however, he stopped abruptly and began to withdraw.

Her eyes fell open with surprise and confusion. She

tried to speak, to ask him why he had stopped, but he placed a silencing finger upon her lips.

"Shhh," he ordered. "Don't ye hear, love?"

"Hear what?" she croaked.

"Horses ridin' in. Someone's comin'. More than one rider, I think."

"Ah, no, Sean," she whispered, almost pleadingly, reaching up and pulling down upon his shoulders. "It's nothin'."

He resisted, however, uncoupling from her and turning over onto his back. "Yes. Those are riders approachin', as sure as the devil."

"Maybe it's only your brother," she suggested, hoping he'd agree and decide to resume their love-making.

"No," he said firmly, hurriedly tucking his male appendage into the flap of his breeches and getting to his feet. "He's not due back yet, and he'd be comin' alone. There's more than one rider out there, and we're too far off the highway for it to be neighbors passin' by." With that, he rushed to one of the front windows and peered out, past its gauzy curtains, into the moonlit night.

"Three riders," he declared uneasily, "headin' straight for us."

"What should we do?" Heather asked, getting to her feet as well and hurriedly bending down to gather up the shawl and cloak she'd shed.

He rushed over to the table and picked up his pistol. "That's simple enough, love. You'll go and hide yourself in the larder, where ya can sneak out the back door if need be. And I'll stay here and see what they want."

"Ah, but, Sean, maybe ye shouldn't. Maybe ye should just leave the door bolted and come and hide with me."

He'd already dashed back to the window to resume his watch, and she was surprised to see that he wore an irate expression as he turned to address her again. "Has it not occurred to ye that your absence has already been noticed and it's your father out there, come to fetch ye?"

"No. It couldn't be. No one saw us leave."

"Well, whoever it is, you're still a virgin, mind. I didn't have time enough just now to change that. So, for Christ's Sake, get yourself back home if aught should happen to me, and pretend ye never left the manor tonight."

"Ah, but, Sean," she croaked again, feeling a terrible, tearful lump forming in her throat.

"But nothin'," he growled. "Get yourself hidden, lass, before I come over there, knock ye out, and do it for ye! Just do as I say! I've had a great deal more experience at this sort of thing than you. I've gotten so I can smell trouble comin'. And mark my words, it's comin' now!"

"But I don't want to go back to the manor. I want to stay here with you."

"And find yourself a gallows' widow?" he asked incredulously. "Without even one night in my bed? That's a ridiculous price to pay for the likes of me, girl, and ye should be quick-witted enough to know it! Now go and hide yourself, I say, or sure as the blazes, I'll do it for ye, and you'll be the sorrier for it," he vowed in a hiss so threatening that she knew she had only seconds to obey.

She couldn't help herself, however. The very thought of having him wrenched out of her arms for good and all now was more than she could bear, and she found herself running over to him and pressing a soft kiss to his cheek before proceeding to the larder as he'd ordered.

His annoyance seemed to recede for a second or two, and he squeezed her to him, looking honestly touched by the show of affection. But then he turned her about and gave her a swat on the bottom. "Now go, girl! The larder's back to the right of the table!"

Heather hurried off to the chamber and, after struggling to get its sticking door open, stepped inside. Then she drew the ill-hung structure shut behind her with a slam. It was pungent and drafty within, and her fingers fumbled in the darkness to get the shawl and cloak tied about her once more.

She wished desperately for a candle and a punk with which to light it, so she could get her bearings. But she knew she couldn't risk letting the candle's glow shine out from under the larder door and tell the callers where she was, so she'd simply have to stand there and wait for her eyes to adjust.

After several seconds, some of the larder's interior became visible to her, and she spied the back door to which Sean had referred. She started moving toward it. Then, hearing a terrible thundering coming from the front of the cottage, she froze in her tracks. It was the riders knocking, she acknowledged, and their pounding was so reverberant, so clearly charged with anger, that she knew she should follow Sean's advice now and sneak outside. But she truly wished to stay and hear what the call was about, so she

226

stepped back behind a cluster of stuffed potato sacks and, squatting down, hid herself there.

The knocking came again, this time accompanied by the shouts of a male voice, and even from where Heather was crouching, she could tell that the party shouting was calling the name of Kerry—Sean and Patrick Kerry.

It was the sheriff, she realized in those horrendous seconds. The visitor had also used the name "O'Neill," and that was what the local sheriff was called.

She squeezed her eyes shut in prayer and began to tremble with indecision. She just wasn't sure whether she should slip out the back way or simply stay and see what happened. It was possible, she supposed, that the other riders Sean had spotted had already snuck around the back and had the cottage surrounded now. And if that was the case, she'd obviously be stepping right into a snare if she chose to leave. On the other hand, there were no guarantees that she'd go undetected if she stayed. So, she really wasn't sure what to do, and the brimming cup of ale she'd drunk certainly wasn't helping her think her options through clearly.

She must stay, she suddenly acknowledged. She had no choice but to stay, because she knew, deep inside, that she cared too much for Sean simply to go home without knowing what fate had befallen him.

In the seconds that followed, the occurrences outside the larder became clearer to her. The sheriff threatened to knock the front door down if it wasn't unlatched at once, and after several bolt-cracking blows upon it, Sean apparently opened it as requested. This was followed by the footfall of at least three people, and Heather breathed a relieved sigh at the realization that all the riders Sean had seen seemed to be present and accounted for now.

Then some conversation took place, and Heather strained to hear it. The sheriff asked Sean if he was, indeed, Sean Kerry, and he denied it, giving the name of Stephen Connors instead. The sheriff then went on to order the others to search the place, and Heather heard their footsteps disperse as the officer continued to question Sean.

While keeping one ear on the questioning in those heart-stopping seconds, Heather managed to note the progress of the searchers. One of them was climbing the steps to the loft, and the other was heading in her direction!

She scrunched farther down behind the sacks and did her best not to make a sound. The footsteps were somewhere near the table now, and there was yet a third set in or around the pantry.

But above it all, to her great relief, she heard Sean complaining. He was uttering some hair-raising curses in between his emphatic claims that he was not the man they sought and that no one had the right to come bursting into a fellow's cottage at such an hour.

Under any other circumstances, Heather would have wanted to laugh at his feigned indignation. She knew, however, that this was a deathly serious situation and that, far from laughing, even her breathing would have to be curtailed soon if she hoped to keep her presence under wraps.

When, at last, the footsteps reached the larder door, Heather heard Sean offer the loudest of his objections. He insisted that the sheriff let him loose so he could accompany the intruder inside and see to it nothing was stolen from the larder during the search. He claimed that he'd had his fill of the authorities preying upon the common folk in the name of the Queen.

This, apparently, was enough to sway the sheriff, because Heather heard two sets of footsteps now— one running in from the fire room—as the larder door was pried open. The walls that surrounded her suddenly became lit by the vacillating light of what was obviously a hand-held lantern, and Heather hunched even farther downward in her hiding place.

"Nothin' in here, ya deuce," Sean snarled seconds later, and Heather could tell that he was just a foot or two away from her now.

Apparently, however, Sean's companion was not convinced of this. Heather heard him make his way farther into the cramped chamber. But he evidently did so in a clumsy fashion, because his movement was immediately followed by the unmistakable sound of a jar falling and shattering upon the floor.

"Ah, now ye've done it, haven't ye," Sean scolded. "Gone and ruined the last of the pickled fruit my poor dead mother left to me! Well, I just hope you're pleased with yourself," he said bitterly. "Comin' into the home of an innocent citizen in the middle of the night and heedlessly knockin' over all he holds dear!"

"I . . . I'm sorry, sir," the other man stammered, sounding amply repentant, and to Heather's amazement, she recognized his voice as being that of one of Jennifer Plithe's brothers. "But Sheriff's draughted me to assist with lookin' for my sister, and it can't be helped that I'm not much good at it."

"Well, I don't have your sister," Sean snapped. "And make no mistake; 'tis you lot who are doin' the stealin'! You're robbin' an innocent man of his sleep, is what!"

Seeming daunted by Sean's words, the lantern bearer clucked and finally began to withdraw from the larder. This, apparently, left Sean an instant or two of light and solitude in which to nudge one of the potato sacks behind which Heather hid. Then he growled something almost inaudible down at her— something about her getting herself home while she still could—and he was gone.

Heather pressed a fist to her lips. She realized, once again, that he was probably right. Nevertheless, she continued to hide there in the darkness as the two of them closed the larder door and walked away.

The next sounds she was aware of were those of two rather heavy-footed parties making their way down from the loft. She'd thought she'd heard a scuffle taking place far above, during the panic-stricken moments when Jennifer's brother had come to search the larder, but she'd been too frightened to pay much attention to it. And now, to her amazement, she heard *Malcolm's* voice as it descended from the second floor.

"He's a madman, this one, sheriff," Malcolm declared. "Had to draw a gun on him to get him down here, and that sounds very much to me like resistin' arrest!"

"Ah, he wasn't," Heather heard Sean interject.

"He's just a bit daft, is all. Doesn't take kindly to anyone wakin' him. Especially in the middle of the night. He's fairly harmless though, sheriff. I swear it."

"None the less, Mr. Connors, or whatever you're called, Mr. Byrne here claims you're the one who shot him last evenin'. So I'm obliged to at least take ye in for questionin'."

"Him, as well," Malcolm insisted. "This fat brute with the greasy black hair. He damn near changed me to a geldin' up there!"

Heather bit her lip and rolled her eyes toward the heavens. Oh, dear God, how she wished Rory had succeeded!

"All right. Is this it, then?" the sheriff asked in a weary tone. "Is this all who live here, Mr. Connors? Just the pair of ye?"

"It is," Sean lied.

"Fine then," the sheriff continued. "Go back with 'em, gents, and fetch their horses, and we'll be off."

"At this hour?" Sean asked, with an amazed rise to his voice. "Can't it wait till mornin' at least, sir?"

"Absolutely not," Malcolm bellowed. "This is the man who shot me, I tell ye, and I want him collared now!"

"Calm yourself, Mr. Byrne," the sheriff ordered, his voice edged with impatience. "I've said we're takin' him in now, and now it is. So get your clothes on, gentlemen."

There were no more words. All Heather could hear were the sounds of someone climbing up to the loft, then coming back down; and she found herself feeling relieved that at least Sean and his friend had had the good sense not to allow the encounter to end in an exchange of gunfire. The situation was grave, admittedly, but as long as Sean was still alive and well, there was yet some hope, Heather told herself.

She remained in her hiding place for a few minutes more, waiting until she heard all of them exit and ride off on their horses. Then, with the utmost caution, she rose and crept to the larder's back door. She cracked it open and peered out in all directions, making certain that no one was waiting outside for her.

Once she was sure of this, she ran to the lean-to and unhitched the remaining horse from the post within. She found herself muttering words of comfort to the animal as she mounted him—assurances that his owners would soon be home and able to care for him once more. She knew full well, however, that these were simply the sorts of lies one tells little children and helpless beasts. Anything to soothe them and keep them from overreacting. And she realized, as she rode away on the steed minutes later, that she was in far greater need of such assurances than he was.

Chapter 12

Heather's biggest problem, once she reached Monaghan Manor, was figuring out what to do with the Kerrys' horse. She couldn't be certain the poor beast would be able to find his way home in the darkness, and she knew that, if she attempted to leave him in the stable or the croft, he was sure to come to the notice of the hands in the morning. So she tied him to a tree not far from the manor, and traveled the rest of the way home on foot.

She would rise before dawn, she promised herself. She would get up before anyone else in the household, and she and her own horse, Nigel, would lead the steed back to Scan's cottage.

With that decided, she began her cautious approach of the manor. Once she arrived at the thicket, behind which Sean had hidden his horse earlier, she scanned the manse and listened for any sounds from within. There were none, and the house was as dark as it had been when they'd left. So, pretty well convinced that there was no one astir, she climbed the oak beside her bedchamber window and went inside as soundlessly as possible.

Her eyes were so well adjusted to the moonlight now, that she found she didn't need to light a candle to find her way along to her bed. When she reached it, she slipped in between its linens and sprawled back upon her pillow with an exhausted sigh.

Sean's cloak, she silently admonished herself. She was still wearing it, and she certainly couldn't afford to be caught with it on when morning came.

She groaned at this realization and rose to remove it. She would hide it under her mattress, she decided. No one, not even the chambermaid, was apt to look under there. As she reached down to stow the garment away, however, she found that she couldn't bring herself to part with it. She simply froze, with the cloak folded up in her hand. Then she clutched it to her chest and, bending her head down, drew in a long, wistful whiff of it.

She closed her eyes with longing. His scent was upon it, and she knew that she simply couldn't bring herself to part with it—even if only to hide it just a few layers beneath her.

They had taken enough of him from her for one night, she acknowledged, gritting her teeth with rage. Malcolm, the worm, had been responsible for wrenching Sean from her arms, tearing their most intimate embrace asunder, and she simply didn't have the strength to relinquish anything more.

She fixed her jaw resolutely and climbed back into bed with the cloak still in her arms. Then, nestling into the mattress, she curled up into fetal position and slid the garment downward, between her thighs. It felt satiny and cool against her loins, and she found a few second's pleasure in it. But she had to admit to herself that it was a sorry substitute, indeed, for what had been there when she and Sean had been so rudely interrupted.

It was better than nothing though. At least it was something that belonged to Sean—more than could be said of her at this point, she tearfully acknowledged.

Well, for what it was worth, she was still a virgin. She could still look her father, or any other man, in the eye and claim to be pure. But what doleful consolation, she thought with a sniffle. She would much rather have had Sean finish what he'd started than to have things end as they had.

She rolled onto her back and again gave forth a light groan. She would have only her memories of it, and they were sure to do little more than torment her. She couldn't help herself, however. All that she'd experienced came back to her now in an overwhelming flood. She remembered how he'd touched her only hours before in this very bed, and most of all, her mind was locked upon the unspeakable link that he'd created between their bodies before they'd been disturbed at his cottage.

It was *torture*, sheer aching, blissful agony to recall it all and wonder how it would have ended if he'd had the chance to finish it. What piece of the puzzle was yet missing that would explain why he still believed her to be a virgin?

Dear God, she thought, squeezing her eyes shut, if she did manage to fall asleep, she was sure to dream of him and nothing else. She was bound to lay there, awake or not, and hunger for that part of him that he'd slipped inside her. Sadly, however, that aching would be nothing, she realized—nothing compared to the torment of wondering what fate would befall him now, in the sheriff's hands.

As planned, Heather slipped out of her room and down the adjacent oak just before dawn. As far as she could tell, she managed not to rouse any of the hands as she took Nigel from the stable. Then she led him to the Kerrys' steed as unobtrusively as possible. From there, fairly well out of earshot of the manor, she mounted Nigel and, with the steed in tow, rode off in the same direction Sean had with her the night before.

It all looked so much different to her in daylight, and she couldn't be certain of any of the landmarks she'd passed en route. But once half an hour had elapsed and she spotted a long, narrow cottage on a dirt road before her—a dwelling that seemed to be the same as what she'd seen of the Kerrys'—she dismounted, untied the steed's lead, and sent him on his way toward it with a slap on his rump. Then she climbed back onto Nigel and raced homeward once more, hell-bent on getting back into her nightshift and her bed before her absence was noticed.

She brought Nigel down to a trot as she neared the manor some thirty minutes later. She would ride around to the east and come in from the stable's side of the property, she decided. However, as she headed for the cover of the grounds' rolling back hills in order to make the trip across, she noted that the croft was already filled with her father's horses.

Panic ran through her. The stablehands were already up and dealing with the horses, and it stood to reason that Nigel had been missed by now. Her heart began pounding like thunder as she continued to ride. How the devil could she explain his absence?

She'd simply have to make it look as it seemed, she concluded after several seconds. She was dressed, after all. It wasn't as though she'd been foolish enough to leave the manor in her nightclothes. So, she'd just tell the hands that she'd taken Nigel out for an early morning ride and pray they believed her. She was usually a late riser, and such a claim was apt to surprise them, but surely it wasn't completely out of the range of possibility.

With this settled in her mind, she spurred Nigel to a gallop once more and hurried on through the hilly back acreage, bringing him up to the croft's gate within just a few minutes. It was best to get it over with, she reasoned. The sooner she faced the stable-hands' questions, the sooner she could answer them and be on her way to the great house. With any luck, she might even be able to get back up to her room before her father rose for breakfast.

"Miss Heather?" one of the stablemen called out to her in obvious disbelief as she dismounted her horse. He had been filling the croft's trough with water, so he apparently hadn't heard her ride up, and his startled expression told her that she definitely had some explaining to do. At this close range, however, she could finally see that there was no one else out-side at present, so at least she would have to lie to only one party, she told herself consolingly.

She nodded and waved at him. "Yes. 'Tis I," she answered with an innocent laugh. "Out for a mornin' ride with my Nige."

He set down his bucket, cocked his head in wonder, and then laughed as well. "But when could ye have left, miss? It only just got light half an hour ago, and none of us heard ye before then."

"Couldn't sleep, I'm afraid," she replied, tying Nigel to the croft's gate. "So I thought I'd pass some time with my dear black beast. He always calms me so. . . . Ye wouldn't mind takin' the tackle from him for me and gettin' him inside, would ye?" she asked in her most charming voice. "I fear Father will think the worst of me if I'm not in for breakfast forthwith."

He smiled broadly and began walking toward her. "Ah, surely, miss. Don't give it another thought. That's what we're here for, after all. . . . But just ye see to it ye have one of us saddle him for ye as well in the future," he added chidingly.

Heather paused long enough to kiss and pat her horse's muzzle. "I will. And thank ye kindly," she added, offering up a prayer that he would ultimately believe her story and see no need to bring her "morning ride" to the steward's attention. Then, giving her windblown hair a casual toss, she headed for the great house.

Once she reached its back entrance, however, she saw that her prayer had been in vain. To her horror, the door swung open in those seconds, and her father and Malcolm stood in its threshold, both wearing chillingly stern expressions.

She stopped in her tracks, searching her mind for something to say.

"Good mornin' to ye," she greeted finally. But she

could feel her smile quiver and fade as they continued to glare at her.

"Where have ye been?" Master Monaghan demanded.

Heather shrugged and tried to smile again. "Just out for a mornin' ride, father. Why?"

"We've been lookin' for ye everywhere, girl! I've told ye not to leave the grounds alone!"

"Yes. I know, sir. But I didn't leave the grounds, ye see. I just rode about for a while, back behind the ridge. I didn't think there'd be any harm in that."

"Well, get yourself in here," he ordered, looking at least a trifle allayed by her claim.

She hated having to lie to him, but these were rather dire circumstances, she reasoned as he and Malcolm stepped aside and allowed her to enter. "Really, you two . . . what is all this ado about?" she inquired, sweeping past them and heading down the corridor in which they stood. "Can't a girl go out for a ride anymore?"

"Into my study," her father directed, and Heather could hear that they were both close behind her as she stopped and turned into the specified chamber.

"Honestly, Father, you're scarin' me now," Heather continued once they were all inside and Master Monaghan had shut the door and headed for his desk. "What is this about?"

She considered directing a convincingly questioning gaze at Malcolm where he hovered near the front of her father's desk, but she instantly decided against it. It was just too early in the morning to be looking such a loathsome creature in the eye. What was more, Malcolm had always had an uncanny ability to see through her.

"Malcolm says he's found the man who shot him night before last," Brian Monaghan replied, settling into his desk chair and propping his elbows on the blotter before him.

She furrowed her brow and kept her eyes fixed upon her father. "The bride snatcher, ye mean?"

"The very same," Malcolm interjected pointedly.

Heather's gaze remained locked on her dad. "So what's that to do with me?" Even as she asked this question, however, she was busy scouring her own mind for any possible answers to it.

But there seemed to be none. She'd remembered to hide Sean's cloak beneath her mattress before leaving her room earlier, and she was certain that no one had seen her traveling either to or from the Kerrys' cottage. So she honestly couldn't imagine what these two wanted from her now.

"Sheriff says he needs to have you and Shannon come down to gaol and help confirm the gentleman's likeness," her father explained. "Bein' that the scoundrel had his face blackened at the weddin' dance, Sheriff feels you and Shannon were the only ones who got a good enough look at him to say if it's him for certain."

Heather crossed her arms over her chest and clamped a hand to each shoulder, pretending to shiver with apprehension. "Oh, Father, I *can't*. I think I'd faint dead away at seein' that villain again! Is it really necessary?"

Even from so many feet away, she could feel Malcolm's glower.

Her father nodded resignedly. "I fear it is. But it should only take a moment or two, and then Malcolm and I will have ye safely home again."

"But must we trouble Shannon with it as well? Won't my word be enough?" she asked hopefully.

Master Monaghan shook his head. "No. I'm sorry to say it won't. . . . There's a man's life at stake here, after all," he added solemnly. Then he leaned farther forward at his desk and looked her squarely in the eye. "But he'll be shackled, my dear. It's not as though he'll be given the chance to swing at ye as ye look him over."

Heather swallowed dryly, but not for the reason her father must have guessed. The very thought of having to see a man as handsome and chivalrous as Sean in irons made her want to weep. If, however, her father thought it was fear she was feeling, then all the better. "I know . . . I know," she stammered. "It's just that I can't help thinkin' what might happen if he ever breaks free. Won't he come after Shannon and me for bearin' witness against him?"

Malcolm let out an ominously low laugh. "Ah, he won't break free. No need at'all to fear that, because I plan to see him hanged for what he did to me! And to Jennifer," he added awkwardly.

Heather couldn't help herself in those seconds. His tone was so confident, vexingly self-righteous, that she turned and addressed him with a challenging gleam in her eye. "Ah, but not without a word or two of testimony from Shannon and me. . . . I mean," she continued with a nervous smile, "that is what you've said Sheriff requires, now isn't it."

It wasn't really meant to be a question, but Master Monaghan responded to it nonetheless. He answered it affirmatively in the second or two it took for Malcolm to meet Heather's gaze. And Malcolm's glare was so threatening that she was certain he already knew that he couldn't rely upon her to cooperate much in this or any other matter.

Sean had to admit to himself, upon reaching the Kilkenny gaol the night before, that he'd certainly seen the interiors of worse lockups. Even now, by morning light, the place looked clean enough. It definitely was not the rat-ridden hole that his father's cell in Derry had been, in any case.

Sean's pallet, if somewhat lumpy, had still been comfortable enough to allow him to sleep fairly soundly. And breakfast, what there'd been of it, had been surprisingly tasty. The best part of all, however, had been his gaoler's willingness to let Rory share his cell. This, at least, had enabled them to talk to one another during the long hours it was taking for the sheriff to conclude his investigation of them. It wasn't that Rory had ever been much for sparkling chat—even before his injury. It was just that he was company, someone who was at least somewhat familiar with the pitfalls of bride snatching, and given the circumstances, Sean found he needed that sort of rapport now.

The sheriff had questioned them until well past 2 A.M. First Sean, and then Rory. Then the pair of them together, answering what seemed to be the same questions over and over again. *Where had they been between the hours of six and ten on the night before last? Did they own any other horses besides*

*the ones the sheriff had seen hitched in the lean-to?
What firearms did they possess?*

Fortunately, once Sean had discovered it was the
sheriff at the cottage door, he'd had the presence of
mind to dispose of the incriminating answer to this
last question. He'd simply slipped his pistol into one
of the potato sacks, behind which Heather had apparently hidden in the larder. He had, thereby, rid
himself of the very weapon that had been used to
shoot that cur who'd come around to finger him.

As for their horses, Sean's bay had been conveniently disposed of as well. The unplanned stop at
the smithy's, which had seemed such a bother to
Sean at the time, had ultimately proven a blessing.
And now, as long as the blacksmith didn't learn of
the sheriff's search for one of the bride snatcher's getaway horses, Sean's involvement in all of it would
probably remain unrevealed.

God knew that he had taken all the usual precau-
tions upon their arrival in Kilkenny. He had used the
alias "Stephen Connors" to rent their cottage from
a local landlord, and Pat, too, had used an assumed
name in what few dealings he'd had with the townsfolk. So, it seemed to Sean that they had exercised
every possible safeguard. And if it hadn't been for
that bloody Malcolm Byrne, Sean thought with a
growl, he'd probably still be a free man.

"Gutless oxgoad," Sean muttered as he lay upon
his rickety bedstead. It was Malcolm who had begun
the shooting, after all. So, it did seem to Sean that
it had been terribly foul of Byrne to have involved
the sheriff in all of it. Especially given the fact that
Byrne would so clearly have shot and killed Sean

without compunction, had he had any kind of an aim. Sean had, sorrily, been in enough of such scrapes to know when a man was shooting to kill, and Byrne had definitely been doing so. Sean distinctly remembered that Byrne's first shot had been meant for his head and that his second had whirred past his chest, very narrowly missing him. Sean, on the other hand, had shot only to wound the bastard, simply to discourage him from continuing to shoot and, of course, to persuade the lot of them to turn back and let him and Patrick be on their way in peace. And Sean couldn't help feeling that he was being given precious little credit now for this show of civility.

He'd only grazed the swine, after all. It couldn't have even been enough of a wound to warrant fetching a doctor. Sean had received far worse several times, in fact, and he'd actually nursed himself back to strength, without even requiring help from Pat and Rory. So it really didn't seem right that Byrne should have rushed off and whined to the sheriff about the incident.

At the heart of it, however, this investigation wasn't about Byrne's flesh wound, Sean reminded himself. It was about the abduction of Jennifer Plithe, and he had, of course, been mindful from the start that anything he said that somehow linked him to Byrne's shooting linked him to the kidnapping as well.

The times were simply changing, Sean acknowledged, feeling a mix of melancholy and relief. For centuries the Irish had revered their bride snatchers, seeing such abductions as admirably daring and usually allowing those found guilty of it to go free. In fact, some of Sean and Patrick's clients had wanted no mention made of the Kerrys when the time had come for the bride's parents to pay out and for the alleged abductor to receive his laud from his neighbors and friends. But the times were definitely changing now, and the authorities, of even such pleasantly provincial towns as Kilkenny, were beginning to recognize it for what it was: kidnapping and, by extension, theft.

"Why do ye think they're holdin' us?" Rory suddenly inquired from his cot, which was just to Sean's right.

Sean gave forth a weary groan at having his thoughts interrupted by such a doltish question. "Ah, come now, Rory. If ye've asked me that once this mornin', ye've asked me a dozen times." Sean knew perfectly well that forgetting such things again and again in the space of just an hour was one of the peculiarities of those who'd suffered Rory's kind of injury, and usually he was fairly patient with it. But given the seriousness of their present circumstances, he was finding that his patience was wearing terribly thin.

"Well, I want to know," Rory returned defensively. "I've the right to know!"

"All right, then. I'll tell ye once again, ye hound. But then I'm done with," Sean snapped. "We're here because that black-haired devil, who woke ye last night, claims I shot him."

"And did ye?"

Sean, having visited more gaols in the course of his life than he cared to number, knew that there were potential informers in the cells all about them.

He, therefore, chose to stick with the answer he'd given Rory each of the other times he'd asked. "Of course not. I was nowhere near the Cassidys' farm Friday evenin', and neither were you."

Rory furrowed his brow, as though deeply confused, and Sean knew that even though he wasn't giving voice to it, he definitely recalled having been out there shortly before the time of the abduction. "Wasn't I?" he asked, rearranging his pillow and then lying back down upon it.

"No. Ye were back at the cottage. Drinkin' with me. Don't ye recall?"

"Maybe I do," Rory answered tentatively.

"Of course ye do," Sean snarled. "Unbound use of my steed and one hundred guineas say ye do," he concluded under his breath.

Always one to accept a respectable bribe, Rory fell blessedly silent once more, and Sean found himself praying that he'd finally drop the subject. He supposed, though, that in as much as Rory hadn't let anything slip out with the sheriff yet and he'd had the good sense not to call Sean by his real name, his prayers had already been answered. Now, if their gaoler would just be good enough to come and release them so they could get out of Kilkenny for good and all, their problems would be over.

But what about Patrick? Sean wondered. He was still in Lismore, expecting word from Sean that the Plithe dowry had been delivered and it was safe to head home and collect his share. And now there seemed no way of telling how long Pat would be kept waiting for this message.

Sean could only hope that his brother would have

the good sense to simply stay put and not risk returning to Kilkenny to investigate the delay. Due to his growing love of drink, however, the quality of Pat's judgment had been waning for quite some time, and Sean sensed now that if Pat proved fool enough to go back to their cottage, he was sure to find himself walking right into the hands of one of the sheriff's henchmen.

The sheriff didn't appear to be a beater, however, Sean told himself hearteningly. So far, O'Neill seemed to be a man who didn't care to resort to torture in order to obtain the answers he sought, and that was at least one thing they had working in their favor.

It wasn't that Sean was particularly worried about being broken by torture. He'd faced it a few times before at the hands of various officials, and he had always had amazingly good luck with holding his tongue. It was just that if they continued to take Rory in for questioning alone, there was no telling what enough flailing could jar loose from that muddled mind of his. He seemed to have no trouble differentiating between a pack of tipplers and a bona fide officer of the law like O'Neill, and Sean knew that he wouldn't be daft enough to launch into his Kerry brothers' ballad during interrogation. But he became quite enraged if hurt in any way, and Sean knew that all hell would break loose and anything was likely to come out of Rory's mouth if O'Neill attempted to bully him.

Sean would simply have to go with him, he concluded as he continued to lie on his bedstead and stare up at the gaol's cobweb-strewn ceiling. He'd simply have to continue to remind the sheriff that Rory was, indeed, incapacitated and insist upon being present for any further questioning.

Just as Sean was making this resolution, however, the cell's door creaked open and the sheriff stepped inside and beckoned to him. "Another word with ye, if ye please, Mr. Connors," he said with a weary drawl, and it was clear to Sean that the officer had gotten even less sleep over the course of the night than he and Rory had.

Sean rose hesitantly from his cot as O'Neill crossed to him with two sets of shackles in his hands.

"What are those for?" Sean asked defensively. "I've caused ye no trouble up to now, have I?"

O'Neill's expression became almost apologetic. "Indeed ye haven't, sir. None at all. It's just that there are some people here to see ye up in my office, and that's our policy, ye see, when visitors are about."

Sean scowled. "Visitors?"

"You'll see for yourself when we get up there," the sheriff replied, reaching out to Sean and shackling first his wrists and then his ankles.

"Take me, too," Rory shouted after them as the sheriff began leading Sean toward the door.

"No," Sean hissed back at him. "I shall return forthwith. Just lie there and be quiet."

Rory, looking amply scolded by Sean's fierce glare, flopped back resignedly on his cot and crossed his arms over his chest with huff.

"What manner of visitors might ye mean, sheriff?" Sean pursued in a low voice as the official led him down the cellar corridor and up the stairs to his office. "Rory and I have scarcely been in Kilkenny long enough to know anyone who might deign to pay us a call. Much less in gaol."

The sheriff's tone was pointed now as he answered. "Why don't we just wait to see if ye recognize 'em, Connors."

A wave of apprehension ran through Sean. He hadn't wanted to let his uneasiness show in front of Rory. No sense in getting him roiled until Sean knew for sure what was in store. But now that he was away from his volatile old friend, his feelings seemed to be coming to the fore.

His trepidation gave way to amazement, however, as the sheriff ushered him up to his office door seconds later and swung it open before him.

Inside he saw Heather, flanked by two well-dressed men, and just to the right of them, stood a yellow-haired lass who appeared to be about Heather's age.

Another quick scan of their faces confirmed for Sean that the man to Heather's left was Malcolm Byrne, and the man to her right had to be Brian Monaghan. His wrinkled face said that he was well along in years, and the periwig he wore seemed to be about the same as the one Sean had spotted on the master of the manor the night before.

Having established this, Sean's eyes returned to Heather, and they focused upon her for as long as he dared let them.

She was now wearing a staid ensemble of light blue and tan, and her hair was swept up into a haphazard bun. It was as though she'd been forced to dress rather hurriedly for this trip into town. . . . But of course she had been, Sean realized. If, indeed, she had made it back to the manor last night without being caught in the act, she must still have been roused at some dreadfully early hour in order to get herself dressed and off to the sheriff by this time.

Sean swallowed dryly, his eyes still locked upon hers in that instant, and he hoped to God that that was all that had happened—that she hadn't been caught trying to make it back to her room and, therefore, grilled about whether or not she was still chaste.

There was no knowing for certain, however, no solid answer in her eyes. He saw only a glimmer of sympathy in them. Just a faint tearful twinkle, and then her gaze dropped to her feet.

Sean, in turn, shifted his stare to Byrne, meeting his venomous expression with one of innocent detachment. But Sean knew that no matter how much guiltlessness he managed to feign, the hostile energy that ran between them couldn't be denied. What was more, he saw that Byrne knew this, too.

Not wishing to risk letting his eyes communicate anything more to Byrne, Sean brought them to light upon the innocuous-looking blonde on the far right. To his dismay, however, he saw, upon this closer examination, that she wasn't as innocuous as she seemed. She was, in fact, the same girl who'd been standing with Heather and Jennifer at the Cassidys' barn dance. And suddenly, it all became clear to Sean. The young ladies had come here in order to confirm his identity, to verify that he was, indeed, the same man who had been disguised as a strawboy at the wedding dance and who had later ridden off with Jennifer Plithe.

It was almost too devastating to be believed. Here

was the very woman he had held in his arms, not ten hours earlier, come, with her girl friend, to bear witness against him now.

Had she gotten caught trying to sneak back up to her bedchamber? he wondered again. Had she been forced to betray him in order to save herself? Or far worse, had her encouragement of his attentions been part of some sort of complicated web from the start? Had she told him how to find her room simply to enable Byrne and the sheriff to follow them both back to his cottage and drop the net over him?

This last possibility didn't stand to reason, though. Not when he considered how far Heather had allowed him to take things the night before. Not when he thought about how she'd clung to him, almost begging him to finish the job and lay claim to her as the threesome had first been heard approaching. Not even now as she'd looked at him, her eyes shining with sympathy.

But what if it hadn't been sympathy at all? What if what he'd seen in them had instead been mere apology? Maybe she'd simply wanted him to know that she deeply regretted having to do what she was about to.

Sean fixed his gaze at last upon the man he believed to be Brian Monaghan. He searched, as surreptitiously as possible, for any indication of rage or indignation. Anything that might confirm that this was a man who had reason to believe that his daughter's virtue had been compromised in the past twenty-four hours.

To Sean's relief, he saw none. He'd become quite expert at reading men's expressions through the years—both blatant and covert. It was a skill that had saved him more than once in the dens of thieves that he and Pat had frequented. And he was as certain as he could be now that Brian Monaghan was simply doing what was expected of him by his right-hand man. It was clear that his interest in seeing Sean convicted was not a particularly personal one.

Nevertheless, what choice did Heather have? Sean thought sadly. Here she stood before him, with her wealthy, powerful father on one side of her and a vengeful would-be betrothed on the other. Surely she could expect some form of retribution if she didn't act in accordance with their wishes now.

But just as Sean was considering running the risk of looking at her again, flashing her a gaze that said he understood her plight, it seemed the decision was made for him. He felt the sheriff reach around from behind him and turn and lift his chin until he was looking squarely at Heather once more.

"Devil take ye, girl! Look at him," Byrne snarled, and to Sean's dismay, the ruffian reached out to her and jerked her chin up as well.

Under any other circumstances, Sean would have seized Byrne for his manhandling. He would have finished the job he'd started in shooting him two nights earlier. But this was clearly not the wisest time and place. So, with great restraint, he held himself back, and clenching his teeth, he met Heather's forced gaze with one of his own.

To his surprise, her eyes narrowed discerningly in those seconds, as though she was honestly trying to study his features. Then she spoke in a calculating tone, like that of an emotionless empress. "Have him say a word or two for me, if ye please."

Sean felt the sheriff jostle him. "Do as you're told, Mr. Connors!"

"But what should I say?" Sean asked awkwardly. "I've never laid eyes upon this woman."

"*Well?*" Malcolm prompted, forcing Heather's chin even farther upward.

To Sean's amazement, Heather jerked free of him in those seconds and began brushing her chest and shoulders off, as though wishing to free herself of the very scent of him as well. "The same is true for me," she brayed. "I've never seen him before. . . . His hair is like the strawboy's with whom I danced. But that's where it ends, I'm afraid. His eyes and voice are wrong," she concluded crisply. And with that, she went over and stood on the other side of her father, as if seeking his protection.

"And you, Miss Kennedy?" the sheriff asked. "Does he look at'all familiar?"

"Well, I . . . I don't know, sir," the girl stammered nervously. "I mean . . . I wasn't the one who danced with him."

Sean saw Heather turn to Shannon in that instant and flash his what appeared, from Heather's profile view of Heather, to be a glower.

"Um . . . but I don't think it's him, sheriff," Shannon quickly added.

O'Neill's tone was deathly serious as he spoke again. "Now you're sure of that, lass?"

Shannon nodded.

"Say it aloud, girl, for the record," the sheriff ordered.

"It's . . . it's not," she stammered again. "He's not the same man," she concluded firmly.

"Very well, Mr. Byrne. It seems we have our answer then," O'Neill said with a resigned sigh.

Byrne looked aghast at this. "But ye can't let him go!"

"Well, I haven't enough evidence to go on holdin' him, don't ye see? The only two people who got close enough to that strawboy to make a definite identification say this is not your man, and I'm compelled to believe 'em. So, unless ye can bring forth another witness of that sort, sir, and mighty quickly, I'll have to set Mr. Connors free."

Byrne exhaled an exasperated breath. "How much longer can ye give me?"

The sheriff took several seconds to answer. "A day, maybe. But that's it," he said firmly.

"A day it is then, sheriff," Byrne replied, his air clearly a determined one.

Chapter 13

The scenery outside Heather's coach window seemed to flash by in a blur as they rode back to the Kennedys' estate to drop Shannon off a short time later. Shannon was seated at Heather's side, while Malcolm and Master Monaghan sat across from them in the cab. And the few times when Heather dared to glance about at each of them, she saw that their gazes were all equally locked upon their respective windows.

None of them had said more than a word or two since they'd left the gaol, and now the air within the coach seemed almost too heavy with unvoiced rage to be breathable.

Heather's good sense told her to just keep quiet. She and Shannon had done all they could to help Sean, and there was nothing to be gained by provoking her father and Malcolm any further.

In spite of herself, however, she felt the angry lump in her throat beginning to swell and slip up into her mouth, and she didn't know how much longer she'd be able to hold her tongue.

"Ye had no right askin' the sheriff to gaol that man

for another day," she heard herself say finally, her glare fixed squarely upon Malcolm. This was the first time she'd ever dared to confront him in front of her father, but she found she didn't care about the consequences now.

Malcolm met her glare with a furious squint. "And the pair of you had no right lyin' about who he was. But ye did it none the less, now didn't ye?"

"Ah, come now," Brian Monaghan interjected uneasily. "Let's not go blurtin' things to one another that we might later regret. . . . I'm sure the girls said what they believed to be true," he added in a diplomatic tone.

"Well, I'm not," Byrne retorted, directing his gaze out his window once more.

"But think about it, Malcolm. Jennifer was as close as a sister to them. Don't ye think they'd have spoken up if they truly thought that man to be one of her kidnappers?"

"Who knows *what* goes on in the minds of such titterin' adolescents? After seein' how flushed with bliss your daughter looked when she danced with that rogue the other night, it wouldn't surprise me in the least to learn that she's harborin' him in her wardrobe!"

"Ah, don't be ridiculous, Malcolm. Heather knows perfectly well that she's soon to be promised to you."

"I know nothin' of the sort," Heather declared, again in a heedless outburst, and the terrible silence that followed was enough to cause all four of them to turn and stare out their adjacent windows again.

"Now, we've talked about this many times, daughter," Monaghan returned in a low growl, "and it's

256

been decided that you and Malcolm will make a very good match."

"I haven't decided it, you have," she shot back, scarcely able to believe her continued boldness on the subject. "I've never been able to bear the sight of him. But of course, no one's asked me how I feel in the matter. For if ye had, you'd know by now that I have no intentions of even speakin' to that monster again, much less marryin' him!"

Before returning her gaze to the passing countryside, Heather chanced to look over at Shannon, and she saw that her face was as pale as a cloud. *Fear,* she realized. Her friend wasn't blushing at the confrontation, as she would have expected her to be. Rather, her face was drained of all color, as though she believed Heather had just signed her own death warrant.

"We'll discuss this when we get home," Brian Monaghan replied, and Heather had no problem identifying the looks on both of the men's faces as those of blind fury.

She settled back against the coach seat with an uneasy swallow. She'd finally said all she'd wanted to say, finally found the nerve to let her father know that his matrimonial plans for her were quite unacceptable, and to her surprise, she felt profound relief at having done so. It was as though a crushing weight had been lifted from her. She'd had no idea how wonderfully liberating really speaking her mind to her father could feel.

She sensed, however, that a whole other set of feelings hovered very nearby for her. Regret and fear came rushing to mind, for instance.

The reason for the regret was obvious. It was only natural to feel that things would have gone better for her had she managed to keep her mouth shut for just a day or two longer. Surely, in that time, she reasoned, Sean would be released and he would have been able to come and rescue her once more from her entanglement with Malcolm.

The reason for her prospective fear didn't seem quite so clear, however. She'd always known her father to be softhearted where she was concerned. She had usually been able to manipulate him with relative ease, and he had certainly never resorted to punishing her in any way. Yet judging from the looks on the faces all about her now, she was beginning to think that might change soon. Malcolm was her father's most prized worker, after all, a man who supported his every decision and plan. She, on the other hand, was merely her father's ward, someone who was sure to cost him much more than she was apt to glean—especially if she continued to refuse the marital arrangement that he thought most beneficial.

"I . . . I'm sorry, Malcolm," she said suddenly, doing her best to sound as contrite as she felt. "I'm sure you and Father only want what's best for me and for the mines, but I simply can't agree to marry ye. I hope you'll find it in your heart to understand."

Malcolm looked over at her for just an instant as she spoke, his face registering a mix of surprise and disgust. Then he turned and stared out his window once more.

She, therefore, shifted her gaze to her father, and she was amazed to see that he didn't appear any more appeased by her words than Malcolm had. Indeed, all she saw on his face in those seconds was amazement. It was as though he couldn't believe that, in her wildest dreams, she thought she possessed the right to refuse the man he had chosen for her.

He pursed his lips, and his next words were more like lightning bolts shooting from his enraged eyes than any kind of utterance. "I said we'll discuss all of this when we get home, daughter, and not a moment sooner!"

In accordance with Master Monaghan's wishes, not another word was spoken as they rode—not on the subject of Heather and Malcolm's engagement or any other. And as they reached the Kennedys' manor and Heather watched Shannon climb out of the coach, she felt as though she was losing hold of the last person who could possibly save her from what was in store.

Once they arrived home, Heather was sent straight to her bedchamber, and though her father didn't say as much, she knew that he and Malcolm would proceed to the study and attempt to sort matters out.

She thought, however fleetingly, about sneaking back downstairs and trying to listen to their conversation through the study door. She knew, however, that her father would be even more furious with her if she were caught eavesdropping. So she stayed in her room as ordered and, pressing an ear to her floorboards, attempted in vain to hear what was being said one story below.

This was her last chance, a voice within her warned. If she didn't want to find herself wed to Malcolm *or* having to endure whatever punishment he and her father decided was fitting in exchange for her refusal of him, she would have to pack a satchel, climb down her tree, and be off to Sean's cottage at once.

The only problem was that Sean was still in gaol, and according to the sheriff, he would be until at least tomorrow night. She could go and hide in his cottage, however, she supposed. She could await his return and pray that Malcolm and her father wouldn't think to look for her there.

But what if the sheriff's men were still watching the place? she thought uneasily. She'd only end up falling into their hands and, thereby, invalidating her claim that she'd never laid eyes upon Sean before. And that, in turn, would jeopardize him all the more.

So, she'd simply have to stay put, she told herself finally. No matter what fate lay ahead for her, she couldn't bring herself to put Sean or his friend in any further danger.

Malcolm sat before the desk in his employer's study, his lips drawn together in a wounded pucker and his arms crossed angrily over his chest. "Ye heard me, sir," he said. "I don't care to continue workin' for a man who breaks his word or allows his daughter to do so. I think I've suffered enough humiliation for one day, havin' to stand there before the sheriff and hear those two petticoats call me a liar. I hardly think I deserved to have your daughter renounce me right there in front of her friend as well!"

"But she . . . she didn't renounce ye really, Malcolm," Monaghan countered gingerly. "I mean, she'll still be wed to ye, if I have aught to say about it."

Malcolm rolled his eyes, doing his best to keep his tone a civil one. "Aye, but that's just it, Brian, isn't it. Ye never seem to have aught to say about anythin' where Heather is concerned. Everyone from here to Coleraine knows ye let her walk all over ye. And don't ye see you've only made matters worse for her husband . . . whoever he might be, by not keepin' a tight enough rein on the girl. Why, when ye get right down to it, havin' a wife who doesn't obey is like havin' a horse who refuses to let ye ride him! Absolutely worthless!"

Monaghan was silent for several seconds. "Aye. I suppose you're right," he said finally.

"Well, I'm only thinkin' of Heather's good, after all," Malcolm continued, sitting forward in his chair and feeling more enthusiasm, now that his boss seemed to be listening to reason. "I mean, what's to become of her when you're gone? She'll need me well enough then, won't she. She doesn't know the first thing about runnin' those mines, and a bloody lot of good it would do any of us to try to teach her. Women weren't created for that sort of work anyway. Let 'em tend to children and cookin', and things that they know . . . I mean, all I'm sayin' is that someone's got to care enough about that lass to see to it she learns to take life seriously before 'tis too late. Those mines have never been run on whims, after all, and I for one don't care to wait and see what idiot husband she'll win to help me with the runnin' of 'em, once you've retired." Feeling confident that he had Monaghan's full attention now, Malcolm rose and began to pace solemnly across the room's painted floorcloth. "I mean, our design from the first, Brian, was that I would marry Heather when she came of age. And eighteen is age enough in the minds of most, is it not?"

Monaghan furrowed his brow with obvious concern. "Ah, but ye heard her, Malcolm. She'll be nothin' but trouble to ye with the way she feels."

Malcolm, feeling challenged by this, met his employer's gaze with an expression that said he was equal to the task. "But I could tame her. I've every confidence of it. After a month or two of marriage to me, I could have her so well forged that you'd scarcely know her, Brian. You have only to give me the chance."

Monaghan looked unconvinced of this. "I'm not sure it's possible, Malcolm. I've paid some of the finest tutors and finishin' schools in Europe to do so, and I'm sorry to say that she's still the same, willful daughter to whom my dear wife gave birth."

"But don't ye see? Mere chidin' doesn't work with a lass like her. You must take a switch to her! If your words don't seem to go into her ears, then you must take her over your knee and beat some good sense and obedience into the other end of her!"

Monaghan was clearly taken aback by this suggestion. "Ah, I couldn't," he replied, shaking his head. "I could never bring myself to do that. She's my only child, after all, and I don't think I could bear to see her suffer."

Malcolm gave forth a dry laugh. "Suffer, ye say?

A simple thrashin' would be nothin' compared to how she'll suffer when you're no longer here to look after her . . . to set right what she does wrong."

Monaghan shook his head once more. "Aye, but I couldn't, Malcolm. I tell ye, I just couldn't."

"Well, *I* could, sir," he said boldly. "I could and I will, if you'll permit me."

"Yes, but it wouldn't be proper. A man not even formally betrothed to her yet, seein' her bared?"

Malcolm couldn't help laughing a bit at the man's callowness in such matters. It was clear that Monaghan didn't know the first thing about raising a child—be it male or female. Malcolm, on the other hand, did. He'd seen enough of his brothers and sisters caned in his youth to know exactly how such procedures were handled. "She needn't be bared, Brian. A switch can sting well enough through a shift to get your point across. And frankly," he concluded, folding his arms over his chest once more, "I shall refuse to come back to the mines until I see such punishment meted out to her! Her lies today before the sheriff will probably help to let a guilty man go free. And that, coupled with her hostile remarks about me in the coach, seems cause enough for me to bring action against ye, in any case. So I hardly think it unfair of me to request that she, at the very least, be properly punished."

Monaghan was silent for several seconds. He folded his hands and pressed his thumbs to his lower lip, staring down pensively at his desk blotter all the while.

"If you'll pardon me for sayin' so, it seems to me that none of us is thinkin' too clearly at present," he said finally. "Perhaps, if given a bit of time, even Heather will come to her senses and change her mind about marryin' ye. I ask, therefore, that ye give me a day or two before we decide to punish her. What say ye to that, lad?" he asked with a hopeful smile.

Malcolm didn't want to wait even ten more minutes to see justice carried out on his behalf. He wanted to storm upstairs to Heather's room and thrash her right then and there. But seeing his employer's entreating expression in those seconds, he couldn't bring himself to refuse this offer of compromise. Some part of him knew how difficult it was for a softling like Monaghan to finally assert himself with the daughter he'd spent the past two decades pampering.

"Very well," he replied after a moment. "A day or two more. But if the lass hasn't had a change of heart in that time, I'll hold ye to punishin' her, Brian. Mind ye, I will!"

Because Malcolm Byrne was apparently unable to produce another witness in the time the sheriff had allowed, Sean and Rory were set free the following evening. They rode back to their cottage with great haste, and once Sean had dismounted his steed, he handed it over to Rory and made a beeline for the back cistern. He circled around it, finally coming to a point at its base where there was a tiny mound of loose dirt. Then, mumbling a prayer of thanks, he dropped to his knees and began digging feverishly.

Rory, always one for nosing in on such undertakings, came and stood over him a couple minutes later. "What are ye doin' then?" he asked blankly.

"Did ye put the horses away?"

"Aye."

"I'm diggin' for the Plithe dowry."

"Ye are? Here in our own back yard?"

"Yes, Rory. Ye know the procedure. We've told it to ye a hundred times. We send our ransom note to the parents of the bride. They deliver the dowry money to a spot of our choosin'. We hire some street urchin to pick it up several hours later. That urchin passes the money on to another and that one to another, until it finally finds its way to our place."

"Oh, aye," Rory replied, as though completely re-enlightened. "I remember now. Ye have it sewn up in a pouch bearin' the seal of the bride's family so you'll know if any of your little hirelin's tried to open it and discover what was in it. Gives some work to the poor ragamuffins, just like you and Pat was," he concluded, reciting this last sentence as if by rote.

Sean smiled up at him for an instant. Then he returned to his digging. "That's right. That's it exactly. Now, let's just hope the little beggars followed through while we were off in gaol. *And* that the sheriff wasn't keepin' the place under too close a watch in that time."

"Aye . . . but Sean, I thought ye told the sheriff we had no part in snatchin' Miss Plithe."

Sean turned and scowled up at him. "Of course, ye daft bugger. Was I supposed to tell him we did have? What was it ye always told Pat and me when we were lads?"

Rory had to give this question some thought.

"Never to tell the truth if ye think it's goin' to get ye into trouble?" he offered tentatively.

"Right again! So, I was just followin' your good counsel, ye see." Sean's words came to a triumphant rise now as he dug an inch or two deeper and finally spotted the edge of what appeared to be a burlap pouch.

"That ye were, I guess."

"That I was," Sean declared, and an instant later, he thrust the packet up into the air with a victorious whoop. "Ah, Saints be praised, here it is at last! My retirement and a new beginnin' for you and Pat! Let's go in and count it beside a cracklin' fire!"

The two of them slipped into the cottage's back door a moment later, and Sean told Rory to go on ahead and search the place for any intruders, before either of them said another word.

Rory returned to the larder a couple minutes later with the report that they were alone, and Sean followed him into the fire room and set the pouch on the dining table.

Hearing the packet touch down, Rory turned back to him with an eager expression. "Let *me* help ye count through it this time, Sean . . . bein' that Pat's not here."

"Ah, now, we all know that you're not really one for cipherin' anymore, Rory," Sean answered charily. "You're much better at buildin' fires, if ye ask me."

Rory looked only a trifle disappointed at this response. "Ah, should I do that then? Should I get a fire goin'?"

"Aye. After two days in that chilly gaol, I think 'tis a grand idea."

Rory, accordingly, crossed to the hearth and, taking up the poker, began pushing the cinders aside so that fresh logs could be placed upon the andirons.

Sean, breathing a sigh of relief at the fact that his refusal hadn't caused Rory to lash out at him, crossed to the pantry and wiped his dirt-caked fingers on a stray serviette. Then he picked up a carving knife and returned to the table to slit the pouch open.

He sank into one of the dining chairs and began at once to inspect the packet. He was pleased to see that its four seams were tightly stitched and that the Plithe seal, which bound the length of ribbon wrapped about it, was unbroken.

He and Pat had never had to act on their threat of hanging any lad who tampered with the packet en route, and he was relieved to see that such a drastic measure was once again uncalled for It had to be remembered, however, that he and Patrick paid the little scamps marvelously well for their services—enough to feed them and any family members they had for a few years to come, so Sean supposed that it wasn't surprising that they had always kept their end of the agreement.

With one slash the coins came spilling out onto the table like a leprechaun's treasure.

"A good take, huh," Rory noted, turning back to face him with a broad smile.

"That it is. Pat will be very pleased, indeed."

Rory suddenly donned a vacant expression. "Where is Pat, by the way?"

Sean was about to tell him once again that he was still with the baker and Miss Plithe in Lismore, but he caught himself. It only stood to reason that what Rory wasn't able to recall, he wouldn't be able to convey to the sheriff, should he come sniffing around again. So Sean chose to gloss over the question. "He's off somewhere, drinkin'." That much, at least, probably wasn't far from the truth, Sean reasoned. "You know Pat. But I'm goin' to bring him home tomorrow mornin', and I'm takin' this money with me, so you won't be bothered with havin' to look after it."

Rory's look of confusion turned to one of concern. "Ah, but you'll return for me, won't ye? Ye aren't just goin' to leave me here alone forever, are ye now?"

Sean rose and crossed to his old friend to give his shoulder a reassuring pat. "Of course not. Don't be daft. We've no intentions of leavin' ye alone here or anywhere else for good and all. In fact, I think Pat wants ye to work with him on the next job."

Rory's eyes widened with disbelief. "He does?"

"Oh, aye. I think he'll be needin' ye more than ye know, to tell ye the truth."

After several seconds, Rory donned a gratified smile. "What? To steal some lassie, ye mean?"

"Precisely. But not until Pat says so, mind," Sean cautioned, shaking a finger at him. "After I've spoken with him, I'm sure he'll agree that it's time for us to move on to another town before startin' up the business again. I've just one more matter to attend to here, and then we'll be off."

Rory gave him a nod. "All right. We came frightenin'ly close with the sheriff this time, didn't we,

Sean?" he asked after a moment, as though the full implications of what they'd been through in the past couple days were only just dawning upon him.

"Aye, Rory. We did indeed."

Chapter 14

Before Sean even had the chance to dismount his horse, Patrick came darting out of the baker's cottage to holler at him.

"Where the hell have ye been?" he exclaimed, waving his fists over his head. "I've been waitin' for ye for *days!*"

"Calm yourself," Sean retorted, fighting a show of amusement as he got down from his horse and tied it to the baker's hitching post. "You're gettin' as bad as Rory with that temper of yours. I've got the money. It's just that we ran across a patch of trouble, is all."

"We? We who?" Pat demanded, looking only slightly allayed by his brother's response.

"Rory and I."

"Rory? What's he got to do with all of this?"

"Oh, nothin', I guess." With that, Sean walked up to his brother and, taking him by the arm, led him back toward the baker's front door. Not wanting anyone within to overhear him, however, he lowered his voice to almost a whisper as he spoke again. "It's just that he was sleepin' up in the loft when the sheriff came."

Pat's eyebrows flared with panic. "The *sheriff?*"

"Ah, 'twas nothin'. Believe me. He simply came 'round to see if I was the chap who wounded that black-haired swine who was shootin' at us as we left the Cassidys'."

"So ye claimed ye weren't, and he left. Right?"

"Well, we had to spend a wee bit of time in gaol over it, but aye, they let us go well enough. And they still seem to believe my name is Stephen Connors."

"Sweet Jesus! That's as close as we've come to the jaws of it, isn't it."

Though it bothered him to have to admit it once more, Sean nodded. Then an instant later, he felt a crushing pain in his upper arm, and he found himself lying on the ground beside the baker's walk.

"And all because you had to go and shoot at that bastard, ye blockhead!" Pat snarled down at him. "I should do a devil of a lot more than punch ye for it!"

Sean thought, for a fleeting second or two, about scrambling to his feet and ramming his brother's head into the front of the baker's cottage. That's what he would have done less than a week before. But he chose to ignore that impulse now. He'd told Pat that he was turning over a new leaf, and he knew that this was one of his golden opportunities to demonstrate that he'd meant it. So, drawing in a deep soothing breath, he rose to his feet once more and, with a wholly dignified air, brushed the bits of dead grass and gravel from his breeches.

"That really wasn't necessary, ye know. I told ye I dealt with the matter, and I did. We're both free men still, and what's more, we've got the Plithe dowry to show for it!"

Pat caught him by the sleeve as he turned to head up to the front stoop. "And how much did it come to? Did all of it look to be there?"

"Ten thousand guineas," Sean replied, continuing to whisper. "I counted each and every one of them myself last night. So that leaves quite a respectable sum for you and me."

Patrick still held him fast, obviously not yet ready to let him carry their conversation in to the baker and Miss Plithe. "Ye left our share behind, didn't ye?" he asked anxiously.

Sean shook his head.

Pat's hold upon him tightened to a bruising firmness. "Why not?"

"Because, with the sheriff nosin' about, I didn't dare to, ye dolt! Now let me loose, before I forget that I'm tryin' to be a gentleman and I flatten ye! And while you're so busy criticizin', I might hasten to note that you're stinkin' drunk again! Why, with that breath of yours, it's a wonder I couldn't smell ye clear back in Kilkenny! You should be ashamed, drinkin' that way in the presence of one of our clients!"

"And what else was there to do? Sittin' about in the man's cottage for three days, waitin' for you to get yourself out of gaol?"

"Well, try to sober up before we ride back, ye sot! 'Cause I'm tellin' ye, right here and now, that I've no intentions of tyin' ye to your horse again if you're too nappy to sit up and ride on your own."

With all of this settled, Sean turned on his heel and

went into the cottage. The scene he saw within was so heartwarming that he almost found it laughable. The baker was seated at the dining table, having what appeared to be a late breakfast, and his bride was standing beside him, pouring him a cup of tea.

"Good mornin' to ye, Mr. Kerry," O'Ryan greeted, smiling up at Sean. "We were just havin' a bit of breakfast, my beloved and I. Care to join us?"

Sean shook his head and returned the baker's smile. He continued to watch with a measure of disbelief, as Jennifer Plithe set the teapot down and took the chair beside her new husband—one of her pale slender hands finding its way into his, where it rested beside her on the table.

They were the picture of domestic bliss, what every man and woman hoped to achieve. And Sean found that, besides feeling happy for them now—even a bit self-congratulatory at having helped to bring them together—he was also experiencing a twinge of envy and regret that things had yet to go so smoothly for him and Heather.

"Come with my darlin's dowry then?" O'Ryan queried, his expression still mystifyingly complacent.

"I have," Sean answered, swallowing back his mix of emotions and striding to the table. He instantly realized, however, that his businesslike air could probably be considered uncouth amid this scene of marital harmony. So he tried to tone it down as he spoke again. "And quite a handsome one it is, too, Mr. O'Ryan. Even after our share. I think 'tis safe to say that you and your lovely bride and any children to come will live very well upon it."

273

To Sean's surprise, the baker held up a halting palm as he extended the money pouch to him.

"No. Give it to my sweet Jen, if ye will. In truth, it's much more hers than mine."

Sean, accordingly, moved to hand the packet to Jennifer instead. "No. No. Take it, Tiernan," she declared. "After all, 'twas you and not I who was clever enough to arrange our bein' brought together."

The baker hesitated for several seconds, and Sean's outstretched hand continued to hover between them.

"Ah well, Christ," Pat interjected, his words slurred where he still stood near the doorway. "I'll take it then if neither of ye wants it!"

Sean turned to glare at his brother's impudence, and before he could return his gaze to the table, he felt the pouch being lifted from his palm.

"Oh, very well, love," the baker said, nervously clearing his throat. "I'll take care of it for ye, if ye prefer. Perhaps 'tis for the best, since I've come to know so much more about the world of commerce than you have."

Jennifer reached out and patted her husband's forearm. "True enough, my dearest. You'll get no argument from me on that."

The couple smiled at one another, locking gazes for what seemed to Sean an interminable amount of time; and then O'Ryan turned and smiled at Sean once more. "We were wonderin', Jen and I, if you'd care to stay and attend our weddin' this afternoon."

Sean furrowed his brow. "Weddin'?"

The baker's cheeks flushed a bit. "Well, yes. We know that, in the eyes of the law and of Jennifer's parents, we're already married. But Jen's the romantic sort, ye see. Wanted it all blessed by the local priest. So anyway, we'd be honored to have ye present for it, bein' that it was the pair of ye who brought us together."

Sean drew in a long breath. Ordinarily he would probably have said yes to such a simple request. He would have considered it best for business to attend. Who knew, for instance, when the baker might scare up a bachelor friend who also wished to engage their services? But with things on such shaky ground in Kilkenny, and with Heather still being offered to that devil, Malcolm Byrne, he knew that he and Pat had to get back home at once and tie up their loose ends. "Ah, we can't, Mr. O'Ryan. But thank ye all the same. We've some pressin' business to attend to back in Kilkenny, so we really must be off. We'll certainly stay long enough, though, to see that you've counted your share of the dowry and you're satisfied that it's all there."

The baker suddenly donned an odd, almost ethereal smile, as though he'd just stepped into the gates of Heaven and all worldly cares were now behind him. "Oh, I won't bother with that, for ye see, durin' these last couple days and nights with Jen, I've come to realize that I'd have married her for free. . . . Such is the depth of our love for one another," he concluded, directing his dreamy expression at his bride once more.

She responded with a contented sigh.

"Ah, sweet Jesus," Pat muttered, coming up behind Sean and obviously doing his best not to be overheard. "Do ye see what I've had to abide while

275

you kept me waitin'? Nauseatin'! Why, 'tis enough to drive *any* man to drink!"

"Get your things, whatever ye brought with ye," Sean growled back. "And go saddle your horse."

"Well, it's none too soon for me," Pat snarled, stomping to the front door and slamming it after him as he made his exit.

Sean cleared his throat loudly in an attempt to interrupt the couple's mutual trancelike gazes. "All right, Mr. O'Ryan, as long as you two are sure you have all that's comin' to ye, I guess Pat and I will go away." He punctuated this by again stepping up to the table to seal their dealings with a handshake.

The baker rose with a smile and shook his hand. "We are, Mr. Kerry. And really, we do thank ye, from the depths of our hearts, for all ye did to make this possible."

Sean felt his cheeks warm a bit with continued embarrassment at having his dubious work elevated to the hallowed level of matchmaking. "You're quite welcome. And indeed, it is we who thank you for bein' a patron."

With that, Sean withdrew his hand, offered the couple a parting smile, and turned to leave the cottage. The last bit of business was concluded, and he could now officially say that he was done, for good and all, with bride snatching. This, of course, brought him a great sense of relief. It was, however, a very fleeting sentiment, given how precarious matters still were in Kilkenny.

Short of asking for his share of the Plithe dowry, Pat had scarcely said a word since they'd left Lismore, and Sean sensed as they rode home that it was more than the deadening effect of liquor that was keeping Pat so silent. The cause of it, most probably, was Sean's announcement that he was retiring from their partnership. Through the years, Sean had learned that his brother was the sort who didn't always react to bad news immediately. Rather, if the tidings were particularly disturbing, he'd silently stew about them, waiting until questioned to let the rage within him come shooting to the surface. Sean was, therefore, quite hesitant to open such a line of questioning. But then again, he reasoned, it was probably better to have it out now than to wait until they were with the ever-volatile Rory to discuss it. So with that in mind, Sean slowed his horse to a trot in the hopes of getting Pat's attention.

Apparently noticing how Sean was falling behind several seconds later, Pat brought his horse to a halt and turned around to face him. "What is it?" he called out irritably. "Has your horse gone lame?"

Sean shook his head, catching up with his brother once more. "No. I just want a word with ye before we reach Kilkenny. Away from Rory, I mean."

Pat clucked with exasperation and brought his horse to a walk. "Fine, then. Say what ye will. I can't promise ye I'll listen, though."

Keeping his horse's gait even with Pat's, Sean began to speak. "It's too dangerous to stay in Kilkenny much longer. What, with the sheriff watchin' us so closely now, I really do think we should gather our belongin's and head to another town."

Pat glared at him. "We, ye say? I wasn't aware ye thought of us as a 'we' anymore, little brother."

"Well, I mean the three of us. You and Rory and

277

me. We all stand to be brought down, after all, if even one of us should fall into the sheriff's hands again."

Pat kept his eyes directed steadily forward as they continued to ride, as though Sean was little more to him now than an annoying fly buzzing about his head. "And what about that green-eyed lass ye became so smitten with at the Cassidys'? Don't go tellin' me ye didn't have a taste or two of her while I was waitin' back at the baker's. I know ye better than that," he added, flashing him a biting smirk.

"That ye do," Sean conceded. "And in truth, I am plannin' on takin' her with us when we leave."

"A good dowry, then?" Pat asked, his tone, as if out of habit, becoming markedly businesslike.

Sean smiled. "Enormous, from the looks of things. But that's not why I want her. I simply love her, ye see. I honestly don't think I can go on without her."

Pat groaned. "Ah, Lord! If you're goin' to start talkin' like those two fools back in Lismore, I'm speedin' up, pup! I can't bear another word of that rubbish!"

Sean waved a palm at him. "Oh, no. No I won't. I promise. I've said all I'm goin' to say about her. I'm just tryin' to let ye know that, given what happened with the sheriff, I think all three of us would be wise to leave Kilkenny as soon as possible."

Pat was silent for several seconds. Then he turned back to Sean with an icy expression. "Well, let me tell ye somethin'. The night ye came to me and declared that you were retirin' from our partnership was the night ye gave up any further say in how it's seen to. As it happens, Rory and I have a job or two yet to do in Kilkenny. Perhaps ye think we've tapped all the riches there are to be had there, but I don't. I'm the master now, and what I say goes!"

"Ah, but you're drunk, Pat," Sean noted cautiously. "Why don't ye wait till you've had a meal and some rest before tryin' to make a final decision on it?"

"I'm still sober enough to remember that you forsook me, Sean Kerry. That ye washed your hands of Rory and me the other night with all your grand talk about wantin' to find a more honorable profession for yourself. And now I'm holdin' ye to those words!"

"But I wasn't washin' my hands of you and Rory, don't ye see? I just don't want to take part in the business anymore. I mean, I'll help ye find new clients and brides. But the actual abductions . . . well, I just don't want to have a hand in them henceforth."

Pat pursed his lips. "Oh, aye. None of the perilous parts for you anymore. Right, ye blue blood?" he exclaimed. "Well, I'm in charge now, and I say that if ye don't take part in all of it, ye take part in none of it! And that's it, for good and all!"

Pat spurred his horse on to a run, and Sean made no effort to catch up with him. Perhaps it would be possible to reason with him later. In the meantime, however, Sean knew it was best to just let him be.

For his own part, Sean would simply ride back to Kilkenny as well, collect his horse from the smithy, and go off to fetch Heather. Even if he couldn't persuade Pat that it was time to get out of town, there was still some hope of saving himself, and he knew he owed it to Heather to act upon it.

* * *

Although he'd been unable to produce another witness against "Stephen Connors" in the time the sheriff had specified, Malcolm Byrne still hadn't given up on the task. He had continued to stop in at the local taverns and other places of business in the last couple days, and he had heard through the grapevine that there was at least one man in Kilkenny who could positively identify the Kerry brothers. This gentleman, a Mr. Tomas McCarty, had purportedly been tracking the Kerrys from town to town for quite some time.

The sheriff seemed to have no knowledge of the fellow; but Malcolm assumed that this was because McCarty was said to be a bounty hunter from a county to the north. It stood to reason, therefore, that he wouldn't care to make his presence known to any other branch of the law and thereby risk having to share the credit for the eventual capture of the bride snatchers.

Enough nosing about at Finney's Pub had gleaned Malcolm not only the gentleman's name, but the number of the room which he was apparently occupying at the inn down the street, and Malcolm went there directly, making certain he had enough guineas with him to help loosen Mr. McCarty's tongue.

To Malcolm's surprise, it was not a young, rugged-looking sort who answered his knock a few minutes later. Rather, it was a white-haired old gentleman, who appeared a bit pained at having been caused to rise and come to the door.

"Mr. McCarty is it, sir?" Malcolm greeted with an unaccustomed smile.

The man looked rather taken aback, as though a caller was the last thing he'd expected. "Yes."

Malcolm reached out to shake his hand. "Malcolm Byrne. I'm a foreman at the local coal mines."

McCarty still looked dumbfounded as he shook Malcolm's hand. "Pleased to meet you. What is it that brings you here?"

"Well, 'tis hardly somethin' to be talked of in a corridor, sir. Do ye think that I might come in for a moment or two?"

McCarty appeared hesitant, but after a few seconds, he stepped aside and gestured for Byrne to enter. Then, to Malcolm's relief, he shut the door and came to join him in the suite's drawing room.

"Have a seat, Mr. Byrne. May I get you something to drink?"

Malcolm settled back into one of the nearby wainscot chairs and smiled up at him. "No. Thank ye kindly. As I said, I'll only take a few minutes of your time."

McCarty, apparently not wanting to pour anything for himself either, sank down in a chair across from him. "All right then."

"Ye see, sir, my visit has to do with the two bride snatchers who made off with Miss Plithe the other night. Ye did hear about that abduction, did ye not?"

McCarty shrugged. "Of course. Who hasn't? Kilkenny seems filled with talk of it these days."

"Well, that's why I've come here. I mean, if I might be so bold, rumor has it that ye came to Kilkenny to hunt those two villains down."

McCarty looked rather surprised by this. Then the corners of his mouth turned up with apparent amusement. "Oh, yes? Is that so?"

"Indeed it is, sir. More specifically, 'tis said that you are a bounty hunter from some county to the north."

He laughed. "Is it really so obvious? I had prided myself on being less conspicuous than that," he added in a slightly wounded tone.

"Well, yes. It is odd that the townsfolk would assign such a title to ye. Ye look and speak more like a nobleman than any sort of deputy, if ye ask me."

McCarty laughed again. "Looks can be deceptive, can't they, Mr. Byrne."

"That they can, sir. That they can. And that's precisely why I've come. It's because the Kerry brothers are such masters of disguise that I've come to ask if you might know them on sight. That is, if ye saw them out of their strawboy masks."

McCarty shrugged again. "I might. And then again, I might not," he answered evenly. "Why do you ask?"

"Well, not to cut into your bounty money, certainly," Malcolm assured. "The truth is I don't care who nets 'em. I simply want to see it done. But I need someone like you to help identify 'em. Someone who's seen 'em out of their masks and would know 'em on the street. Might that be you, sir?" he asked anxiously. "Are you the man I seek?"

McCarty picked up a tobacco pipe from the butterfly table beside him and began examining its bowl. It was as though he hoped that feigning a sudden interest in it would somehow hide the fact that he was actually weighing the pros and cons of collaborating with Malcolm.

"Truly," Malcolm began again, "I have no interest in whatever bounty money ye may have comin' to ye, and ye have my word that I'll testify before any official in the land that it was, indeed, you and not the sheriff who apprehended the Kerrys, if you'll only agree to come with me and identify 'em."

McCarty sat forward in his chair, his face registering great interest. "Come with you where?"

"Well, to the Kerrys' cottage, of course."

"You know where they live?" he asked, clearly surprised to hear it.

"Aye, sir. If, in fact, these men are the Kerrys, I certainly do. Don't you?" Malcolm inquired, equally surprised to hear that a man who had supposedly been following them for so long did not possess such information.

McCarty shook his head. "Can't say that I do, Mr. Byrne. I mean, I'd have arrested them by now, wouldn't I, if I knew just where to find them."

"Aye," Malcolm conceded, feeling duly embarrassed. "How daft of me. But of course ye would have." An instant later, he sat back in his chair and donned a satisfied expression. "Well, then. It seems we'll each be doin' the other a good turn in this, doesn't it."

McCarty smiled. "Yes it does. But you still haven't told me what particular interest you have in seeing the Kerrys captured, Mr. Byrne. Are you kin to Miss Plithe?"

"No. I was simply one of the men who saw her hied off at the Cassidys', and I led the chase a few minutes later. And while doin' so, one of the Kerrys turned back and shot at me. Wounded me," he added in a quavering voice, slipping back his waistcoat and shirt so that McCarty could see the bandage on his shoulder.

McCarty leaned forward and politely eyed the dressing. Then he nodded sympathetically, biting his bottom lip as though he were tempted to laugh for some reason.

Malcolm felt his face redden a bit, and he quickly slid his garments back over his wound. It must have seemed rather childish to a lawman, he realized, making such a fuss over what was so obviously a mere flesh wound. "Well, it bled somethin' fierce," he added defensively.

McCarty nodded again, continuing to bite his lip. "I fancy it did. They can smart, those shoulder wounds."

"Have ye had one then, sir?"

"A few. So, 'tis on your own behalf, as well as Miss Plithe's, that you seek the Kerrys?"

"Aye. And because . . ." Malcolm's words broke off as he realized that what he was about to say might also sound rather petty to one as hardened as a bounty hunter.

"Because," McCarty echoed in a tone that said he expected full disclosure from Malcolm in exchange for his agreement to participate in whatever he had in mind.

"Well, it may strike ye as a bit triflin' on my part, but one of the Kerrys . . . Sean, I believe it was. Well, he seemed to take a fancy at the weddin' dance to a woman to whom I am soon to be betrothed."

McCarty's face reflected great interest once more, and again he seemed to be fighting a smile. "Oh, did ye now?"

"He did, indeed. And I must tell ye that I didn't find it the slightest bit amusin'."

McCarty sobered, evidently out of a sense of courtesy. "No. I don't suppose I would have either, Mr. Byrne, had I been in your place. . . . And so, this young lady of yours. Who might she be? That is, if ye don't mind my asking."

Malcolm scowled. "I don't know that it has much to do with all of this, sir. But seein' as how it was who brought her up, I guess 'tis only polite to answer ye. She's my employer's daughter, Miss Heather Monaghan."

McCarty nodded. "Ah, yes. Your employer's daughter, and you said you work at the mines, which would seem to indicate that the young lady promises a considerable dowry."

Malcolm again felt embarrassed, but he did his damnedest not to let it show. "Aye."

McCarty turned his palms upward. "Thus the bride snatcher's interest in her, you see."

Malcolm nodded; but in truth, he really hadn't thought about it from quite that angle before. It hadn't occurred to him that Kerry's interest in Heather could have been purely a professional one, that he had simply been sizing her up as his next quarry for another client. Malcolm had focused fully upon the desirous gazes that had passed between the two of them as they'd concluded their dance. Consequently, he'd viewed the bride snatcher solely as a rival for Heather's hand.

"No. His interest seemed a good deal more personal than that," Malcolm said bitterly.

"Well, in that case, your interest in seeing him and his brother finally brought to justice makes a great deal more sense to me. I understand it entirely, sir, and I am, therefore, more willing to put faith in your claim that you will see me credited with their capture before any of your local officials are."

Malcolm rose, smiling at this, and stepping forward, reached out to shake McCarty's hand on the agreement. "Splendid. Will this evenin' be soon enough for me to come back here and lead ye to 'em then?"

McCarty rose as well and nodded. "It will, sir. At what hour?"

"After dark. I think that best, with the sheriff keepin' such close watch over everythin' these days. Will eight o'clock be agreeable?"

"It will," McCarty confirmed, seeing him to the door. "And thank you for calling upon me, Mr. Byrne."

"Not at'all, sir. My thanks to you as well."

Malcolm felt a warm glow spreading within him as he made his way back down to the street minutes later. He had, at last, found someone who could positively identify the Kerrys and who, moreover, had a vested interest in doing so. To top it off, he was going now to personally see to it that justice was served to his vixenish bride-to-be. Something he'd been looking forward to for a very long time.

He just couldn't help smiling. If matters went as

lanned, he was about to be completely avenged—
eeing Heather and that rogue, to whom she'd
eemed so attracted, both receive their due punish-
nent in the same day.

Chapter 15

Sean knew it was risky, attempting to fetch Heather again in broad daylight, but he also knew there were risks with waiting until after dark to do so. He'd encountered enough men like Malcolm Byrne to realize that they weren't easily shaken off. He sensed that, even if the sheriff didn't care to pursue his arrest any further, Byrne did, and he'd do everything in his power to see Sean brought to justice. So, after purchasing a hooded cloak in Kilkenny town and picking up his reshod steed at the smithy's, Sean raced off to Monaghan Manor.

As on his first visit there, he chose to tie his horse, as well as his newly reclaimed steed, to a tree, well away from the estate, and proceed the rest of the way on foot. Again he hoped that this precaution would prevent anyone from hearing or seeing him approach. He also put the hood up on his cloak so that if he was spotted, his identity wouldn't be revealed.

Once he reached the thicket near the oak that led up to Heather's room, he stood studying the place for a minute or two, listening for any telltale sounds from within. There were none. So, clenching his teeth with a do-or-die sort of spirit, he dashed to the old oak and began climbing it.

When his eyes became level with Heather's window, he clung to the tree's trunk and stared through the diamond-shaped panes for several seconds. He hoped to catch sight of Heather, hoped to find her in there alone, eagerly awaiting his return for her.

It seemed he'd done nothing but rush about, attending to business, since the sheriff had set him free. But now, at last, he was finally getting back to his beloved Heather, and he hoped, with all his heart, that she'd welcome him and sneak out with him much more willingly than she had a few nights before.

But perhaps she didn't realize that he'd intended to come back for her, a small voice within him suggested. God knew there had seemed no safe way for him to get word to her that he wouldn't leave Kilkenny without her. So he hadn't tried. He'd simply assumed that the look in his eyes at the gaol had made it known to her. He'd merely let the hours, the days, tick by, never once giving thought to the possibility that Malcolm Byrne could have pressured her into marrying him in that time.

But that didn't seem likely. Only a day or so had passed since the sheriff had released him and Rory, and surely nothing that drastic could have happened in such a short while. He was just tired, he concluded, worn-down by the difficulties of the past couple days.

One glimpse of Heather, any shred of evidence that she was nearby, would be enough to reassure him that all was still well with her, he told himself.

Yet as much as he sought it, there was no stirring in her chamber now, no noise to confirm that she was anywhere within.

So, he'd go in search of her if necessary, he suddenly decided. She'd ruddy well been kept waiting long enough! And with a kind of recklessness, he ventured out onto the limb to his right and jumped up to catch hold of the branch that hung just overhead.

With a thrust or two, he was able to touch his feet to the window, and one stomp was all it took for the two sashes to separate and open to him.

He began swinging from his waist again, building up the momentum he needed to propel himself inside. Once he attained it, he let go of the overhead branch, and he slipped into the room, landing beneath the window with a surprisingly quiet thud.

He froze, listening intently for anything that would indicate that someone had heard him and was coming to investigate. Thankfully, there was nothing of the sort. And having established this, he looked down and finally realized why his entrance had been such a soundless one. He was lying on a *gown,* a thick nest of billowy satin, and as he slowly rose and got a better look at the garment, he saw that it was, without a doubt, Heather's size.

He furrowed his brow as he continued to study it. He hadn't thought Heather the sort to leave such costly apparel lying about on the floor. She was, he'd learned, a bit of a tease and rather spoiled—two traits he'd come to find strangely attractive in women through the years. But he'd been given no reason to think of her as slovenly as well, and he sensed that something was very amiss in the Monaghan household. Before he had an instant more to ponder it all, however, he heard footsteps approaching from the corridor. He freed his feet from the tangle of clothing and hurried into the adjacent wardrobe, leaving one of its doors just far enough ajar so he could peer out between its hinges.

To his delight, he saw that it was Heather who entered the bedchamber an instant later. She was wearing nothing but a shift, and she was, fortunately, alone, unaccompanied by any sort of governess or handmaid.

Probably about to dress for dinner, Sean surmised. Why else would she be wearing nothing but a shift at such an hour? But just as he was about to step out of the wardrobe with a teasing smile and a suitable gown in hand for her, he heard more footsteps approaching. He moved farther back, behind the concealing garments that hung within, and continued to watch the scene with an odd sort of anxiousness.

Something was definitely wrong. He could see it on Heather's face now as she turned toward the wardrobe, then began pacing about her hooked rug and wringing her hands.

He wanted to call out to her in those strained seconds as the footsteps grew louder and louder. He wanted desperately to know what was troubling her, but he realized that there wouldn't be time enough for her to answer, nor time enough for him to hide himself again, before the caller entered. So he simply stayed where he was, holding his tongue and praying that whoever it was would keep his or her visit brief.

An instant later, a man dressed entirely in black

stood in her threshold with something in his hands. Sean couldn't seem to make out what it was, since it rested against the equally dark ground of the gentleman's clothing, but he could see that it was long and thin.

A second or two later, as the man turned his face toward the wardrobe, Sean could also see that he was Malcolm Byrne, and the look he wore as he turned his gaze to Heather, in her gauzy shift, was an unmistakably lecherous one.

To Sean's surprise, Heather did not respond to this with a gasp or a chaste recoil as he would have expected. Rather, she simply groaned, as though he'd come to collect a debt of some kind. Then, to Sean's amazement, she scurried to her bed and bent over the foot of it, with her posterior thrust out quite suggestively.

Dear God, Byrne *had* married her in Sean's absence! They'd been wed, and he was about to lay claim to her, before Sean's very eyes!

But as Byrne began heading toward the bed, his hands hanging at his sides now, Sean saw that it was a switch he was carrying, and the whole scene became even more nightmarish for him. Sweet Jesus, the bastard was going to beat her! Here, in her own room, under her father's own roof, Byrne was going to take a switch to her, and no one but Sean seemed to have any mind to stop him!

This last point was underscored an instant later as another man—the fellow Sean had seen with Heather and Byrne at the gaol and assumed to be Brian Monaghan—entered the room and shut its door behind him with a shockingly passive expression.

Then, before Sean could even seem to grasp all that he was seeing, Malcolm Byrne was standing behind Heather and the gut-wrenching sounds of it began—the sounds of the switch being slashed through the air and coming down upon the cushions of flesh beneath. And in a horrible flash, it suddenly occurred to Sean that this was all because of him, that Heather was now paying the price for the lie she'd told on his behalf at the gaol.

His mind froze in those minutes as he heard the switch come down again and again upon Byrne's victim. They were punishing her for that lie or for refusing to marry Byrne—or both—Sean acknowledged, and he wasn't sure how much longer he could bear to stand there and simply listen to it go on.

But he couldn't reveal himself, a voice within him warned. If he came dashing out to Heather's defense now, it would mean having to contend with both men at once. He would be forced either to knock them out or to shoot them in order to facilitate his getaway with Heather, and he knew that neither of those alternatives would seem very wise in the long run.

"No," he exclaimed under his breath, gripping the clothing bar above him in an effort to keep himself from moving. He would simply have to stay where he was and endure the torturous sounds of it and of her resultant outcries until it was over and the two men left.

How many strokes had there been so far? he wondered. Ten, maybe. Twelve, perhaps. Each delivered with such whipping force that the urge to lunge from his hiding place and strangle Byrne was almost overwhelming.

Sean realized that he would have given almost anything to have had the switch turned on him instead. He, after all, had had the chance to grow calloused to such pain through the years. But Heather, with her soft, ivory skin still so fresh in his memory, wasn't meant for such things. And he found that the very thought of the welts that villain was leaving upon her now was causing an unbearably painful lump to form in his throat.

But just when he knew he couldn't stand it any longer, just as his hands were breaking free of the bar overhead and he was about to burst out of the wardrobe like a cannon blast upon those two ruffians, the beating came to a merciful end, and he slipped silently down to his knees upon the wardrobe floor in a trembling mass of shattered self-restraint.

His heart was beating like thunder as he peered out and saw the two men leave a moment later. And even after they'd shut the bedchamber door behind them and been gone for several seconds, he had all he could do to steady himself and gather his wits about him. Once he did so, however, he wasted no time in heading for the bed.

Heather had pulled herself farther up onto it by this point, and she lay sobbing quietly into its linens, her torso heaving.

Sean squeezed his eyes shut as he finally reached her. He wanted to make his presence known. He wanted to comfort her, to take her into his arms. Yet he knew that anything he did might cause her to cry out with surprise, thereby betraying his presence to the others.

So finally, almost without thinking, he let his hand come to rest upon one of her bare feet. To his surprise, she did not look back to see who had touched her. She simply lifted one of her hands and gave him an angry backward wave. "Be off with ye, Myra," she bawled. "There's nothin' ye can do for me now."

Apparently, she thought he was her handmaid. But perhaps it was for the best. At least she knew there was someone in the room with her, and she wasn't as apt to screech with shock as he revealed that it was he and not one of the servants.

"No. 'Tis I," he whispered in response. " 'Tis only I."

She instantly turned and faced him, her tear-filled eyes registering an odd mix of surprise and horror, as though these were absolutely the last circumstances under which she wished to have him see her.

He pressed a silencing finger to his lips, and he slipped down beside her on the bed.

All of Heather's other feelings gave way to one of great need as he wrapped his arms about her and she reciprocated his embrace. Instead of speaking to him, however, she only seemed able to continue sobbing, now with sniffling gasps, as he rocked and shushed her.

"They knew I was lyin' about ye at the gaol. They knew and they beat me for it," she croaked.

"I know. I know," he murmured, reaching up to brush some wisps of her tear-dampened hair from her eyes. "And I shall find some way to make it up to ye, love. I swear it! I would have come back for ye sooner, but there've been so many complications. And by the time I got here, those two brutes were just comin' in for ye, and I knew it would only have made matters worse if I had let my presence be known. But I'm here for ye now. And ye won't ever have to let 'em lay hands upon ye again. . . . Come on. Come along down the tree with me, and let's away before someone comes back to look in on ye," he urged, easing her over to the side of the bed. "I've two horses awaitin' us in the woods to the west."

"But I can't ride, don't ye see? Not after what's been done to me," she whimpered.

"So, we'll take a blanket along. Pad ye up good in the saddle. You'll be all right, angel. You'll live, I promise ye. Take it from someone who's known more than his share of beatin's. Why, that one didn't even draw blood."

She arched her head back and tried to get a glimpse of her posterior. "Didn't it?" she asked with amazement. "Sweet Jesus, it surely felt like it did!"

Sean offered her an unconcerned laugh. As thrashings went, hers hadn't been the mildest he'd seen, certainly. But there seemed no sense in encouraging her to become any more wrought up over it than she already was. The main thing now was to get her calmed down and out of there, for both of their sakes. "Naah. You're just warmed a bit, is all. I'll cool ye down with some cold, wet towels when we get to my place. Now come along," he coaxed again, rising from the bed and reaching down to slide her out onto her feet as well. "Let's be gone while we still can."

Heather stood upon shaky legs for several seconds.

The beating had left her feeling as though her entire backside was aflame, and the last thing she was up to now was climbing down a tree and riding a horse for several miles. But as Sean continued to hold her steady and she stared up into his entreating blue eyes, she could see how crucial it was that she overcome her pain and simply concentrate on fleeing with him. So, biting her lip and doing her best to swallow back her tears, she began moving with him toward her wardrobe.

"Your gown," he noted as they passed the window. "Do you want to put it back on now, before we leave?"

She shook her head. "No. I've . . . I've better clothes for ridin'. Let me find a habit," she stammered, wincing a bit with each step they took.

"No. You just lean up against this," he directed, stopping to deposit her beside a nearby chair, "and I'll fetch one for ye. What should I look for?"

Heather clutched the back of the chair, putting what seemed all of her weight upon it. "Look for kidskin. A reddish-brown color."

He turned and flashed her a gentle smile before stepping into the wardrobe. "Ah, to match your bonny hair then, love?"

Heather tried to reciprocate his smile, but found she was still in too much discomfort to do so. "Aye," she choked.

"And will ye be wantin' anythin' else? Now's the time to say so, it seems," he added in a low voice as he finally returned to her with the requested costume.

Her eyes began to well up again as she reached out

297

to receive the habit. "I . . . I packed a satchel the other day. It's in the wardrobe on the floor. 'Twas the day we saw ye at the gaol. I packed it to come to ye, Sean. But then I didn't know when you'd be set free. I didn't know if I'd ever be seein' ye again . . ." Her words broke off into a sob, and she dropped the habit over the chair. Then she felt her head and torso collapsing over it as well.

Sean instantly reached out and hugged her to him. "Now, now," he whispered. "Matters aren't as black as all that, are they? I'm here now for ye, and we'll both be set free once we're out that window and on our way." He kissed the crown of her head, then continued to stand and gentle her for several seconds more, until her weeping subsided.

"Ah, Sean. 'Tis just that my father sanctioned it, don't ye see? I always thought he loved me, and then he went and let *this* be done to me, and there was just nowhere to run! I didn't know when you'd be released . . . if ever," she added with another sob.

He patted her on the back and continued to shush her. "But I'm here now, love. As free and determined as ever. And I swear to ye, you'll be treated like a queen from this day on. The next time your father sets eyes upon ye, 'twill be he who's doin' the cryin'. Cryin' for your forgiveness. And as for that bloody Byrne, if our paths should ever cross his again, I promise to hold him down while you get in a few good licks of your own! That is, if you'll only put this ruddy habit on, and let me button ye, so we can leave here," he added, his tone reflecting a mix of teasing and genuine annoyance.

Heather laughed a bit at this, and her smile seemed

298

to Sean like the sun breaking through a mass of storm clouds.

"Now come along," he urged once more, reaching out to blot her tears with one of the ends of his cloak. "Let us make haste, while we still can!"

Heather drew in a deep breath and did her best to ignore what was left of the ache in her throat. "Very well," she agreed, stepping into the habit's gown as he held it open to her. "That's all behind me now, isn't it," she said more brightly.

Sean hugged her again. Then he turned her about and hurriedly began buttoning the garment. "That it is. Why, most duchesses don't live any better than you shall in my care. You'll see," he pledged, kissing the nape of her neck as he finished the buttoning. "Now, follow after me. Out the window and down the oak." With that, he returned to the wardrobe to get her satchel. Then he rushed back to the bed with it and tossed it upon the mattress.

Heather looked on in confusion. She couldn't imagine what he was doing. Then, as she saw him move about the bed, drawing all of the coverlet's ends together, it began to make sense. He would wrap the satchel up in the counterpane, and it would later be used to cushion her ride to his cottage.

An instant later, he had the ends of the coverlet all gathered together in his right fist, and with the cumbersome-looking bundle slung back over one of his shoulders, he made a hasty return to the open window.

He set the truss down and bent over to tie the counterpane's ends together. Then he turned and walked over to Heather. "Let me help ye to the win-

299

dow," he said, wrapping an arm about her waist and guiding her along. "Let's make certain you're close enough at hand, before we take matters any further."

Heather couldn't believe how gentle he was in those seconds, how caring and patient, given the perilous possibility that someone might walk in on them at any moment. He seemed to know just how impaired the beating had left her, and he handled her now as though she were some poor old woman hobbling with a cane.

When they reached the windowsill, he propped her up against it, then bent down and picked up the bundle once more.

"Anythin' breakable in here?" he asked.

"Not that I recall."

"Ye won't mind then if I simply toss it down?"

"No."

He cocked his head at her and offered a teasing smile. "Are ye quite sure now, lass? I just got ye quieted down, after all, and I'd hate to be givin' ye cause to start up cryin' all over again."

She laughed and waved him off. "No. I'm all right," she said stoically. "Just heave it down."

Sean stuck his head out the window and took a good look in all directions. Then, once he was convinced that there was no one about, he lowered the coverlet as far as he could before finally letting it drop. To his relief, it landed fairly soundlessly some four feet from the base of the oak.

"No harm done, it appears," he confirmed. "Now, let me go out ahead of ye, love, and help ye along the way. I'm sure your legs are still a bit unsteady."

Heather stepped back, and he slipped out the window, his hands and feet coming to rest upon the tree's limbs with such fluidity that one would have thought he was simply stepping out onto a docked raft. Heather, on the other hand, already knew she was going to face a terrible struggle just trying to persuade her body to scrunch down and straddle the windowsill.

"Come on," he called up in a whisper. "I'll catch ye, Heather lass. Don't ye fear. 'Tis just a few steps down, really."

He watched empathetically as she lifted her skirts seconds later and stuck one leg out over the sill. Her nose was crinkled with obvious pain, and her eyes looked teary again as she eased her head and torso out as well.

"That's it, love, and there'll be a nice, cold bath for ye to sit down in when we reach the cottage," he encouraged, waiting until she swung her other leg out and then reaching up with his free hand to take hold of her waist. "A nice cold sit-down, and all the ale you'll need to help ye forget."

Still hanging on to the tree with one hand, he slid her out onto the limb that was situated just above the one he occupied.

"But you'll fall if ye don't take your hand off me and get it back upon the trunk," she countered, having already taken her own good advice and wrapped her arms about the bole for dear life.

"Ah no, I won't. I've done this in the dark before, remember. Just let me get a couple feet farther down, and I'll reach up for ye once more. Keep holdin' on."

She had no intentions of doing otherwise, as the

wind began whipping through the tree's budding boughs in those seconds. On the one hand, she resented the wind for making their escape all the more difficult, and on the other, she was grateful for it, hopeful that it would drown out any noise they were making and prevent the servants from overhearing their descent.

"Can ye sit again for me, love? Sit down on that limb and let me slip ye farther down. Or shall we just try it with ye squattin'?"

Neither sounded particularly comfortable to Heather, but sitting did sound safer. So, with a grimace, she eased her derrière, ever so carefully, down upon the limb.

"Ah, there's a brave girl. Come to me now. Slide down," he said, reaching up and, with great effort, wrapping his free hand around her torso once more. "Take a good hold on me."

She did so without hesitation, her hands locking about his neck with such desperate tightness that she thought for certain she was hurting him.

He made no complaint, however. He simply brought her to rest on the next branch down and gingerly eased out of her grasp.

"Just two more," he encouraged, "and we're to the ground, where I can carry ye."

"Carry me?" she echoed in amazement, still managing to keep her voice low. "Ah, Sean. Ye won't get far carryin' me. I'm slowin' things down enough as it is."

"You just let me worry about that. You're light enough to manage, don't ye fret. Now, two limbs more and we're down."

Heather's left foot slipped out from under her several seconds later, as they were negotiating the last of their downward climb, and there was an instant or two when she thought she'd fall face-first and end up with her head as battered as her bottom. But Sean, with his outlaw reflexes, caught her in the nick of time and held her fast, until she could regain her footing.

His instincts were amazing to her, awe-inspiring, and she stood for several seconds, staring down at his hooded figure as he finally got to the ground and reached up to help her down as well. He'd certainly shown himself to be much stronger and more enterprising than her father or Malcolm had ever been, and she was really beginning to believe his claim that he'd managed to stow away a small fortune amid all his dubious adventures. There was just something so noble about him, so gentlemanly, that, had she not met him only seconds before he committed an abduction, she would never have guessed him to be a kidnapper.

An instant later, he told her to jump down to him, and as she squatted and leapt from the last limb, he caught her in his arms and hugged her so tightly that his flowing cloak seemed to envelop her as well in the chilly wind.

"Ah, that was grand, darlin'," he praised, setting her down and kissing her forehead. "I'm so proud of ye! Now, pick up the coverlet, and let's be off to the horses, before anyone spots us."

No sooner had Heather gathered up the bundle than she felt him sweep her up into his arms again and begin walking with her—being chivalrously careful all the while not to put any pressure upon her smarting posterior.

"But ye can't carry me all the way," she objected again.

He smiled down at her, not missing a beat as he walked. "It's not far, really. And please don't take offense at this, but 'tis still faster this way, I think, than with you tryin' to trail behind."

Heather offered no further protest, sorrily deciding that he was probably right. She simply settled back in his arms, with one hand clamped upon her bundled satchel and one arm wrapped behind his neck. He, after all, was the expert at this sort of thing, she silently reminded herself.

But just as it seemed they were in the clear, just as he was heading for the cover of the thicket and then on to the nearby woods, she heard heavy footsteps coming up behind them and a male voice yowling something which she couldn't seem to make out.

Sean turned in that instant to see who it was. Heather, still in his cradling arms, naturally turned with him. And in that split second, she saw a black-haired man running toward them.

At first she thought that he might be Malcolm. His height and build seemed right, but he was dressed so differently now, in a flowing, moss-green cape, and his facial features were too distorted with rage for her to really identify him.

Before she could cry out, before she could drop her bundle and free her hands to help Sean, the man lunged at them and struck Sean over the head with what appeared to be a pistol.

Sean's arms opened from beneath Heather, and

she fell to the ground at his feet. Then his body slumped down upon hers.

Forgetting about her debilitated state, not even really feeling the lingering pain in her backside, with both her weight and Sean's crushing down upon it now, Heather did her best to slide out from underneath him and scramble to her feet.

But there wasn't enough time. Before she could get away, their attacker took hold of her by the hair and began pulling her upward, and then she felt a heavy blow upon the back of her head. After that, there was nothing—only sudden enveloping blackness.

Chapter 16

Patrick Kerry was starting to feel a bit woozy where he sat upon his steed in the nearby woods. Though he rarely made such admissions, he had to concede that he'd had too much ale at dinner that afternoon. But in truth, he didn't care. To his way of thinking, his compromised state offered the perfect test for Rory: finding out whether or not he could carry out a bride snatching pretty much on his own.

How long had it been now since he'd gone off? Pat wondered. Still wobbling in his saddle, he reached under his cape and felt about his waistcoat for his pocket watch. After fumbling irritably for several seconds, he finally let the matter go with a shrug, and he returned his hands to his saddle horn. He'd realized, at last, that it wouldn't do much good to consult a watch, since he hadn't bothered to note what time it was when Rory had gone off on foot.

Pat thought he'd heard Rory shout something a few minutes earlier, from the direction of the estate, which stood just to the east of where Patrick was waiting. Then there had been a bit of rustling in the thicket nearby the manse. After that, however, only silence had ensued, and Pat had spent it drifting in and out of lucidity, wondering, from one second to the next, if he should go to all the trouble of dismounting, tying up his horse, and staggering off to see if the bugger needed any help.

No. no, Pat thought again, waving the idea off. Putting his accursed new partner to the test, that was what he was doing. How better to determine whether or not Rory was still clear-witted enough to succeed in the abduction-for-dowry business?

What was more, Pat didn't really know where he was at present. He'd allowed Rory to plan this entire undertaking on his own. He'd let him choose their quarry and decide when to lead Pat to her. So, being totally unfamiliar with this turf, Pat knew that there was some danger of his getting lost if he ventured out after Rory now.

He lifted himself a bit in his saddle and had another wavering look at the estate. "Monaghan Manor," he'd thought he'd heard Rory call it. Quite palatial really, he concluded, sitting down again. There might even have been some truth in Rory's claim that the master of the estate owned the nearby coal mines. God knew Rory spent enough of his time hanging about in pubs to have caught wind of such prey. So, Pat had simply chosen to take his word for it.

What was there to lose, after all? It was Rory who'd be caught if things went awry. Pat, on the other hand, had been careful to stay just far enough away from the estate to outride anyone who might come after him as well.

But what was keeping Rory? he wondered again. Even under the worst of circumstances, he'd certainly had enough time to get hold of the lass and return with her by now. Why, Pat's bladder—widely known for its capacity and serving as his unfailing timekeeper in such drunken states—was nearly bursting at present with all the alcohol he'd consumed with his afternoon meal, and he'd urinated just before they'd left their cottage. So, on that basis alone, he was sure that plenty of time had passed since they'd reached the Monaghans' grounds.

Well, he'd just get down from his horse, "pump bilge," and set out after the dolt, he resolved finally. It was probably best to relieve himself, in any case. God only knew, after all, what kind of a jarring getaway they'd have to wage if Rory did return with the girl as planned.

With this decided, Pat freed his feet from his saddle's stirrups and slid over to his right in an effort to swing his left leg up and over the steed. Before he could jump down from the horse, however, he lost his balance, and he landed face-first on the ground.

He looked up an instant later and saw his horse staring back at him as though it feared he had taken total leave of his senses.

" 'Tis nothin'," he hissed at the animal, struggling up to his unsteady feet and reaching down to brush off his cape. "Just need a wee bit of relief. You'd fall too, ye great, daft beast, if ye had to climb down that far to take a piss!" And suddenly, in spite of all of his efforts to avoid it, Pat's thoughts turned to Sean and what he'd say if he had seen what just happened.

Pat's stomach tightened with a mix of remorse and continued resentment.

He would never, as long as he lived, understand why his brother had retired, leaving him to fend for himself in their perilous business and, worse yet, forcing him to depend upon the likes of an imbecile like Rory. Pat honestly felt he'd done his share in their partnership through the years, and he was still deeply wounded and perplexed by Sean's insistence upon resigning.

But just as Pat was beginning to give up on Rory altogether, just as his unsteady fingers managed to open the front flap of his breeches, and he bared his privates to the nipping wind so he could empty himself against a nearby tree, he heard Rory call out to him in a low voice. He turned back to see the brunet approaching with a beautifully clad maiden lying limply in his arms.

"Ah, Rory. God bless ya," he exclaimed, keeping his voice equally low. "Is that the right lass, then?"

Rory donned his usual dumb grin. "That she is. And I didn't even have to go inside for her!"

Pat was surprised at this. "Ye didn't?"

"No." Rory stopped where he was, several paces away, and threw the girl back over one of his shoulders. Her body seemed like a cloth doll's against his huge form. "Some other fella had a hold of her, ye see. Some gent in a hooded cloak. And I just hit him on the head and took her away from him," he explained proudly.

Pat furrowed his brow. "In a hooded cloak, ye say? Did ye get a look at him?"

Rory shook his head and walked over to where his

horse was tied beside Patrick's. "Can she ride with me?" he asked with a childish, pleading rise to his voice. " 'Twas I who fetched her, after all."

"Ah, all right, if ye want. Just don't go droppin' her along the way, ye oaf. It lowers our share, mind, if the bride is damaged in any way."

Grinning again, Rory hurried to his horse, flung the girl over it, and began tying her ankles and wrists together with some lengths of rope that he'd attached to his saddle string.

Pat finally relieved himself. Then he quickly rebuttoned his pants and climbed back onto his horse. "So ye didn't see his face, this hooded gent?"

"No," Rory answered irritably. "I just told ye that, ye fool."

Pat recoiled a bit with indignation at being addressed so by one of such dubious wit. "Well, there's no need to snap at me. I was just askin', is all. I simply thought that maybe he was that man who's been followin' Sean and me off and on since Dublin. Must be someone wantin' a measure of our business, I guess," he concluded with a shrug.

"Must be," Rory agreed, mounting his horse and reaching out to stroke the young lady's auburn mane, where it hung over the horse's right shoulder.

Pat tilted his head to the side and sat studying her for several seconds, but his vision was a little too blurred for him to make much out. "Looks a wee bit familiar, that one," he said in passing.

"Aye. Could be you've seen her about town. Word in the public houses is that she 'hath got a gadfly,' " Rory declared with a laugh.

"Well, let's just be off, before she's missed. If she's

this Master Monaghan's only daughter, he's sure to be keepin' a ready eye on her these days. You go first, and I'll bring up the rear, in case there's any shootin'."

Rory, still seeming uncontainably pleased with his performance on this, his first bride snatching, offered no argument. He simply turned his horse about and spurred it to a gallop, and Pat followed closely behind.

Sean groaned, and his eyes fluttered open as he finally began to regain consciousness. There was a sharp pain at the back of his head, and he reached up to touch the throbbing area, only to have his fingers return to his view with blood upon them.

"'Sdeath!" he muttered, struggling to sit up. "Heather? *Heather?*" he called out, suddenly recalling his circumstances. He looked about in all directions and saw that she was nowhere in sight. Only her bundled-up coverlet remained.

He got to his feet and, still hunched over, staggered to a nearby tree and leaned up against it. Using its support, he raised himself to a fully upright position. Then, having accomplished all of this, he pressed his forehead to the trunk, shut his eyes, and let out another pained groan.

Someone had hit him. Some crazed giant of a man with black hair and the yowl of a banshee. Then, realizing who it had been, his eyes fell open to a stunned wideness and he stood shaking his head in disbelief. "Ah, no. *No!*" he whispered against the

311

tree. It couldn't have been *Rory* who'd struck him and made off with Heather. *Could it?*

How much time had passed since he'd been hit? He pushed himself away from the tree and strained to scan the late-afternoon sky. An hour, maybe, he estimated, given the position of the sun.

Christ, of all the idiotic stunts for Rory to brave, this one won the laurels! Stealing his beloved Heather off, when he'd specifically told Pat that he intended to take her for his own!

But maybe Pat didn't realize that the girl with whom Sean had become enamored at the wedding dance was Heather Monaghan. Or worse yet, maybe Rory had simply decided to take the business into his own hands and kidnap Heather by himself.

In either case, Sean knew he must gather his wits about him now and hurry back to their cottage. Perhaps he could still catch up with Rory before he hied Heather off to a prospective bridegroom!

So, mustering all his strength and will against the almost blinding pain in his head, Sean took up Heather's satchel and set off for the point where he'd left his horses tied.

"When will she wake, Pat?" Rory asked dully, sitting beside the fire and staring down at Heather's still-unconscious form.

Pat sat across from him in one of the other dining table chairs, scraping a fortnight's accumulation of dried mud from his riding boots. "I just felt for her pulse five minutes ago, ye dullard, and I'm tellin' ye,

312

she's not dead. So please take mercy on my achin' head and stop askin' about it, will ye?"

"Can we swive her while she's still out? She'll be not one wit the wiser, after all."

Pat laughed, a laugh that faded to an appreciative smile as he gazed down at the girl again where she lay between them on the hearth rug. Her legs were curled up to the right, beneath the clingy skirt of her riding habit, and her long, auburn hair was swept off to the left, as was her face. Her hands rested, palms up, at her sides, and as Pat thought about it, he realized that she looked very much like one of the seraphim he'd seen painted on the ceiling of a cathedral in Dublin. "Sure is lovely, I agree. And don't think the idea's not temptin' me, as well. But all that wrestlin' about is bound to wake her, and even if she doesn't realize what we did to her, her husband-to-be surely will. You'll find our clients quite concerned about that sort of thing."

"Well, we wouldn't have to push ourselves all the way in," Rory suggested hopefully. "We could just poke around a bit, ye know, until we've each had a minute or two of Heaven."

Pat gave this proposition some thought. "Naah. I don't think so, Rory. Ye must learn to restrain yourself when it comes to the lasses we steal. They're more like a crate of fruit than anythin' else, ye see. They're goods, like huge sacks of grain."

Rory smiled sportively. "Ah, she didn't feel a thing like grain when I was carryin' her. Grain's not warm and soft like that, I'll tell ye!"

"Don't argue with me, now," Pat snarled, bending

over to deposit one boot at his feet and begin cleaning the other.

"Could I . . . could I just take a peek at her breasts,
then? I mean, what harm could that do?"

Pat nodded wearily. "Oh, all right, ye hound. If
ye must. But that's it, mind! I don't want ye takin'
matters any further than that."

Rory, smiling with delight, slid off his chair and
landed on his knees beside their captive. For an instant, Pat thought he might pounce upon the poor
girl and tear the bodice of her gown in his zeal to see
her bared. To his surprise, however, Rory simply sat
stroking her long hair for several seconds.

"Ah, you should smell her, Pat," he said reverently, bending down to her collarbone and taking a
long whiff. "Scented just like roses, she is. Ye know,
when ye get your nose right down into their tight little velvet petals. Come have a sniff. I've never encountered anyone who smelled this much like a
flower!"

"But that's how ye know they're really rich, don't
ye see? They're the only ones with the means to
spend their days floatin' around in great pools of per-
fumed water."

"Well, ye don't know what you're missin'. Ye really ought to come closer and have a sniff and a look,
before she wakes."

"Naah. You go ahead for the pair of us. I prefer
to wait until we get to our next town and I can buy
a whole night with a wench."

Rory shrugged, obviously too engrossed with their
captive now to care what decision Pat made in the
matter. With some hesitation, he let his huge fingers

come to rest upon her bared neckline, just above her bosom. Then, having paused, apparently to gather up more nerve, he slid two of his fingers down into her cleavage and rested them there between her soft white breasts.

"Ah, Pat, ye really should have a feel," he murmured, closing his eyes dreamily. "They're divine, they are! Like somethin' between warm plum puddin' and bread dough. Absolutely enough to make a man pour forth on the spot!"

Pat glared at him. "Contain yourself, or I'll take her away from ye and lock her in the larder! We'll get ye a whore as well, once we've moved on," he assured.

"Ah, but they're never as enjoyable as one like this, are they," Rory noted with obvious disappointment. "I mean, one like this who's never been with a man."

Pat continued to glower at him. "Just have your look and get back up to your seat, now! I'm not warnin' ye again!"

"Oh, all right," Rory agreed with a disgruntled sigh, and he hurriedly propped up Heather's head and torso and peeked down her bodice. " 'Tis pretty dark down there, Pat. Would ye be mindin' if I just undid a button or two in the back, so I could slip a hand in?"

"Very well. If ye must," Pat snapped. "But don't go tearin' the thing. We want her gown lookin' its best for our client."

"Who is our client?" Rory inquired, tipping Heather forward and beginning to go to work on her gown's buttons.

"I bloody well told ye already, ye fool. I don't know who he is! We haven't found one yet. Can't ye remember a ruddy thing from one day to the next?"

Rory donned a wounded expression, but having gotten their captive's bodice pretty well unfastened by this point, he wasted no time in gathering the fruits of his labors.

He carefully laid her down again. Then, with his back to the fire and his knees straddling her head and neck, he slipped both of his palms down into the front of her dress and caressed the two mounds of flesh beneath with an ecstatic sigh. "Ah, Patrick! Come feel. Like silk she is," he continued, beginning to stroke her rather heatedly.

"That's enough of that! You get yourself back up to your chair this instant!"

"Ah, can't I just have a feel up her skirts first? I promise not to rip anythin'. I'll be very careful, Patty lad, I swear it! I mean, I never denied you boys your mischief when you were growin' up, now did I?"

Pat fixed his jaw in annoyance. The truth was that Rory had been more than lenient with him and Sean, back when they were lads, and this was the one argument that Rory knew Pat couldn't fight. "Very well. One little feel, then. But you lift up her gown first, so I can see your hands all the while. I won't have ye spoilin' what we went to such trouble to snatch!"

Heather moaned and suddenly became aware of a tickling sensation along the insides of her legs. She was lying upon a mat or rug of some kind. She could feel its very marginal cushioning beneath her. But her pounding head, the one part of her that seemed to need the padding most now, lay upon what felt like a flat stone surface.

Her eyes fell open, but her vision was too fuzzy for her to make out much of what she was seeing. There were rafters overhead, and the smell of a wood fire filled her nostrils. Then, just as her sight began to clear a bit, all went black again, and she felt something lying over her face—a cloth of some kind.

Her *gown,* she suddenly realized. The skirt of her habit had been pulled up over her face, and she felt her shift being pushed upward as well now. She panicked, feeling large strange fingers upon her, and with a gasp, she shoved her skirts back down and hauled herself up to a sitting position.

She saw a huge dark-haired man kneeling at her feet, and in that frenzied instant, he looked almost as startled as she must have. She jerked her legs away from him, curling them up under her gown. Then she slid herself backward, up against the stone wall that stood behind her. It was then that she noticed that her habit was unbuttoned, and its bodice began to slip downward, away from her. With another gasp, she clasped it tightly to her chest and glared at her assaulter.

"Sweet Jesus," she hissed. "Who are ye? And just what do ye think you're doin' to me?"

The stranger was clearly mortified at having been caught in the act. "Well, I didn't do anythin' to ye, really, miss. I was just havin' a peek, was all. Tell her, Pat," he beseeched, turning and looking off to his left.

Heather followed his eyes, and to her horror, she saw another man sitting just across the hearth rug

317

from them. She studied him for several seconds, taking in his flame-red hair and blue eyes, and even without his strawboy mask, she was sure she recognized him. "Dear God, you're Sean's brother!"

He looked equally intent upon identifying her. His mouth dropped open slightly, and his eyes widened as he leaned forward in his chair to have a better look.

He was drunk, Heather realized. The way he teetered in his seat and squinted at her told her that he was more than mildly intoxicated.

"Ah, Saints help us, Rory," he exclaimed, dropping the boot and knife he'd been holding. "You've stolen the wrong lass!"

"But I can't have. This is Heather Monaghan, sure enough. Aren't ye, girl. Isn't that your name?"

Heather continued to ease away from them both, keeping her gown clutched to her all the while. She wasn't sure if she should answer them. She just couldn't be certain at this point whether admitting to being Heather Monaghan was a wise thing to do or not.

"Ah, Christ, her name is not the point here," Patrick Kerry scolded, his speech sounding somewhat slurred. Then, after glaring at the brunet for several seconds, he got up and began pacing anxiously about the room.

His companion clucked with exasperation. "What is then, prithee?"

"She's Sean's lass. Didn't ye realize that? Didn't Sean tell ye about meetin' her at the Cassidys'?"

Heather shifted her gaze to the brunet, who was looking pretty aghast by this point.

"Sean's lass?" he echoed, furrowing his brow. "Well, how was I to know? He said nothin' of it to me."

Pat stopped his pacing and began gnawing pensively on his right thumbnail. "I suppose he wouldn't have, now that I think on it. I mean, I don't fancy it ever occurred to him that we'd attempt to snatch her. But now, ye see, we've gone and done so, haven't we. And he'll surely *kill* the pair of us if he learns of it!"

"But we . . . we've done her no harm, really," Rory stammered. "Couldn't we just sneak back and leave her where we found her?"

Pat gave this some thought. "Aye. I suppose we could. No harm done, as ye say. Just a little rap on the head, right, miss? And I hardly think ye need hold that against us. I mean, Sean will never know of it . . . unless, of course, you tell him," Pat concluded, looking down entreatingly at their captive.

Heather donned a pained expression. "He'll know," she offered gingerly. "He'll know because it was he who was carryin' me when ye took me." She returned her gaze to the dark-haired gentleman, whom Patrick had referred to once or twice as "Rory." If he was the same Rory who had supposedly punched Sean in the mouth a few days before, then it stood to reason that she should use the utmost caution in addressing him now. "It was he ye struck with your gun," she concluded warily.

Before he had a chance to respond, however, Patrick came rushing across to him and grabbed him by the hair. "Ye bloody dolt," he thundered, his face turning scarlet with rage. "Ye crazy, reckless bastard! I trusted ye with one simple little snatchin', and ye end by knockin' out *Sean* and stealin' his lady from him! Then, as if to top it, you're brazen enough to bring her back here and sit fondlin' her by the fire!"

Heather winced at hearing more about what went on while she was unconscious. Before she could find herself truly humiliated by it, however, Patrick began raging again, and all she felt was fear. She'd never been in the company of anyone so obviously violent and so dangerously intoxicated to boot; and even the beating she'd suffered earlier seemed civilized and tame by comparison.

"I should flay ye, is what! I should carve ye up and feed ye to the fish in the brook!" Patrick shouted, punctuating each exclamation with a swift kick to one of the brunet's legs.

Rory attempted to tear free of Pat's grasp upon his hair. "But whoever was carryin' her was wearin' a hooded cloak. So how was I to know it was Sean, of all people?"

"Ye should have stopped to look at his face, ye blockhead! Ye can't just go leavin' bodies lyin' about like that, without stoppin' to see who ye've hit!"

"But I had to get hold of the girl and run, Patty! Don't ye see? What if someone had come 'round the side of the house in those seconds? What if I'd tarried too long and someone had seen me?"

Pat let his hands slip down around Rory's neck, and Heather thought for certain she was about to witness a murder. Then suddenly, Pat's whole body began to tremble with fury, and he tore himself away from Rory as though having second thoughts about killing him, and rushed over to the chair he'd been occupying.

Heather covered her eyes with her forearms, for fear of flying splinters as he began dashing the chair against the hearth's mantle an instant later. He was roaring all the while, like a huge wounded beast, and the stream of obscenities he was issuing made Heather's mouth drop open with shock.

"Jesus God, Rory! Here it was, our first abduction without Sean, and you have to go and make us look like complete imbeciles in his eyes! How are we goin' to right things, I ask ye? How are we goin' to get the lass back to her home and convince Sean that nothin' went awry when *he's* the one we crossed in order to steal her?"

Before Rory could answer Pat's tirade, however, the cottage's front door swung open and Sean stood, breathless and seething, in its threshold.

In that same instant, Heather noted that Sean held her bundled-up counterpane in his arms. And unable to contain her relief and great joy at seeing him again, she sprang to her feet and ran to him with a sob.

Sean dropped her satchel and returned her embrace. "Ah, thank God you're here," he whispered. "I thought perhaps they might have already takin' ye off to a client."

Heather shook her head and tearfully buried her face in his waistcoated chest.

"They didn't hurt ye, did they?" he asked through clenched teeth.

"I don't think so. But then I only just awoke, ye see, because they knocked me out, too."

He shushed her and stood stroking her back for several seconds. "Well, have no fear. I'm the only man who'll touch ye henceforth. You have my word on that!"

He slipped one of his hands down inside the back of her unbuttoned bodice, sending an aroused chill running through her. Then he pulled up rather sternly upon her sagging gown and clapped its back shut with one of his large palms. "So, Rory," he began again, his voice much louder now, "would ye care to tell me why ye laid me out earlier and made off with my beloved here?"

Rory looked tongue-tied, almost as though he were on the verge of tears himself. "I didn't . . . I didn't know it was you, Sean. I just didn't see ye well enough under that hood. I mean, I don't recognize that cloak you're wearin'. Ye must have only just acquired it."

"That I did," Sean answered coldly.

"Well, and then," Rory continued, "the other thing was that no one told me Miss Monaghan was promised to you. I mean, I'd heard talk in the pubs of what a prize she'd be. But no one said aught about you havin' any claim upon her."

"We're outlaws, Rory," Sean retorted. "Sought from one county to the next. So, given that alone, I hardly think the local folks are likely to be able to tell ye much about my amorous pursuits. Do you?"

Heather could feel Sean's harsh tone reverberating in his chest as he turned and addressed his brother as well. "And Pat. What have you to say about all of this? Surely ye recognized Heather when the pair of ye took her. The green-eyed lass at the weddin' dance, remember?" he added pointedly. "Might ye, by chance then, know what she's doin' here with her dress hangin' open?"

"Now, Sean," Patrick began defensively, dropping the shattered chair he'd been holding and waving his palms out before him. "Ye have to understand that I was lettin' Rory handle this particular job . . . I mean, with her knocked out, her eyes were shut all the way home and she was draped over Rory's horse. So I didn't even get a good look at her until just a couple minutes ago. And by that time, Rory had stolen a little peek at her. And I was just railin' at him for it when you came in."

"Is that true?" Sean whispered down to Heather. "Is that all that happened?"

"As far as I know."

"So that's why her gown was opened, gentlemen?" Sean pursued in a growl.

Pat turned and stared at Rory, and Rory stared back at him as though completely lost for a reply.

"We were just . . . just, uh, goin' to give her a bath, ye see," Pat offered finally with a sheepish shrug. "Ye know, before takin' her off to our client."

"And who might that be?" Sean queried, clearly not believing a word of it.

"Um . . . well, we hadn't really settled upon one just yet. We thought we might, um, mind your good counsel and take her on to another county before tryin' to get her married off."

"Mind my good counsel, huh? Well, that would really be a turnabout, wouldn't it, Pat?"

Pat nodded.

Sean cleared his throat authoritatively, obviously

having lost all patience with his brother's suspicious claims. "Now, you listen, the pair of ye, because this is how it is!"

"Yes?" Pat interjected hopefully, obviously wishing to agree to just about anything that might help to get him and Rory off the hook.

"I'm goin' to turn Miss Monaghan around to face ye, and I want ye each to apologize to her and give her your vows that you'll never lay hands upon her again. And after that, I want you, Rory, to run down to the brook and get me a couple buckets of the coldest water you can find. And then fetch us a towel. And as for you, my dubious brother, I think a light supper and a pitcher or two of ale, delivered to us up in the loft as soon as possible, would be in order."

"Oh, yes," Patrick agreed with a grin. "That we can do in the twinklin' of an eye. Right, Rory?"

Rory, looking markedly relieved that Sean had decided not to kill them, as Pat had claimed he would, nodded zealously.

"All right then," Sean prompted, reaching down and easing Heather around to face them.

She still felt too embarrassed by it all to look up at them, however.

"Come now, darlin'," Sean whispered, lifting her chin. " 'Tis they who should be hangin' their heads, not you. You've nothin' on earth to be ashamed of, a beauty like yourself," he added, bending down and kissing the crown of her head.

"I'm sorry, Miss Monaghan," Rory blurted.

"That goes for me as well, miss," Patrick chimed in.

"But really, we hardly saw a thing," Rory continued. "I mean, I had a bit of a feel under your gown, I confess. But it was too dark to really see much. I have to say, though, that ye *felt* wonderful anyway, miss. Like silk, as I told Patrick. I mean, Sean's always had excellent taste in ladies, so I knew that you'd be—"

"That's enough, Rory," Sean snapped. "I'm sure the young lady would prefer that ye neither speak nor even think of the matter again."

"Ah, right. Right ye are, Sean," Rory replied, clapping a finger to his lips. "Not another word of it. I swear!"

"Well, then, gentlemen, it seems ye each have somethin' to see to now. Miss Monaghan and I shall retire to the loft for a time. We've both had a rather difficult day, and we wish to be left alone for a while. We will, of course, listen for your knocks *at the bottom of the stairs,* as ye come with what I've requested."

Heather felt suddenly seized with nervousness at what obviously lay ahead. On the one hand, she knew that Sean intended to ease the lingering pain of her beating with the things he'd asked Patrick and Rory to fetch. But she also knew that he probably meant to deflower her up in the loft as well, and she felt an almost childlike dread of it now.

"Not to question ye, Sean," Pat began again gingerly, "for 'tis indisputable that ye know more about the business than either Rory or I. But don't ye think the young lady will be missed sooner or later? Don't ye think it might be best for us not to tarry, but to leave Kilkenny before her father and the sheriff come here lookin' for her?"

"Well, it might, Patrick. But Miss Monaghan was . . ." He paused, obviously searching for the right word. "Was injured earlier today, an injury that could keep her from bein' able to ride out with us if it is not seen to. And as I said, we do need to retire for a short time before we leave. We shan't be more than an hour or two, though, I promise ye. So perhaps in that time, you and Rory can see to packin' what we'll need to bring with us."

Pat offered him another amenable smile. " 'Tis as good as done," he replied, catching Rory by the arm and pulling him along as he made his way out of the fire room and headed for the larder.

Once they'd gone, Sean turned Heather back to face him and bent down to kiss her forehead. "Ah, we're finally alone again," he said with a soft laugh. "Shall we go up to the privacy of the loft and see to those matters?" he asked with a provocative edge to his voice.

Heather swallowed dryly and nodded. Between the continuing pain of Malcolm's thrashing and her virginal abashment, her legs felt like jelly beneath her. Nevertheless, she knew she'd have to try to make her way up the stairs with him.

An instant later, however, she realized that this wouldn't be necessary. To her relief, Sean swept her up into his arms and, with fitting carefulness, carried her off to their temporary hideaway.

Chapter 17

As they reached the top rungs of the stairs, the loft became visible to Heather. It was surprisingly spacious, but like the first floor, it contained very little furniture. What there was, though, appeared to be welcoming enough. The three pallets were up on wooden bed frames, rather than simply laid out upon the floor, as Heather had seen in the servants' quarters at the manor, and each had a wholly presentable night table stationed next to it. Moreover, the loft smelled as though it had already received an adequate spring airing. It wasn't at all the musty chamber that Heather had expected, and she was sure this was due, in no small part, to the two opened windows in its back wall.

Sean set her down when they reached the top of the stairs, and before Heather could even take a step back from him, he grasped her upper arms and kissed her long and hard. Then, finally noticing that she wasn't yielding to him at all, that her body remained tense in his embrace, he eased away from her with questioning eyes.

Heather's voice caught in her throat, and only an

airy rattle seemed to come forth as she tried to respond. "It's just . . . just *everythin'*, Sean. I don't know. I'm still wrought up, I guess," she confessed, her eyes glistening with emotion.

He hugged her to him once more. "I know. I know. You've been lashed, knocked out, and kidnapped, all in one day, love. All within just a couple hours. 'Tis a pity, isn't it, that I must add layin' claim to ye to that list. But I promise ye, you'll find it a great deal more pleasant than anythin' else you've been through," he added in a winning tone.

"Ah, well, we really don't have to take care of that today, do we?" she asked, almost entreatingly.

"Yes, bonny Heather, we must," he said softly, reaching out to stroke her hair as he continued to gaze down at her. His look, however, was not the desirous one she would have expected, but clearly apologetic. "I let them come and take ye from me before, but I shan't a second time. You're mine now. My spirit is filled with the need of ye. And I'm afraid my body must take ye unto itself as well."

"But lyin' down with ye, with my backside in such a state . . ." Her words trailed off into a whimper. Then her eyes shone with anger and frustration. "Sweet Jesus, it's as though Malcolm plotted it, isn't it. It's as if he beat me expressly to keep me from bein' able to ride away from him and from comin' to lie down with you!" Feeling trapped and tongue-tied by it all, she crossed to one of the open windows for a breath of fresh air.

She heard Sean laugh under his breath as he walked over to her.

"I wasn't tryin' to amuse ye," she snapped, turning back to scowl at him. "I ask ye—how can I possibly keep my mind on you, with the back of me burnin' so and reminding me of him all the while?"

He stepped behind her, lifted her auburn mane, and pressed a kiss to the back of her neck. "Oh, there are ways. And after I've seen to your lash marks and we've had a bit of dinner and ale, I'll happily show ye one of 'em."

Heather's whole body seemed to tingle at these words as he whispered them into one of her ears. "Are there really?" she choked.

His whisper swept over her once more. "Oh, yes. In fact, I read once that Roman women used to be deflowered while standin' up. Right there, before God and guests, at their weddin's."

Heather leaned more heavily against the windowsill, feeling in no shape at all to go on discussing such a knee-melting subject with him. "That couldn't be," she said tremulously. "Where could ye have heard such a thing?"

There was a mischievous smile in his voice. "I didn't hear it. I read it. In the archives of a monastery outside Derry. Pat and I were wards there for a time, and we snuck about and found records of such things kept in some secret chambers. Remnants of the darker ages, I fancy. And all in Latin, of course."

"And you read Latin?" she asked with obvious surprise.

He laughed softly. "Enough to tell what was bein' described in this case, anyway. Our father always encouraged us to read and write as lads. Said it was crucial to makin' one's way in the world. And mercy, you can well imagine how glad I was I'd minded him when Pat and I stumbled upon those!"

"Well, 'tis rubbish. It must be. I've never heard of such a thing."

He wrapped his arms around her waist, not seeming to care now about how her still-unbuttoned bodice drooped before her. "Judgin' from what you were sayin' in your father's tackle room the other day about thinkin' that a man lays claim to a woman by makin' water inside her, I'm sure there are many things you've never heard of . . . I mean, ye haven't even given me the chance to tell ye the oddest part about what I read."

"And what was that, prithee?" she retorted, feigning annoyance in the hope that it would mask her continued abashment at having to discuss such a subject with a man as attractive as he.

"Well, that it wasn't their bridegrooms who claimed these women at their weddin's, but stone statues."

She clucked. "Stop teasin' me now. 'Tis cruel of ye, considerin' all I've been through today!"

He turned her about to face him. "But I'm not teasin'. I'm tellin' ye, almost word for word, what I read. They lifted their skirts, straddled the . . . the male parts," he added awkwardly, "of a pagan statue. And then they lowered themselves down upon it, until . . ." Again his words broke off, and even he looked a bit embarrassed by the subject now. "Until they couldn't be called virgins anymore."

Heather winced. "Mother Mary! Like impalin' themselves on a sword, ye mean?"

The corners of Sean's lips turned up with obvious

amusement, and he stood running his palms up and down her back as he answered. "Well, hardly on anythin' as long as that, I'm sure. At least ye won't be findin' aught quite that fierce in our weddin' bed," he assured with a smile. "There's far more profit for a man in bringin' ye pleasure than pain, after all. Because, if he pleases ye, you're much more likely to keep comin' back, ye see. And we gents do so want ye to come back," he explained, slowly lifting her chin and kissing her lips again.

Heather felt her cheeks heating with a blush, and she declined to look up at him when he ended their kiss.

"Ah, but it's duty, Sean. A lady goes on lyin' with her husband because 'tis expected of her."

Again he responded with a quiet laugh. "Tempted as I am to say I'll take it in any way I'm able, I want ye to swear to me, darlin', that that will never be the reason why you consent to lie with me." He raised her chin again and met her gaze, his eyes burning with earnestness. "Swear it, please."

She bit her lip and nodded, still feeling too apprehensive to know *what* principles were guiding her now.

He looked pleased by her response, and as he bent down to kiss her once more, Heather could feel the swollen male part of him pressing up against her with an intensity that couldn't be ignored. But before he could take matters any further, there came a loud knocking at the foot of the loft stairs.

"I've the cold water ye asked for," Rory called up to them. "Should I leave it down here for ye then?"

Sean, clearly vexed by the interruption, drew away

from Heather with a pained groan and reached up to smooth his disheveled hair. "No. It's all right, Rory. You can bring it up," he answered, still somewhat breathless from their kiss.

Rory obliged him, appearing at the top of the steps seconds later with a bucket in each hand and a huge towel draped over his right forearm. "I thought you'd be wantin' this poured into the tub beside the fire, except that ye asked for it to be cold," he noted awkwardly, his brow furrowed with confusion.

"Aye. Well, set one of the buckets and the towel on that night table, please. And the other bucket ye can just leave there by the stairs," Sean said, and Heather could tell, from the slight waver in his voice, that having had their amorous encounter interrupted for the sake of dealing with such mundane matters was nothing less than agonizing for him.

Rory did as he was told and disappeared back down the stairs a moment later.

Sean, in turn, directed his gaze at Heather again and offered her a diplomatic smile, one that said he was now somewhat resigned to tending to those things he claimed would precede their lovemaking.

He extended his hand to her. "Relief has arrived at last, my dear. Why don't ye come lie on the bed for a bit and permit me to have a quick look at Mr. Byrne's handiwork." When she failed to respond, he added, "You'll feel worlds better for it."

After a second or two more, Heather finally took his hand and followed him to one of the beds. In spite of her seeming cooperation, however, she knew there was no hiding her feelings from him. Her limbs were all atremble at the very thought of having to bare herself to him once more, and he surely must have felt this.

He sat down at the end of the bed and patted the mattress invitingly. And his tone, as he spoke again, was so matter-of-fact that Heather found it almost shocking—given the circumstances.

"Well, come on then, love. Off with that ruddy gown, will ye? 'Tis not as though I'm some crazed surgeon with a saw in hand. . . . I really do mean to help, ye know," he added, his voice whisper-light and his eyes irresistibly sincere. "I'm Sean, remember, not that switch-wieldin' associate of your father's," he concluded, finally giving her hand a downward tug.

Heather tried to return his smile, but found that her lips were too quivery to sustain it. So she simply nodded and, easing her hand out of his, bravely began removing her habit.

"That's right, my dear," he encouraged. "I helped ye into the thing, so I've surely seen how ye look out of it. . . . Have ye forgotten, then, just how far things went between us the night the sheriff rode up?"

"But that . . . that was different."

He donned a puzzled smile. "Why?"

She didn't answer. In fact, she looked too embarrassed to choke out a single word. So Sean knew he'd have to try to arrive at the answer on his own. "It's not that time of the month for ye, is it?" he inquired in a low voice. "Is that what ye wish to hide from me?" He had hoped to put her more at ease with this question, had hoped that such candor would make her realize that there was no subject she couldn't broach with him. But to his dismay, he saw that it seemed to be having just the opposite effect.

"No," she gasped, looking horrified. "How would you know about that?" She had only dared to discuss that subject with two other people in her lifetime: Shannon Kennedy, of course, and her second governess. Both of whom she'd chosen not only because they were confidantes, but also because they were female. She would never have dreamed of making mention of such a thing to a male, no matter how close, and she was appalled that Sean even had knowledge of it, let alone that he'd give voice to it.

To her further amazement, he simply hung his head now and laughed to himself at her response. "Sweet Jesus, lass. That's been happenin' to women since the Creation. Can ye possibly imagine that word of it wouldn't have gotten 'round to us men by this time?"

She lifted her chin indignantly. "Well, that's not why I've reservations now."

He reached up and, with an allaying smile, stroked the back of her hand. Then his fingers began playing at intertwining with hers. "Why, then? You can tell me, ye know."

She felt rather foolish at this point, her answer being such a seemingly marginal one. "Well, only that it was so dark the other night, and it's so light at present."

Again he seemed amused. "Oh, that night was light enough, believe me, for a man of any experience to know what lay beneath nightgowns and shifts. Now, come on with ye, darlin'. The sooner ye lie down, the sooner I can help ye to feel better."

Though still somewhat reluctant, Heather eased her arms down onto the bed. Then, lifting her legs up after her, she finally lay facedown upon the mattress, and she reached up to clutch one of the bed's pillows to her.

"All right," Sean began again. "Hold still, please, while I lift your shift."

Heather did so, and an instant later, she felt him leaning over her and rolling the garment up and away from her with the utmost care.

Try as he might to fight it, Sean couldn't help drawing in a wincing breath as he saw what lay beneath. He'd known, from the outset, that seeing his dear Heather's ivory skin so red and welted would sting him to his core, and he'd been dead right. "Bastard," he exclaimed under his breath.

"Am I bleedin'?" she asked uneasily, only half wanting to know.

His voice betrayed more of his repressed rage. "No. But given his means, Byrne brought ye as close as he could to it. . . . Ruddy swine," he growled again. Then his tone became more heartening as he rose and drenched the towel in the water Patrick had left beside the bed. "Ah, it's cold enough," he noted with an exaggerated shudder. "By God, so it is, bein' that winter's ice has only just left along the brook. I'd brace myself for this, love, if I were you," he warned.

Heather did so, her fingernails digging deeply into the pillow before her. She bit her lip, doing her best not to cry out at the shock and the subsequent pain of it.

"Aye. I know it smarts at first," he murmured. "Almost as though you're bein' beaten again. But just lie still and give it a moment or two to cool and numb ye."

Heather couldn't help groaning. Then she exhaled a long breath seconds later as the freezing towel began to interact with her inflamed flesh and her body finally started to relax.

Sean, meanwhile, moved up beside her and sat stroking her long hair.

"Feelin' better?"

She nodded. "I guess you really have been through this before. You couldn't have known what to do to relieve it if ye hadn't been."

"Aye. More times than I care to say, actually," he returned with a sheepish laugh. "Oh, never at my father's hand, mind. Nor at Rory's. But headmasters and priests haven't the same compunction, I've found. And you know how lads are. Always into trouble of some kind or other. Until finally, one day, ye get wise enough to realize that a stolen apple or the thrill of playin' a prank isn't worth quite so high a price. But what you did, Heather love, lyin' for me at the gaol," he went on, sounding almost choked up with gratitude. "Now, that was worth almost any price we had to pay. And I shall strive, all my days, to help ye believe that."

Heather reached back to him, and he caught her hand in one of his and bent down to kiss it. "I know," she said simply.

He still sounded as though he was fighting back his feelings. "No one's ever done anythin' quite like it for me."

"Ah, you'd have done the same in my place. Ye did, in fact, in a way, when ye heard the sheriff and

336

Malcolm ridin' up and ye chose not to go through with claimin' me."

"Perhaps. . . . But I won't this time," he continued in a warning tone. "I want ye, Heather Monaghan. I want ye, and I love ye, and I don't intend to let anyone or anythin' stop me from claimin' ye. Ye do know that, don't ye?" he asked, his voice smolderingly low.

Her words caught in her throat as she tried to answer, because the warning was so obviously directed at her as well—at that frightened little part of her that had been showing itself, off and on, since he'd brought her upstairs. "Uh-huh," she said finally. But just as she was beginning to fear that he was growing aroused again and that matters would escalate between them, they were interrupted a second time by a knock at the foot of the stairs.

"Must be Pat with our food and ale," Sean declared, getting up. "I'll go down and fetch it from him."

He returned a couple minutes later with a platter containing what looked like two small meat pies, a pitcher of ale, a couple of spoons, and two cups. "Not quite dinner, I admit," he said, setting it on the night table. " 'Tis really more like supper. But then, again, I suppose it's best for us to eat lightly with all the ridin' we have ahead."

Heather groaned. "Yes."

She felt him reach down and touch her towel ever so gently. "Time for another drench, I think."

She couldn't argue. She knew he must have felt, as she did, how cooled down the cloth had already become against her fevered skin.

He peeled the towel from her. Then she saw him submerge it in the bucket beside the bed and wring it out, the musculature of his forearms twisting a bit with the wringing. An instant later, he disappeared from view once more, and she braced herself for the second round.

It came. Freezing. Breath-stopping. But to her relief, her body seemed more ready for it now, acclimated by the first dose of it. And within just a second or two, she was relaxed once more and actually feeling hungry for the steaming hot pies that awaited them on the platter.

She remembered now that she hadn't eaten since the night before. She'd simply been too filled with dread about her beating to eat either breakfast or dinner. But now that matters had finally settled down a bit and she was safely back in Sean's hands, she found that she had quite an appetite.

"Some ale, my dear?" Sean offered, returning to her line of sight and beginning to speak with a teasingly stuffy English accent. "I know, of course, that you are hardly the sort to partake of such strong drink, but I do highly recommend it, given how besetting your day has been."

Heather laughed at his mockery. "Oh yes. I quite agree, sir. Do serve me a brimming cupful, if you will."

"Ah, ye do that accent very well," he said, moving over to pour her some. "Was your mother English, perchance?"

She reached out and accepted the ale from him seconds later. Then she propped herself up a bit and drank deeply of it. "Ah, Heaven forfend, Mr. Kerry!

How could ye even think such a thing? In fact, I may well be the wealthiest *all-Irish* heiress in the land. And proud I am of it, too!"

"That ye should be," Sean concurred, pouring himself a cup as well and settling down next to her again. "A toast to ye, then," he declared, catching the rim of her cup in his fingers and raising the vessel up to be tapped upon his own. "To the 'all-Irish' Heather!"

Heather lowered her glass again, and they both drank.

"And what about you? Where did you learn to speak the Queen's English, pray? From all the landlords' daughters ye've snatched?" she asked, raising a taunting brow.

Sean might have taken offense at this, had it not been so clear that she'd said it in jest. He took another swallow of ale. "Well, though it's rather embarrassin' to admit it, it seems to come naturally to me for some reason. Probably because I've read so many English books."

Making certain that her breasts were amply buried in the pillow, Heather propped herself up on her left elbow and regarded him with renewed interest. "I'd hardly have thought it, ye know. That kidnappers spent much time readin'."

Sean laughed. "Well, I can't speak for all kidnappers, mind. But, aye. 'Tis true of me, I guess."

Heather crinkled her nose with distaste. "I don't like to read. I would rather have learned about the world as you have, I think . . . from revelin' about from one town to the next. How very excitin'," she declared, her eyes twinkling with admiration. "How

339

thrillin' to find one's self bein' chased and shot at and such!"

He donned a weary expression. "Ah, 'tis not as grand as all that, believe me. Ye tire of it surprisin'ly soon."

"Yet not of readin'?" she asked with an amazed rise to her voice.

He smiled and shook his head. "No. Not of readin'. Because there's always somethin' new and different to be found in books, isn't there. Why, I've read of lands I'll probably never have the chance to see in my lifetime. And all the colors and sounds and smells of 'em just seem to come alive with the written word, don't they."

Heather shrugged. "I suppose. Never as good as goin' there yourself, though," she grumbled.

Sean reached up to the night table, lifted the serving platter, and brought it to rest between them on the bed. "Ye better eat some now, darlin', for there's no tellin', once we're on the ride, when we'll have the chance to dine again."

Heather, knowing this was sound advice, picked up a spoon and helped herself to one of the hot pies. "Ah, this is wonderful," she declared between bites. "Pardon me for sayin' so, but I wouldn't have thought bachelors capable of such cookery. Did Pat bake these, then?"

Sean laughed. "Mercy no! With all he drinks, we daren't let him too close to the fire! Rory does the cookin' usually. I'm sure Pat simply warmed 'em for us."

"Well, perhaps, one day Rory can teach me to

cook. As it is, I couldn't make toast if my life hung upon it."

Sean elbowed her teasingly. "So, 'tis true what they say about you rich lasses? Spoiled and worthless?"

"But it's not my fault," Heather protested. "Our cook never lets me anywhere near the fire room. Not even to take a taste now and then. So how was I ever to learn?"

Sean donned a mocking pout. "Poor dear. I weep for ye, I do. We'll simply have to keep Rory on as cook for us, won't we, once we've settled in somewhere."

"And where will that be, do ye think, Sean?" Heather inquired, doing her best to sound confident in his judgment and whatever decisions he made for them both.

"Somewhere to the north, I fancy. It's been a while since we brought off a job up there, so perhaps the authorities have forgotten. And all my saving's are there, too, mind. Safely stowed in a bank in Derry, under an alias. So I guess we'll have no choice but to head that way."

"Aye," Heather replied, feeling a wave of apprehension run through her. For the first time in her life, she would have to rely upon someone other than her father to keep her fed and clothed, to look out for her very survival. And she had to admit to herself that, even as much as she'd come to trust Sean, this was a frightening prospect indeed. "How does it feel, havin' to look after yourself in the world?" she began again in a wavering voice. "I mean, havin' to earn for yourself every shillin' ye need just to stay alive?"

He looked as though he was tempted to laugh at this, as if he really couldn't tell whether or not she was joking.

"No. I mean it, Sean, really. I'm truly wonderin'."

He sobered a bit and then shrugged. "Oh, God. I don't know. I guess we've been doin' it for so long, Pat and I, that I don't remember a time when we didn't have to."

"How old were ye when your father died?"

"Eleven."

She reached up and brushed his mop of blond hair back from his eyes. "Lord, so young," she said sadly.

"Aye. I guess I was. Old enough, though, to know that Pat and I would end up in an orphan home or debtors' prison if we didn't learn to fend for ourselves posthaste."

Heather offered him a soft, respectful smile. "And so ye did."

"Yes. But not without old Rory's help. We would surely have failed if not for him."

"What, um . . . what is it that ails him?" Heather asked gingerly. "I mean, not wishin' to offend, but, he does strike me as bein' a bit half-witted."

Sean nodded. "Aye. A little. He was hit in the head by a constable's musket butt a couple years ago. We got into a wee bit of a scrape with a job, ye see, and Rory, bein' the oldest of us, was the slowest to get away, it seemed. Anyway, we just counted ourselves lucky that he didn't die after that." He shook his head grimly. "Nursed him for weeks, we did. So dead and still, we'd have buried him if not for the fact that his heart kept on beatin' and beatin'. And then, one day, like a thunderbolt from a cloudless sky, he opened his eyes and started to speak again, and it was then we finally knew he wouldn't die. But he was just never the same, though. It seemed that musket actually knocked some of his memory and many of the words he'd known right out of his brain."

She grimaced. "How tragic."

"Aye. But it comes with the turf, doesn't it. Our work has never been what one might call honest exactly."

"Ah, well, ye made a little fortune at it anyway. And even I've come to know enough of the world to realize that every rich man is dishonest in his own fashion. Even my father does his share of cheatin' his workers out of their due. And as I said, he's Irish through and through. So, we can't go blamin' that on the English gentry, now can we."

"I guess I wasn't even tempted to," Sean said evenly. Then he offered to pour her more ale, and she gladly raised her cup. He helped himself to more as well and lay back down beside her. "But as to what you asked earlier, about havin' to look after one's self, it seems to me ye have to come to love yourself, as the Bible says. You know, to love and take care of yourself the way your parents once did. It's just that, for some of us, that day comes sooner than expected. And, it seems, *your* time for it came today when ye left your bedchamber with me. But don't worry," he added in a jocular tone, finishing off his ale. "You shan't do it alone. I'll help ye along with it."

She smiled. "Aye. I know ye will. It's just a bit scary around the edges, is all."

"Well, I think you'll find it rather freein' in the

long run . . . not havin' to answer to your father and your governess anymore." He reached over to her and slowly ran his hand down the curve of her back. "You're sure to find me much more obligin' than they."

"But it's not just leavin' my father that concerns me," Heather continued uneasily. "It's leavin' my life, my friends."

"Little girls worry about leavin' their friends. Grown women, like yourself, on the other hand, know they must follow their husbands."

"Aye. I suppose you're right," she conceded, though somewhat glumly.

"Ah, cheer up. We'll have the means for ye to come back to Kilkenny and visit whenever ye wish."

She flashed him a joyous smile. "Will we?"

"Of course. I simply ask that ye wait until we've had a priest marry us to do so, is all. Just so I'm assured of gettin' ye back when you've finished your visitin'." He wrapped an arm about her waist and hugged her to him.

She continued to smile. "I think I'll really like bein' your wife, Sean."

"I think ye will, too," he agreed, taking her now-empty cup from her hand and reaching up to return it to the night table. "Need that towel cold again?" he asked as he turned back to face her.

"No. I think I'm as numb as you're goin' to get me."

He laughed under his breath. "Probably. . . . So tell me, angel," he began again, bringing his face, his lips stirringly near hers in those seconds, "since seein' the world seems of such interest to ye, what country should we visit first?"

She cocked her head and gave the question some thought. "China, maybe. Yes. And all of Anatolia, I think," she answered with a laugh. "How about you? What do you want to see first?"

He reached up and ran his fingers through her long hair. "Someplace a bit closer to home, I think," he said with a seductive smile. "Say Rome, perhaps." And with that, he slipped his hand purposefully down between her breasts and the pillow, with which she'd taken such care to shield them from his view.

This, she supposed, was his not-so-subtle way of letting her know that even what she sought to hide from his gaze wouldn't be kept hidden from his touch.

His next words were a fervent flow in her ear. "Could I interest ye in bein' my *Roman* lady for a while, love? I promise to make your stay a most pleasurable one."

She'd been wrong earlier. It hadn't been the darkness of their previous night together that had made her so submissive to his advances. It had been the strong ale she'd consumed. And to her relief, it was happening again. She was suddenly quite tipsy and filled with that sense of drunken abandon and adventurousness that he always seemed to bring out in her in the end.

"Oh, yes," she replied in a quavering whisper. Then she shut her eyes with an enraptured sigh. "I think ye can."

Chapter 18

She felt him rise from the bed and remove the wet towel from her. Then, knowing that he'd probably disrobe at this point, she simply chose to keep her eyes shut as she rolled back onto her stomach.

Sean, noticing that she was choosing not to look over at him as he shed his clothes, smiled to himself. Then, when he was finally naked, he lay down beside her again and began kissing the curve of her neck. "Ye know, what I've come to learn about shyness through the years, my dear, is that it's strongest from across the room. Ye don't really feel it when you're up close to someone, as ye are to me now."

She let her eyes drift open, and as she turned to look at him once more, he took her in his arms and claimed her lips with his own. His tongue plunged deeply into her, and she again felt that swollen male part of him pressing up against her legs.

She shut her eyes and gave forth a pleasureful groan as his hands moved down to her breasts and began caressing and squeezing the tender tips of them.

He was right. They were so close as to be almost

one now, and his fondling was causing such over-whelming sensation in her that she was hardly even aware of her bashfulness anymore.

"Let's get in under the linens," he whispered, finally ending their kiss and reaching down to pull the coverlet and sheets open.

They both wriggled in beneath, and then Sean turned onto his side and lay facing her again. Instead of returning his amorous attentions to her breasts, however, his hand slid down between her legs as he began kissing her once more. Then he eased her soft reluctant thighs apart and slipped two fingers up inside her. She gasped a bit as he did this, but to his relief, she didn't try to stop him.

Heather had an urge to roll onto her back as his fingers quickly closed down upon the pleasure point within her and began slowly massaging it. She knew, however, that in spite of the numbing effects of the icy towel and the ale, her posterior was still too scourged for her to risk it. She feared that the pain of it might simply overpower the pleasure he was bringing her, and she didn't want to risk letting that happen. So she forced herself to stay as she was, her legs parted, scissorlike, upon the bed and her arms wrapped about Sean's neck for balance.

"That's it. Just try to relax," he murmured, his fingers quickening their pace. "Shut your eyes again, and simply let me guide ye through it."

She did as she was told, having incurred the wrath of enough males for one day, and the side of her began to feel almost locked upon the mattress—his steady motion seeming to bobble her like a fishing boat anchored in a wind-swept bay.

"Ah, God, Sean. 'Tis happenin' again," she exclaimed under her breath, "that crazed feelin' ye brought me in my bed."

"So just let it happen," he whispered. "Lie still, and simply let it wash over ye, love. It'll ready ye for what's to come."

Again she obeyed. But his manipulations became so unbearably rapid and well aimed that she found she had to silence herself against his stubble-roughened cheek in order to keep from being overheard by the others downstairs.

"Shhh. I know," he said, and it was as though he somehow really did know precisely what she was feeling.

Then, as the last of the explosion within her subsided, he withdrew his fingers and hugged her to him once more. And she found that his subsequent tugs actually eased her up onto him, to a point where her right leg was astride his torso.

Still breathless from her climax, Heather opened her eyes and stared questioningly down at him.

"You'll have to lie over me," he said softly. "It's the only way I know of to keep from hurtin' your backside."

She was hesitant, but she slowly obliged him, coming to rest upon his warm form with his arms encircling her. She felt the huge swelling between his legs rubbing tellingly up between hers, and again her expression was pained and questioning as her eyes met his.

He gentled her, reaching up to run his fingers through the long hair that streamed down her back. "Ah, don't worry. Not just yet. We'll give ye a bit more time. And besides, you might like it this way," he suggested with an enticing smile. "It has its advantages, after all. It allows me do this, for instance," he whispered, bringing his hands around to the front of her and letting them slip beneath and cup her breasts. "And this," he added, drawing her upward a bit and closing his lips around one of her nipples. Then he pulled her closer to him and lay with his tongue stroking its tip, ministering to it, until she was once again forced to silence herself against one of her forearms.

"Take hold of the bedstead," he directed suddenly.

She demurred, not having the faintest idea what he had in mind.

"Just do it, love," he coaxed again. "It will make things easier in the end."

He sounded so sure of this that Heather knew better than to continue resisting. He was, after all, much more experienced in the realm of lovemaking than she. She, therefore, reached up and grasped the head of the bedstead. But then, realizing what unspeakable part of herself became flush with his face as she did so, she gave forth a chaste gasp and slid back down to her previous position.

He laughed softly at her modesty. Then he took hold of her wrists and placed her hands back up on the headboard. "It's all right, angel. That's precisely where I want ye to be."

"But, Sean," she countered in a mortified whisper, staying where he'd put her.

To her amazement, his lips did not answer her with words in those seconds, but with action. In one fell swoop, his hands gripped her about the waist and pressed the lower half of her downward upon his mouth. And in spite of her schoolgirlish titters and an attempt or two to squirm free, she found him holding her fast—his tongue probing quite expertly and his teeth nibbling here and there. And she found that she was simply too astounded by this, too shocked to do anything but squeeze her eyes shut and freeze.

Her mind suddenly raced back to that "tasting" kiss he'd bestowed upon her hand the night they'd first met, and recalling how it had provoked and titillated her—how his tongue was titillating her now, she had to bite down upon her lower lip until it bled to keep herself from crying out. Then she dug her nails into the burnished wood of the bedstead and simply let a long, quiet groan seep out of her as his mouth continued to ravish her for what seemed a torturously long period of time.

She continued to try to pull away, to free herself of the pulsating stimulation that seemed to be driving her to madness. But again she found that he was just too strong for her, and her efforts finally ended in her whispered pleads for him to stop.

He must have heard her, because an instant later, he slid her back down over him, until her hands broke free of the headboard and they were face to face once more. He kissed her, and again she felt that huge, aroused part of him awaiting her below. And for some reason, she found that she no longer feared it, that she actually craved it now in the ready state in which he'd left her.

As if he sensed this, he reached down and guided

it into her, like a dagger being capped by its sheath. And it felt so stout and long, so strangely fulfilling, after the tickling light teasing of his tongue, that she couldn't help letting an enraptured moan escape her.

Still clasping her waist, he pushed farther downward, clearly to the point to which he'd entered her a few nights before. Then he reached up and, with a heart-melting twinkle in his large blue eyes, he drew her chin level with his and kissed her.

Issuing a relieved sigh, she let her face slip down to one of his ears as he ended their kiss. "It dooon't hurt," she told him softly.

"That's because we haven't seen it all the way through," he whispered back, his voice almost apologetic.

She felt a twinge of renewed uneasiness at this. "We haven't?"

He gave forth a hushed laugh. "No. Not quite. You'll know it, believe me, when we have. Now, do you want to do it, my Roman bride, or shall I?" he asked with an imperative edge to his voice, and Heather finally realized how tormenting it must have been for him all this time, having to spend so much effort trying to ready her for the act and not having had any such attentions directed to the beckoning part of him that still waited within her.

"You," she answered with a tense swallow. "I haven't the courage, I'm afraid."

"Take hold of somethin' then," he whispered.

She did so, her fingers reflexively sinking into the brawn of his upper arms. And an instant later, with compassionate swiftness, she felt the stabbing pain in the depths of her as he pushed down upon her hips once more and the tearing length and width of him was thrust even farther into her—farther than she had thought possible.

"Is that all?" she asked after a moment.

"Aye."

"Are ye sure?"

Sean hadn't, to the best of his knowledge, ever lain with a virgin before, but he had distinctly felt the barrier within her finally give way with the thrust. "I am."

She looked markedly relieved. "Ah, good." She pulled away from him, as if to break the carnal link between them.

He laughed and held her fast. "Hey then, lass," he said with a chiding smile. "I may have said I'd laid claim to ye, but I didn't say we were finished. . . . It should stop hurtin' in a minute or two. Just give it some time," he assured, hugging her head to his chest and shushing her.

Closing her eyes with continued relief, she let her weight sink down upon him. The piercing ache deep within her was beginning to wane, and she took great comfort in knowing that she was finally his now and that her father could do nothing to change that. This realization brought her such peace, in fact, that she actually felt herself beginning to drift to sleep, lulled into slumber by Sean's rhythmic stroking where his fingers rested upon her back, and by the now-slowing beat of his heart.

Just as she was on the edge of awareness, however, just as she felt the inviting oblivion of a nap begin to envelop her, he began to move within her once more.

At first, she thought he was going to withdraw from her. But then she felt him push down upon her hips again, plunging himself deeply into her a second time—an action which he repeated over and over. And it finally dawned upon her that *this* was that unutterable "swivin'" motion she'd seen Shannon's brothers imitate once in a while when they were sure there were no adults about. This was nothing less than the way her father's horses mated, and she honestly believed she would have been mortified by it if not for the fact that it felt so damnably good—his stern male hardness seeming to speak to her soft female depths in a language of touch that both soothed and mesmerized her. And now, with the pain of her deflowering finally passed, she again became aware of that throbbing part of her that his fingers and mouth had left so swollen and hungry for more. And as he caused her body to glide up and down over his, again and again, she found herself instinctively bearing down and joining in with the motion.

"That's it," he said with an impassioned sigh, looking suddenly seized up with sensation as she continued the movement. "That's it, my lovely bride. Just like that."

She'd done everything that he'd asked up to this point, and she wanted, with all her heart, to cooperate now as well, to bring him the same rapture that he had her—both today and on the night he'd first come for her. And as if she'd known all her life what men and women did together, as if her body remembered what her mind had never before experienced, she let this intimate part of her embrace the most intimate part of him, moving over him like a splashing, sun-warmed tide, until finally, as if apart from his own will, he took the power back upon himself. He began thrusting up into her with such speed and force that she was again compelled to silence herself against him, upon the warm musculature of his heaving chest.

Then, as his crazed motion reached some sort of peak seconds later, it was he who finally broke down and let his ardent outcries be heard. And they settled, at last, into a satisfied stillness.

A minute or two later, she felt his body shaking a bit, and she looked up to see him laughing to himself.

She furrowed her brow defensively. "What is it?"

"Oh, nothin', love. I was just thinkin' that that wasn't too bad, for a first effort."

She continued to scowl. "Did I do somethin' wrong?"

He reached up and wrapped his arms about her. "Not at all. You were splendid. Sheer heaven, in fact. So much so that a bit of sarcasm seemed fittin' somehow."

Pleased by this praise, she laid her head back down and nestled it against him. "I am yours now, aren't I, Sean? For good and all?"

He stroked the crown of her head. "That ye are, Mrs. Kerry. And once we've settled up north somewhere, we'll have a proper weddin' to prove it."

"Ah, good! And we can invite my friends?"

He gave forth a soft laugh. "If ye wish . . . anyone but that fella Byrne," he added pointedly. "I'm sure ye understand."

"*Understand?* Ah, perish that thought! Devil take him!"

"You're sure quiet all of a sudden," Sean observed, when several seconds of silence had fallen between them.

"Aye. I was just thinkin' of Shannon, is all."

"The blond lass who was with ye at the gaol, ye mean?"

"Yes."

"What about her?"

Heather reached up and let her fingertips play upon his chest. "Well, only that, with Jen and me married off, she'll be on her own now. And I find it rather sad, really."

"Oh, I don't know. She struck me as comely enough. I'm sure she'll find a husband by and by."

"Maybe," Heather said tentatively, simply trying to grasp how drastically her life and Jennifer's had changed in the course of just the last few days.

"From a well-shod family, is she?"

"Yes. Rather. Why?"

"Well, I could have Pat and Rory steal her for some gent, if you'd like," he suggested in a mischievous tone.

"Ah, stop teasin' me," she protested, her eyes glimmering with indignation. " 'Tis overwhelmin' for a girl, findin' her whole life changed in just an hour or two."

"I know," he murmured after a moment, his arms closing around her. And how well he did, having swept off more than his fair share of unsuspecting maidens through the years. But this time was different, a voice within him reminded, because he'd taken

Heather for himself—not to be passed on to some stranger. What was more, she'd come along with him quite willingly. "But I do have somethin' that might make it easier for ye," he declared after a moment.

"What?" she asked hopefully.

"Let me get it." He slid out from beneath her and rose from the bed. Then he bent down to the nest of clothing he'd left on the floor.

She noticed that he was holding a tiny cloth pouch as he stood up again, and to her surprise, he simply tossed it to her, and it landed just an inch or two from her on the mattress. "What is it?" she inquired, eyeing it with an intrigued smile.

"The key to my treasure, of course."

She flashed him a befuddled look.

"It will open my savin's box, at the bank in Derry. And there are also enough guineas in there to sustain ye until ye reach the bank. 'Twas all deposited under the name 'Tomas McKay.' Not a total alias, I suppose, since my middle name really is Tomas," he added with a smile.

"But what am I to do with it?"

"Hold on to it, for safe keepin', of course. In case anythin' should happen to me along the way. I'd give it to Pat or Rory, but the truth is, I really don't trust 'em to share the wealth with you, when all is said and done. And since you're my lawful wife now, you're clearly the one who should have it."

She felt her eyes glaze with tears as she finally reached out and let her fingers close around it. "Ah, but Sean, 'tis all ye have in the world."

He gave forth a dry laugh. "And quite a bit, really. A great deal more than most men have, I assure ye!"

"Oh, I know. But to trust it to me," she choked, shaking her head. "Why, I've never been given charge of more than a shillin' or two in my life."

"I find that hard to believe, as rich as your father is."

"No. It's true. My governesses always controlled the purse strings when we went to town—a sure way to keep the reins on me, I guess," she added ruefully.

"I'd say so," he agreed. Then his tone became more heartening. "Well, those days are in the past, my dear. You're a married woman now and surely old enough to be entrusted with a little key."

"Ah, but maybe you should carry it, just the same," she said, extending it to him. "What if I lose it?"

He flashed her a confident smile. "Ye won't. Your life may depend upon it, girl, so believe me, ye won't. You've got to come to trust yourself more if you're ever to leave your maidenhood behind."

After several seconds, she pressed the velvety purse to her chest. "Well then, I'll carry it here. Next to my heart, Sean. Just for you," she replied, still feeling deeply touched by the gesture.

Clearly pleased by this, he sank down upon the bed once more and lay gazing dreamily into her eyes.

"But what could happen to ye that you'd want me to have it?" she pursued in an apprehensive whisper.

"That's obvious, isn't it? You're now missin' from your father's house, after all, and I'm sure I'm still under suspicion with Kilkenny's sheriff. And that's just one county, mind. We've many more to cross before we reach Derry, ye know, and I dare say I'm sought after in most of them."

"Ah, don't talk that way. I can't bear to even think of losin' ye now, love."

He smiled. "All right. Don't think of it then. But ye did ask, ye know."

She couldn't help marveling at him. He was so nonchalant about it all, so unruffled at the prospect of finding himself arrested or shot by some enraged constable along the way.

"We must go now, then," she suddenly declared, sliding herself away from him and stepping off the bed with its coverlet draped in front of her and the cloth pouch still clutched to her chest. "If ye think there's real danger for ye in stayin' in Kilkenny, we must away at once, while we still can."

A knowing expression tugged at one corner of his lips as he continued to lie there, propped up quite casually on his elbow. "But what about your bein' too scourged to ride?"

"Ah, forget that. Your life is far more important than my backside!"

He seemed to be fighting a laugh.

"What is it?" she asked, her voice edged with annoyance.

" 'Tis just that you're soundin' like a wife already, darlin', and I hadn't expected the transformation to come quite this soon."

"Ah, stop it now, and let's just away," she exclaimed, reaching down and tugging on one of his arms with continued fretfulness. How on earth could he go on being so maddeningly calm about it all? she wondered.

"All right, Heather love," he agreed after a moment, seeming almost flattered by her concern for

358

him. "Now that I've seen ye properly fed and bedded, I suppose this is as good a time as any. . . . It does seem to be threatenin' to get dark soon," he added, squinting toward the window as he rose and slipped back into his breeches. "I'll go downstairs and see if Pat and Rory have us packed."

Chapter 19

"It seems we've got some visitors comin'," Sean declared with a scowl when he returned to the loft a short time later.

Heather had re-dressed in his absence, and at hearing this news, she sank down upon the foot of the bed they'd occupied with a worried expression. "Who are they?"

"Can't say for certain yet. Rory just spied them when he went out to saddle the horses. But they're pawky, whoever they are. They apparently left their horses behind somewhere, so they could near the place on foot and not be heard."

"Did they see Rory?"

"He doesn't seem to think so. We'll just drown the fire a bit so it looks as though we left it to die out on its own, and then we'll draw the curtains and pretend not to be here."

Heather's face was pale now with obvious trepidation. "And what should I do?"

"Just stay in the loft, and don't light any of the candles. There are stairs that lead down to the larder over to the far right, beside the window, if ye should need to make an escape."

She rose and rushed over to Sean, and her trembling fingers felt like ice as she reached up to kiss him. "I don't like this, love. This is just what happened last time."

He wrapped his arms about her waist and stood swaying with her tenderly. "Aye. But with one important difference," he said with his usual easygoingness.

"And what's that?"

"You're mine now. And I don't care who's comin', I intend to tell 'em so."

"But shouldn't we go and slip out the back? There's still time enough for us to ride away, isn't there?"

He shook his head. "Not without havin' 'em on our heels all the way out of the county. I mean, they can't have left their horses too far behind, after all. And besides, if it is the sheriff or some of his henchmen, what have they got on us, really? Your presence is the only thing that can incriminate us now, and I know you've the good sense to get out of here in time, if ye think it necessary."

"And what about your key? Shouldn't ye take it back, in case we're separated?"

"Where is it?"

She took hold of his right hand and guided it up to where the pouch rested in the bodice of her dress, between her breasts. "Where I said it would be."

He pressed it lightly, then smiled. "No. You're to keep hold of it, remember? Especially if we're separated."

She bit her lip and continued to stare up at him, her eyes glistening with fear.

"It's all right," he assured her, giving her hair a playful sweep. "There are only two of them as far as we know, and four of us, angel. So in numbers alone, we already have the clear advantage."

She sighed uneasily, doing her best to take comfort in his words. That was precisely what it came down to with a man like him: whether or not he had the fighting force to shoot his way out of a bind. And clearly, he believed he had it now.

"Very well," she said after a moment. "I'll stay up here out of sight, if that's what ye think best."

"And you'll slip down the back way if necessary?" he asked pointedly, pressing an admonishing finger to the tip of her nose.

Her tone was a reluctant one, but she nodded nonetheless. "Aye."

Before he could say anything more, however, there came a heavy knocking at the front door, and she knew he'd have to go back downstairs and lend a hand in fortifying the place.

He kissed her forehead, and withdrawing his pistol from his breeches, he turned and climbed soundlessly back down to the first floor.

Heather, in turn, dropped to her hands and knees and crawled over to the angled front frame of the loft, so that she could peek around it and keep a stealthy watch of what happened.

Either Patrick or Rory had already pulled the fire room's curtains shut. And in the minutes that followed, both Pat and Sean crouched beneath the two front windows, each on either side of the door. Their pistols were drawn, and they were clutching them out before them, as though more than willing to shoot if necessary.

Rory, on the other hand, didn't appear to be armed. Nor, to Heather's surprise, was he making any attempt to hide. In fact, he was standing out in full view, calmly tending to what was left of the fire, and after several seconds, Heather realized that he'd been stationed there to act as a decoy of some kind.

The front door rattled a bit. Someone was attempting to open it from outside. Then apparently feeling that it was barred, whoever it was desisted.

"Open up," an all-too-familiar voice suddenly thundered. "We know you're in there," the caller exclaimed, and Heather's heart seemed to sink to her feet as she realized that it was Malcolm who was speaking.

The Kerrys remained silent, not seeming to move a muscle where they both continued to poise for attack. Rory, too, seemed unfazed by Malcolm's frightful bellowing. He simply slid his chair closer to the fire and sat down to warm his hands over what flame remained.

"We're kickin' the door down," Byrne continued, "if ye don't open it at once!"

This was evidently a risk the Kerrys were willing to take, for again, they didn't make a sound in response.

Several seconds later, Malcolm began to follow through on his threat, and with intermittent blows—blows too heavy for he alone to have produced—the door's thick wooden bar started cracking in half.

Even in that dim light, Heather saw Sean turn and

glare up at the loft, as though warning her to head out the back way. She chose to ignore him, however. It wasn't just his future that hung in the balance, after all, she rationalized, but her own, and she'd be damned if she'd be torn from him a second time.

Sean's admonitory glance was certainly well timed, for not even an instant later, Malcolm and an elderly-looking gentleman came bursting into the cottage, and seeing Rory sitting before the fire, they leveled their guns at him.

"Where are they?" Malcolm demanded.

"Who?" Rory asked, continuing to look in their direction but sounding quite unruffled by their forced entry.

"Ye know perfectly well who I mean. The Kerry brothers," Malcolm snarled.

Rory shrugged. "Don't know any brothers by that name. But the fella who shares this cottage with me, Mr. Connors, and his friend are standin' right behind ye, and I don't think they're pleased with what ye've done to our door."

Before Malcolm and his companion could turn on their heels and confirm this claim, Sean began issuing his orders. "Stay right where ye are, gentlemen, and put your guns down."

The white-haired fellow did so without hesitation. Malcolm, on the other hand, wasn't as quick to obey.

"I mean it, Mr. Byrne," Sean growled. "Are ye havin' trouble hearin' me, then?"

"Ye know him?" Heather heard Patrick inquire of Sean in a surprised voice.

Sean nodded. "The cur who had Rory and me gaoled a couple days ago." His tone became threatening once more as he again directed his words to Malcolm. "I'm still waitin', sir. Do ye need some shootin' to remind ye of what I've asked?"

Malcolm squatted and set his gun down with a huff. "Well, given that you've already shot me once, Mr. Kerry, I really shouldn't be fool enough to think ye wouldn't do so again."

Heather breathed a sigh of relief where she still hid. She hadn't been sure how stubborn Malcolm would be about surrendering his gun. And even though he'd done so in quite an incitive manner, he had, nevertheless, done so—finally relinquishing all control to the Kerrys.

"I've told ye before that my name isn't Kerry," Sean said coldly, gesturing for Pat to go and collect the intruders' weapons.

Pat did so, still appearing to Heather to be a bit tipsy as he moved. Then once he had the pistols in hand, he simply set them a foot or two away, on the seat of the chair upon which he'd wreaked such havoc earlier.

"That ye have, Sean," Malcolm countered. "But you were lyin', and Mr. McCarty here can prove it."

Sean, seeming intrigued by this claim, circled around to have a look at the stranger. "Oh, can he now? And what would ye be tellin' the sheriff, sir? That you're my 'ally', as ye claimed the other day in town?"

Malcolm chimed in again with a discrediting laugh. "If he looks familiar to ye, 'tis because he's been trackin' you and your brother for quite some time. He's a bounty hunter from the north, ye see. Come specially to seize the pair of ye."

Sean had his back to Heather now. But he was standing at such an angle that she could see him part the stranger's cloak with the barrel of his pistol and look him up and down with a cocky leisureliness. He sounded amused as he spoke again. "Oh, really? Well, ye made no mention of that, sir, when last we met."

"How could I?" he asked. "You were strangling me. Remember?"

Sean gave forth a dry laugh. "Ah, that's right. So I was." But far from remaining amused, Sean's tone became almost bloodless as he spoke again. "So then, ye've come to turn us in to the sheriff, have ye?"

"No," the gentleman answered evenly.

Sean's voice rose with taunting amazement. *"No?"*

"What Mr. McCarty means is, he intends to arrest ye himself," Malcolm interjected. "He hasn't come all this way, after all, just to see the local sheriff collect the bounty for ye."

"Oh, I fancy he hasn't," Sean replied, feigning concern for the stranger's interests. "Someone must pay ye for all that time you've spent on our heels, after all. The only rub I see in your scheme now, though, is that it's the pair of you and not us who seem to be before the guns. . . . Tie 'em up," he hissed suddenly to Pat, backing away from McCarty so that his gun could be fired with equal ease at either him or Byrne, while Pat went off to find some rope.

Heather breathed another sigh of relief at hearing that the intruders were finally to be dealt with and that she and Sean and the rest wouldn't have to tarry much longer. Despite Malcolm's claims that the gentleman with him was a bounty hunter, a man with no interest in involving the local authorities in all of this, she couldn't help feeling that the sheriff wouldn't be far behind, and this made her all the more anxious to get going.

But just as it looked as though she and Sean were in the clear, just as Patrick stepped away from the broken chair, upon which he'd set the men's guns, and began heading toward the larder for the rope, Malcolm seized the opportunity to lunge over and recover his weapon.

Sean shot at him in that same instant, but to no avail. With lightning speed, Malcolm managed to dash over to Rory and press the muzzle of his gun firmly to Rory's right temple.

"Now you drop your gun, Kerry," he ordered, sounding both victorious and winded.

"Ah, Sean, no," Rory groaned in response as though aghast at the prospect of having to see him and Patrick surrender on his account.

"Yes, Rory," Sean said resignedly. Then he flashed Pat an imperative look and they both set their weapons down in reluctant unison.

"And don't ye be fightin' Mr. Byrne, mind," Sean continued to Rory. "He has a pistol to ye, remember."

As Sean concluded this warning, he glanced up in Heather's direction, and perhaps it was just the shadowy lighting in the cottage, but she could have sworn she saw him motion with his eyes in that instant.

What could he have been trying to tell her, though? Not just that she should flee again. . . . No. Because his gaze would have traveled back behind her, toward the rear set of stairs, if that was what he'd been attempting to say. Instead, his eyes had focused off to her right, upon the top of the steps that led up to the loft.

The bucket, a voice within her suddenly exclaimed. His gaze had lighted upon the second bucket of cold water that Rory had left for them at the top of the stairs. And having deduced this, it all fell into place for her. He wanted her to sneak over to where the bucket still rested and pour its freezing contents out over Malcolm's head. And in that way, Malcolm might be distracted just long enough for Rory to break away from him without being shot.

Having finally grasped all this, Heather wanted to offer Sean a nod of agreement, some assurance that she would follow through with the plan. But he had long since returned his gaze to Malcolm and Rory. So she didn't hesitate an instant longer. Delighted at this golden opportunity to lash out at Malcolm, she receded into the shadows of the loft and made a furtive beeline for the water.

As she was doing so, however, she heard Malcolm begin speaking once more. He was talking to the bounty hunter in an annoyed tone. He was telling him to pick up one of the Kerrys' guns and reinforce his efforts by getting a weapon trained on Pat and Sean as well.

This would complicate matters, Heather realized, quickening her pace. Even with Malcolm distracted for a few seconds, they might not succeed in turning the tables on him with his companion armed again, too.

She continued to crawl along, however, her efforts to remain quiet as she traveled seeming to make this the lengthiest space she'd ever had to traverse. The odds were long, she acknowledged, but it might well be their only hope, and she couldn't help praying a bit under her breath as she finally came within reach of the bucket.

Before she could take aim and tip it over, however, she froze at what she was hearing below. Malcolm's companion was speaking now, and his words made Heather's mouth drop open with amazement.

"No. You drop your gun, Mr. Byrne," the bounty hunter brayed. "I'm changing allegiances, as I have some misgivings, you see, about arresting my own son."

At this, Heather peered over the loft floor to have a better look.

"Your *son?*" Malcolm repeated in disbelief. "Whatever are ye talkin' about?"

The stranger smiled. "Well, only that Sean Kerry was sired by me, some twenty-four years ago, and he's been on the wing so much in the past several months that it finally took someone like you, someone equally as intent on finding him, to lead me to one of his ever-changing places of residence."

A flabbergasted silence ensued among them, and it was clear to Heather that they were all too stunned by this declaration to even notice how her head protruded from the loft now.

"That's quite a claim, Mr. McCarty," Sean choked at last. "Would ye be havin' any proof of that?"

The stranger, still keeping his gun fixed on Malcolm, reached up into the neckline of his cloak and tore what appeared to be a long gold chain from around his neck. Then he tossed it to Sean.

Sean, in turn, stepped back to the firelight and studied the locket that hung from it, turning it over in his hands.

"Open it," McCarty urged. "Look inside. I'm sure you'll recognize the face. Or perhaps if you were too young at the time, your good brother will do so for you."

Sean popped the locket open and stood staring down at whoever was pictured within it. Then he beckoned to Pat.

His brother hurried over to him and stood studying the golden oval as well.

"Is that Mother?" Sean asked in a low voice.

"Aye. I'm pretty sure it is," Pat replied, his voice reflecting both wistfulness and resentment. "And that does look to be her locket as well. I remember it from when she used to hold me on her lap."

"She died, boys, I'm sorry to report," McCarty went on in a wavering voice. "About two years back. And after that, you see, I realized that all I had left in the world was you, Sean. So, of course, I came looking for you." He suddenly issued a wry laugh. "How could I have known then what a wild-goose chase I would have to wage simply to overtake you? You do keep a brisk pace, you know," he added, chuckling and wiping his brow.

Another silence fell over the room, and then Sean took a couple steps backward and sank into the chair that Rory had been occupying earlier. His face was so shadowed, as he continued to stare down at the locket, that Heather couldn't make out his expression. She was relatively sure, however, that he still wore the same stupefied look.

"Tie Byrne up," Sean said to his brother as he lifted his gaze again. Then as Patrick headed off in the direction of the larder once more, Sean shifted his attention back to the stranger and his tone became quite quizzical. "And how are we to be certain that ye really are who ye claim to be? Have ye any way of provin' that ye didn't simply steal this locket from our mother so you could come to us with this story?"

The stranger gave forth a confounded laugh. "Now, why on earth would I do that?"

Sean leaned back in his chair and ran his fingers through his hair, the locket chain still dangling from his right hand. "For a number of reasons, I fancy. 'Tis no secret that my brother and I make a good wage at what we do. So ye surely won't be the first to come to us wantin' to join in on it."

Again the stranger laughed, but this time he sounded genuinely amused by Sean's words. "Bride snatching? At my age? Oh, you do flatter me, my boy! No. The fact of the matter is that, unlike yourself, I never had to work for my wealth. My title and holdings were well in place before I was even born. Surely William Kerry must have at least informed you that your mother had the good sense to run off with someone moneyed."

"He did," Sean conceded with a scowl as Pat returned with the rope he'd requested.

Then, apparently noticing that Malcolm had yet to relinquish his weapon as Patrick tried to get near him, the white-haired stranger addressed him again.

371

"Oh, come now, Mr. Byrne. Do put down that gun, will you, before I'm forced to shoot it out of your hands! I mean, it only stands to reason, doesn't it, that your life means a great deal more to you than that stranger's does to me? And I really must confess that I'm beginning to lose all patience with you."

Though it was worded rather facetiously, Heather could tell that the gentleman's threat was heartfelt. Malcolm, however, couldn't seem to, and it wasn't until the stranger cocked his pistol that Malcolm finally complied with his wishes and handed him his gun.

Seeing that there was no longer any threat of Malcolm shooting Rory, Heather seized that instant to finally do what Sean had seemed to be requesting earlier. She took hold of the brimming bucket, angled it out over Malcolm's head, and emptied it squarely upon him.

"Thanks, love," Sean declared, laughing up at her. "Better late than never, I guess."

Malcolm, wiping the water from his eyes, glared up at her. "Who the devil is that?" he demanded, apparently unable to make out her features from that upside-down angle.

"My bride, Byrne," Sean replied coolly. "And I promise to better acquaint ye with her once Pat's finished tyin' ye up."

Meanwhile, the elder Kerry, seeming undeterred by Byrne's suddenly soggy state, was busy doing just that.

"So, Sean," the stranger began again with a smile. "I've found you on your wedding day, have I?"

Sean continued to sound less than cordial toward

372

him. "Somethin' of the sort. The young lady and I intend to be married by a priest as soon as possible."

"Oh well, I do hope you also intend to invite me to the ceremony. I'd be quite wounded, I must admit, if you didn't."

"What do you want from us?" Sean asked, his tone a markedly pained one now.

The stranger emitted a nervous laugh and bent down to set both his gun and Byrne's at his feet. "How unmannerly of me to have gone on holding those when the danger has so obviously passed. . . . Well, but I thought I had made my purpose clear."

"Apparently not, since I'm inquirin' about it, sir," Sean snapped.

"Well, I do hesitate to go on speaking of such matters in Mr. Byrne's presence," he said charily.

"I advise that ye do so, however, unless ye relish the thought of endin' up tied in the larder with him!"

"Well, I've . . . I've come to claim you, son," he stammered. "I, *Tomas* Craswell, have come to name you, Sean *Tomas*, my heir. Now granted, I've aged quite a bit through the years, and I know that one old face looks essentially the same as the next to a young man such as yourself. But surely you must see some resemblance. I know I do in you."

Sean declined to reply.

"Well now, your sweet mother must have expected this response from you, mustn't she. I mean, as I just pointed out, look how she thought to give you my Christian name as your middle one, just as if to help convince you. Always the tenderhearted one, she," he concluded, shaking his head fondly.

Sean's tone was biting as he spoke again. "Aye, but

not quite tender enough, it seems, if she could go off with you and leave a sucklin' babe and a four-year-old behind."

"You're angry, aren't you," Craswell acknowledged. "I'd guessed you might be. We Craswells have always been a rather self-righteous lot, so it comes as no surprise. But you must understand that your mother and I did try to persuade William Kerry to let you boys come and live with us when it was decided that your mother wished to marry me. And in spite of our best efforts, the man adamantly refused the request. And the law favored him, I'm afraid. But once word of his"——he paused and cleared his throat, as though searching for the right words——"untimely end reached us, we knew we were free to seek custody of you once more. And we set about searching every orphan home and abbey for you, but to no avail. The two of you had, evidently, already begun lying low, even at those young ages. And it wasn't until we received news that one of William Kerry's closest associates, a Mr. Rory something or other, had been struck down by a constable in Derry a couple years back, that your mother and I got wind of you again. But by that time, she was already terribly ill with consumption, and I didn't dare leave her to set out after you. I was afraid she might pass away while I was gone, you see," he explained, his voice again shaky with emotion. "In any case, this did strike me as the sort of tidings that 'tis best to receive from the source, rather than a message bearer. So, do forgive my delay in finally reaching you to deliver them in person. I had intended to tell you all of this the other day in town, but you must admit that you gave me very little opportunity," he said with an awkward laugh. "First choked. Then brained. I'd hardly thought a Craswell capable of such violence, really."

"Stop callin' me by that name," Sean warned, jabbing a finger at him.

"Or you'll kill me?" Craswell asked with knowing amusement. "Yes. I haven't any doubt that you would . . . that you could, even though I'm the only man here with a gun still close at hand." His tone became an admiring one as he continued. "So, I shan't apply the name to you again until you give me your permission to."

At this, Sean glowered at him, as though still not sure what to make of his story. "Ah, Christ, Pat," he said at last. "Just drag Byrne to the larder and lock him up in there, so we can be off. I've listened to all the malarkey I care to for one day, Mr. Craswell!"

Seeing Pat and Rory about to take Malcolm out of there, Heather finally called down to Sean. "But ye promised I could hit him first."

Sean looked up at her and laughed. "So drenchin' him wasn't enough for ye?"

She shook her head.

"Well then, come on down, love, and have another try, and quickly, please."

"Oh, she's beautiful, Sean," Craswell declared as Heather began making her descent. "I daresay, even lovelier than your sainted mother. Miss Monaghan, I presume," he continued, reaching out to kiss her hand as she got to the bottom of the stairs.

Heather was surprised to hear him call her by

name, and looking up, she could see that Sean was as well. Before either of them could question him about it, however, Malcolm let out an enraged roar.

"Heather! What, in the name of God, are *you* doin' here?"

"But that should be obvious, shouldn't it?" Sean retorted. "She's mine now. I laid claim to her not half an hour ago. And she has simply come down to have a swing or two at ye for what ye did to her earlier. . . . All right then, darlin'," he continued, giving Heather a nudge toward Byrne, "go kick him or spit on him, or whatever it is ye have in mind. Time's a wastin', so have at him!"

Heather, feeling she'd already had to wait far too long in the matter, didn't hesitate to storm over to Malcolm with the intent of slapping his face. But just as she reached him, just as she was going up on her toes and bringing her hand back to strike his cheek, Rory jumped in front of her and, in a crazed fit, began pounding upon Malcolm's head with his fists.

Patrick tried to pull their old friend away from their captive in those frenzied seconds. Then Sean and Craswell stepped in as well. But by that point, it seemed to be too late. Byrne had sunk to the floor, his head drooping forward against his rope-bound torso.

"Dear God, Rory, I think ye've broken his neck," Pat exclaimed upon closer examination. "Look, Sean, at how queerly his head is hangin', and I'm feelin' no pulse!"

Rory stashed his hands behind him and began backing away from the gathering. "Well, ye said to

376

'have at him,' Sean," he muttered defensively. "I heard ye clear as day."

"Yes. But I didn't mean you, Rory. I was talkin' to Miss Monaghan!"

"Well, I did it *for* her," he declared, lifting his chin. "And I surely did it better than she ever could have!"

"That's for certain, ye madman," Patrick snarled. "Ye've gone and killed him, is what!"

"Well, I didn't . . . didn't mean to," Rory stammered. "It's just that he made me cross, holdin' that gun to my head all that time. And then I remembered that he was the same bastard who yanked me out of bed the other night, and I just flew out at him, lads. I'm sorry."

"Sorry?" Pat echoed in amazement. "Ye've murdered the man, for mercy's sake, and all you can say is you're sorry?"

Rory, looking even more mortified, slunk farther away from them and continued to keep his hands locked behind him.

"Ah, stop it now, Pat!" Sean ordered. "Shoutin' at Rory isn't goin' to bring Byrne back. . . . We'll simply have to think of somethin', that's all. We'll just have to find a way to make the sheriff believe it was an accident, because really, in a way, it was."

Pat furrowed his brow. "What? Are ye crazy? The sheriff will never believe that, comin' from us! Not with Byrne havin' pointed at you just a day or two ago. So, I say the best course is just to leave him here to rot, while we flee, as we intended."

Sean looked equally disturbed now. "But we've never sunk to murder. Not in all our years. We've never just left a man for dead, and I can't help balkin' at doin' so now."

"So, I'll stay behind and deal with the matter," Craswell suddenly volunteered. "Most of the local folk think I'm a bounty hunter searching for the pair of you, anyway. And since Byrne there made no secret about being after you as well, I'm sure they'll believe me if I simply return to town with the claim that he fell from his horse as we gave chase and was killed."

The room was silent at this proposition, and Heather bit her lip nervously. Her eyes traveled from Sean's face to Pat's and back again in her effort to determine what they might say in response.

"I think it a good idea, Sean," she declared after a moment, having summoned what seemed a great deal of courage to do so. "I mean, Malcolm would probably have killed you with even less remorse than you're all feelin' now. Let us not forget that."

Sean's gaze locked upon her for several seconds, and unable to read his expression, Heather began to feel a bit guilty at having shown support for the suggestion. She swallowed back that twinge of conscience, however, and met his eyes more squarely, convinced now that she was guilty of nothing more than practical-mindedness. Malcolm was dead, in any case, she reasoned. It was a shame, yes. A terrible accident. But it was the sober truth. So what was the point in risking any more lives over him? What sense was there in jeopardizing the futures of everyone who remained?

"I have to agree with the lass," Patrick chimed in. "I mean, if this gent is willin' to stand buff for our quick-tempered friend, then why not let him? Why stay here any longer and take the chance of all of us bein' put on trial, just because Rory doesn't know his own strength sometimes? After all, when ye think on it, 'twas an officer of the law who left him in such a dangerous state in the first place."

Sean weighed his brother's words for several seconds. Then he turned and addressed Craswell. "And what if the sheriff doesn't believe ye and you end by bein' blamed for the death?"

Craswell shrugged and offered him a forbearing smirk. "Well, at least I'll go to my grave knowing I found my only heir and that I managed to pass my address and my holdings on to him," he replied, reaching into one of his waistcoat pockets and withdrawing a folded slip of paper. He promptly pressed it into one of Sean's hands. "And that's all that matters to me in the end."

Sean continued to look a bit nonplussed by the offer. "You'd risk it all? Your life, your fortune, simply to save us?"

A smile tugged at the corner of Craswell's mouth. "If it will bring you any closer to believing that I'm your father . . . yes."

Sean unfolded the paper and saw a house name and street written upon it.

"My address in Derry, as I said," Craswell clarified. "I'd advise the four of you to go there forthwith, as I'm sure you'll be seeking a safe place to stay. My steward will show you the provisions I've made for you and your brother in my last will and testament. And you'll be well looked after there, I promise. . . . And in the event that I should get into a bit of difficulty back here in Kilkenny, I'm sure you'll be good enough to send some of my servantry and my savings down to my rescue." He reached out and sandwiched Sean's right hand between his, patting the back of it affectionately all the while. "I'll trust you to do that for me, son," he added in a compelling whisper. "And one other thing I must tell you before you go," he continued, his voice returning to a normal volume, "is that, whatever else you and Patrick may come to think of me in the future, please don't believe for a moment that I stole your mother away. Unlike all the maidens the pair of you have hied off in the course of your profession, she did come with me by her own choice twenty-four years ago."

"As I am now," Heather whispered, taking hold of Sean's other hand and giving it a heartening squeeze.

Craswell smiled, looking most hopeful for the couple's future, and in that split second, Sean could almost see a lifetime of happy memories shining in his eyes—coupled with some sadness at how quickly the years had passed. "Yes, my dear," the old man said. "As you are now."

Epilogue

Sean, Heather, Pat, and Rory headed off for Derry that evening and ultimately decided to take Craswell up on his offer of hospitality. In the days that followed in the palatial manor, they stumbled upon many personal effects that Pat and Rory remembered as having belonged to the late Mrs. Kerry Craswell. And this, combined with finally seeing himself named as the principal heir in the last will and testament that Craswell had claimed to have on hand, pretty well convinced Sean that old Tomas was, indeed, his real father.

Craswell returned from Kilkenny a couple days later, having succeeded in persuading the town's sheriff that Malcolm Byrne's death was accidental. And Sean and Heather, complying with his wish that he be present at their wedding, postponed the ceremony until his return.

It was a lovely affair, held in the back gardens of Craswell Manor on a warmish April afternoon. And to Heather's delight, both Shannon Kennedy and her old friend, Jennifer Plithe O'Ryan, were able to travel up and attend.

Heather's father, however, declined to do so, simply sending her dowry money along in his place. He claimed that the shock of having lost both his only child and his trusted business assistant in the same week had left him bedridden. But he did concede, in the note that accompanied Heather's dower, that he would consider traveling up to visit his daughter and son-in-law when he was feeling better.

Now sharing in the Craswell wealth, Patrick and Rory were able to retire from bride snatching. And Sean and Heather, in the interests of continuing to preserve Sean's anonymity, would eventually dispense with the name "Kerry" and legally adopt "Craswell" as their surname.

In the meantime, however, they had more enjoyable matters to attend to—such as a honeymoon, spent, at the bride's request, traveling about China and all of Anatolia.

FIERY ROMANCE

CALIFORNIA CARESS   (2771, $3.75)
by Rebecca Sinclair

Hope Bennett was determined to save her brother's life. And if that meant paying notorious gunslinger Drake Frazer to take his place in a fight, she'd barter her last gold nugget. But Hope soon discovered she'd have to give the handsome rattlesnake more than riches if she wanted his help. His improper demands infuriated her; even as she luxuriated in the tantalizing heat of his embrace, she refused to yield to her desires.

ARIZONA CAPTIVE   (2718, $3.75)
by Laree Bryant

Logan Powers had always taken his role as a lady-killer very seriously and no woman was going to change that. Not even the breathtakingly beautiful Callie Nolan with her luxuriant black hair and startling blue eyes. Logan might have considered a lusty romp with her but it was apparent she was a lady, through and through. Hard as he tried, Logan couldn't resist wanting to take her warm slender body in his arms and hold her close to his heart forever.

DECEPTION'S EMBRACE   (2720, $3.75)
by Jeanne Hansen

Terrified heiress Katrina Montgomery fled Memphis with what little she could carry and headed west, hiding in a freight car. By the time she reached Kansas City, she was feeling almost safe . . . until the handsomest man she'd ever seen entered the car and swept her into his embrace. She didn't know who he was or why he refused to let her go, but when she gazed into his eyes, she somehow knew she could trust him with her life . . . and her heart.

Available wherever paperbacks are sold, or order direct from the publisher. Send cover price plus 50¢ per copy for mailing and handling to Zebra Books, Dept. 3326, 475 Park Avenue South, New York, N.Y. 10016. Residents of New York, New Jersey and Pennsylvania must include sales tax. DO NOT SEND CASH.

THE BEST IN HISTORICAL ROMANCES

TIME-KEPT PROMISES (2422, $3.9)
by Constance O'Day Flannery

Sean O'Mara froze when he saw his wife Christina standing [
fore him. She had vanished and the news had been written abc
in all of the papers—he had even been charged with her murd
But now he had living proof of his innocence, and Sean was r
about to let her get away. No matter that the woman was claimi
to be someone named Kristine; she still caused his blood to boil

PASSION'S PRISONER (2573, $3.9
by Casey Stewart

When Cassandra Lansing put on men's clothing and entered t
Rawlings saloon she didn't expect to lose anything—in fact s
was sure that she would win back her prized horse Rapscalli
that her grandfather lost in a card game. She almost got a sm
satisfaction at the thought of fooling the gamblers into believi
that she was a man. But once she caught a glimpse of the vir
Josh Rawlings, Cassandra wanted to be the woman in his e
brace!

ANGEL HEART (2426, $3.9
by Victoria Thompson

Ever since Angelica's father died, Harlan Snyder had been a
gling to get his hands on her ranch, the Diamond R. And nc
just when she had an important government contract to fulf
she couldn't find a single cowhand to hire—all because of Sr
der's threats. It was only a matter of time before the legenda
gunfighter Kid Collins turned up on her doorstep, bac
wounded. Angelica assessed his firmly muscled physique a
stared into his startling blue eyes. Beneath all that blood and d
he was the handsomest man she had ever seen, and the one p
son who could help beat Snyder at his own game.